TIME
HEALS
NO
WOUNDS

TIME HEALS NO WOUNDS

HENDRIK FALKENBERG

Translated by Patrick F. Brown

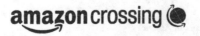

Text copyright © 2015 Hendrik Falkenberg

Translation copyright © 2016 Patrick F. Brown

Previously published as *Die Zeit heilt keine Wunden* by Amazon Publishing in Germany in 2015. Translated from German by Patrick F. Brown. First published in English by AmazonCrossing in 2016.

Published by AmazonCrossing, Seattle

www.apub.com

Amazon, the Amazon logo, and AmazonCrossing are trademarks of Amazon.com, Inc., or its affiliates.

ISBN-13: 9781503933477
ISBN-10: 1503933474

Cover design by Shasti O'Leary-Soudant

Printed in the United States of America

The Beginning

i have been watching you
for years
ever since i discovered who you are and who you were

i see what you do and what you have done
i feel the pain you have caused this world
i behold the sorrow for which you must answer
i endure the lifelong wounds for which you bear the blame
day after day

don't think you can escape me
turn around and you won't see me—but i am there
run, try to escape me—and i will be waiting for you
the time has come for you to pay—god won't be the one to
     judge you

you will experience the pain so many have suffered because
     of you

sorrow will knock on your door and you will wish you had
    never been born
perhaps you have forgotten, so i am here to remind you
there is no mercy, no forgiveness
time heals no wounds

There was no indication of sender or recipient. The letter was simply found lying on the doormat one spring morning. But the person who picked it up knew for certain that it wasn't meant for anyone else.

Sunday Evening, Ten Years Later

The waves crashed against the outcropping of rocks with such force that the spray flew several feet high. Dark clouds drifted across the blue-gray sky, a harbinger of the shifting weather. Seagulls cried and circled over the rugged coastline. In the distance, a combine harvester traced lonely paths across a rapeseed field. A rumble of thunder came from far off, then a bolt of lightning illuminated the horizon. It had not rained for weeks, and the community longed for it. The wind was still calm and the air muggy, but the waves intensified.

The beach lay deserted in the fading light. A lone figure trudged along the surf with quick, determined steps, his black rubber boots continuously bathed by whitecaps. With each wave, the water rose higher, ready to pull the old man out to sea. His boot prints in the coarse sand were immediately washed smooth by each breaker.

He stared out to sea. Time had not been kind to his face. Deep ridges traversed his brown, leathery skin, creating a unique map of life. He wore a crooked blue wool cap over his bald head, old-fashioned corduroys, and a moss-green parka that showed signs of deterioration. He carried a small fishing net over his shoulder and gripped his cane with a shaky hand.

He scanned the beach as he walked through the foaming water. Sometimes he poked around the seaweed and picked up tiny items and placed them in his leather belt pouch. The threat of severe weather did not hurry him. The old man raised his head, as if he could hear the voices of a bygone era amid the mounting roar and rumble of the elements.

Suddenly, he fixed on something. From a hundred yards away, the cries of the seagulls sounded like a deafening chorus as they flew over the section of the beach at the foot of the cliffs that the locals called "the shark fin" on account of their unusual shape. Some of the birds swooped down to the beach, while others swarmed above.

He charged toward the protruding rock formation. The seagulls flew away and watched as the wide-eyed man pushed aside a clump of seaweed with his cane. He emitted a few unintelligible sounds, then recoiled. He turned and rushed to the cliffs, stumbling up a narrow path, using his cane to steady himself. His chest heaved as he struggled to reach the top of the cliff, then he staggered toward the combine rolling over the rapeseed field.

The first heavy raindrops hit the dusty ground, while gusts of wind ruffled the dune grass.

Exactly four and a half miles from the beach, Merle also heard the thunder of the approaching storm. The room remained unchanged, shrouded in darkness, its stale air musty. Even the dazzling flashes of lightning, which now struck at ever shorter intervals, failed to penetrate the confines of the enclosure.

The darkness awoke in the young woman memories of her childhood. Memories that she still found difficult to bear. Her mother had changed partners so quickly that she could barely keep the names straight, but the pain that emanated from their venomous insults never changed.

One evening, another of her mother's lovers had scrutinized her as she foolishly snuck to the fridge for a cold soda.

"Aren't you fat enough already?" he had said before turning to her mother, who had been lying listlessly on the sofa, her face puffy. His next words had been the purest of poisons. "Put your daughter on a diet, otherwise she'll never get a boyfriend!"

Merle had glared at her mother and tried to shield herself against the alcoholic haze that permeated the room. She wanted her mother to defend her just this once. "You're fat and ugly too, you know!" Merle wanted to say. "You spend your life in this shithole, letting yourself get fucked by any bum who comes your way, and you're drunk before you've even had breakfast! You disgust me!"

Instead of saying anything, Merle ran up the stairs to the bathroom. She heard chairs being knocked over downstairs, followed by a nasty, guttural laugh.

"It's true. I really am ugly!" she had said to herself that night as she looked in the mirror. "The boys at school laugh at me and the girls ignore me. I'm fat and covered in zits, and my breasts haven't started growing!"

Merle's bedroom gave only the illusion of a safe retreat, because her mother had hidden the key to her door. Lately Merle felt an urgent need to transform her room into an impregnable fortress, especially since a strange lust had now crept into the glances of her mother's boyfriends.

Since her mother rarely came upstairs, Merle's changes to her room went unnoticed for a week. But when her mother opened the door one morning, she was shocked.

"Have you lost your mind? What is this? Some kind of tomb?"

Merle had painted the walls black and glued dark, opaque fabric to the window. All the furniture had been painted black, and she'd tossed everything she couldn't paint into the closet. Merle had even found black latex bedding.

"So you want to be a vampire? Fine by me! It's no wonder, given where you come from!"

Merle's mother never alluded to her father and ignored all questions about him. Before Merle could dig any deeper, her mother took off down the stairs to have another drink.

"Great idea! I might as well become a vampire!"

And so the transformation of Merle's room was soon followed by the transformation of Merle von Hohenstein herself. The somewhat chubby, shy girl with mysterious green eyes and a distinctive birthmark under her right eye morphed into a forbidding figure. Her baggy black clothing, dyed hair, dark makeup, and pale skin ensured she would be left alone.

These measures allowed Merle to enjoy a peaceful teenage existence for the next two years. But the morning after her graduation, Merle had undergone another radical change.

She laid out items from trendy fashion boutiques on the bed. Not a single piece of clothing was black. Merle stripped naked and walked into the bathroom. She ripped a sheet off the small mirror. For two years, it had prevented her from scrutinizing her looks. She stood, shoulders back, eyes fixed on the image in the mirror. No trace of fat or pimples—even her breasts had developed into apple-sized mounds.

"A little pale, but that will soon change," she had said.

Half an hour later, Merle stepped into the cool morning air wearing a flowery sundress and carrying a large sports bag. She looked at the house of her joyless childhood and took several deep breaths, then walked through the rusty garden gate, never to return.

Goose bumps ran down Merle's arms as she stood almost ten years later in that dark room, reflecting on her childhood. She jumped at another clap of thunder. The sudden scare also reminded her of the past.

She had wondered why her mother always had enough money despite never getting a regular job. Merle's grandparents had died early and except for their aristocratic last name had left nothing worth mentioning. Nevertheless, the wallet in the old hall dresser was always well stocked, and Merle had been able to swipe a considerable amount over the years without ever being caught. This money had gone a long way in helping her start her new life. Later on, while getting her degree in journalism, she'd discovered the source of all the money by sifting through the past.

The last several years had been bright and cheerful, and in ten hours and forty minutes, at 5:16 a.m., she would celebrate the ten-year anniversary of when she'd fled this hellhole and was born again into a brand-new life.

Another thousand yards to go. Johannes Niehaus pulled the paddle through the water with all his strength, propelling the canoe to the finish line of the regatta. The bass hammering in his headphones was rounded out by wailing guitars. Fast rock music always psyched him up when he practiced. Had MP3 players been allowed in competitions, he probably would have already achieved his goal of qualifying for the Olympics.

The sky grew darker, and the rain soaked Johannes's workout clothes. A blustery headwind grew stronger by the minute. The trees along the shoreline waved, and the almost glassy water rippled. He heard a loud clap of thunder over his music and jumped. The change in weather did not actually bother him: he had managed many storms in his canoe. However, since the amount of time between the lightning and the thunder was getting shorter, he pushed himself harder despite the wind.

A few hours ago, he had been sitting on a train on his way back from his parents' house, which was about three hours away in a tiny town. A big departure from the bustle of the city, where he had moved six years ago. He had applied to an athlete-development program and been accepted to the Olympic Training Center, along with an offer from the police academy for a job reserved for top athletes. Upon finishing police training, Johannes was assigned an administrative role that consisted mainly of filing, copying, and writing memos. When he'd asked for something more challenging, he was assigned to the Criminal Investigation Department, but little changed in his day-to-day work. Since his time as a competitive athlete was coming to an end, Johannes had tried to improve his job prospects by applying internally to another position. As a result, he was assigned to Detective Chief Fritz Janssen from homicide, who was known as a tough old man who believed in unconventional detective work. Behind his back, he was known as "Old Fritz"—loved by some, hated by others.

When Steffen Lauer, head of the department, had informed Old Fritz that he would have to spend his last three years working with a young partner, he exploded.

"What am I supposed to do with a rookie who barely shows up?"

"I thought it'd be a perfect fit," Lauer said. "Not much will change, and with your experience and . . . somewhat unorthodox work habits, Mr. Niehaus will quickly get the hang of being in the field. The boy has paddled his arms off for our country, so give him a chance!"

Lauer stroked his bald head and twirled his mustache—a common tic. He was short and wiry, and as a passionate amateur triathlete, he had a soft spot for athletes. He was extremely popular with his staff because he gave them lots of leeway and always defended them in critical situations.

"At least he'd earn a living doing real work," Fritz said. "Still! I have no desire to be someone's nanny. Make someone else do it!"

Johannes stood outside the half-open door and was unsure if he should enter. Ingrid Meier, the energetic and portly secretary of the

Criminal Investigation Department, made the decision for him. She came up from behind and swung open the door.

"Mr. Niehaus is here," she said.

Fritz turned to Johannes, his face bright red, obviously unsure how much Johannes had overheard. Mrs. Meier smiled cattily.

"Glad you came in, Mr. Niehaus," Lauer said, giving Fritz a look of warning. "This is Mr. Janssen, who will introduce you to the practical side of police work and murder investigations over the next few years."

"Two years," Fritz said. He looked at Johannes and was confused by his different-colored eyes. "So you're the rower," he said, and Johannes's ears glowed with embarrassment.

"Canoeist."

Confused, Fritz looked at Lauer. "What's the difference?"

"There are several differences," Johannes explained. "Canoeists use different boats, either a Canadian—as I do—or a kayak. Canoeists also use a paddle and face the direction they're going, rowers sit opposite."

"See, you already have something in common," said Lauer. "Mr. Janssen is also in his element on the water. Isn't that right, Fritz? You spend every free minute on your old shrimp boat!"

Fritz stared at Johannes through his rimless glasses. With his thick eyebrows, he was somewhat reminiscent of an owl, and it was impossible to glean anything from his faded blue eyes. Lauer quickly put an end to the awkward meeting and left the details for another day.

It was not until the following Monday that Johannes had seen Old Fritz again.

"Morning," Fritz said when he arrived at work. With a coffee in hand, he shuffled through the small anteroom, which had been transformed from the copy/storage area for Johannes's use, and went into his office.

Uncertain if he should approach him, Johannes spent the morning trying to make his "office" a little more appealing. Only after lunch did he knock on Fritz's door. When no answer came, he opened it. Apart

7

from two locked floor-to-ceiling closets, an almost empty desk, and two chairs, there was nothing.

Over the next few days, Johannes did not see Fritz. However, by Friday, he could no longer contain himself. In the small break room, he spoke to a young colleague about Fritz's absence.

"Fritz? I saw him just now in the hallway, and yesterday he was at a meeting."

Johannes was confused. "Does he maybe have another office?"

"Nope." She took a closer look at him and pushed a strand of brown curly hair from her face. "Aren't you the athlete who was assigned to him? You'd be the one to know where he's hiding!"

"I . . . um . . . I only saw him briefly on Monday," he mumbled.

"Ah, well then, the rumors must be true: Old Fritz will move heaven and earth to get rid of you," she said and smiled. "Don't read too much into it. I had to work with him before too. He may seem a little grumpy at first, but he's actually a really nice guy."

He did not know what to say. "Nice guy" and Fritz did not exactly go hand in hand. His thoughts must have read like neon letters across his forehead.

"Don't believe everything people say about him. Fritz may have his own way of doing things, but he gets away with it because he's so successful. For some, that's cause for resentment. Not to mention that most people here don't really get his sense of humor."

Unless this game of hide-and-seek was meant to be some kind of joke, he had yet to encounter any humor in Fritz. Johannes walked to Fritz's door and opened it. Fritz sat in the chair behind his desk and eyed Johannes.

"Well, look who decided to show up!"

Johannes gulped. "I . . . um . . . thought you had gone on vacation," he said.

Fritz ran a finger over a large scar on his left cheek. "Fine!" He slammed his hands on the desk. "I've spent the whole week trying to

8

avoid you, but obviously everyone has conspired against me, so we'll have to learn to get along somehow. However, let me make one thing clear: I will not change anything about my work habits, nor do I want you to do anything without speaking to me first! Your place is next door in the copy . . . uh . . . in the office, and you're not to touch anything in here. I don't want any clutter in my space!"

Johannes looked around the room. It was clinically sterile. Even the desk, with its computer keyboard pushed aside, showed no evidence of actual police work. The only personal accessory he'd noticed was a small picture frame holding a faded photograph of a slender, good-looking woman with her arm around a little boy.

"My mother," Fritz said.

Johannes studied the photo and recognized the vestiges of the boy's facial features in Old Fritz. As a child, he had also worn glasses, looked puny, and had an unruly mop of hair. The resemblance to his mother, who looked absently into the camera, was astounding.

Fritz stood, walked around the desk, and stuck out his hand. "Fritz," he said. Johannes was unsure if he had just seen him wink.

"Johannes. But you can call me Hannes like everyone else."

Fritz released his vise grip and fumbled with a cabinet lock. "All right, Hannes. At the moment, we have no case, so it's best that you take a look at some old ones. Think of it as the theory phase. But hurry up, because a body can pop up anywhere at any time!"

Fritz stacked several black file folders in front of Hannes and stretched his back. "These are the last three cases I've solved. Start with these, and next Tuesday, we can talk about the first case. Say three o'clock?" He glanced at the practice schedule through the door—the only spot of color on the wall next to the desk. "Provided your Olympic preparations don't get in the way. I won't be to blame for the national rowing team's defeat." He grinned devilishly and patted Hannes on the shoulder. "So now you have plenty of work. I have some things to deal with. We'll talk next week." Fritz grabbed his jacket and left

9

through a side door hidden behind a filing cabinet that led to the hallway. Evidently, he had been using it these past few days.

The following week, Hannes had engrossed himself in the case of a housewife who had been stabbed by her husband's jealous lover. And Fritz actually kept his word. On Tuesday, he'd discussed the case with him and showed great patience in answering all his questions. He no longer used the side door, and his hoarse "Morning" boomed throughout the former copy room each day. Over the next few days, Hannes had studied the other two cases, and wondered when his new life as a homicide detective would actually start.

It was soon Sunday evening. Hannes was not too enthusiastic about the coming week. Fritz would be back in the office on Tuesday after spending a long weekend on his old cutter.

With one last stroke of the paddle, Hannes reached the dock and carried his canoe through the cascading wall of water into the boathouse. Lightning flashed almost without interruption, and a permanent rumble filled the air. Shivering, he closed the boathouse door and listened as the storm rattled the building. Hannes went to the locker room. In the hallway, he ran into his training partner and archrival, who had gotten out of the water in the nick of time.

"Another lap, dork?" said Ralf. "You look like a wet rat."

"That's what happens when you do water sports," said Hannes before he slammed the dressing room door behind him. *Stupid jerk!* he thought to himself. What bugged him the most was that Ralf had better times on the water.

Hannes quickly peeled off his dripping clothes and massaged his muscles in the hot shower. He considered the hot tub, but decided his couch, a loaded pizza, and a DVD were the way to round out his weekend.

He dried himself off, his body overcome with fatigue. His cell phone rang, and Hannes answered. Steffen Lauer was on the other end. Hannes listened for a few minutes as a rush of adrenaline washed away his tiredness. He threw his gym bag over his shoulder and sprinted to his old truck in the rain. The stubborn engine started after the third try, and Hannes was soon speeding to police headquarters.

SUNDAY NIGHT INTO MONDAY MORNING

The dream begins as it always does. It is amazing and at the same time frightening how stories can turn the memories of others into nightmares. Impenetrable darkness, no light, no form, no outline, only nothingness. The rhythmic sound of boot steps drawing closer, a smell of sweat, blood, and smoke in the air.

Suddenly, the darkness is shattered by a sea of outstretched arms. The identical expressionless faces attached to these arms all stare in the same direction. An army of white masks—uniform, standardized, robotic.

A child's laughter, then the sweet voice of a woman singing in a foreign language. The heads all jerk to the right, and the white masks distort into hateful grimaces.

An explosion. Full of stroboscopic images, thrashing hordes of young men, fleeing children, women, elderly, desperate faces, raised arms, pools of blood. Shots ring out, flames lap at houses, and windows shatter as smoke, thick and acrid, shrouds the hellish image fragments.

The dream ends as it always does. Sweat-soaked sheets under a trembling body, a racing pulse, endless hours of tossing and turning. Until finally the first rays of light creep through the narrow crevices of the shutters.

Monday at Noon

In the small harbor there was an abnormal hive of activity. People were busy trying to repair the damage from the severe storm the night before.

Fritz Janssen sharply turned the wheel of the former shrimp trawler. He was heading to his berth on the pier. The city's main port lay a few miles south, where the edges of the city stretched to the old fishing village. Little distance separated a rural idyll and the new housing developments for young, affluent urbanites.

Through his binoculars, he spotted Hannes leaning against his old Jeep. Fritz was irritated. Although the vehicle had become prone to breakdowns, he had not been able to bring himself to purchase a new one. He had picked the car out with his wife shortly before her death, which was why the somewhat dented vehicle was full of happy and painful memories.

As *Lena* chugged past the lighthouse, Fritz saw a white speedboat off the starboard side. Apparently, it had not been properly moored by its owners and had rammed its bow into a fishing boat during the storm. Fritz sneered. He was sure that the owner was some landlubber from the city who knew nothing of even basic boating.

He saw a fisherman gesticulating wildly at a man in a white suit who had just climbed out of a BMW 3 Series convertible. The man punched the furious fisherman in self-defense, and a fight broke out. Fritz accelerated to the dock and watched as Hannes awkwardly tried to mediate the dispute only to be thrown aside by the berserk fisherman. He lost his balance and fell to the ground. Distracted, Fritz rammed into the dock and scratched up his cutter.

"Shit!" He threw his rope to a freckled boy. "Fiete, tie me up!"

Fritz hustled over to the brawl. Several men had now detained the driver and the old fisherman.

"Okay, okay, Ole, calm down. Don't get yourself so worked up," Fritz said in the local dialect, placing his hand on the quick-tempered fisherman's shoulder.

However, it took much more persuasion before Ole truly calmed down. "I'm not gonna get my hands dirty because of that guy," he said.

"This brat belong to you?" Ole asked Fritz with a nod to Hannes, who was sitting on the ground clutching his knee. "He asked when you were coming back and wanted to wait around until you docked."

"That's Hannes. They saddled me again with a newbie I have to teach how to be a cop."

"Then you should tell him not to meddle in other people's business," said Ole. "Next time he might get more than just bruises . . ."

"Teaching a young police officer not to get involved in other people's business? I'm gonna suggest that to the guy in charge of training new recruits."

"We can solve these things on our own. We don't need the police!" said Ole before he walked away.

Fritz sat down on a bollard and winced as pain shot through his back. The last few days on the rough sea had left their mark. "Damn it," he said. "If this continues, I'll have to dry-dock my boat for good." Hannes limped toward him. "What are you doing out here?"

"Are they always so welcoming here?" Hannes asked. "When that old fart tossed me aside, I twisted my knee, and we're in the middle of competition season!"

"Old fart," Fritz repeated. Was that what Hannes called him when he was not around? "Well, at least you can see what old farts still have in them. Be glad Ole was too busy with that yuppie, otherwise you'd be worrying about more than your leg. And when some little snot makes me scratch my boat, he had better see to it that he wins the national championship. You know, Ole and I sat next to each other in school. Does that make me an old fart too?"

Hannes quickly changed the subject. "I didn't know you spoke the local dialect. I barely understood a word."

"How are you going to solve any crimes here if you don't understand the locals?"

"Maybe you can give me a few private lessons."

"When the time comes," said Fritz as he pushed himself up from the bollard with a groan.

"More back pain?" asked Hannes, who had often seen Fritz hobbling at the station.

The pain was now running up and down Fritz's entire back. He repeated his previous question. "So, what are you doing out here?"

"A body's been found on a stretch of beach about three miles from here," Hannes said. "An old man stumbled upon it last night. I couldn't tell you sooner because I was unable to reach you. Incidentally, Mr. Lauer wants to speak to you about that. Anyway, it's a woman. Everything points to drowning. The body's with forensics now."

"If she drowned, then that's not really a case for us," said Fritz.

"The cause of death has not yet been determined. And the new medical examiner—you know, the short one with black hair—mentioned there were a few inconsistencies."

"What sort of inconsistencies?" Fritz asked.

"No idea. She wants to complete the autopsy first and send us the report."

"Jeez, Hannes! If we waited every time for the forensic report, our investigation would go nowhere. You could've at least teased some preliminary information out of her. Or"—he cocked his head—"did the young lady get your tongue?"

Hannes's face turned bright red at the mention of his exchange with the highly attractive medical examiner.

With a husky laugh, Fritz hit him on the shoulder. "At least now you have a reason to see her again, because I'm certainly not waiting for the official report!"

Hannes couldn't understand Fritz's rapid mood swings—let alone predict them. He'd learned that the old detective had been grappling with loneliness ever since his wife died of a heart attack after a long illness about fifteen years ago. "We should head to the spot where the body was found," he suggested, eager to steer the conversation elsewhere.

"We're not going to find much after the storm," said Fritz. "Were the crime scene investigators able to tell you anything? Or was there another young doe-eyed newcomer too?" Chuckling to himself, he walked over to Hannes's patrol car. "Let's head to the beach now. We're already halfway there. My car can sit here for a while. With my bad back, I can't drive, anyway. And the kid over there's already tied up my boat."

He waved at the boy and shouted something across the square, which sounded like "Well, Fiete, *stenjhiawfugsn?*" as he pointed at Hannes.

"Dat's right," the kid replied with a grin and gave a thumbs-up.

Amused, Fritz looked at Hannes's quizzical face and slumped into the passenger seat of the car. Annoyed, Hannes got behind the wheel. When he started the engine, Fiete came over, waving his arms. Fritz rolled down the window, and the boy held out a bronze brooch with a recessed red stone.

"I found that in *Lena*'s bow," he said and darted away.

"Well, Fritz?" Hannes said with a wink. "Did you meet a little mermaid on your trip?"

Over the past few days, Hannes had begun to wonder about Fritz. His boss had been receiving a number of phone calls and would leave the station conspicuously early. So the old codger was back on his feet. Grinning, Hannes drove off. For once, he had the last laugh, while an angry Fritz quickly stuffed the brooch in his pocket. "Not a word to anyone!" he said.

The patrol car's rattling engine died just as they reached the end of a dirt road near the "shark fin" cliffs.

"What, you couldn't find a crappier car?" Fritz said as he carefully got out. "Didn't know we had such clunkers in the fleet!"

"It was the only one available."

"I want to tell you something," said Fritz, poking his index finger at Hannes's chest. "You're way too naive! On the second level of the parking garage, there are several practically new patrol cars. But let me guess who assigned you this one. Old Ingrid, right?"

Hannes nodded. It had indeed been the secretary of the Criminal Investigation Department.

"Ever since I started this damn job, that old witch has harassed me whenever she can," Fritz said. "In the future, you've got to insist on a decent car because I'm not going to keep squeezing into this box!"

With slightly uneasy steps, he approached a narrow path leading down to the beach. At the edge of the cliff, he slipped and fell backward, arms flailing, and disappeared down below. Despite his injured knee, Hannes ran after him. Fritz was hurtling down the trail to the beach and only came to a stop when he hit the sand.

Hannes raced down and leaned over him, worried. "Man, Fritz, are you okay?"

"Another fall like that and you'd be driving me to the nearest hospital." Fritz rolled over onto his knees. His black jeans were slightly torn and dirty.

"There were two trails up there. Fortunately for you, you at least chose the right one to fall down, because the crime scene should be right in front of us."

"You're a real optimist. I'm so happy!"

"No seriously! The left path leads to the other side of the beach, and there's no passage between the two sides because of the rocks."

Fritz warily eyed the path. "I wonder if I'll ever be able to get back up. Anyway, what now? Where was the body found?"

Hannes looked at the beach. "It was completely dark when I was here last night, but probably over there by the remnants of the barrier tape."

The two men stepped over clumps of seaweed that had been washed ashore and made their way through the driftwood.

"That was the storm of the century," Hannes said. "I'm sure it was no fun to be at sea in that weather."

"It's usually less severe out on the open sea than closer inland. But it really wasn't fun."

They reached the shreds of barrier tape flapping in the wind. Otherwise, this stretch of beach looked just as desolate and ravaged as the rest of the coast.

Fritz turned, surveying the scene. "Although we won't find any new evidence, it's important we get a good look at the crime scene, so we always have it in our minds. Maybe at some point we'll make a connection we don't see right now. Where exactly was the woman?"

"Right next to this rock. The forensics team took pictures."

Fritz trudged to the spot, and his black jeans got soaked up to the knee. He turned in a circle, taking in the scene, seemingly storing a mental picture. The beach formed a small secluded headland at this point and was shielded on one side by a large number of rocks. The narrow strip of sand was dotted with shells, and a few yards from the waterline rose the coast's mighty cliffs. A lone, slightly stunted tree grew in the rocks, but otherwise dune grass was the only vegetation in sight.

"The medical examiner assumes drowning?" shouted Fritz. "If it was murder, she also could have been thrown off that cliff." He pointed to the edge of a cliff thirty feet above.

"Drowning was Maria's first impression," Hannes said.

"Who's Maria?"

"Oh right, our new colleague in forensics."

"She could have definitely been pushed and drowned in the water after being seriously injured. Or she was simply placed in the water."

"Maybe she was neither thrown nor drowned," Hannes said. "Right now, murder's only one possibility."

"Right. Hopefully, that young doctor will be able to give us some clues."

"If our colleagues are able to find something," said Hannes. "Of course, there was some time between the discovery and our arrival, and the storm had already kicked into full gear. Believe me, the body really wasn't a pretty sight! I wonder if it's possible to determine if her injuries were caused by the storm or not."

Fritz grew queasy at the thought of this: it was clear he would not be able to avoid a visit to the autopsy table. He had always hated dealing with bodies.

"There's not much else we can do today, so let's crawl back up, and tomorrow we can learn more from the beautiful Maria."

"Tomorrow? I was supposed to pick you up, so we could head back to the station and start the investigation. The chief was very clear about that and—"

"I don't give a damn what he says. I'm your direct superior, and I'm telling you we'll start tomorrow morning! Now, help me get up that damn hill, and then go home or to practice or wherever."

Hannes gave up and helped him climb the cliff. "My back hurts too much to sit. I'm going to walk. See you tomorrow," Fritz said when they reached the top. Ashen-faced, he staggered toward the harbor. Hannes shook his head. He wondered what he should do with his unexpected free afternoon, because practice was out of the question due to his aching, swollen knee.

Just then his phone rang. "Hello, Maria! Find something out already?"

"Hannes." He loved her faint Spanish accent. "There's no doubt the woman drowned."

"Accident or suicide?" he asked.

"We're not sure. We discovered abnormalities that we need to look at more closely. For example, there are tiny abrasions on her wrists that could be from a rope. Best you come over tomorrow morning."

"But there was no rope when she was pulled out of the water."

Maria laughed. "Then it's up to you to find this rope. Welcome to your first case!" She hung up.

"Your first case." That sounded both appealing and disconcerting! With no clues, Hannes felt helpless. He looked at the barely visible path that led to the cliffs along the harbor. There was no trace of Fritz. Hannes called him, but his phone was still off.

The restless night was now behind Merle. The eye of the storm seemed to hover just above her. For hours, she had listened in the dark to the whirling and howling and thunder. Merle had been afraid of thunderstorms her entire life, but that night, she would have given anything to be handed over to the forces of nature. Sometime in the morning, it had all subsided, and Merle had fallen into a dreamless sleep that lasted for hours.

When she woke up, there was silence. Her right hand automatically reached for the bedside lamp. Then reality set in and drove the last sticky threads of sleep away. Wide-awake and panicked, she felt the adrenaline pulsing through her body and sat upright. She should not fall asleep! What if someone snuck in and found her completely defenseless? Her breath grew uneasy at the thought; she listened to the darkness. Then she reached out and was met with no resistance. A sob rose in her throat, and she did all she could to swallow the surge of despair.

After all, she found herself on the same comfortable mattress she had seen in the soft glow of her watch when she'd first opened her eyes in this room two days ago. She had been surrounded by total darkness and had sensed a soft surface on which someone must have laid her. She had noted the stale taste in her parched mouth and felt relief when she ran her hands over two granola bars and a bottle of water. She had unscrewed the lid and quickly quenched her thirst.

She had only gradually shed the feeling of being trapped in a dream. Where was she? In a hospital? Had there been an accident? She had shouted these questions into the darkness, but the silence that had followed seemed only more profound. Distraught, she had curled herself into a ball, her mind filled by a viscous fog.

After an hour, she had been able to regain some of her determination and carefully scanned the room. Whenever she had bumped into something, she had cried out in fear. An object had rattled as she knocked it over. She had cautiously felt the object with her fingers, her time spent in the darkness as a teenager aiding her in the process. "A metal bucket!" she had whispered in surprise as she then felt the matching lid.

She measured the room to be exactly sixteen small steps wide by twenty steps long. Apart from the bed and the bucket, she had found no other items. A spot on the wall had caught her attention. Her fingertips had sensed a slight unevenness—so slight, however, that Merle had almost ignored it. She had run her fingers up and down the narrow gap until she had been sure that she had found a door. The door to freedom, to light! But she had been unable to find a handle. Someone must have brought her here and locked her up! But who? And how? And above all, why?

Again her fingers had run up and down the barely noticeable gap in the wall. It felt different: the wall was cool and smooth, not rough. "It's the way out, it's the way out," she whispered over and over. But no matter how much she had scratched at the gap and no matter how much she had thrown herself against the possible door, her attempts were unsuccessful.

The purpose of the bucket had become apparent when, two hours later, she'd had to go to the bathroom. Merle's thoughts had then turned to the unknown person who had locked her up. She'd racked her brain in search of a clue, but her memory always faded after recalling the old tree she had been sitting against as she watched the sea.

Merle moved along the bed until she came to a wall. She cautiously stood up and took several small steps from her sleeping spot. She was careful to keep one hand on the wall so she did not lose her bearings. She hated the darkness; her mind and body yearned for light. She felt defenseless and shuddered at the thought of everything that could be hiding in the dark. She needed to go to the bathroom. She moved to the corner of the room farthest from her bed where she had carefully placed the bucket and tightly closed the lid.

"No one can see me!" she said as she pulled down her tight jeans and squatted over the pail. Then she froze. But what if? What if she had fallen into the hands of some perverted kidnapper who had installed a camera that could record her in total darkness? She forced the rising panic back down. Just as she was about to stand up, she heard a noise for the first time since the raging storm.

Footsteps were slowly coming closer! Merle raced back to the bed, almost knocking over the bucket. She hit her shin against the wooden edge of the bed and crouched in a ball on the soft mattress. She pulled her legs close to her body and trembled. Cold sweat ran into her eyes as the noise of footsteps suddenly ceased at the exact spot where Merle had sensed the narrow gap in the wall many hours before.

MONDAY EVENING

Hannes leaned back in his seat and pressed his head against the window. The Ferris wheel slowly began to turn, lifting him with a swing into the darkening evening. The colorful sea of lights from the annual carnival glittered below. It was a sharp contrast to the solitude of the beach he had visited with Fritz that afternoon.

Earlier, he had participated in a singles event and had tried hard to make the best of a bizarre game in which six males and six females were unleashed upon one another. He had ended up sharing his entire life story with five of the women and had been met with both approval and rejection. He'd been completely bored and walked off unnoticed, disappearing into the carnival crowd. The smell of roasted almonds, sticky cotton candy, sweat, and vomit wafted in the air.

Hannes had left the fairgrounds and crossed the street to a gas station, where he bought a six-pack of his favorite beer and stuffed it in his backpack. He had already started heading toward the waterfront when, leaning against a tree, he had seen the blinking Ferris wheel. Floating just above everything else, it was exactly what he needed. He now sat in his seat, enjoying the distant mix of voices and carnival music, glad to have escaped the pushing and shoving of the fairgrounds below.

His thoughts wandered back to the failed Singles Night. Those stupid questions! How do you answer a question like "So, who are you?" or "What do you do?" Who was he? He had been searching for the answer to that question for so long, and if he found it, he most certainly did not want to share it with the first stranger to come along.

His gaze drifted to his reflection in the window of the gondola. *Who am I? Name: Johannes Niehaus, known to all as Hannes. Age: thirty-two. Height: six foot two. Place of birth: some small town in the middle of nowhere. My dark-blond hair is never the way I want it, and due to a pigment disorder, I have one green eye and one blue eye. My ears stick out and have a tendency to blush when I'm embarrassed. I'm an athlete and a police officer, and I live in a small one-bedroom apartment.* Pretty basic profile, he thought. But it was also a complicated question—the million-dollar question, so to speak. *Who are any of us?*

A jerk and a terrified scream yanked him from his thoughts. The lights in the gondola flickered, and a brief look below revealed a pyrotechnic spectacle of flashing and dying lights. For a moment, the lights all shone without interruption, and a collective sigh of relief drifted up to him from the crowd. Then the power went out for good, and the fairgrounds and much of the city sank into darkness. His gondola remained stuck at the top at the highest possible position.

He looked around the gondola for the first time. There were six seats, three on each side, five of which were occupied. Opposite him, a frightened young couple clung to each other. The guy in the seat farthest from him said, "Well, this fucking sucks!" and looked at the pitch-black fairgrounds below.

The woman to Hannes's right looked at the man in annoyance. "It's just a power failure," she said.

"I don't know who you are or where you're from, but a power outage on a Ferris wheel definitely sucks. Right?" the man said.

"You got that right," the other man said. "Hopefully, they have an emergency generator or something. But power outages usually only last a few minutes."

"Don't jinx us," the woman said.

"I was stuck for four hours on a train last year because of a power outage. In the dead of summer too!" the first man said.

And while the story was eagerly shared down to every last detail, an uninterested Hannes let his thoughts wander.

"Your first case," Maria had said, and he was still uncertain whether he should be delighted or terrified. Up until now, he had led a rather innocuous life and had really only confronted crime on TV or in the paper. He had at first been euphoric when he arrived last night at the police station and was sent down to the beach.

Once there, his euphoria had promptly subsided and was seamlessly replaced by violent nausea as he stood in the middle of a raging storm, looking at the corpse of a woman in a tattered business suit. She seemed to have been tossed around for a while by the wind and water before being deposited there. Her body, with its wounds and twisted joints, looked gruesome. Before Hannes was able to take a few steps back, he threw up in the seething water next to the body.

"You still at it?" one of the forensics men yelled. "If you're so squeamish, then keep your distance and don't barf all over the crime scene!"

His ears glowing, Hannes muttered an apology and walked away. Was this a scene he would have to get used to from now on? He couldn't have had a worse start to his new career: half the station soon knew he had puked all over his first corpse. He rinsed his mouth out with salt water. In the distance, he could see two very old men being interviewed by a colleague. Another officer came up and provided Hannes with some background.

"The one on the right stumbled upon the woman while he was out collecting amber; he's supposedly an artist who lives in the area. The one on the left is a farmer who had been harvesting his field nearby and was dragged here by the artist. Both seem pretty flustered. How about you? Has your stomach calmed down?"

"I feel so embarrassed," Hannes said.

"Nonsense! How do you think we reacted when we saw our first bodies? Some of these guys here had the exact same reflex as you—myself included. Next time, it'll be easier. At the very least, you probably won't heave on the body."

His frank words helped put Hannes at ease. Nevertheless, he continued to keep a low profile until the body was removed and was glad when he was finally able to go home. At first, he assumed he was only sent to the crime scene in order to observe, but Lauer told him later that morning that the dead woman's case had actually been assigned to him and Fritz.

"An unidentified victim and no leads—Fritz is the perfect man for the job. And I couldn't think of a more fitting challenge for you to dip your toes into."

Hannes had spent the morning at forensics and tried several times to get in touch with Fritz. Thankfully, he had followed Lauer's instructions and intercepted him at the port.

Someone asked, "What are you doing up here?" and suddenly Hannes was back in the gondola. Everyone was staring at him.

"Sorry, my mind wandered," he said.

"We hardly noticed," joked the young woman next to him. She had long blonde hair and a pretty face, and came quite close to his idea of an angel. She wore a number of silver bangles on her left arm, and her tall, slender figure left nothing to be desired.

The girl opposite him, however, seemed to have a somewhat sunnier disposition. "Let me summarize the last ten minutes for you," she said, smiling to reveal a small gap between her front teeth. She pointed to the young woman. "That's Elke. She just arrived in our beautiful city and wanted to get an overview of the urban jungle from up here. She has plenty of time for that now." The woman giggled. "Our comedian's name is Ben. He's originally from Berlin and is a student at the university, right?"

Ben nodded, and one of his blond dreadlocks fell into his light-blue eyes. He was wearing a faded green T-shirt with neon-yellow letters that read "Fuck the system before it fucks you!" His face was covered in blond stubble, and he had an elongated silver rod in his eyebrow.

Placing her arms around her boyfriend's shoulders, the woman continued, "This is Kalle. He was born here, and that's why he doesn't really appreciate this awesome view anymore. And I'm Ines. I just returned from a year abroad in Africa. We wanted to celebrate our reunion by going to the carnival."

"Celebrate!" said Kalle, wheezing.

"Kalle's afraid of heights. I convinced him to go on the Ferris wheel, and of course this happens."

It had grown so dark that he could barely see the others in the gondola, though the outlines of the booths and the rides were somewhat visible. A few spots were illuminated by the rotating blue lights of the various emergency vehicles.

"I'm Hannes," he said in an attempt to catch up. "I've lived here for six years. But this is the first time I've been stuck one hundred and sixty-five feet in the air."

"There are some pluses," Ben said. "I've managed to get away from my girlfriend. She was making my evening a living hell. As far as I'm concerned, we can chill here for a while. Apparently, the cell network is overloaded and has also gone out, so for once, I'll get some peace."

Elke cleared her throat. "Some boyfriend you are! Do you realize your girlfriend is probably worried sick?"

Ben shrugged and made the gondola shake. "Whatever. We're through. I would have told her that after coming here."

"As if that makes it any better!"

"I've also done some ditching of my own tonight," Hannes said, and he immediately felt as though Elke was making him her next target.

"I was on one of those organized singles outings. Twelve lonely hearts in search of love. I escaped at the first opportunity."

"What made you go on that?" asked Ben. "You must be pretty desperate!"

"I had no choice. It was a birthday present from my sister, and I had to promise her I'd actually participate. Which I did . . . for twenty-two minutes."

Ines laughed while Kalle continued to be preoccupied by his fear of heights. "Was it so bad that you actually counted the minutes?"

"Overall, yes. I never thought I'd participate in singles events. I felt like some reject who had to pander to potential customers."

"Singles events? Plural? So that was not your first time?" Ben asked. "Who sent you on the other dates?"

Shit, he had said too much. As a part-time police officer who would be investigating murders, he would have to choose his words more wisely.

"No one. But since people have told me all sorts of amazing success stories, I thought it couldn't hurt. However, my sister didn't know I'd given up on this type of dating. Well, now I'm definitely not doing it anymore!"

"Wait a minute," Ben said. "The spirit is willing, but . . . You know the rest."

The guy was starting to pick on Hannes, but Elke saved him. "You, of course, have no need for that, right, Romeo?" she asked Ben.

"If you knew," he said and grinned. "I have a wealth of experience. My latest speed dating achievement is now somewhere down there wandering in the dark. So I'm the living counterexample to all the success stories."

"You can't just go making generalizations," Elke said.

Ben shrugged. "Maybe you're right. It's hard to say. But whatever. Better alone than to give up and settle no matter what the cost."

Ines butted in. "Don't limit yourselves. It worked for Kalle and me—we met each other on the Internet. So there's also a success story sitting in this gondola."

"You're kidding," said Ben. "Obviously, it's hard to say. Eighty percent of this gondola has had some sort of experience with dating services. Or . . ." Grinning, he turned to Elke. "Should we make that an even hundred?"

"No! And just so you know: I'm not into boys, especially ones like you. So don't even try it."

"Take it easy. I have nothing against you. And as for your orientation, it doesn't matter to me."

"I've tried online dating services several times," said Hannes, turning to Ines and Kalle, "but it was too overwhelming. I always mixed up the women I met. I once asked the wrong woman how her grandmother's funeral went. I almost fell to the floor! Then I created an Excel spreadsheet with the most important facts about each of them. Before every date, I'd go over their information just to make sure I didn't commit another faux pas."

The laughter shook the gondola.

"How romantic!" said Ben, wiping tears of laughter from his eyes. "But not a bad idea. I'm going to remember that!"

"That's good, because no one in this gondola's going home with you," Elke said.

"Don't be so sure. Maybe I'm so fed up with women that I want to try something else." Ben stared deeply into Hannes's eyes and raised his eyebrows.

"Do you ever take anything seriously?" Elke asked.

"Sure, I'm just a little on edge because I finally decided to break up with my girlfriend. These last few weeks have been an utter nightmare, and I keep putting it off."

"On that note"—Hannes patted his backpack—"let's toast! I have a six-pack in here. We may be high, but we don't have to be dry."

This news seemed to bring even Kalle back to life. "I can throw in a bag of licorice and a few roasted almonds."

"A campfire in the middle, and this would be a perfect evening," said Ben.

Hannes opened five beers with a lighter and passed them around. They all clinked their bottles together.

Ines snuggled with Kalle. "That hits the spot. By the way, we've been taking this all pretty well! Better than being stuck hanging in a roller coaster . . ."

"How long have we actually been sitting in the dark now?" asked Hannes.

"About half an hour," Elke said and sipped her beer.

Hannes was beginning to feel comfortable, and the conversation was starting to get lively. Ines shared a few anecdotes about her year in Africa, where she had been an aid worker. Hannes told them about his rather unexciting life as an athlete and police officer.

"Really, you're a cop?" Ben asked. "I could have guessed you were an athlete judging by your build, but you don't strike me as a police officer. That could be because I've only met police officers in . . . other situations."

"That's such a cool combination," Elke said to Hannes. "You get paid to do what you love, and police work seems pretty exciting!"

Hannes sighed and told her what his actual workday was like at the station.

"I know how it is," said Ines. "With me, everyone thinks development work must be really exciting and motivating. But I often spend so much time doing paperwork that I sometimes think I'm more of a bureaucrat than an aid worker. That's why the year in Africa was a good change."

Elke did not have to deal with such difficulties. She worked as a teacher at a nursery school, where she was confronted with other challenges. Nor did Kalle, who as an event manager was always traveling.

"Anyway, the last hours of my twenties have been pretty exciting," Ines said.

"What do you mean? Is your thirtieth birthday coming up?" asked Hannes.

She nodded. "After tomorrow, I can no longer use my youth as an excuse. Damn, how time flies! It used to drive me insane when my grandma and parents said such things. But now I realize just how short a year actually is."

"Same for me," Hannes said. "At twenty, I thought I'd have children by the time I was thirty, and it felt like that was still way off in the future. I always wanted to be a young father, but today I feel exactly as I did then. As if I had all the time in the world."

"How old are you?" asked Kalle.

"Thirty-two. What about the rest of you? Are you still in your roaring twenties or are you old like me?" he asked, and it turned out the others were also over thirty.

Hannes could already feel the effects of the alcohol; but this was not surprising, since as an athlete he almost never drank. Ralf, his rival, had been correct in calling Hannes a dork. At Hannes's former club, he was nicknamed "the Workaholic," because he placed everything second to his athletic success and frequently had to be sent home from the gym late at night.

"Are you going to celebrate your thirtieth?" he asked Ines.

"No, I just got back and have no desire to organize a big party right now. But you know what: if you'd like, you can come over tomorrow night. We're having a few people over. Nothing much, just a few beers. No big to-do. No gifts. What do you say? It can't be just a coincidence that we met each other this way."

"Great idea!" said Ben, and since everyone else agreed, they arranged to meet at eight.

Nearly two hours had passed, interrupted only briefly by a worker who tried to reassure them over a megaphone that the Ferris wheel's manual override was unfortunately defective.

"Why is it taking so long for the power to come back on?" Ben said and shifted in his seat. "I don't know about you, but I could use a bathroom break soon!" He pointed at the empty beer bottles by their feet. "As soon as this thing starts moving again, let's find a toilet and then drink another round in the main tent. What do you say?"

Everyone except for Ben looked at their watches.

"You can see the difference between those with jobs and you," said Kalle with a laugh. "We've all got to get up early."

"Oh come on," he begged. "You can't let a special evening peter out like that!"

After a while, they all gave in.

"Okay, but only if we get our feet back on the ground in the next few minutes," Elke said.

And at that very moment—accompanied by "Oohs!" and "Ahs!"— the power came back on, and a sea of lights flashed below. The gondola jerked forward and floated slowly down toward the ground. As soon as they got off, they stormed the nearest restroom and gathered out front.

"Where to now?" asked Kalle as Ben's cell phone rang. He looked at the display and walked a few feet away. After a few minutes of heated conversation, he hung up and returned.

"I have to go," he said.

"Now?" asked Ines. "You were pretty insistent that we go out for another drink. Did your girlfriend just rip into you?"

"No, that was someone else. Something's come up. Anyway, we're still on for your birthday. Sorry, guys. I'll see you tomorrow."

Ben disappeared into the crowd.

"There's something fishy about him," said Elke as they all watched him leave.

"You got that right," said Hannes.

Monday Night into Tuesday Morning

These dreams are a scourge. Like the ghosts of long-dead souls, they come and go as they please. They follow only their own rules. Rarely do they vary: their actions seem predetermined and immutable.

Throughout the night, the rattling of the cattle-car wheels can be heard, and in the total darkness, this noise is the only warning of the impending descent into hell.

Suddenly, the door of the car is quickly rolled open. The glaring light blinds the eyes, angry shouts ring out.

"Come on, faster, faster, line up!" Unbearable cold pierces the body. The orders are obeyed by running. "Faster! Faster!"

Cursing, insults, beatings, a mountain of clothes, an ocean of shorn hair. Nakedness, ice-cold water from pipes in the ceiling, more running, and more beatings and humiliations.

Clothes striped blue and gray—at least no longer naked.

Wooden shoes that make every step torture.

A stab in the arm, cold—inside and out.
Helpless, defenseless, joyless—hell on earth.

TUESDAY MORNING

When Fritz entered the office the next morning, Hannes had already been sitting at his desk for an hour. It didn't look as though Fritz had had a particularly good night. He was pale and clearly still suffering from severe back pain.

Fritz leaned against the door frame with a cup of coffee. "This really sucks! You know, I've put in so much overtime through all these years, and never once did I make a big deal about it. I worked weekends and holidays. So when I take some time off, I want to enjoy that time off! Steffen just lectured me about how I should always be on call and how we should have actually started the investigation the day before yesterday. As if it matters to the body whether we start sooner or later. If it's really so urgent, he could have transferred the case to someone else!"

"Lauer told me you're the right person for the case since we have no clues," Hannes said in an attempt to calm him down.

"I'm honored," Fritz said, then his mood suddenly brightened. "Come into my office, and we'll try to figure something out."

Fritz plopped down in his leather swivel chair and stretched his legs. He was wearing his usual black jeans and blue polo shirt.

"Any news from forensics? Is there actually a reason to suspect foul play, or are we getting worked up over nothing?"

"Maria called me yesterday afternoon. It's been confirmed that the cause of death was drowning. However, small abrasions were found on the woman's wrists, maybe caused by a rope. When we pulled her out of the water, her hands weren't tied. Maria also mentioned other abnormalities."

"Why didn't you let me know? That's important!" said Fritz.

"Your cell phone was off, and your voice mail has not been activated."

"Fine. Did Maria specify the abnormalities?"

"No, she suggested we come see her in person."

"I really hate how medical examiners always have to be so secretive. Did she say when we might honor her with our presence?"

"She's there all morning."

"Then let's get this over with. What's your schedule look like?"

"I'm here all day. When I fell down at the harbor, I twisted my knee so badly that my doctor said I can't even get into a canoe."

Fritz got up from his chair and walked around his desk toward the door. "You row with your arms, not your legs."

"True, but since I canoe, it's still a problem," Hannes said, following Fritz down the hallway. "You kneel on one leg while the other lunges forward. If I were paddling a kayak, it'd be a different story."

"Then why don't you use a kayak while you're injured?"

"Because that's a completely different type of motion. With a kayak, you use a double paddle."

Fritz shook his head. "That's a funny way of getting around. Makes me grateful for my *Lena* with her motor and wheelhouse."

***

Later that morning, Maria met them at reception. Hannes's ears began to glow at the sight of her short wool skirt, suede boots, and white top. Something about the expression in her hazel eyes unsettled him.

Maria extended her hand to Fritz, then Hannes. "Thanks for coming early. I'm lecturing later on at the university. Anyway, let's head to the autopsy room. Right this way."

"You're Spanish?" asked Fritz as they walked down a poorly lit hallway.

"My father's German and my mother's Spanish. I grew up in Barcelona, but because I went to a German school, I learned the language at an early age. And then I went to college in Germany. Unfortunately, my parents didn't raise me to be bilingual, so I had some difficulties at school, at least in the beginning. And as you can tell, it's still possible to hear where I come from."

"Think nothing of it," Fritz said. "You speak perfect German. I've spent a lot of time with foreigners and have worked with youth to combat violence and right-wing extremism, so I can pinpoint accents pretty easily."

"That's comforting," Maria said while she slipped into a white lab coat. She opened the door to the autopsy room, where a man was bent over a body.

"Hey, Andi. This is Fritz and Hannes, the investigators. I'll give them a brief overview."

The young man gave a nod. "The table's yours."

Hannes and Fritz paused at the sight of the battered naked woman on the steel table. The room had no windows and was very sterile, with steel cabinets on the walls and various instruments on a metal tray. This stood in stark contrast to the mutilated body. With a sinking feeling, Hannes registered a slightly sweet odor.

Maria noticed the officers' discomfort. "The woman looks a little more decent now. When we first got her here, it was a bit grotesque."

Fritz coughed and had difficulty breathing. His voice was huskier than usual. "Please, give us a brief overview," he said as he rubbed the scar on his left cheek.

Maria smiled. "I'll do my best. We don't want another unfortunate accident." She glanced at Hannes, whose ears glowed again. Obviously, word of his nausea at the beach had spread. Fortunately, not to Fritz.

"Nonsense, we're not that squeamish," Fritz said.

Maria walked behind the table, so the dead woman was between them. "As you can see, the body has been badly injured," she said, "but the injuries are mostly superficial. Although we did discover a few minor fractures and chips in the bones, they could hardly have been inflicted by a person. They were more likely the effects of the storm. She was in the water for quite some time and had been tossed among the rocks. She drowned. That much is certain."

"You had mentioned something to Hannes about marks on the wrist?"

"Exactly, look here." She raised the dead woman's right hand and pointed to the reddish abrasions. Hannes and Fritz reluctantly approached the table. "But we cannot say whether these impressions were caused by some form of restraint or from contact with the rocks."

"Could she have fallen from the cliff?" asked Hannes.

"We just don't know."

"How long was she in the water and when was the time of death?" Fritz asked.

"When she was found, she had been in the water for twenty to thirty hours. And determining the time of death for drowning victims is extremely difficult, but it should be somewhere in that time frame," Maria said.

"And the woman's age?" asked Fritz.

"Between fifty and fifty-five. Unfortunately, no ID was found on her. Since she's not wearing a ring and has no corresponding impression of one, it's safe to assume she was unmarried. Her hair was dyed blonde but is actually gray."

"Did anyone check her against the missing-person reports?"

Maria nodded. "No matches."

"You mentioned several abnormalities," Hannes said.

"Yes, but to see these you two must unfortunately come closer."

Fritz and Hannes reluctantly approached.

"Here." She turned the left forearm in order to give them a better view. Hannes flinched and heard Fritz swallow. "There is a tattoo right here. It's nothing unusual, even for a woman of her age. But this tattoo is very new. Unfortunately, it's impossible to make out. You can see for yourself it's quite faded and blurry—and not done by a professional, because the spot's also inflamed. We figure the tattoo was done only twenty to thirty hours before she was recovered—because of the inflammation, probably before her death. I think it's unrealistic that she got it voluntarily."

"Why?" asked Fritz.

"Even an amateur tattoo artist would be ashamed of such a botched job. Besides, I can hardly imagine a woman of her caliber would get a tattoo. She was wearing a business suit, and a tattooed forearm makes for a bad impression at a business meeting. Incidentally, we made another discovery on her arm. You can see a small elongated scar here. Due to the tattoo and the inflammation, it doesn't immediately stand out. Unfortunately, it's hard to tell how old this scar is. Compared to the tattoo and other wounds, it's definitely older. As you can see here"—Maria pointed to a wound on the upper arm—"the difference is . . ."

"All right," Fritz said. "We get it."

Maria shrugged and placed the arm back on the table. "Except for the marks from the rocks, there are no signs of external violence. She was definitely not raped. And there was no blow to the head. We also found no foreign material in her clothes or under her fingernails, though such things would have been completely washed away by the water."

"Hmm," said Fritz, massaging his scar. "Can you take a photo of the tattooed arm for us?"

"Already done." Maria pulled out a thick envelope from a desk drawer and handed it to him. "In here you'll find photos of all the injuries and the tattoo. There's also a detailed report, but I've already shared the essentials. There's one more thing: we found traces of a sedative in her body. Ingestion was also most likely between twenty and thirty hours before her discovery. Of course, that's dependent on the concentration of the drug."

"If you had to make a guess about the cause of death, what would you say?" Fritz asked.

"Accident, suicide, murder—any of these would correspond to her condition."

Back in his office, Fritz opened a drawer and slammed a stack of paper on the desk. "Let's summarize what we know! First, the facts."

He wrote "Victim (female)" in big letters and added a list of bullet points underneath:

Name: Unknown
Age: 50–55
Clothing: Business suit
Time of death: Probably Saturday
No jewelry, no ID
Dyed blonde hair
Recent tattoo and scar on left forearm
Tattoo unclear
Sedative in blood

Fritz pushed the sheet of paper to the edge of the desk and placed two photos of the tattooed forearm next to it. Then he pulled the next sheet from the pile and wrote "Discoverer of Body."

"Hannes, what do we know so far?" He tapped his pencil on the paper.

"An old man who lives nearby was walking along the beach and stumbled over the body. That was Sunday evening, prior to the storm, so before six thirty. Or that's what the farmer he flagged down stated. The old man has not said anything and appears to be a little crazy. The farmer said that the old man lives by himself in a small hut and calls himself Merlin. Supposedly he's a famous painter."

"Merlin?" Fritz looked at his notes. "He's world famous for his insane work! I went to an exhibition of his a few years ago. If you stare at his paintings long enough, it takes a while before you can collect your thoughts."

"Really? I've never heard of him."

"Maybe you should treat yourself to a little culture once in a while and not just sports. I didn't know the guy lived near here. And what do you mean he hasn't said anything?"

"Nobody could get a word out of him. Maybe he was in shock. The farmer said he never makes a sound, not even during his rare visits to civilization."

"We should pay the old boy a visit. No statement? That's unacceptable." Fritz placed the sheet of paper with Merlin's info diagonally below the photographs. "Let's go visit the farmer. Did he say anything else?"

"He did. He was quite knowledgeable, unfortunately more on issues unrelated to the victim. Our colleagues got a crash course in agriculture. His name's Lutz Olsen, and he was riding his combine harvester when Merlin flagged him down. It must have been around six thirty because it had just started raining. He then climbed down to the beach, saw the body, and drove his combine back home to call us. Evidently, he doesn't have a cell phone. The emergency call came at exactly 7:38 p.m., and our colleagues from the crime squad arrived shortly before eight. The storm had been raging for more than an hour."

"Had the farmer seen anyone that day?"

"No, he'd been working in the fields since that morning and didn't notice anything. No one asked him what he saw Saturday, because we only just found out that the body had been lying there for quite a while."

"So we don't really have much to go on," said Fritz. But he was accustomed to tough starts. "Hopefully, it won't take long to learn the victim's identity."

He pushed the piece of paper with Lutz Olsen's details next to the information about Merlin and took a long sip of coffee. Then he stood and leaned on the desk.

"What about ship traffic?" Hannes asked.

"What do you mean?"

"Well, the woman could have fallen overboard and washed up on the beach. Maybe she was pushed. That would explain the lack of a struggle."

Fritz looked at Hannes and nodded. "You're right! You should contact the Coast Guard. They can put together a list of which ships have been in the area since Friday and radio them. After that, we can go for a little ride in the country and see the two witnesses. Let's start with the farmer, then we'll look for the old artist."

After the Coast Guard promised to get back to them, Hannes and Fritz headed for the coast. Earlier that morning, another storm had passed over the city, but it had been significantly weaker than the one on Sunday. The sky was still overcast, and Fritz's Jeep snaked through a gray sea of houses. Around noon there was hardly any traffic, so they reached the outskirts of town very quickly. Fritz's favorite classical music was playing through the speakers. More than a few cases had been solved while he was attending the symphony. Hannes, who was more a rock music guy, stoically endured it.

As the Jeep left the big city behind, the sun broke through the clouds and bathed the landscape in a golden light. The green of the still-damp meadows and trees seemed especially intense.

Fritz rolled down the window and happily breathed in. "That's it with the rain," he said. "The next few days will be boiling hot again. Glad my garden got a good soak."

"Where do you live?"

"Close to the harbor, where you picked me up yesterday. I bought a small house there two years ago. I got fed up with the weekend traffic to my boat and back. It was torture. Besides, it was never my dream to grow old in the city. I just rent a small room there for the weekdays. I'm looking forward to spending my time gardening or on my boat, and my nights smoking a pipe on the terrace, listening to the seagulls. But that's still a long way off."

Hannes turned toward him, surprised. He had never once thought Fritz had a romantic side.

"Surprised?" Fritz said and laughed. "My wife and I always dreamed of owning a house by the sea. Only now I'm living that dream alone. But if my back keeps acting up, I'll probably have to hire a gardener and sell my boat. That leaves just the terrace, a rocking chair, and my pipe. Let me tell you something . . ." He glanced over at Hannes and straightened his glasses. "Don't put your dreams on hold. Don't wait for the right time to come. And don't wait for this or that to be finished. Things change quicker than you think, and suddenly it's too late. And then you'll regret it for the rest of your life."

"Did your wife die a long time ago?" asked Hannes.

Fritz avoided the question. "So how was last night? Are your days as a single man now finally over? The big night was yesterday, right?"

"No success," said Hannes.

"Maybe you need to rethink your requirements," Fritz teased.

Hannes rolled his eyes and told him about the power failure and his unexpectedly long ride on the Ferris wheel. The incident had been making waves in the papers. A complaint had been filed against the owner of the Ferris wheel: even though the power had gone out and manual override hadn't worked, the gondolas could have been pulled down by hand. A woman with a heart condition had also been on the Ferris wheel, and she had collapsed.

"I met four nice people, so there was a plus side to the situation," Hannes said.

The well-maintained farm was abuzz with activity when the Jeep rolled up. No one took much notice of them as they walked up to a group of four men. Three were kneeling on the stone-paved courtyard, trying to keep a cow on the ground, while the fourth rummaged through a small suitcase.

"Rumen acidosis," Fritz said.

"Huh?" asked Hannes.

"Rumen acidosis. It's a metabolic disorder that leads to colic and diarrhea."

The rearing cow was given an injection, and seconds later, she calmed down. The men stood, dripping with sweat. One of the larger ones stared at the two police officers.

"Can I help you?"

"Detective Janssen from the Criminal Investigation Department. This is my partner, Niehaus. We want to talk about Sunday evening with Mr. Olsen. But if now's not a good time . . ."

"It's all right," said the big man. "I'm Lutz Olsen. I already told your colleagues everything, but I'll gladly do it again. Tom and Hauke, take Sina back to the barn." He turned to the third man, who had shut his suitcase—obviously the vet. "Come back tomorrow around noon?"

"Will do," the vet said and made his way over to his beat-up car.

"Come in," Olsen said, pointing to a thatched building. He had on a red plaid shirt and brown corduroys. His face was chiseled, and his cracked, pawlike hands were proof of a life dedicated to hard work.

He came across as warm and friendly, and his cheeks, flecked with red, suggested that he knew how to appreciate the finer things in life.

"You know your way around animals?" he asked Fritz as they headed toward a white front door wreathed in wild climbing roses. "I heard your diagnosis. You hit the nail on the head. We don't have much dairy cattle anymore and focus on growing rapeseed. Since biofuels are on the rise, rapeseed's a much better source of income. Now that it's July, I have to direct all my attention to the harvest, and since Hauke—that's one of our two workers—was at his sister's wedding this weekend, Tom had to take care of the animals by himself. Unfortunately, he doesn't have a knack for it and used too much concentrate feed. You saw the result."

"Some good hay and sodium bicarbonate work wonders," Fritz said.

"Wow, you really know your stuff!"

Olsen flung the door open and ushered them into the hall, its walls decorated with old tools.

"Inga! Two men from the police are here. Can you make us some coffee?" he shouted.

From an adjoining door, a plump woman with short gray hair and chubby red cheeks stuck out her head and waved to them with a smile.

"I'm Inga Olsen. Welcome to Hohenberg Farm! Please, have a seat in the living room. I'll bring you some coffee and pastries."

"My Inga," Olsen said and led them into the living room, which was full of bright rustic furniture and a fireplace. "She's always happy when we have guests. It's not often that someone goes out of their way to come here. Most of the time, it's just our workers and the cattle. Actually, my wife owns the farm. I shrewdly married in." He winked and plopped down into an old-fashioned armchair. While they waited for coffee, Fritz and Olsen discussed past and present farming practices, and Hannes could not get over his amazement at Fritz's expertise.

Mrs. Olsen rolled in a cart with steaming coffee and a colorful cake plate. She distributed flowered plates and gave each of them a considerable slice of cheesecake, while the cackling of hens could be heard through the open window. Hannes was hungry and grabbed another slice from the cake plate, which pleased Mrs. Olsen.

"My partner's a competitive athlete. He can always use a few calories. Just don't eat too much, Hannes, otherwise your canoe won't float."

"Says the coffee junkie . . ." Hannes said.

Fritz quickly turned to business. "Can you tell us what happened Sunday night?"

"Well, there's not much to tell," said Olsen. "We farmers follow the weather reports with particular interest, so I had tried to harvest as much rapeseed as possible before the storm. Unfortunately, I don't wear a watch, but I think it was around six thirty when the crazy old painter appeared in my field, waving his arms and running toward the combine."

"Do you know the man?" Fritz asked.

"'Know' is too strong of a word. He's lived in the old cottage not far from the lighthouse for probably ten years. I know he's a famous painter. But do I really know him? No."

"He rarely comes to the village," Mrs. Olsen said. "His daughter provides him with the essentials. She drives a yellow sports car, and since we're on the road leading to the old hut, I sometimes see her drive past. We have a small farm shop, and she once bought fresh eggs from me. She was very curt and well dressed. Otherwise, she buys everything for her father in the city, which is a shame because we have a lot of fresh things out here."

"When the painter arrived, what exactly did he say he found?" Fritz asked.

"Say?" Olsen chuckled, and his wife answered for him.

"He hasn't spoken for years! At least not when someone from the village has been around. Perhaps he speaks to his paintings or his daughter. He was taciturn when he moved here, but after a while, he went silent."

"So how did you know what he wanted?" Hannes asked.

"At first, I thought he was having a seizure. He always carries a cane with carved symbols. Maybe he's a member of some sect and conjures spirits. Anyway, he just made strange sounds and was completely beside himself. He repeatedly pointed to the cliffs and finally pulled on my shirt. At first, I was annoyed, but then I understood that he wanted to show me something. So I followed him, and he led me to the place where the two narrow paths start. He pointed down the path on the right, and I immediately saw something floating in the water. At first, I thought it was an animal and climbed down. But I could quickly tell it was a woman. Her eyes were open, and at first, she didn't seem to be dead. Her arms and legs moved in the waves. But when I jumped into the water, I noticed her eyes were fixed. You know, on a farm, you see dead animals all the time, and I immediately realized she was dead. Her skin was so . . . unnatural, not at all alive! Nevertheless, I felt her pulse, but there was nothing. I felt nauseous, and I ran as fast as possible back to my combine and drove here to call the police. Later, some detectives of yours came and asked me to drive back with them."

The farmer had clearly been caught up in the memory. Beads of sweat hung on his forehead, and his face had lost some of its healthy color. His wife patted his hand.

"Had anything changed at the crime scene or with the woman in the meantime?" asked Fritz.

"Well, the corpse already looked pretty . . . chilling. But of course, the storm had been raging for some time by then and . . . Well, it was not a pretty sight, so bruised and twisted."

"Does that mean you couldn't see any injuries when you found the woman?" asked Fritz, glancing at Hannes.

"I didn't look very closely. But I can't recall any injuries."

"Did you know the woman, or was she vaguely familiar to you?"

The farmer shook his head.

"According to the police report, you called at 7:38. How long did it take you to get from the beach to here, and when did you return with our colleagues?"

"Like I said, I don't wear a watch. But it probably took half an hour. When I was down by the water, it had started to rain and the wind had noticeably picked up."

"And what time was it when you returned to the beach with our colleagues?" Fritz repeated.

Olsen turned to his wife. "Maybe ten?"

"Did you notice anything unusual on Saturday or Sunday?"

"No, nothing. Tourists rarely get lost here. They all stay a few miles up the coast, where the sand is finer. We unfortunately have a lot of rocks lying around here. Because of the rocky outcrops, you can't walk from the sandy beach to here directly. There is a fairly overgrown path along the cliffs that only the locals know about."

"What did the old painter do in the meantime?" asked Hannes.

Olsen looked at him in surprise. "Now that you say it . . . When I climbed down to the beach, I stopped paying attention to him. I don't think he came down with me. But when I came back with the police, he was there again. Since he doesn't speak, I told the police he was the one who led me to the body."

"He probably found the dead woman while collecting amber," added Mrs. Olsen. "There was an article about him in the paper with a small picture of one of his paintings. Pretty awful, by the way, so gloomy and chaotic. He supposedly uses amber in some of his paintings. That's why you see him sometimes on the beach."

"We wanted to meet with him," said Fritz. "You said this road leads to his house?"

"Not quite. The road ends at an abandoned farm. We purchased that farm's fields several years ago from the heirs of Mats Petersen. They let the farm completely deteriorate. But then again, it was never really a beauty. Drive down the road to the old lighthouse, where you'll see a small dirt road on your left. It ends at the old cottage where he lives. It was empty until he moved in."

"Thank you very much for your time," Fritz said. "And of course for the wonderful cake. I have to roll my colleague to our car now, and then we'll try to get a few words out of the old maestro. Should you think of anything, even if it seems unimportant, please call us immediately." He patted his pockets. "Hannes, I forgot my business cards again. Did you get yours yet?"

"No, not yet. Would you happen to have a piece of paper?" Hannes asked their hosts. He left his cell phone number on an agricultural magazine before they parted.

"How come you know so much about farming?" he asked as Fritz started the car and slowly drove away. "You'd think you've been working on a farm for years."

"My adoptive parents . . ." Fritz hesitated as a Brahms violin concerto filled the air. "They actually had a farm I was supposed to take over. But my romanticized notion of becoming a cop ultimately won out. Anyway, we now have a clue. The body apparently had no visible injuries before the storm tossed it about. Let's hope that you make another good impression on the old painter and loosen his tongue. Maybe Merlin likes to paint nude portraits of young well-toned athletes . . ."

When they arrived at the old lighthouse, Fritz parked the car. The lighthouse had long been replaced by a modern steel structure. The front door of the old tower was half overgrown with ivy, and some stones from the walls had fallen out. A half-splintered window hung in its frame next to the door.

"So much for the romance of the sea," said Fritz.

"You're right, the lighthouse really is something. They could at least fix it up for tourists."

"We already have enough tourists. It's nice this small section remains untouched. Now, where's this dirt road? Or maybe it's more of a trail."

Soon they were rounding the old walls of the lighthouse, staring at the fifty-foot drop. A jumble of small and large rocks jutted out even farther into the water. The air was muggy, and even by the coast, the breeze was moderate. Fritz took pleasure soaking in the sea air, while his gaze was lost in the distance.

"Fritz, over here!" Hannes pointed to some flattened grass. "A car must have recently driven down here. Can you see the tracks? They lead over there, behind that small grove. Doesn't seem like anyone drives down here often."

"Yeah, well, evidently, the old man's daughter is the only one who visits him. Let's try it."

"So your Jeep can actually serve its purpose," Hannes said as Fritz drove it down the barely visible lane. "Poor thing must be so bored in the city!"

"Be glad I have this poor thing," said Fritz as he bounced over potholes. "We wouldn't have gotten very far with your piece of junk. I wonder how the daughter of this Merlin guy can drive down here in such a low sports car."

As the field gave way to a small pine forest, the ground eventually flattened out. The trees were not particularly thick and had been twisted by the wind into odd shapes.

"I wouldn't want to be alone here in the dark for too long," said Hannes.

"Wait until you see the old man's paintings. This bizarre forest seems to inspire his imagination in a similarly eerie way."

A small clearing with a half-collapsed house appeared between the trees. Fritz brought the Jeep to a stop in front of a small porch.

"Let's hope our painter isn't out collecting amber," Fritz said.

The treetops at the edge of the clearing rustled in the breeze. Upon closer inspection, the house looked even more dilapidated, with a chair and small table on the porch. A half-empty glass of water stood beside an opened book on the table.

Fritz and Hannes climbed the rickety porch steps. Fritz picked up the book and turned it over. "*The Wehrmacht's Crimes during World War II*," he read. "Apparently our silent artist is interested in history."

Hannes sniffed the glass. "Vodka! Looks like Merlin gets his inspiration from more than just stunted pines." He smiled and knocked on the half-open door. "Hello? Anybody home?"

Everything was quiet. Fritz kept flipping through the book, and Hannes pushed the door open and stepped into the dark, empty hall. He saw three closed doors and a narrow staircase that probably led to the attic. "Hello?" Hannes opened a door on the left and stepped into the next dark room.

A few rays of sunshine came in through the narrow slits of the wooden shutters, and specks of dust danced in the thin bands of light. As his eyes adjusted, Hannes screamed and stumbled back. A demonic grimace with yellow eyes and long claws. Flames flickered in martial colors, and skull-like faces looked up at him in torment. Hannes's heart, hardened by competition, pounded. Suddenly, he felt a hand on his shoulder and screamed again.

"What did I tell you?" said Fritz. "This guy's images are really bizarre. And yet they sell all over the world!"

"Bizarre? That's probably the understatement of the year! Are all his paintings this terrifying?"

"I think so. It's his trademark."

"Who would hang such horrifying pictures on their wall?"

"Apparently plenty of people." Fritz shuddered. "I'm going to take a look outside. When you're done being scared, we can head back to the city. We obviously came here for nothing."

Fritz disappeared through the door, and Hannes looked around in the dim light. Demons danced across canvases large and small, while others, lacking any recognizable features, created unsettling scenes with jarring colors. In some paintings, fragments of amber had been used, which explained the artist's lonely walks along the beach.

These images had a dramatic effect on Hannes. He felt they deeply touched something in him, something dark and carefully hidden. It was a feeling that scared him. The paint was applied so thickly in places that the protrusions from the canvases made the gallery seem like a 3-D nightmare.

Hannes began lifting a cloth that hung over a canvas of gigantic proportions when he heard shouting outside. He quickly ran down the hall to the porch. Fritz was yelling at an old man, who uttered only confused sounds while waving and repeatedly thrusting a slightly curved cane at Fritz. Suddenly, the old man let out a scream, his eyes rolled back, and he slumped over.

Hannes, without thinking, jumped over the porch railing and ran over. He carefully felt for the man's pulse and was relieved when he detected a faint beat.

"He fainted! What did you do to him? Why were you yelling at him like that?"

"What . . . what did I do?" said Fritz, his face red. "I walked over to the outhouse. Suddenly, this guy jumps out of the trees and hits me on the head with his stick!" He pointed at the scrawny, motionless figure on the ground.

"Since we're not uniformed, he probably thought we were burglars. Help me carry him into the shade."

"Sure, I'm the one to blame," Fritz said and grabbed the old man's legs.

They carried the limp body onto the porch and laid it down gently. Hannes raised the old man's legs and placed them on the chair, then put the chair's cushion under his head.

"Maybe we should call an ambulance: at his age, you can't be too careful," Hannes said, looking down at the pale face.

"The doctor would be better off taking a look at my bump. He's fine. I didn't even get close enough to touch him." Fritz leaned forward and looked at the man with concern. The artist's wool cap had slipped to the side, exposing his bare, liver-spotted scalp. He had a large circular birthmark just below his right eye, and his sallow complexion and dirty clothes created a pitiful impression.

A moment later, Merlin opened his eyes and winced when he saw Fritz's flushed face. Hannes pushed Fritz aside and spoke slowly and clearly.

"We're police officers. There's no need to be afraid. Look!" He pulled out his badge. "I'm going to help you get into this chair, and then we'll calmly explain why we're here. Please don't worry." Gently, he grabbed the man under the arms, and Merlin let himself be helped into the chair. "Rest for a moment, and we'll bring you a glass of water. May we use your kitchen?"

The old man did not answer. Hannes took the silence as consent and went with Fritz into the house. "Let's let him collect himself. He's a tough old man, all right."

"Your first aid skills are pretty up to date," Fritz whispered.

"That's true, but I also used to volunteer helping the elderly. You learn to be careful with people who are disturbed . . ."

They walked into the kitchen, which looked reasonably modern. Hannes took a glass from the small dining table and filled it with water.

Back on the porch, Merlin was drinking the glass of vodka.

"All right," Hannes said and laughed, trying to make the best of the situation. "Alcohol might do you some good, but you should also drink some water."

Merlin took the glass and downed it. Then he eyed the detectives suspiciously.

"We're from the police," Hannes said again. "We knocked, but heard nothing and assumed you weren't at home. That's why we looked around. We wanted to make sure everything was all right. Apparently, you mistook my colleague for a burglar." He leaned against the railing. "Are you feeling better? I can get you another glass of water."

The man nodded yes and Hannes disappeared into the house. From inside, he heard Fritz's muffled voice and fragments of words: "body," "woman," "beach." Apparently, Fritz was done messing around. Hannes rolled his eyes and sighed. Empathy was not Old Fritz's strong suit! As Hannes stepped out into the sunlight again, Fritz repeated his last question.

"So what time did you find the body?"

Merlin stared at him, then took the glass from Hannes, drank it in one gulp, and placed it on the table. He wobbled to the front door and went inside.

"You've got to be kidding me!" Fritz said.

"The best thing to do is to return tomorrow. I can come by myself if you don't want to."

Fritz thought for a moment. "All right, Mr. Social Worker. Maybe that's for the best. This guy's really driving me crazy. Maybe your skills are better suited here. But let me make one thing clear: if you can't get him to talk on your terms, then I'll pay him another visit. We're investigating a death! If need be, I'll have him write a statement—or paint one!"

They walked to the Jeep and got in. Fritz started the engine and took off toward the forest. The bumpy road lulled them into silence. Hannes's eardrums began to vibrate as Fritz turned the speakers all the way up. At the lighthouse, he turned onto the deserted country road and, ignoring the speed limit, floored it, reaching 80 mph before slowing down at the first bend. Only then did his pent-up anger seem resolved.

"Not exactly a successful day," said Fritz after he had turned down the music. "We know a little more about the state of the body at certain points in time, but not who she is. Nor do we have the slightest idea who the suspect is or if there even is one."

"Does it usually take this long to get a lead?" asked Hannes.

"When no one has seen anything, the victim's identity is unknown, and no evidence can be found, it's pretty damn difficult," Fritz said.

After another curve, the Olsens' farm came into view. As they approached the house, a plump figure hurried over and flagged them down.

"I wonder if the farmer's wife wants to give you a slice of cake for the road."

Fritz stopped in front of Mrs. Olsen. She walked to the passenger side and knocked on the window. Fritz grinned at Hannes and motioned for him to open it. "Come on, roll it down! The good lady wants to chat with you."

"Good thing I caught you," said Mrs. Olsen. "I figured you hadn't driven by yet. Did you get him to talk?"

Fritz said, "We're very grateful for your assistance, but we can't comment on the investigation."

"I just wanted to say that our worker noticed something on Saturday. He just now told my husband. But if you don't have time, then okay. I just thought we were supposed to contact you if anything else came up."

"You're absolutely right," Hannes said. "It's a good thing you stopped us. What did your worker notice?"

"It's best you come by. He can tell you himself. You know, nothing ever goes on around here, and now one thing is happening after the other! Maybe dead bodies are run of the mill for you in the city, but out here, we never have any problems. We rarely head into town, and that's a good thing. The smell, the noise, the riffraff." She shuddered.

"I always say to my husband: the best thing about the city is the road that leads out of it."

Fritz and Hannes got out of the car and followed Mrs. Olsen into the yard.

"Over there, that's Tom," Mrs. Olsen said, gesturing to a young man. "Tom, come over here and tell the two policemen what you saw!"

Hannes and Fritz recognized the burly farmhand as one of the men who had wrestled the cow to the ground. Tom approached, confused and fiddling with his baseball cap, and Hannes noticed his slight limp.

"Well?" Fritz said. "Mrs. Olsen said you had something to tell us."

"Don't know if it's really that important."

"We'll be the judge of that," said Fritz.

"So on Saturday, I went down to the beach, near where my boss found the woman on Sunday. Because whenever I have some time off, I like to go fishing and just chill out for a bit. So I climbed down and sat on the rocks. Then I unpacked my fly kit."

"He does fly-fishing," Mrs. Olsen said. "That's the hardest way to catch fish, right, Tom? He once brought us such a big trout, we ate for days."

Fritz rolled his eyes. "So what happened?"

"Well, I was considering what fly to use, and while I sat there thinking, I heard voices on the other side of the cliff. The cliffs are pretty steep there."

"Yes," said Fritz. "And where were the voices coming from?"

"I asked myself that same question." Tom said, scratching his head. "Because . . . usually there's nobody around here. And when I didn't see anyone, I thought it must have come from the other side of the cliffs. I climbed over the stones and saw a boat anchored in the water. A man and a woman were on it."

"Hang on! Which side of the rocks were you on? Where the body was found or the other side?"

"Where was the body? I was on the left side of the cliffs because I always have more luck there."

"The body was found on the other side," Hannes said.

"Oh, well then, so I was on the other side, the side where there was . . . nothing."

"What did the people and boat look like?" Fritz asked.

"Well, I'm not exactly sure. The man and woman were arguing, and I felt embarrassed. I didn't want them to see me, so I climbed back over as soon as possible. But I slipped and hit my shin." To prove it, he pulled up the leg of his pants and pointed to a bruise.

"But you must have noticed something," Fritz said. "The size or color of the boat, hair color, anything?"

"Um . . . so the boat was not a fishing boat, but one of those fast ones. A speedboat. And it was white. Perhaps the same length as a fishing boat. And there was a red fish painted on the bow. The man was slim—and well dressed! I was surprised he was wearing a suit. You don't really wear that on a boat. The woman was also well dressed. Dark clothes, long blonde hair."

Nobody noticed that Mr. Olsen had joined the group. "The dead woman also had long blonde hair and was wearing dark clothes!" he said.

"Right," said Fritz. Suddenly, a suspicion began to take shape. "Do you have a pencil and paper?" he asked Mrs. Olsen.

Mrs. Olsen disappeared into the house. Fritz rocked back and forth on his heels and nodded at Hannes. Tom fiddled with his cap until Mrs. Olsen reappeared. With rapid strokes, Fritz drew a rough outline of a boat with a dolphin on the bow.

"Did the boat look something like this?" he asked Tom.

Tom looked at the sheet. "Pretty much."

Fritz looked to Hannes in triumph. "And now we have a lead!"

***

Merle lay still on the mattress. Her longing for light was almost painful. It had entered the room only once, and that was a day ago. When the sound of steps outside her prison had finally ceased the night before, a thousand thoughts had gone through her head. What would happen to her? Beatings, shackles, rape? Would anyone come in? A man? A woman? Or would she be released and it would all prove to be a horrible joke?

She had sensed scraping, followed by a slight creaking noise. Suddenly, a small flap had swung open—at the exact spot where Merle had suspected a door. A bright beam of light shone into the room. The long period of darkness had made her eyes incredibly sensitive, and she had quickly closed them because of the pain.

There had been another scraping noise and then a loud bang. She peeked warily through her fingers. She saw nothing, only darkness. Just as she was about to dismiss the experience as a figment of her imagination, she again heard footsteps growing softer and moving away.

"No!" she had screamed. "Who are you? Please, tell me what you want!"

Without thinking, she had jumped off the bed and run to the spot where she believed the door to be. She threw herself against the wall and pounded it in desperation.

"Let me out! I want out of here! Please!" She'd dropped to the floor and carefully felt around, bumping into hard and soft objects. Then she had noticed a new smell. Food! Someone had brought her food! She identified fresh bread, sliced cucumber, and a big piece of cheese. A bottle of water had also been placed inside. Merle had forced herself to take only small sips in order to ration the liquid.

Now, a day later, Merle's stomach was rebelling. She pressed the button on her watch; it was almost 6:00 p.m. She was terrified to discover that the hands now had a weak glow: the watch's battery was running out. She had turned the light on too often over the past few days, using the soft light in an attempt to make out the details of the room, though her efforts had been in vain.

If only she could talk to someone! She had never been a particularly communicative person, even though her social skills had vastly improved in recent years. But after days of silence and the absence of human contact, she noticed that her mind gradually began to drift.

"Not anymore!" she shouted into the darkness. It sounded wrong: her voice was hoarse and strange. "I can't lose my mind! If there's no one here to talk to, then I'll talk to myself!" Again her thoughts slid back to the past, and she shivered. "I escaped the darkness once before, and I'll do it again!"

Merle sat up in the bed. She had succeeded! She had found a weapon against the darkness and loneliness. Her bright voice became more certain, and she felt calmer.

"I still don't understand why Mom hated me. She got a lot of money from the government because of me, and she spent it on herself. Had I not taken what belonged to me, I'd probably still be stuck in that awful house."

It was only by accident that Merle had found out her mother's secret. A professor had given them an assignment to write a short biography about any relative of their choosing. Since Merle had known virtually nothing about her grandparents or her mother, she had first tried to make up a story. But her thoughts had wandered as she wrote, so she tore up the paper.

In the days that followed, Merle had constantly thought about Mrs. Bernstein, a friend of her mother's who had always been kind to her. Strangely, she'd been unable to remember her face but could recall her hands. They were soft and delicate, and Mrs. Bernstein had lovingly caressed Merle's hair and given her affection like she had never known.

Merle had read a newspaper article about the famous Amber Room, which had been lost during the Second World War, and the memory had come flooding back to her. Amber had received an amber brooch from Merle's mother for her birthday. Merle, who at the time was eight years old, had greatly admired the brooch. "What a wonderful gift," Amber had said. "Now I have jewelry to match my name. Amber is wearing amber, what do you think about that, Merle?" Amber! Amber Bernstein! Merle had quickly flipped through the phone book, and sure enough, there was an Amber Bernstein living in Merle's hometown. But it had taken three days before Merle had gathered enough courage to call her. She had dialed and wanted to hang up when a warm female voice answered. Was this really a good idea?

"Uh . . . hello, Mrs. Bernstein," Merle had finally said. "This is Merle von Hohenstein. Do you remember me?"

For a moment, there was only static.

"Merle von Hohenstein? My God, it's been so long! Twenty years? Of course I remember you. How are you?"

"Good. It . . . it might sound strange, but I'm calling because I'm trying to find out something about my family history and my past. My mother never told me anything and . . ." She had sounded desperate and did her best to fight back tears.

"And now you're hoping I can tell you something?" Mrs. Bernstein's voice had grown warmer. "Merle, I'm very glad to hear from you. Your mother was a bit . . . peculiar. I've been wondering all these years how you've been."

"What do you know about my father?"

"Not much, your mother rarely spoke openly to me. I had to promise her that I would not tell anyone about it."

"Mrs. Bernstein, you're my only hope! Please!"

"Well, your mother and I have had no contact for almost twenty years, so I don't think I owe her anything anymore."

"She'll never know anything about it," Merle said.

"Fine! I have always regretted abandoning you to your mother. You certainly have not had it easy. But I would prefer not to speak about it over the phone. I just had a hip operation and can't leave the house. Would you like to come visit?"

Merle had at first been hesitant but nevertheless arranged to meet Mrs. Bernstein the following weekend at her apartment.

"And the visit was one of my best decisions," Merle said in the darkness of her cell. "If I had known what Amber had to say, I would have visited her so much earlier."

Then, just like the evening before, she could hear slow footsteps approaching. Merle's mind raced. The door opened, and a tray was pushed inside. This time, Merle was cautious and did not look directly into the light. Even if it streamed in for only a few seconds, it was enough to memorize the shadowy outlines of the room. The walls were gray with no plaster, and there was a single lightbulb dangling above. The bed seemed well built and made from dark wooden boards. In the corner, she saw the metal bucket and thought about its awful smell. She looked back and saw some kind of dog door installed in a heavy metal door. She tried to make out more details, but it slammed shut, and Merle heard a bolt slide into place and click. She did not see a door handle. Obviously, it could only be opened from the outside.

Merle smelled cooked vegetables. She carefully got out of bed and groped along the wall toward the door, feeling the cold iron. She got down on her knees and almost immediately discovered the spot where the dog door had been installed. She pushed against it, at first carefully and then with all her strength, hoping to move it, even just a little. But it did not budge.

Merle leaned back against it. She found a bowl with a spoon on a small tray and wolfed down the vegetable stew.

"Well, at least I know more than I did before," she said after she scraped the bowl clean with a finger.

Merle shivered. Suddenly, she was slightly dizzy and then overcome with sleep. Her arms felt heavy, and it was only with great difficulty that she could keep her eyes open.

"Damn it, the . . . food. There must . . . a sedative . . ." Powerless, she fell to her side and fought against the fatigue. "Can't fall asleep . . . who knows what . . ."

TUESDAY AFTERNOON

Hannes left the doctor's office in a bad mood and stepped out into the balmy afternoon. Music flowed from the cafés and mingled with the customers' snippets of conversation and laughter. Fritz had dropped him off on his way back to the station, and he had sat for an hour in the waiting room before he had finally been allowed to show his swollen knee to Dr. Mey. The sobering diagnosis had only further fanned his resentment toward Ole, the old fisherman who had caused his injury.

"Mr. Niehaus, there still has been no improvement. You'll need to keep off your knee," the doctor had said. "I'm writing you a prescription for an ointment, which will help, but unfortunately, you're going to have to postpone any further athletic activity. If you don't, this relatively minor injury could turn into something much more serious that could keep you out for the season."

Hannes had reluctantly decided to follow her advice. The World Cup was in less than two weeks, and the competition was his last chance to qualify for the world championships. There was also the possibility of qualifying for the Olympic Games next year, and he was secretly still hoping for a miracle. At thirty-two, this would be his last chance to compete as an athlete in the Olympics. The thought of Ralf paddling his canoe through the Olympic course while Hannes sat at home watching on television was painful and motivating.

On his way home, Hannes remembered he had to find a gift for Ines. He had almost forgotten about her spontaneous birthday invitation, but now he had no real desire to attend. Since he had not managed to build a real social network, he decided the birthday party would be a unique opportunity to make some friends. And although Ines had said no gifts, he could not come empty-handed.

After considering several ideas, Hannes was struck by a familiar sound a couple of blocks away. Like on most afternoons, Anton was standing next to the entrance to the city park, playing his violin. Anton was a true character and well known in the neighborhood. He had been a professional musician and now lived off a small pension. But he had not given up music, and with his snow-white hair, suit, and bow tie, he maintained a dignified appearance.

Hannes watched Anton play. As he went to drop a coin in the red-velvet-lined box, an idea popped into his head. Anton did not play on the street to supplement his pension. The money he earned went to a charity he had devoted himself to. The neighborhood was not hip or trendy: there were no mothers driving their kids to piano lessons in Range Rovers. Anton gave free music lessons to poor children from the neighborhood. With the proceeds from his busking, he rented a rehearsal room and bought several instruments on which children from around the world could try their first notes. Last spring, he and his students had given a concert in the park, and even if there had been a few slipups here and there, the children's excitement and joy had deeply moved the audience.

Since Ines worked in development, surely she would appreciate it if he gave her something meaningful instead of some sort of embarrassing gift. When Anton put down his violin, Hannes walked up to him and told him about his idea. He requested that Anton play a birthday song while he filmed him with his phone. Anton obliged with a cheerful version of Stevie Wonder's "Happy Birthday." He then bowed and waved sheepishly at the camera.

Hannes handed Anton thirty euros, and his eyes lit up. "I know what I'm going to do with the money. There's a little boy from Africa in my band who's very talented. I'll take him to the symphony."

"Great idea! That's perfect!" Hannes said, then told Anton that Ines had been an aid worker in Africa.

Hannes continued on his way, his knee hurting a bit less. He entered the small park through the gates near the old fire station and took a shortcut through a field. After the long day, he looked forward to a cool shower. As he rounded a bush, he almost collided with two men. A guy with blond dreadlocks exchanged some cash for a small bag. Startled, the men looked up at Hannes before running away. He couldn't believe it! That was . . .

"Ben!" he shouted at the fugitives. "Ben, stop!"

Ben, who had taken the small plastic bag, hesitantly slowed down and turned around. He was embarrassed as he walked over to Hannes. "So I guess this is what you'd call caught in the act. Are you going to cuff me now?"

"Normally, I would! What are you doing?"

"This is just to relax!" Ben waved one of the bags full of marijuana.

"Still! There's a playground over there! Why do you have to conduct your drug deals here of all places?"

"Drugs, drugs, drugs . . . Such a strong word for something so trivial. Others get drunk, I get stoned. What's the difference?"

"The difference is that selling marijuana is illegal, as is purchasing it."

"So what are you going to do?" Ben asked and sighed.

Hannes thought for a moment and then pulled himself together. "I have a party to go to! There's a good chance I may forget about what I saw here."

"Man, I knew you were all right."

"Don't go around saying I caught you and let you go. Not even at the party. You're still coming, right?"

"Yeah, man, I'll keep it between us. You can count on me."

Hannes shook his head.

"No, really. I'll never forget it! If you need something, just contact me . . . You can of course also have some." He grinned and waved the plastic bag.

"I'm a competitive athlete, you know. Anyway, are you coming tonight?"

"Of course! I have a really cool gift for Ines. See you later—and thanks again!" He playfully punched Hannes on the shoulder, turned around, and jogged away.

Hannes looked around, hoping no one had seen anything. Fortunately, no one was there, and he rushed home to get into the shower.

An hour later, he got off the bus and studied the map of the neighborhood posted at the bus stop. Ines and Kalle lived across town in an area he was completely unfamiliar with. He walked past a noisy group of teens in front of a pool hall and passed the blinking lights of a sex shop which threw a kaleidoscope of colors onto the street. Two blocks later, he was surrounded by silence broken only by the excited barking of a terrier. He walked by a row of houses and stopped in front of number 72. He glanced through the names listed next to the doorbells. Seconds after he had pressed the top button, the door buzzed and the fluorescent hall lights switched on.

"You have to walk up to the fifth floor. Unfortunately, there's no elevator," a tinny voice said through the intercom.

He sighed and readied his knee for the climb.

"Man, and you are a competitive athlete?" Ben greeted him as he reached the final landing. "That took forever!"

Ben laughed and leaned against the open doorway. Ines and Kalle came to the door, beaming.

"It's great you could come!" Ines said and gave him a warm hug. "I was afraid you might all change your minds and last night would just be a one-time encounter."

"How can you live so high up with your fear of heights?" Hannes joked to Kalle and then shook his hand.

"Be glad you didn't help us move," he said with a laugh. "That was the day we lost our friends."

The apartment was in excellent condition and tastefully decorated. Ines brought several plates of finger food into the living room.

"Elke's not here yet, but we should probably start. Hannes, would you like something to drink?"

"Beer," Hannes and Ben said in unison, and in no time they were holding cold bottles.

"To the final hours of my youth," said Ines, after which they all clinked their drinks.

At that moment, the doorbell rang, and Ines sidled over to the intercom. "Elke's on her way up," she said from the hallway.

"Anyone else coming besides Elke?" asked Hannes. "Or did you actually lose all your friends in your move?"

"We still have a few," Kalle said, laughing. "But Ines didn't really want to have a big party, and you know how it is: it's hard getting people to come at the last minute. Sometimes we have to schedule something weeks in advance, otherwise we would never get to see our friends."

"Yeah, it was so much easier back in college," Hannes said, and as if on command, they all turned to look at Ben.

He laughed and shrugged. "Hearing you say that really makes me want to finish school . . ."

"I'll say this: enjoy every day! How much longer do you have until you're done?" Ines asked.

Ben shrugged. "I'm not going to stress myself out. My father died early and left me enough money to get by the next few years."

"And it doesn't bother you that you live off of your father's money?" asked Hannes.

"Not at all. It's not taking me so long because I'm lazy. I devote a lot of my time to fighting neo-Nazis. There are more important things than finishing your degree on time. Besides, my father would have been proud. He spent his entire life fighting the far right and was active in a victims association. His father, my grandfather, was murdered in a concentration camp."

There was an apprehensive silence.

"Was he Jewish?" Elke asked.

Everyone looked at the door because no one had heard her come in.

"Hello, Elke," said Ben. "No, he wasn't Jewish; he was a Communist. And for that he was shot in the back of the head . . ."

The conversation turned to Ben's activism, and with each successive story, Elke seemed to hold him in greater esteem. Hannes too realized he had great respect for Ben's commitment, especially since he didn't come across as a show-off when he told his stories. Instead, he seemed very determined, and his knowledge of the Nazi era and current neo-Nazi scene was impressive. It made sense why he had decided to study history, even if later he would probably have trouble staying afloat financially.

"Well, enough of that," Ben said, getting up from his chair. "After all, this is a birthday party . . . I'm going to go have a smoke. May I use your balcony?"

Hannes followed him to the balcony door. Ben looked at him in the reflection of the windows and grinned. He pulled a pack of cigarettes out of his pocket and shook one out.

"All perfectly legal," he said to Hannes and disappeared onto the balcony.

"What's that supposed to mean?" asked Ines.

"No idea," Hannes said.

When Ben came back into the room reeking of stale cigarette smoke, Hannes was already recounting the events of his day. He was unsure how much he was allowed to say and avoided details. Nevertheless, they hung on his every word.

"You really have an exciting job," said Kalle. "You're lucky."

"Don't say that," Hannes said, and he described his morning visit to the medical examiner. "And besides, we're just groping in the dark right now. We have no leads and no clues. So, as an events manager, you probably have some good stories."

But Kalle was dismissive. "It sounds more exciting than it is. At first, I thought it was great, working with real stars and making these big, lavish events happen. But the majority of my work is routine, and celebrities are not always known for their cooperation. They're accustomed to being treated like royalty and develop an attitude."

"Speaking of which, I just remembered. Ines, I have a present for you."

"But I had said—"

Hannes waved aside her protests and pulled out his cell phone. "It's not a gift in the traditional sense," he said and explained the story.

Touched, Ines watched the old violinist's performance and excitedly hugged Hannes. Apparently, Ines's job as an aid worker had also made a big impression on Ben, who had sponsored a girl in Africa on her behalf, as well as on Elke, who had made a donation to Doctors Without Borders in Ines's name.

"This is really unbelievable," Ines said and laughed. "Thank you so much! You've really made my day. And it's definitely better than a bottle of perfume or some stupid knickknack."

"Yeah, and we already have enough of those," said Kalle, and everyone laughed.

Ines wagged her finger at him. "You're not so innocent yourself, my dear! Kalle collects coasters from around the world, and there are three drawers full of them in the cabinet."

They turned their attention back to the finger food, and the discussion became less serious. Kalle demonstrated his skills as a DJ. Old party hits boomed from the speakers, livening everyone up.

"It almost makes you feel old," Elke said, rattling her bracelets. "Teenagers probably consider these songs oldies now."

"If they even recognize them," said Ines.

At midnight, Elke looked at her watch and jumped up in surprise. "I should head home now, I've got a bunch of kids waiting for me tomorrow morning."

"Oh come on! They might be easier to deal with if you're hungover!" Ines joked. "Tonight's been really fun. Let's not think about work for once. There's no reason why we can't go a little crazy from time to time. We should really let loose!"

Ines walked over to a chair and pushed it against the wall. Kalle supported her efforts to keep the party going by dimming the lights and turning up the volume.

"We'll see when your colleagues come and ask us to keep it down," Elke teased Hannes, then kicked off her shoes and began to hop around the room. Soon the group transformed the living room into a dance floor. It was only when the morning light crept through the windows that Elke at last acknowledged how tired—and perhaps old—she felt.

Promising to get together again sometime soon, they exchanged phone numbers and headed out into the early morning. The birds were already chirping as Hannes, slightly swaying, attempted to hail a cab. A feeling of happiness flowed through him, and he vowed to enjoy life to the fullest. The dead body and the station were far from his thoughts.

Tuesday Night into Wednesday Morning

Dreams have different origins. They are based on imagination, stories, fears—and memories.

As in the dreams of years past, it begins pitch-black. A beam of light appears when the hand of a small child pushes the door open, allowing for a glimpse into the adjacent room.

A young woman with a battered face and gray hair sits in a poorly furnished living room. The dull glow of the single lamp in the room falls on her hunched back. A sewing machine sits in front of her on the rickety wooden table, a mountain of fabric next to it.

The child enters the room. The previous night, he slept at a friend's house and received a set of pajamas as a gift from the friend's mother. The child knows his own mother earns very little, and any purchase poses a heavy burden. His own pajamas are old and worn, and he had outgrown them.

The child beams and innocently skips in the light of the lamp and, spinning in circles, presents his gift. He figures his mother will be so happy when she sees the new blue-and-gray striped pajamas!

Tired, the mother raises her head, and her eyes widen. A scream comes out, and she stretches out her arms in defense. Panicked, she jumps up from her chair and backs away. Inarticulate sounds are all she produces before she throws herself on the threadbare sofa, buries her head in the pillow, and sobs. Shivers run up and down her body. The forlorn child stands in the center of the room, his arms at his sides, before he leaves, closing the door behind him.

Darkness is all that remains.

WEDNESDAY
MORNING

It's cold, Merle thought as she slowly regained consciousness. She felt déjà vu as she lay on the soft mattress, trying to get her brain to work again. It was as though she had been transported back in time to when she had first woken up in this room. Everything still felt the same, right down to the chill that gave her goose bumps.

Then she remembered the food and the subsequent grogginess. She became restless. She listened to her body and then moved slightly. No pain. No handcuffs. Everything seemed fine. So why the sleeping pill in the food?

She touched her thigh and froze. She had been left in only her underwear.

Merle trembled uncontrollably and moaned. Without clothes, she felt even more vulnerable and helpless. Someone had entered the room while she'd slept and undressed her.

Merle began to sob. As she turned on her side and curled up in a ball, she felt something soft next to her. She examined the item with her hands and unfolded it. It was too small to be a blanket. The item had two buttons and an elastic waistband. She realized it was a pair of pants and a long-sleeved shirt. She slipped on the garments. The material was thin but warm.

I don't understand! Why would someone put sleeping pills into my food, undress me, and place a pair of pajamas on the bed? What do they want? And why won't they talk to me?

When Fritz came into the room, Hannes was sitting at his desk, his eyes slightly bloodshot. He was badly hungover.

"What's wrong? You look like you spent half the night hugging the toilet," said Fritz. He was wearing his typical black jeans and blue polo shirt and was carrying a coffee cup.

Hannes shook his head. "I told you about the people I met on the Ferris wheel. Ines's birthday was yesterday, and she invited all of us. I didn't get to bed until five, and now I'm feeling it."

"How many beers did you have?"

"I lost count."

"Well, it's about time you started training again, otherwise you'll lose sight of your goals and get completely out of shape. Was there at least a woman you're interested in?"

"They're all interesting, but Ines has a boyfriend and Elke's a lesbian. You'd like Ben. He's a committed Nazi hunter and has even gone to jail for it."

"Well, looks like you've got yourself a fine group of friends. Probably better not to tell me everything this Ben character is up to . . ." Fritz leaned against the desk. "I called the Coast Guard again yesterday evening. The owner of that unmoored motorboat's named Florian Schneider, and the report reveals he was negligent in properly tying his boat up. Mr. Schneider has naturally tried to make up excuses, but the circumstantial evidence is clear. It wouldn't surprise me if it was his boat the farmhand saw on Saturday."

"Did the Coast Guard send you photos?" Hannes asked.

"They e-mailed me a picture of the boat, but they don't have a photo of Mr. Schneider. Persons involved in accidents aren't booked or fingerprinted."

"What does Mr. Schneider have to say about the deceased?"

"So far nothing, because he hasn't been questioned. I drove past his house yesterday, but it was deserted, and he was also unreachable by phone. But I know where he lives and where he works. He runs a real estate office downtown, so we can grill him in person. And I have a special job for you while we're there. This isn't official, but it'll certainly speed things along."

Fifteen minutes later, they were studying the window display at the Schneider Real Estate office. It was a bright, cloudless day, and the sun's reflection glared in the windowpane. Fritz squinted as he examined the listings and then shook his head.

"I should buy myself a condo downtown! Here, look at this crappy place: eight hundred square feet, three rooms, balcony, centrally located, great potential. Only 450,000 euros!"

"And in addition to that bargain price, you'll also shell out 3.57 percent in commission directly to Mr. Schneider," Hannes added, beginning to feel better. "That's got to be around 15,000 euros. I don't want to know how many hours I'd have to work to afford that."

"Doesn't sound like you're best friends with real estate agents."

"I'm looking for a new apartment, and almost everything has to go through a real estate agent, no matter how rundown the place is. You have to fork over a month's salary just to move."

"And I now understand why Mr. Schneider can afford such a fancy speedboat. According to the info from the Coast Guard, he's only thirty-nine. And his house is more of a villa with a small park," Fritz said. "Now let's see what he has to say."

They entered a bright waiting room which, thanks to the black leather couches, palm trees, and modern art, exuded a sophisticated atmosphere. The glass reception desk was empty, and a short electronic buzz announced their arrival.

Hannes looked at the colorful paintings on the walls. "This is insane," he said. "I could give my little nephew a couple of colored pencils and sell the work as"—he studied one of the titles—"*A Blind Woman's Morning* for a fortune."

"Don't tell me you prefer Merlin's paintings," Fritz said and grinned.

"At least his paintings convey emotion and take talent. But this . . ." Hannes shook his head.

"Well then, you've found yourself another job, because you're certainly not going to get rich being a police officer," said Fritz. He drummed his fingers on the counter. "Is somebody going to come or what?"

The door at the end of the room opened, and a staid-looking gentleman wearing horn-rimmed glasses and a suit stepped out. "Thank you for choosing us" came the canned response from inside, and a tall, slender man with slicked-back blond hair and tan skin appeared in the doorway. "Let me know if I can do anything for you. I'm sure we'll find a buyer for your little gem soon."

While a scowling Hannes stared at the floor, the portly gentleman was ushered out. The real estate agent approached them with an out-stretched hand, his grin revealing teeth as white as his suit.

"Forgive me for making you wait. My assistant called in sick today. What can I do for you? Are you interested in buying or selling?"

"Are you Mr. Schneider?" Fritz asked.

"Yes, I am. I'm the owner of the company, so you're in the best hands." His teeth illuminated his suntanned face.

"Detective Janssen." Fritz pointed to Hannes. "You already met Niehaus this weekend."

"I thought your faces looked familiar. And how can I help you? My lawyer's taking care of the matter." His initial friendliness waned with each subsequent word.

"We're from the homicide unit," said Fritz. "We're not here about the fishing boat."

Schneider's face lost some of its color. "What about my *Dolphin*? My boat was seriously damaged in that accident."

"Like I said, we're not here because of the accident."

"So why are you here? Did my boat hit someone as well?"

"I hope not," Fritz said. "However, a woman's body was found on the beach about three miles east of the port. Does that mean anything to you?" He watched him closely. "We have evidence that your boat was anchored at the exact same spot on Saturday."

Schneider turned slightly red. His jaw dropped. "What's this? You want to pin a murder on me now? Is this your private vendetta for the old bum with the dinged boat?"

"The one incident has nothing to do with the other. I'm only interested in what you were doing on Saturday at said beach area and who was with you on board your boat."

"I didn't anchor my boat near any beach on Saturday, and there was no one on board. What makes you think it was me?"

"There's a witness who saw a boat near the beach on Saturday, and it bore a striking resemblance to your speedboat."

"It resembled my boat? That doesn't mean it *was* my boat!"

"Where were you on Saturday?"

"I don't think I need to answer that."

"And I don't think we're getting anywhere," Fritz said. "We're only asking because you could be an important witness. Nobody has assumed you did anything, but your responses do make me a little suspicious. If you believe you don't have to cooperate, then we'll gladly continue our conversation down at the station. However, you'll have to

79

close early today. Hannes, why don't you call our colleagues and give them a heads-up."

While Hannes pulled out his cell phone, Schneider looked on in shock. "You're not fooling me with your dumb tactics. You think you've got me shaking in my boots? I have absolutely nothing to do with any corpse. I have no idea why you're making up this story."

"I'd watch what you're saying!" Fritz roared in a hoarse voice, and Schneider jumped back. "No one's making up any story! A woman's mutilated body was discovered at the same site where someone in all likelihood saw you on your boat on Saturday afternoon. In other words, on the exact same day this woman died. Fittingly, a woman was also seen on your boat. So I'd better not hear any more lies out of you!"

"Fine. I was out on the boat Saturday. So it's possible someone saw me in the harbor. But I went straight out to sea and was alone. I have nothing more to say without my lawyer present."

"Fine. You'll be hearing from us. We already have your address, and I recommend you promptly get in touch with your attorney. Have a nice day."

Fritz and Hannes left the office.

"And? Did you get a picture of him with your phone?" asked Fritz as the two of them walked toward the illegally parked Jeep.

"Sure," said Hannes. "You really unnerved that guy with your fake outburst."

"That wasn't fake. It was obvious that creep just told us a load of crap. You don't need to be a psychic to know that. Why didn't he admit he was on the water Saturday? I'm sure Tom will recognize him in the photo. I expect Mr. Schneider will have a few more excuses for us, because after his performance just now, I have my suspicions."

"Maybe we should arrest him now? What if he tries to take off?"

"That won't happen! We'll wait here until our colleagues arrive to keep an eye on him . . . Damn it, you've got to be kidding me."

Confused, Hannes looked at Fritz. Fritz pointed at a parking ticket under the wiper. In order to get out of the fine, he would have to explain why he had parked illegally, and there was nothing Old Fritz hated more than paperwork.

Fritz hurried down the hall to his office, followed by Hannes. "That was dumb of me. I should have printed out the photo of the *Dolphin* and taken it with me. We could have saved ourselves the detour!" He pushed his office door open and turned on his old computer.

The door flung open again. "Can I have a word with you tomorrow, Fritz?" a heavyset colleague asked, leaning against the desk.

"How about knocking first?" Fritz asked and moved his coffee cup to safety.

The police officer grinned. "No time! I just want to hear your opinion about this case." With that, he slammed a file on the table.

"Marcel, I'm flattered that you appreciate my advice, but we're in the middle of an investigation. Can't it wait until later?" Fritz eyed the brown folder. "What's it about?"

"A missing-person report," said Marcel, opening the file. "A young intern at the evening paper hasn't showed up to work and hasn't been reachable since the beginning of the week." He pulled out a photograph and slid it over to Fritz. "Her name's Merle von Hohenstein, twenty-seven years old, and there's been no trace of her."

"She looks sweet," said Hannes.

"May I introduce you, Marcel? This is Johannes Niehaus, my current student. And as you've just noticed, I've been unable to break him of his impertinent behavior. He's in that phase when you check out every woman to determine if she'd be a suitable partner."

Embarrassed, Hannes stuck out his hand, and Marcel shook it with a grin. Fritz opened an e-mail from the Coast Guard and clicked print. The printer in the corner of the room started churning.

"I'm really sorry, Marcel, but my case has first priority," Fritz said and shut down his computer. He grabbed the printout of the boat and nodded at Hannes. "Come on, we've lost enough time!"

The two investigators headed out of town. Hannes called the Olsens to let them know that they would be dropping in for another visit.

"Well, this is quite a stir," said Mrs. Olsen as Fritz and Hannes got out of the Jeep. "Come in, I've baked another cheesecake. It might still be warm, but my husband says it tastes better that way."

"That's nice of you, but unfortunately we don't have time for your delicious cake," Fritz said. "Tom is an important witness. We may have found a lead because of him."

Mrs. Olsen pushed Tom forward while Fritz opened a folder and held out the image of the battered speedboat.

"Is this the boat you saw on Saturday? And"—he waved to Hannes—"we would like to know if this is the same man you saw on the boat."

Hannes opened the photo on his cell phone and held it out.

Tom grabbed the photo of the battered boat and scratched his head. "Hmm, yeah, I think it looked like that. I remember the painted red dolphin at the bow." Then he took the cell phone and looked at the screen.

"We have three photos of him, so you can scroll," Hannes said and took over after Tom gave him a quizzical glance.

"Yes . . . well . . . I only got a brief look at him, but he really reminds me of the man on the boat."

"Do you think he does, or do you know he does?" Fritz asked.

"Hmm . . ." Tom scratched his head again. "Will he go to jail if I say he's the guy? Because I'm not quite sure, the photos are kinda small."

"But at first glance, do you recognize a distinct resemblance?" asked Fritz, and Tom nodded. "Then we should organize a lineup for you to see him in real life. Don't worry; you'll stand behind a two-way mirror so you can see him, but he can't see you."

After Mr. Olsen agreed to release him for a few hours, Tom climbed into the backseat of the Jeep, and they took off toward the station. As they entered the city, Fritz barely eased off the gas, continuing to barrel down the road toward the police station, when his cell phone rang.

"Janssen here," he said and blew through a red light. A light flashed from a small box near the intersection. Fritz swore. "What? No, that wasn't because of you! I was just caught running a red light. But what's up? Talk to me!"

A few seconds later, Fritz cursed again and abruptly stopped the car. Furious, he slammed the phone on the dashboard. "Those amateurs! Our surveillance team did a great job. Just as they were about to arrest the suspect, they found the real estate office locked and a sign hanging on the door saying the office was closed. Once they finally managed to get the door open, there wasn't a single person in the office. If we're actually investigating a murder case, then our prime suspect has just managed to escape through a back door."

On the way back to the farm, Fritz railed against the decline of the police force and his colleagues' incompetence. Not even the gentle sounds of Vivaldi could appease him. A relieved Tom jumped out of the car when they reached the farm. Even a piece of Mrs. Olsen's cheesecake was unable to brighten Fritz's mood.

"Now what?" asked Hannes while Fritz wiped the last crumbs from his mouth and drove the Jeep back toward the city.

"Now we pay a visit to Mr. Schneider's residence. This guy's obviously hiding something."

"What about Tom and the Olsens? Aren't they under suspicion too? All three live near the crime scene. And then there's Merlin."

Fritz rubbed the bridge of his nose. "Tom was fishing on the beach, Mr. Olsen was in his field, and his wife was at home. We still don't know what Merlin was up to on Saturday. Do any of these people seem suspicious to you? But you're right. Just because the focus is on Schneider right now doesn't mean we should lose sight of other possibilities. Even a crazy old artist, a somewhat simple-minded farmhand, and an unpretentious farmer and his wife may have their dark sides too. So long as we're unsure of the victim's identity, it's unfortunately quite difficult to make any connections. If we still don't know who she is by tomorrow, we'll probably have to show our country bumpkins a photo of the corpse. There's no way around it. But at least Mr. Olsen has already seen it and stated that he doesn't know the victim."

Fritz stopped the Jeep in front of a modern estate in an upscale residential area on the outskirts of the city. High walls and massive steel gates blocked the view of the mansion. It was already noon and well over ninety degrees.

"Six Lake Street. This is Schneider's home," Fritz said, pointing to the gate.

"Where's the lake?" asked Hannes. "I'm a little disappointed."

"It's probably behind the property, with private bathing platforms for members of high society."

Fritz opened the glove compartment and pulled out a badge, business cards, and his gun. He threw on a linen jacket despite the heat and stuffed his gun into the inside pocket.

"Do you think it'll get that serious?" asked Hannes.

"No idea. But in the event that Schneider has something to do with the woman's death and feels cornered, I'd rather play it safe. I don't think he's actually home. But perhaps his wife will let us in. Then at least we'll know she's still alive."

Hannes rang the bell, and a woman's voice came over the intercom.

Fritz got straight to the point. "Hello. This is the police. Are you Mrs. Schneider?"

"I am. Did something happen?"

"We'd like to talk to you. Would you please open the gate?"

"Did something happen to my husband?"

Fritz shot Hannes a meaningful glance. "Could you please let us in? We'd prefer not to communicate through the intercom."

"Of course, come in!"

A moment later, the gate swung open. A white house with odd angles stood on the other side of a well-kept lawn with meticulously trimmed hedges. Porthole-shaped windows alternated with protruding walls. The house was surmounted by a bold roof that looked like a bent triangle that extended to the ground. Each room seemed to have a private balcony or winter garden, and the first floor consisted almost entirely of glass.

"Wow," Hannes said. He stared in wonder at the unique mansion.

Even Fritz seemed enamored. He scratched his head and looked around. "I would never have thought you could make so much money off commission," he said. "And look at the size of the plot. All this must be worth a fortune. Maybe he inherited something."

Hannes followed Fritz along a gravel road, which must have been meticulously raked shortly before. When they had made it halfway, a massive brown wooden door opened, and a tall, slender middle-aged woman stepped out. Her high-heeled sandals and dress were white, and her light-blonde, artistically ambitious hair and pale skin completed the enchanting scene. She floated atop a sweeping staircase in front of them.

Mrs. Schneider turned to a shirtless young man who was weeding at the edge of the stairs. "Lars, please take a look at the rhododendrons on the lakeside terrace. I believe they're in desperate need of water."

The young man wiped beads of sweat from his forehead. "Of course, Mrs. Schneider, I'll take care of it right away." He nodded to Fritz and Hannes and disappeared around the corner.

Fritz took out his badge and droned the usual greeting. "You asked about your husband," he continued. "Do you have a reason to believe we're here because of him?"

"I don't know why you've come. Please, explain," Mrs. Schneider said, taking a puff from a thin cigarette. Fritz tried to ignore the perfumed smoke.

Hannes broke in. "We're looking for him. He left a note at his office stating it was closed. He's not at home?"

"No, he's not. Maybe he went to the doctor. He complained about a headache earlier. I've tried to call him because we're hosting a small gathering this evening, and he should be here already."

"That's odd. This morning, we met him at his office, and he seemed completely fine. Was your husband forced to close for the day because he suddenly felt sick?" Fritz asked.

"He's in good shape. Maybe he caught a summer cold. Or maybe he has an appointment. You can ask his secretary if she knows why he suddenly disappeared."

"The office was, as I said, closed. He had told us earlier that his assistant was ill and had not showed up to work."

"Why are you searching for my husband?"

"Mrs. Schneider, were you with your husband on his boat on Saturday?" Fritz asked.

She exhaled. "That ship is his favorite toy. I have not been on it in ages. He races it so fast that I feel sick every time. But sometimes he takes important customers out with him."

"That's strange . . ." Hannes said, but Fritz cut him off.

"On Saturday, your husband had apparently not only raced his boat. He laid anchor by a section of beach where, a day later, a woman's body was found."

"He told me nothing of the sort. However, I returned from New York yesterday late in the evening. My sister lives there, and I stayed with her for a week."

"Do you remember your flight information?"

Mrs. Schneider flicked her hair over her shoulder. "You do not think I . . . I arrived on a Lufthansa flight at nine thirty. You can verify that if you would like."

"You're not under suspicion," Fritz said. "But we do need to investigate all possible leads."

"You said your husband sometimes takes special customers out on the boat. Do you know if he had anyone on board on Saturday?" asked Hannes.

Mrs. Schneider turned to him, paused at the sight of his unique eyes, then looked him up and down. "I have no idea. He runs his business on his own. You'll have to ask him."

"Unfortunately, we're running out of time. Who else would know his schedule?"

"His secretary, of course. Leonie Kustermann. She lives at 20 Post Street. Was that everything? I still have to take care of the preparations for the party."

"That's all, thank you," Fritz said. "Could you please inform your husband when you speak to him that he should contact us? Here's my card."

Mrs. Schneider nodded. "I'll tell him. Now, if you'll excuse me."

She held out her hand, and Hannes wondered if she expected them to kiss it. However, he followed Fritz's lead and merely clasped it. As Mrs. Schneider turned back inside the house, Fritz and Hannes followed the gravel path back to the gate.

Hannes shook his head. "She didn't come across as too worried."

"Or particularly sympathetic," said Fritz. "That white princess radiates cold arrogance. There doesn't seem to be a close relationship between the two. Who knows what services the young gardener provides here?"

"You don't mean that he . . ."

Fritz waved his hand. "I wouldn't be surprised. She eyed you up and down. At least now you've got another job option. Gardener for a rich, neglected wife." He chuckled. "Anyway, at least we know the body isn't Mrs. Schneider's."

"Why didn't you tell her a woman was on board?"

Fritz shrugged. "Just a feeling. If she's having an affair with her gardener, maybe her husband eventually returned the favor and fooled around with a customer. Perhaps the woman pressured him on Saturday, making him commit an irrational act. We should have initially maintained the impression that we only wanted to question him as a witness, but at the same time monitor the property and continue searching for Mr. Schneider. I'm going to visit his secretary. Perhaps she can tell us if he took a customer out with him on Saturday. I'll leave you at the office. Find out everything you can about this man! Sift through our archives, use the Internet to track him down, try to find his friends."

After dropping Hannes off, Fritz continued to Post Street. Nothing happened when he rang the doorbell. It was a nondescript apartment building, same as any other. Although its best days were long gone, it gave the impression of being clean. The faint sound of a radio came from an open window on the first floor, and a baby screamed from somewhere in the house. Fritz rang again, holding the buzzer down for a while. A few seconds later, a gray-haired woman appeared in the open window.

"Excuse me!" shouted Fritz. "Are you Ms. Kustermann?"

"No, Ms. Kustermann lives above me and left about an hour ago."

"Oh, I thought she was sick."

"Well, she didn't look very good. Maybe she went to the doctor."

Fritz thanked the old woman and strolled back to his car. Once inside, he scanned Post Road in the vain hope of discovering a bakery or café somewhere. As a consolation, he popped in a CD of piano concertos and reclined in the driver's seat to reflect on his next steps. A searing pain in his back catapulted him into a vertical position. His cell phone rang.

"Fritz, it's Hannes! We now know who the victim is. A missing-person report just came in, and the description's an exact match!"

***

Fritz raced down the hall and opened the door to Hannes's office.

"That was fast! Did you run a couple of red lights again?" Hannes joked.

"I did, but this time I remembered to put my lights and siren on. So I'll only have to explain two tickets from today."

Fritz stepped closer and looked over Hannes's shoulder at the computer screen. "Is that her?" He pointed to a photo of a woman with long gray hair.

"That's her. Helene Ternheim was reported missing by her brother, Christian Ternheim. The two head the drugmaker Lagussa, and he has not heard from her or seen her since Friday. She's fifty-seven and lives in a penthouse near the harbor bridge. She was supposed to attend a board meeting yesterday afternoon, and when she didn't show, her brother called the police."

"There's no possibility of a mistake, is there?"

"No. Maria's already been in touch with Ms. Ternheim's dentist and compared the dental records. There's no doubt this is Helene Ternheim."

"Has her brother been notified?"

"No, that's been left to us."

Fritz exhaled. "This case is really starting to take off. We'd better not put off visiting Mr. Ternheim, even if there's nothing worse than informing someone about a loved one's death. But still, he has a right to know as soon as possible, and he might be able to shed further light on the case."

"When did we want to stop by the Coast Guard? They promised the initial data for today."

"Why don't you head there on your own. It makes sense if we split up. The manhunt for Schneider is already underway; Matthias and Steffi are coordinating it. You can take my car, and I'll take the bus. Lagussa's headquarters are only a few stops away. I'll meet you back here, and we can share what we've learned."

Fritz threw the car keys to Hannes and was already halfway out the door when Hannes hesitated. "Um . . . wouldn't it be better if we did everything together? I was taught that detectives should only split up in exceptional circumstances."

Fritz eyed his young colleague before taking a deep breath. "Well, let me teach you a few more things, smart alec. First: welcome to reality! Second: a murder investigation always counts as an exceptional situation to me. Third: I told you when we first started working together that I won't change the way I work because of you. Still, you shouldn't go telling everyone how we carry out our investigations. In the end, the only thing that counts is the result; I can tell you that from years of experience. So why don't you go and get the passenger lists of all the ships that were in the area. I don't think we'll get anywhere looking at them, but if we can rule the ships out now, it will help."

Three hours later, Hannes and Fritz met back at the station. Fritz furrowed his brow as Hannes brought the Jeep to a screeching halt in the parking lot and rammed it into first gear before he finally turned off the engine.

"Maybe you treat your own car that way, but I'd like to keep my Jeep for a few more years," Fritz said as Hannes opened the door.

"I'm sorry," said Hannes without the slightest hint of remorse. "I couldn't resist. It's really fun to drive a car where everything works and you don't have to deal with funny noises or backfiring. Your car's still in good shape and—don't worry—no scratches." He pounded happily on the roof and looked in amusement at the vehicle, which had seen better days. "Or should I say, no further scratches, because here . . . and there . . . and over here . . ."

Fritz took the key from Hannes and slammed the car door.

"The trip was worth it," Hannes said and patted a bulging blue bag with the yellow Coast Guard logo. "Everything's in here. It's amazing all the info the Coast Guard collects."

"Big Brother's watching you," Fritz said. "Let's hope our brothers and sisters at the Coast Guard also filtered the data into something useful. Let's go eat, I'm really hungry."

"How did it go with you?" asked Hannes as they walked toward the cafeteria.

"I have always hated being the bearer of bad news. In all these years, I still haven't found a suitable way to do it. Especially since those left behind all react differently. Some collapse, others are silent, and others attack you because they don't want to believe it."

"And Mr. Ternheim?" Hannes asked.

"He was shocked, and obviously wasn't expecting to hear that his sister was dead. However, he was quick to regain his composure. And I did learn some interesting tidbits. But one thing at a time. Let's deal with the food first." Fritz studied the menu at the counter. "Spelt patties with sprouts and mashed potatoes! Who comes up with this crap? Mrs. Öztürk, is it health-food week again?"

Mrs. Öztürk wiped her hand on her apron and winked. "Ah, Detective Janssen! You haven't been here in a long time. There's healthy food on the menu every day. You don't like it?"

"Healthy's good, but taste matters too," Fritz said.

"Either way, there are no more patties! You got here too late. There're only leftovers now. But if you want, I'll make you currywurst, okay?"

"Two, please, and a large plate of fries," said Fritz, his mood brightening.

Hannes pulled a bulging salad bowl from the refrigerator and cracked open a soda bottle of sparkling water while Fritz grabbed a bottle of beer and poured himself a cup of coffee.

"You don't seem to mind the health campaign," said Fritz.

"And you seem more concerned about your taste buds than your health," Hannes said. "Because I can't work out at the moment, I have to adjust my diet. I'm burning almost nothing right now."

Fritz shook his head and steered them toward a secluded table in the corner by the window. "When I hear you talk like that and compare our trays, it makes me feel bad." He put his tray down and slid into the booth with a groan. "Our brains have to kick into high gear now, so maybe I'll burn off at least one of my currywursts."

He speared his first piece of meat and shoved it into his mouth. Satisfied, he watched as Hannes balanced a leaf of lettuce on his fork.

"Enjoyment trumps everything," Fritz said. He took a long sip of coffee before switching to his beer, which he drank with a satisfied sigh. Hannes looked at him in disbelief and shivers ran down his spine. Fritz shoveled another bite of sausage into his mouth. "Put that down for now and tell me what the Coast Guard has for us. Then I'll tell you about my meeting with the victim's brother."

Hannes fished a stack of papers out of his bag and placed the documents next to his plate. Then he unfolded a sea chart.

"This is a map of the area in question. As you can see, the various sectors are labeled. Ms. Ternheim was found here"—he pointed to a cross near the shoreline—"at six thirty on Sunday evening and pulled from the water just before eight. By Maria's estimations, she died twenty to thirty hours prior. They've divided the waters around the crime scene into four zones according to calculations of current and wind conditions. As a precaution, in case there was a mistake determining the time of death, they extended the window to between fifteen and thirty-five hours."

Fritz leaned over the map and studied the four zones, which spread out like a fan. "A fairly large area. Basically, the zones extend like a somewhat wobbly triangle from the crime scene out into the sea, and only the first zone touches land. That means . . ."

". . . that the woman did not drift from somewhere else along the coast," Hannes completed the thought. "Where she was found, the coast juts out a little farther into the sea like a sort of promontory or small headland. Since this headland is shielded on the left by rocks, the body could not have floated there from elsewhere, otherwise it would have gotten stuck on the other side of the rocks. That leaves only the right-hand side, which leads to the lighthouse. But the direction of the current precludes this possibility."

"That's very important information. If she wasn't thrown overboard but was placed in the water, it must have happened right at the site. How many ships passed through these marked areas?"

Hannes slid a piece of paper across the table. "In total, twenty-five ships were recorded, one of them a big passenger ferry."

"Hold on! That's just the boats that have been recorded. What's with all the recreational boaters like our real estate agent? There's tons of them floating around on weekends!"

"Actually, that's a problem, because yachts, speedboats, and fishing boats aren't recorded. Some smaller boats, including virtually all fishing boats, are still equipped for safety reasons with a radar system that automatically sends information to the Coast Guard. All other boats are detected by radar but are only a blip on the screen."

"Which is perfectly fine," said Fritz. "At least there's still freedom on the water. But let's get back to the topic. So how many of these unidentifiable blips do we have?"

"Fortunately, the stretch of coast in question isn't highly trafficked. I saw a screenshot of a tourist area, and it was teeming with recreational skippers. All in all, there were just twelve smaller boats in our area."

"So we're talking about a total of thirty-seven vessels, twenty-five of which we already know. That doesn't make me particularly optimistic," said Fritz.

"Maybe. All recorded ships were radioed and checked. None of them reported any incident or noticed anything unusual. So we can cross them off our list."

"So long as what they said is the truth," said Fritz. "And it's not really possible to verify. We would have to board all the boats, question all the crew members, review their statements, and possibly make further inquiries. We wouldn't be done until winter."

"Especially since the ships are now all over Europe."

"Since we can't inspect the ships, we should consider the responses accurate and concentrate on the investigation here on land. Figuring out which boaters were in the area would most likely be impossible. We must be judicious in our use of resources, and after my conversation with Mr. Ternheim, I doubt we have to look on the water. According to him, his sister would instantly get seasick and avoided boats like the plague. So why would she have been on Schneider's boat? She would never have willingly boarded, at least when she was alive."

When he saw Hannes's disappointed expression, he offered rare and encouraging praise. "Still, your information helps. We can rule out the big ships, and thanks to the sea chart, we have a more accurate picture of the situation. Who knows, maybe we'll take another look at it later."

Hannes dabbed a ketchup stain on the chart with a napkin and gathered the papers. "What was the outcome of your visit to the drug company?"

Fritz speared the last piece of sausage and stared at the plate, then told Hannes about his visit to Lagussa.

As Fritz had exited the bus, the steel-and-glass facade of the company's headquarters towered before him. The forecourt was spacious and attractively laid out with trees, planters, and seating. There were several covered bicycle racks in addition to a fountain.

Fritz had entered through one of the building's revolving glass doors. He glanced down at himself and realized that he in no way fit into this environment. He was relieved to have at the very least polished his leather shoes that day.

"Can I help you?" a woman had asked.

"Yes. I'm Detective Fritz Janssen. I'd like to speak with Mr. Ternheim."

"Do you have an appointment?"

Fritz shook his head. "It's very important that I see him."

The receptionist did not seem convinced. "Do you have a badge?"

Fritz had held his badge out without saying a word.

"All right. Would you please come to the reception desk? I'll see if Mr. Ternheim has time for you now. But I cannot make any promises, since he has a very busy schedule."

"I'm sure he'll spare time for me," said Fritz, following the young woman. She was dressed formally and balanced atop a pair of high heels. She picked up the phone at the reception desk. While she negotiated with Mr. Ternheim's secretary, Fritz looked around the huge hall.

Lagussa's specialty lay in the manufacture and distribution of psychotropic drugs. The walls were covered in oblong banners with descriptions of the company's products. Dispersed throughout the hall were thematically appropriate art installations, like the sculpture of a brain made from iron. Large planters and rippling water flowing through glass at the end of the hall were intended to create a friendly atmosphere. However, Fritz felt uncomfortable and completely out of place.

"Mr. Janssen?"

He turned around and saw a lean elderly lady with a stern face and gray hair pulled into a bun. She scrutinized him through her glasses, and Fritz noticed that her green eyes were set too close together.

"I'm Ruth Wagner, the executive assistant. Mr. Ternheim is waiting for you in his office. If you would kindly follow me." She pointed toward the glass elevators next to the fountain.

While the elevator zoomed up, Ms. Wagner said, "Have you found Ms. Ternheim? I couldn't sleep last night. It's not like her to not call."

Fritz ignored the question. "Are you the assistant to both Ms. and Mr. Ternheim?"

She nodded. "There are actually three assistants. The other two are subordinate to me and work more behind the scenes."

Fritz noticed her firm tone and the pride that emanated from her. "How long have you worked for the Ternheim siblings?"

"Thirty years. In the beginning, I worked as Mr. Ternheim Sr.'s secretary. When his two children took over ten years ago, I remained their assistant."

Fritz had noted her name. Well-informed secretaries were always a treasure trove of background information.

The elevator stopped at the twentieth floor, and the doors opened to a completely different scene than the one in the foyer. The nicely furnished room with dark-brown carpeting and moss-colored upholstery was home to three tidy desks. Two younger women looked up from their flat monitors and warmly greeted Fritz.

"Ms. Maler and Ms. Stahl," said Ms. Wagner, introducing her colleagues. Fritz politely greeted them. She'd then steered him to the leftmost of three doors and turned to him. "Have you found Ms. Ternheim?"

Fritz had faced the massive wooden door and opened it after a brief knock. The room was decorated with wood paneling and comfortable upholstered furniture, suggesting that Mr. Ternheim placed no great value on modern functionality.

A gaunt gray-haired man stood by the large panoramic window, with his back to the door. He turned around and looked at Fritz. He was clean shaven and had no wrinkles, even though he was well into his fifties. Only a birthmark under his right eye marred his otherwise flawless face. At the sight of Ternheim's suit, which perhaps might have been stylish in the 1980s, Fritz no longer felt so badly dressed.

"Mr. Janssen, you're the lead detective in charge of finding my sister?" asked Ternheim.

Fritz cleared his throat and decided not to beat around the bush. It did not look as if it was necessary to take a cautious approach.

"I am. However, we had already found your sister before you notified us. Mr. Ternheim"—he cleared his throat again—"we unfortunately found her body Sunday night on a beach located about three miles from the old fishing port. We were only able to identify her after you filed a missing-person report. I'm sorry."

Mr. Ternheim shifted slightly back toward the window and stared out over the city. Fritz knew there was nothing he could say and remained silent.

Quietly, almost as if to himself, Mr. Ternheim said, "I was afraid something happened."

"What do you mean?"

Mr. Ternheim turned around. "How did she die? An accident?"

"We don't know yet," Fritz said. "I very much hope you can help us in this matter." He'd described what had happened, without getting into too many difficult details.

"And how should I be of any use in the investigation?" asked Ternheim. "That's clearly your job. After all, you should have enough experts who are familiar with such cases. If you want to know if she had enemies, she had none as far as I know. Of course we have competitors that would prefer to get rid of us. After all, we're the industry leader! But otherwise my sister had few contacts. Like me, she devoted her life to the company. That leaves little time for a private life."

"Excuse my next question, but I have to ask: Do you think she might have committed suicide?"

"Out of the question."

"Of course, there's the possibility of an accident. Your sister could have fallen from the cliff. Do you have any idea what she might have been doing on that section of the beach?"

Ternheim scratched his chin. "She was probably visiting our father. She sees him at least once a week and provides him with the essentials. In recent years, he has greatly declined. However, he lives in a place near the cliffs. Maybe she went for a walk . . ."

"Hold on! What did you say? She may have visited your father? Who's your father?"

"The former owner of Lagussa, Heinrich Ternheim. You might know him as Merlin."

Fritz paused. Hannes dropped his fork and stared at him in disbelief. "What? Merlin is the victim's father? That means Helene Ternheim is the daughter the farmer's wife told us about? That crazy old man once led a pharmaceutical empire?"

"Yes," said Fritz with a grin as he adjusted his square glasses. "He left the company a decade ago, which at his age is remarkable. Since then, he's devoted himself to his true passion: painting crazy pictures. His son seems to share our opinion on them."

Hannes was barely listening. He poked at the lettuce. "That explains why he was completely beside himself. Poor old man. Walks along the beach to collect amber and suddenly stumbles over his dead daughter."

"He was crazy and taciturn before, according to the Olsens. But at least this sheds new light on the matter. My instincts tell me it was no coincidence Ms. Ternheim was found on that stretch of beach."

"So what now?" asked Hannes.

Fritz looked at his watch. "In two hours we meet with Mr. Ternheim at the medical examiner's office. He has to officially identify the dead woman as his sister. Unfortunately, he can't be spared that."

"She had no husband or partner? Are there any children or other family members?"

"No, she was never married, nor does she have any children. Her mother's no longer alive, and after our experience with their father, I certainly wouldn't want to drag him to the medical examiner's office . . ."

While Hannes cleared their trays, Fritz strolled over to the counter and asked Mrs. Öztürk about the changes to the menu. When Hannes joined him, Mrs. Öztürk smiled.

"Ah, the young man with the green and blue eyes! Very good karma! In my village, it's said that a man like you can look into other dimensions. The green eye to what was and the blue eye to what is. You're at home in both worlds! You must learn to look correctly and take advantage of your great gift!"

Hannes's ears turned red. Fritz laughed and patted him on the shoulder. "And with these ears, he can even hear the voices from the other side. If that doesn't help us in our investigation . . ."

Fritz pulled Hannes toward the exit and waved good-bye to Mrs. Öztürk. She glared at him.

Christian Ternheim arrived at the medical examiner's office in a modest car. Hannes had expected a cold, stiff businessman and now marveled at the pale, slightly bewildered face. On the other hand, who would arrive bursting with life at the place where you have to identify your dead sister? Mr. Ternheim seemed to want the matter over with as quickly as possible. Maria was already expecting them, and after a brief introduction, they headed for the elevator.

"Since we're done examining, we have to go to the basement," she said to Hannes. "The bodies are kept in the refrigerator down there."

She sensed everyone wanted to get this over with and quickly led the group down a bright corridor to the tiny room. It was almost too small for all of them since the stretcher took up most of the space. Hannes realized it was impossible to distance himself from the dead woman beneath the white sheet.

Maria glanced at Mr. Ternheim. He nodded, and she gently lifted the sheet to reveal a pale face framed by light-blonde hair. For a moment, Christian Ternheim's face relaxed.

"That's not my sister," he said and sighed. But only a moment later, his face contorted into a confused grimace. "Where . . . but . . . it's her! Oh my God! Helene! But what happened to her hair?"

"Did you not know your sister had blonde hair?" Maria asked.

"No. She had brown hair that turned gray around her fortieth birthday. She never dyed her hair."

Ternheim leaned over the stretcher, trembling as he touched his sister's body through the thin cloth. He wiped his brow.

Fritz said, "We have a few brief questions about some abnorm—"

"Please!" Mr. Ternheim raised his hands. "Can't we put this off until tomorrow? I . . . I need some time now. You can come to my office tomorrow, but . . . please, not now."

Fritz nodded. "We'll lead you upstairs. Thank you for coming here so quickly and . . . Well, we're truly very sorry."

As Hannes tried to leave the room, Maria held him back. "Wait. Let them go ahead. I need to show you something."

Fritz looked puzzled but said nothing and closed the door behind him. Maria pulled the sheet to the waist so the battered torso was visible. Hannes leaned over the stretcher and looked intently back at Maria. *What a contrast*, he thought. *In front of me is this horribly disfigured, lifeless body, and behind me is this attractive young woman.*

"Here." Maria lifted Helene Ternheim's left arm. "We studied the tattoo in more detail. This is not a typical tattoo. I mean, not some rose or anchor. Nor Asian characters, which are all the rage now. We examined it through a microscope and analyzed it on the computer. We're convinced this is a series of numbers. While we couldn't identify all of it clearly, a series of six or seven digits were tattooed on her arm around the time of her death."

"It was so nice to see Amber again after so many years." Merle was still trying to fight against the loneliness with the sound of her voice. "Even though I only recognized her delicate hands."

Unfortunately, Mrs. Bernstein was hardly able to help Merle research her family history. She did know one thing, though, and it was of significant interest to Merle.

"Your father was a deadbeat. I'm sorry for being so frank. He was a little older than your mother and had rented a cabin in the mountains with three friends. Your mother, two other girlfriends, and I were on a ski trip and stayed in a nearby house. It didn't bother us, of course, that four young men were staying just around the corner. On the second night, we went to après-ski with them." Mrs. Bernstein sighed at the painful memories. "Your father had an eye on your mother, and she was very interested in him too from the start. He was not really her type—a little standoffish and cranky. One of his friends had told me that there had been some incident between your father and another woman in school, which his father was only able to straighten out with a great deal of difficulty. I warned your mother about him, but she wouldn't listen."

"Why was she so attracted to him then?"

"Your mother had always been . . . well, interested in money, and your father comes from a rich manufacturing family. She had always fantasized that she would someday marry a rich man and be worthy of her noble title. Maybe she was hoping your father would be her savior."

"But he wasn't?"

"Not at all! And then the inevitable happened. They spent several nights together, then continued to write after the vacation was over and talked on the phone every now and then. But this was more on your mother's initiative than his. When she finally realized she was pregnant, she thought he would marry her, of course."

Mrs. Bernstein had laughed in discomfort and refilled Merle's coffee. Then she had gotten up and hobbled to a closet.

"I have a few photos of the trip. Your father's in one."

Merle had considered the somewhat blurry image with curiosity. Her mother stood in front of a ski lift with her arm proudly around a large, stiff-looking man. He gazed at the camera with a forced smile. Merle had felt nothing. Absolutely nothing.

"You can keep the photo."

"Thanks. What happened next? Did my father ever know about me?"

"Oh yes. Your mother immediately told him she was pregnant, but his reaction was different from what she'd expected. A lawyer appeared at her door and made it clear a marriage was out of the question. There were two possibilities: either she would stay silent and refrain from any contact with your father in return for a monthly payment, or the paternity would be challenged in court." Mrs. Bernstein looked sadly into Merle's eyes. "You already know what your mother decided to do."

"Do you know my father's name?"

"I've tried to remember, but it won't come to me. However, I still keep in contact with a friend from back then, maybe she can remember. If I find out, I'll get back to you."

"Fortunately, the friend had a better memory than Amber," Merle said to the darkness.

She tried to ignore her growling stomach because she had promised herself she would not touch any more food. She did not want to be knocked out again. She was restless and got up from the bed to walk in small circles around the room. Three times clockwise, then three times counterclockwise, and over again. "I have to keep moving. But if I move, I use energy and have to eat again. Whatever I do, it's wrong."

But the fear of being drugged again was greater, and Merle leaned against the wall next to the bed. She remained there in a trancelike state for an hour. Only the sound of footsteps shook her from her lethargy.

"You can keep your fucking food," she whispered. At the same time, she hoped the light would allow her to discover more about the room, details she had overlooked last time.

The footsteps stopped in front of the steel door, and Merle heard a faint groan. Then the bolt was pushed aside, and she turned her head away to avoid being blinded. The room seemed unchanged: a large cobweb was all she had previously missed. Her eyes then fell on herself, and she looked at the clothes she had found that morning and put on while shivering. They seemed to be pajamas; the shirt and pants were striped blue and gray.

She noticed the door had been open for a while now without anything being pushed inside. She looked toward it, and a blinding flash of light hit her face. Merle screamed and put her arm over her eyes. A soft click, then another flash of light. Merle threw herself on the bed.

WEDNESDAY EVENING

Hannes's thoughts raced. He stared out the bus window. So the tattoo on the victim's arm represented a series of numbers. A code? What did the perpetrator want to tell them? He was now convinced there was a perpetrator. Ms. Ternheim's sudden disappearance, the secluded location of the crime scene, the dyed hair, the tattoo, the sedative in the blood—the list was too long for it to be a coincidence or for there to be an innocent explanation. But what really puzzled him was the role of the real estate agent, who had disappeared without a trace. Hannes had been glad when Fritz had let him go early.

Hannes got off the bus, and as he turned the corner onto his street, he was met by several flashing police lights. A large crowd had gathered in the middle of the narrow road. Traffic was blocked by emergency vehicles, and an ambulance was parked in front of the building where he had lived for the last six years. He saw his neighbor Richard, who lived with his girlfriend in the apartment next to his. Hannes quickly pushed his way through the crowd over to him. "Hey, what's going on? Was there a fire?"

"No, the weird guy who lives above us has a large terrarium, and a python escaped. They're now searching for it."

Hannes's face went pale. "A . . . a snake? In our building? You're kidding me!" He had been afraid of snakes since he was a child, and they haunted his dreams. "How long has it been missing?"

"No one knows. The guy left yesterday morning, and when he came back an hour ago, the terrarium was empty. He probably didn't close it properly after feeding the snake."

Hannes broke out in a cold sweat, thinking how he always left a window open because of the heat. "So it might have been slithering through our building yesterday?"

"Maybe. You don't need to worry. At the moment, the snake isn't dangerous because it was just fed yesterday. The fire department's combing the building, and when they're done, we can return to our apartments. Evidently, it's a nine-foot python, so it should be pretty easy to find."

"What if they don't find him?" Hannes imagined waking up the next morning and looking directly into the eyes of a python dangling from the ceiling lamp and had to suppress a gag reflex.

"Then it's definitely no longer in the house," Richard said and seemed to wonder about Hannes's overreaction. "Besides, pythons aren't normally aggressive toward humans. Anyway, the police officer over there just told us we'll be able to go back inside within the hour."

"How come that loser was able to keep a snake in our building? Isn't it illegal?"

"Apparently not."

Hannes sat down on the curb and wondered how he could ever get a peaceful night's sleep in his apartment again. Even if the python was found, it still meant it was going to be living directly above him, and if it had already escaped once, perhaps it had developed a taste for freedom . . .

A firefighter announced through a megaphone that the search was over. The python, however, had not been spotted. Hannes jumped to his feet and scanned the area. There was no way he was spending the night there! He would look for a hotel room, preferably on the other side of town. He needed a change of clothes and some toiletries, but he had no desire to enter the building.

He suddenly had an idea and pulled his cell phone from his bag. Ben picked up after a few rings.

"Ben, it's Hannes. Remember yesterday afternoon in the park? You know, when you were a completely law-abiding citizen? Well, I've got a favor to ask . . ."

"Man, that was fast. Okay, what's the favor?"

"Could you please come to my apartment as soon as possible? You live close by, right? Twelve Tower Street."

Hannes was surprised that Ben didn't ask any questions. "All right, I'll swing by in ten minutes."

Ben got there in eight minutes. Hannes had kept his eye on his watch the entire time. He really wanted to get out of there as soon as possible.

"What's up?" Ben asked as he pulled alongside Hannes on his Old Dutch bike.

"Some idiot neighbor keeps a snake, and it's loose." Hannes painted a brief picture of the situation, and Ben scratched his head through his dreadlocks.

"That's one for the papers . . ."

"Well, I'd prefer that it stayed in the papers."

"And what would you like me to do? Fumigate the place with marijuana?"

"I'm terrified of snakes! I can't sleep here tonight. I'd rather pay for a hotel somewhere. I just need a few things from my apartment." Hannes handed him the key. "Could you please get me some clothes?" he asked in embarrassment.

He prepared to be teased, but Ben remained serious. "Hold on, I have a better idea! I'll get you a couple of things from up there, and then you can bunk with me until they find it. I have a guest bed, so it's no problem."

"Really? That's so nice, but . . . I mean, we barely know each other."

"Well, it never hurts to have a police officer in the house, right? So long as you consider me a law-abiding citizen and turn a blind eye, it's no problem," Ben said and laughed. He pushed his bike up against a rusty bike rack and unstrapped his gym bag from the back. He reached for the key. "So what do you need and where can I find it?"

He returned with a full bag. Its contents, including clothes, would tide Hannes over for the next few days. The sun had set, and Hannes followed Ben to his house, which stood slightly back from the road in a large garden dominated by tall broad-leafed trees. The old house seemed to have been recently renovated and had a sophisticated elegance. Hannes never would have imagined that Ben lived in such a place.

"By the way, Elke called me a little while ago," Ben said as he pushed open a rusty gate. "She suggested our fairground group get together Saturday night. Kalle and Ines are free. What about you?"

"Good idea! Where are we meeting?"

"We can meet here at eight. I'll let Elke know tomorrow."

Just before the front steps, Ben turned down a paved path lined with bushes. Confused, Hannes followed him as he disappeared around the corner. Ben turned around and gave his trademark grin.

"Impressed, huh?" He lifted his arm and pointed to the back of the garden. "I live over there. A doctor and his family live in the big house, so there are toys all around. Watch your step."

"So you live in the bushes, or . . . ?"

"What are you implying? Don't worry, I've got a little more style than that. Come on!"

Hannes was careful not to step on one of the numerous toys and followed Ben deep into the garden. He could see the outline of a small structure between two trees.

"This was once the gardener's home," Ben said as he walked toward the little house. "But since there's no gardener—as you will easily see in the daylight—they rent out the cottage. And since the family likes a little diversity, I got the place."

Ben hit a light switch, and a dim outdoor light lit up a small but very well-maintained brick house. The red shingles of the gable roof were overgrown with moss, but otherwise the house seemed in very good shape. There was even a small tiled patio with a table and chairs next to the front door. A book lay facedown on a chair next to an over-flowing ashtray.

"I'd just curled up with a book when you called. Don't look too closely at the ashtray," he joked.

"So how many joints do you smoke a day?"

Ben shrugged. "Depends. Why do you think people are so suscep-tible to drinking? The desperate attempt to feel real. To finally be their true selves, even if it's only an illusion. I'm no better than them."

He opened the unlocked door and turned on the light. Hannes followed him into a tiny hallway with coat hooks and two shoe shelves. Ben put his bag on the floor.

"Although it looks very small from the outside, I have everything I need. In here to the left is the living room plus a small kitchen, then there's my bedroom, next door to that is the bathroom, and right here's the room where you can sleep. It's a bit Spartan, but at least you have a sofa, wardrobe, and a small table and chair. But you can use the kitchen and living room too—and the bathroom of course."

"As long as I don't have to share your bedroom," Hannes joked, remembering Ben's suggestive remarks on the Ferris wheel.

Ben suddenly looked embarrassed. "Oh, I was just kidding. Sometimes I get carried away. Let me show you the rest of the place."

The bathroom was small but clean and even had a washing machine and a laundry basket, which made it nearly impossible to turn around.

Ben's bedroom was no bigger than the guest room; it had a double bed and a wardrobe, which took up an entire wall.

"And now, the holiest of holies," Ben said as he opened the door to the living room. Hannes was terrified as a large ball of wool rushed at them and jumped up on Ben.

"It's all right, Socks!" Ben patted the big dog's head, and after seeing his four white paws, Hannes realized the name was entirely justified. "I surprised you, didn't I?" he said to Hannes. "I trained him so well that he rarely barks. That was a prerequisite to living here. He's also very good with children."

Apparently Socks was also fond of police officers. He sniffed Hannes and put his front paws on his chest to lick his face.

"You can leave him at home and he won't destroy your apartment?" he asked, scratching the animal behind the ears. Socks panted, his breath reeking of dog food.

"I only leave him here for a few hours. He can wander around the garden freely. My landlord also looks after him, so he goes in and out as he pleases."

The living room surprised Hannes the most. He had expected complete chaos, but it looked tidy, and the furniture—a comfortable couch, a dining table with four chairs, and a wall shelf—seemed cozy and stylish. Only the open kitchen was as chaotic as he had expected, with piles of dirty dishes and various packages of food and plastic bags. He even noticed a half-eaten, dried-out cheese sandwich.

"Yeah, the kitchen's unfortunately a little messy. I've been considering getting a dishwasher, but I'm not sure where I'd put it."

"Are you kidding? This place is a dream! If you ever move, let me know!"

"Expected something different?" Ben teased. "You don't have to live in a pigsty to show how countercultural you are. I really like it here, and besides, what's important is what's going on in here." He tapped his forehead.

Hannes again revised his thoughts on Ben. He really appreciated that Ben had showed up to help without asking a single question or making up an excuse. He seemed to be very levelheaded and thoughtful, even if he had hidden this side of himself when they'd first met.

"Okay, dude. Socks has to go outside again. We can let him run around the garden. He knows where he's allowed and where he's not, and the children know it too. We can make ourselves comfortable on the patio and toast your traumatic experience with a cold beer."

While Socks roamed the garden, sniffing, Hannes stretched out in the deck chair that Ben had generously offered him and took a big gulp from the bottle of beer.

"This is insane! I've been looking for a new apartment for a long time and would be grateful for a reasonably decent and affordable one in an apartment building. And you live right here in the middle of paradise," Hannes whispered.

"You don't have to whisper. My landlord left on vacation today. Anyway, their bedroom's on the other side, so they wouldn't hear a thing. Trust me, I've tried . . ."

Hannes looked at Ben's book. *The Anti-Nazi Handbook.* "You really are engrossed in the topic. How many people are in your organization?"

"We're not an organization in the classic sense. We have no name and no fixed structure. There's only an e-mail list, and those who have the time or desire come to our irregular meetings or participate in our activities."

"What was the last thing you organized?"

"We had something on Monday, which was why I had to disappear so suddenly. A few morons from the neo-Nazi scene had gathered at the war memorial to hold a spontaneous tribute to fallen German soldiers. The monument's location was perfect—one of its sides sits about thirty feet below the park's balustrade, so while the skinheads stood there proudly holding their stupid banners, we threw firecrackers down at them. Their memorial was quickly over." Ben laughed. "You should have seen it! Suddenly they weren't so cool anymore. Since there were only three of us, we made a run for it. We didn't want to get into a fight with thirty Nazis. We're not that crazy!"

Hannes laughed. He was amused by the image of the skinheads frantically jumping around to avoid the firecrackers. "Have you been attacked by guys like that before?"

"Sure, several times. I even once fell into the hands of some sort of neo-Nazi women's group. I had to spend a week in bed after that."

"What drives you to do this? Your grandfather's death?"

Ben thought for a moment. "Perhaps it plays a role subconsciously. I mean, the story was always a recurrent theme in our family, and it has certainly influenced me. But actually, I see it like this: some people now argue that we should finally let go of the past. But these people overlook an important point. It's not a question of collectively donning sackcloth and ashes. I wasn't even an embryo during the Nazi regime and am therefore not guilty. To me, it's not about passing judgment on the guilt or innocence of our grandparents. It was a completely different time with very different circumstances. Education and media coverage back then certainly didn't compare with today's. Not to mention the fear of what might happen to you if the Gestapo didn't take a liking to you. Who can really say how you would have behaved back then?"

He paused for a moment and took a swig of beer. "Of course there were heroes who didn't buy into that perverse game, and I can only hope that I would have been one of them. What concerns me the most is what we can learn from history. I can't just sit idly by and watch as these asshole Brownshirts band together and shout idiot slogans to lead us right back down the road to hell."

Hannes nodded, impressed. Ben pulled a pack of tobacco and a small plastic bag from his pocket and rolled a joint on the table. He pointed to the greenish-brown mixture in front of him. "Like I said, if you want some, it's not a problem."

Hannes declined. "Maybe I'll take you up on your offer once I'm done with sports."

"I heartily recommend it," Ben said as he flicked his lighter. "How's your investigation going, by the way? Made any progress?"

Hannes told him an abbreviated version of his busy day. As he described the Coast Guard's capabilities, Ben furrowed his brow.

"Isn't it scary that everything we do can be traced? That may be a plus if you're fighting crime, but I don't particularly like the idea that our society's becoming so transparent."

"As a private citizen, I think you're right," Hannes said. "But since we have no leads in this case, I'm grateful for every resource. At least we now know who the victim is."

"Oh yeah? Who is it?"

Hannes squirmed a little, feeling somewhat guilty. "This stays between you and me, okay?"

"Of course, man. You're not the only one who can keep a secret," Ben said and winked as he waved his joint around.

"All right, so the victim is a woman named Helene Ternheim. She is, or was, the managing director of a pharmaceutical company."

"What's the name of the company?"

Hannes second-guessed himself before responding. "Lagussa. It makes money selling psychotropic drugs and . . . What's the matter?"

Ben's joint had fallen out of his mouth, and he looked aghast. "Lagussa? Are you sure?"

"Why? What's wrong?"

Ben picked up the joint and took another deep puff. "Well, Lagussa has a rather checkered past. We've stumbled upon this company in our research. It wasn't always called Lagussa. It was founded by the pharmacist Heinrich Ternheim as the North German Chemical and Pharmaceutical Works, or NGCP, shortly before the First World War. At first, the company only developed medicine for the treatment of respiratory diseases, but with time it expanded its portfolio. It was not a well-known company, and its drug sales remained primarily in north-west Germany. During the Nazi era, the company was considered 'vital to the war effort,' and as a result, its situation fundamentally changed."

Ben stubbed out the spent roach in the full ashtray. "That distinction had its advantages, and the company quickly aligned itself with the Nazis. For one, the company was given priority in the allocation of much-needed materials, so production wasn't threatened by a nasty shortage. Secondly, workers lost to military service were soon replaced with forced laborers. And there was yet another advantage, if it can be called that: the company's products were tested on prisoners in the concentration camps without deference to the law or morality. It had, in short, secured itself a steady supply of human guinea pigs. So NGCP first took off under the Nazi regime and clearly profited off the war."

"But didn't the Allies overhaul it after the war?"

"Well, back then there were a number of companies that needed to be overhauled. Ultimately, the Allies focused on the bigger fish. In comparison to the Americans, the British were a little more moderate in their approach to denazification, and NGCP apparently slipped through the cracks. Shortly after the war, the company was renamed North-South Pharmaceuticals. Maybe they were hoping to soon operate throughout the country. In the nineties, it changed its name again following a drug scandal, and since then the company has been called Lagussa."

"I had no idea," said Hannes. "So the Ternheim family has a dark past. I'm surprised none of this is public information."

"Well, that's going to change in a couple of days!" Ben stood up and collected the empty beer bottles. "Lagussa will be holding court on Friday night, celebrating their commitment to corporate social responsibility as part of a charity event benefiting children with leukemia. This will be the perfect setting for me and my fellow activists to show the world Lagussa's other, darker side."

"What are you planning?"

"You'll read about it in the papers on Saturday morning."

Wednesday Night into Thursday Morning

Again this sinister darkness! What nightmare lurks inside this time?

Quiet whispers ring in the ears. When the eyes open, the curtains of the dream stage are drawn.

"He's awake, quickly now!" a bright, familiar voice shouts. A chubby boy with curly blond hair enters the field of vision and empties a bucket over the sleepy face.

It burns the eyes, stings the nose. A torrent of urine and feces rushes across the face and mixes with tears of shame.

"He did it again! Bed wetter, pants shitter! Bed wetter, pants shitter!" sounds a chorus of children's spiteful voices.

The orphanage room with its bunk beds and bare walls blurs behind a curtain of tears.

THURSDAY MORNING

Merle's dream had transported her back to two weeks before. Back to a day that had gotten off to a pleasant start.

She had been coaxed from her sleep by the warm sun and the sound of birds chirping outside. She was to go on a day trip with her boyfriend and was scheduled to meet him at 11:00 a.m. He had kept the destination and reason for this trip a big secret, and Merle had reluctantly promised to wait for him at the East Cemetery. *Maybe it won't be so bad,* she'd thought as she lounged under her duvet. *Maybe a day trip will be a good chance for finally letting him know my decision.*

Her boyfriend had jumped out of the car just as she was leaning her bike against the cemetery gates. "There you are! I could hardly wait!" He passionately kissed her, and Merle was disgusted to taste his cigarette breath.

"So where are we going?" she asked. Her boyfriend only smiled.

In a while the city was behind them, and they were heading north along an empty country road.

"Are you taking me to the beach?"

Her boyfriend shrugged. Merle looked out the window. They'd been together for almost two years, yet she had recently come to the realization that they were not made for each other. She was annoyed by his jealous rages, and lately they had become more frequent and more violent. Although he always gave what seemed to be a sincere, heartfelt apology after every outburst, Merle had become fed up with his constant mood swings. Because of her past, freedom wasn't just a pretty word for her: it was an indispensable part of her life.

She glanced at him. Sure, he was very attractive with his unconventional hairstyle, slim body, and light-blue eyes. But she had also recently discovered a chilling coldness in those eyes. She had even wondered if he was secretly doing drugs—at least that would explain his mood swings.

Today, however, he was in a very good mood. He stopped the car on a hill, and the sea stretched out before them, merging on the horizon with the deep-blue summer sky. He pointed to a narrow path that led down to the beach.

"There's a surprise for you down there! Come on!" He jumped out of the car and held the door open for her.

Merle was surprised at his chivalrous gesture. She followed him down the path, and when they reached the beach, he guided her toward a small group of rocks. *I have to tell him,* she kept thinking and finally worked up the courage.

"Hey, hold on. I've been thinking a lot about us over the past few days and—"

"You're not the only one! You'll see. Right behind this rock."

"Wait! Just listen to me for once!" Merle said. "Maybe you've been thinking how nice this is—I know I once did! But I've realized this really isn't working out. Your crazy jealousy, your mood swings— sometimes I'm really afraid of you and . . ."

His smile had disappeared; he stared at her in disbelief. "You're breaking up with me?"

She gently grabbed his arm. "I like you, I just think we're not right for each other."

He pushed her hand away. "Oh yeah? And who's behind it this time? Is it the bartender from last Saturday? I saw how he stared at you all evening, and you . . . you encouraged him and—"

"That's it! I've had it!" Merle cried. "Do you even hear the things you say? Could you listen to me just once without becoming insanely jealous?"

His face twitched, and his cold, fixed stare bored hypnotically into her eyes. For a moment, she was afraid he would hit her.

"You'll be sorry," he said. Then he turned and trudged through the sand. Merle sighed in relief. That certainly wasn't the gentlest way to break it to him, but at least she had finally gotten it over with!

Merle had wondered how she would get back to the city, but first, before leaving, she peered behind the little rock. She looked down at a small wooden box with a red heart painted on it. Next to the small box was a lit candle, and inside the box was a small gold ring atop a velvet cushion.

A cold snout nudged Hannes awake. Socks licked Hannes's face all over, wagging his tail. Hannes looked around until he finally remembered where he was.

"I thought I'd send Socks in here to gently wake you," Ben said.

Hannes turned and saw Ben standing at the door.

"It's a little after eight thirty. I have to go to class soon. Socks comes with me to campus. Help yourself to whatever you need."

Hannes sat up. "Damn it! It's already eight thirty? I'm supposed to be at the station by eight! My boss is going to kill me!"

Ben shrugged. "The world's not going to stop spinning if you solve the crime an hour later. Do you want to sleep here tonight too?"

"If that's okay with you."

"Sure, man, not a problem! Just pull the door closed behind you. I put a key on the patio table for you. Come on, Socks!"

After the front door closed, Hannes jumped up from the sofa bed and rummaged for his cell phone. He had forgotten to turn the alarm on and had three missed calls. Just then the phone vibrated. Hannes answered.

"Man, finally! Unless you just lost your leg, I need you here! Where the hell are you?"

"Fritz, I'm really sorry. It'll never happen again, honest! It's a long story and I—"

"You can tell me the story in the car," Fritz said. "We have a nine o'clock meeting with Mr. Ternheim at Lagussa's headquarters. I'll pick you up in ten minutes!"

Hannes heard an engine start in the background. "Stop, Fritz, I'm not at home! Pick me up at 10 Park Avenue."

"Ah," Fritz said and hung up while Hannes was already trying to put on the jeans he had worn the day before. He would have to do without a shower.

"A snake?" Fritz asked. "People. I'll never understand. Well, I went to Ms. Ternheim's penthouse last night with four of our colleagues; her brother gave us a key. The view of the harbor was stunning, but we didn't find much. Ms. Ternheim seemed to be very interested in history: in addition to pharmaceutical literature, there was an entire shelf of books devoted to the Nazi era. Everyone's gotta have a hobby, right?"

"There was a book about the Nazi era at her father's place too! I think I know why Ms. Ternheim had such a strong interest in it," Hannes said and shared Ben's background knowledge about the victim's company.

"Well then! Your new buddy's really knowledgeable. And what do these activists plan on doing at the charity event?"

"No idea. And I'd prefer if you would disregard that last part. Ben's been like a buddy to me."

Fritz sighed and took a big gulp of coffee. "You know, I've also tried to make life difficult for neo-Nazis over the years. So you're lucky I didn't hear what you just told me. But did you say anything to Ben about the victim?" He pointed to a crumpled newspaper on the floor of the Jeep. "Look at the front-page headline."

Hannes picked up the paper. Fritz hit the brakes, slamming Hannes's head into the dashboard.

"Sorry," said Fritz. "A dog just ran in front of the car."

Hannes couldn't see a dog anywhere and rubbed his forehead while staring in disbelief at the front page: "Managing Director of Pharmaceutical Giant Lagussa Found Dead. Murder?"

"Maybe your buddy has a contact at the morning paper?"

"I can't imag—"

"Well then, how the hell did this shit get in the newspaper?" Fritz roared. "What were you thinking, discussing the identity of the victim with civilians? Next time, why don't you just contact the paper directly. Hell, it'll probably make the evening paper!"

"But that's impossible! We sat out on the patio until really late last night, and by the time we went to bed, the paper would have already gone to print. Someone else must have tipped them off."

"Yeah? Who? It wasn't me, I'm assuming you're also not that stupid, and our medical examiners hopefully know how to be professional."

"Maybe Mr. Ternheim—"

"Mr. Ternheim called this morning and was furious. He demanded an explanation as to why his dead sister was already appearing in the papers."

"But there's got to be other people who know. The dentist, for example, who we got the matching dental records from."

With weary, bloodshot eyes, Fritz glanced over at him. "Whatever. We couldn't have kept it a secret for much longer. We'll just have to deal with it now. But in the future, please keep your need to share things under control. There will be serious consequences if you don't!"

They arrived at Lagussa's corporate headquarters. The company's white flags fluttered at half-mast, clearly a gesture in honor of their CEO.

"Where are we going to park?" Hannes asked.

Fritz turned and grabbed his detachable police light from the backseat and rolled down the window. He placed the light on the roof while steering the Jeep with his knees and drove onto the plaza in front of the large building.

"That should be enough to keep the traffic cops from doing anything rash," he said and turned the engine off.

As they rode in the elevator to the twentieth floor, Fritz said, "Let's split up. We'll make better progress that way. It's fine if only I talk with Mr. Ternheim again. You take care of the assistants. Two of them are around your age, and maybe that'll get them to talk. We're not going to be able to get much out of the head secretary, Ms. Wagner. She's been with the company for decades and seems so loyal she probably considers herself a part of the family. Don't zero in on any particular topic. Just try to learn as much as possible about Ms. Ternheim. What kind of person was she? What did she like? Dislike? Did she have any hobbies? Friends? Enemies? And so on."

Hannes nodded as the elevator doors opened. The assistants greeted them politely, but it was clear they had great difficulty maintaining a professional demeanor. Ms. Wagner got up from her desk and walked over. Her eyes had the telltale shimmer of tears.

"I read it in the newspaper this morning." She sobbed for a moment, then covered her mouth. "It's so awful! I can't believe it! Why didn't you tell me yesterday?" She stared at Fritz.

"I'm very sorry. But you understand we have to inform the family members first and then decide together who to tell and when. This is my colleague, Mr. Niehaus. He'd like to talk with your two assistants while I speak with Mr. Ternheim. May I go in?"

Ms. Wagner nodded and led him to the office. "He's already waiting for you."

A slightly embarrassed Hannes walked over to the two young women. They introduced themselves as Irene Maler and Anna Stahl. This was the first time Hannes would question people on his own, and he did not want to let Fritz down.

"Did you come straight from a fistfight?" Anna asked.

"Life as a police officer can be dangerous. Anyway, is there a quiet place I could talk with you individually about Ms. Ternheim?"

Irene pointed to a corner of the office. Four chairs sat behind several planters in a waiting area. "I'll go first. Might as well get it over with," she said and walked over there. She sat cross-legged on the edge of a chair, her black miniskirt revealing her flawless legs.

Hannes followed her and worried his ears might turn red. He made a conscious effort to focus on her face. He sat down in the chair opposite her and noticed out of the corner of his eye that Anna was furtively looking at him.

"How long have you worked for the Ternheims?"

"Not long, and I'm leaving soon. I gave my notice last Friday."

"Oh, why? Did you receive a better offer?"

"I did. In less than three months, I'm outta here."

"And when did you start?"

"Two months ago."

"Ah, and how well did you get to know the heads of the company in this time?"

Irene snapped her gum with a loud pop. "Well, I've never really worked with them. Actually, I've only really worked for Ms. Wagner."

"What can you tell me about Ms. Ternheim?" Hannes asked.

"What do you mean?"

"Well, what kind of boss was she, for example?"

"My boss is Ms. Wagner. I only worked for Ms. Ternheim in a tangential capacity. Basically, I'm Mr. Ternheim's assistant. I only ever saw her go in and out. My coworker can definitely tell you more. She works—er, worked for Ms. Ternheim."

"Ah. Well, what kind of impression did you have of her, and what were you told about her?"

"Well, I don't know much. She was a career woman. She was always in the office before me, even when she didn't have anything on her calendar, and whenever I left, she was usually still there. I often wondered if she spent the night here. She never said much; she probably thought it was below her. She could be very determined when things didn't go her way."

"Did you notice any changes in her recently?"

Irene laughed. "Changes? Nope! I've heard she wore the same hairstyle and clothes for years."

"Not just her appearance. Were there any changes in her behavior?"

"Like I said, I didn't have much to do with her. Work was all that mattered for her. That's why she always seemed a little aloof. She probably only had enough room in her head for the next product launch: a new antidepressant is supposed to hit the market at the end of the year. She wasn't really interested in us."

"Do you know anything about her social life? Friends, for example?"

Again Irene chuckled. "I don't think she had the time for friends. The company was all that mattered. At least, I don't know of any friends or acquaintances."

Hannes nodded. He was tempted to ask whether Irene knew of any connection between Ms. Ternheim and the real estate agent Florian Schneider, but he had no idea if he was allowed to divulge the name of a suspect.

"Is there anything else you can tell me about Ms. Ternheim?"

Irene shook her head. "I'm sorry, but I really don't know much about her."

"Thank you. Please send over Ms. Stahl," Hannes said, happy to be done with the first part of his questioning. However, he feared Fritz would be unhappy with his results. He could only hope Anna had something more to share.

Irene made a show of standing up and smoothing out her skirt. "Are you in a special unit or something? You're certainly in awesome shape."

Hannes looked down at the floor. In the morning rush, he had chosen his tightest T-shirt. "No, I'm a canoeist. Anyway, thanks for your time, and I wish you all the best at your new job."

But Irene did not seem to get the message or ignored it. "Oh, you're an athlete? How amazing!"

Fortunately, Ms. Wagner rescued Hannes. "Irene! When you're done, I have an urgent task for you."

Irene rolled her eyes and lowered her voice. "Maybe you can take me out on your boat sometime? You know where to find me," she said before walking back to her desk. Hannes loved her shapely figure and how she looked in high heels.

Anna sat down; she was a sharp contrast to Irene. She wore a skirt that ended at her knees, a conservative striped blouse, and only a trace of makeup—Hannes was able to make out the freckles on her nose.

He looked over and saw Fritz leave Mr. Ternheim's office and disappear with Ms. Wagner behind another door. He turned back to Anna. "This must all come as a surprise to you, Ms. Stahl. Definitely not an easy situation."

Anna brushed a strand of brown hair behind her ear and blushed. "No," she said and wrung her hands in her lap. "That was really an awful surprise this morning. I read the headlines at a newspaper stand while waiting for my bus. I couldn't believe it. Just last week, I was discussing the gala this Friday with Ms. Ternheim, and now . . ." She shrugged and looked back at her desk, as if she could find the answers there.

"How long have you been working here?" Hannes asked.

"Oh, I've been at Lagussa for almost ten years now. After high school, I entered a training program here and then worked in market research. Lagussa is a very good employer, and I've always felt challenged. I've never had a reason to change jobs."

"And how long have you worked as an executive assistant?"

"Three years last month. I know because . . . Ms. Ternheim gave me a bouquet of flowers on my anniversary."

Hannes wondered about Irene's statements. The picture she had painted of Ms. Ternheim was hardly one of a CEO who would bring a bouquet of flowers on her assistant's third anniversary.

"Ms. Ternheim must have been very pleased with you," he commented.

"Yes, we always got along great. She was a nice woman, though very demanding. But she was always fair. And she was a sympathetic audience."

"Could you give me an example?"

"Well . . . To this day, I'm still grateful for what she did. Two years ago, my mother got really sick. She . . . her health declined very quickly, and it soon became clear she was near the end. Ms. Ternheim was understanding and gave me a lot of leeway. She even told Ms. Wagner I could work flexible hours. This went on for about four months. She even came to the funeral."

Hannes began to wonder if the two assistants were talking about the same person. "That's very extraordinary and definitely says something about Ms. Ternheim."

"Yes. Perhaps she was especially sympathetic in my case because she had taken care of her father for many years. He worked here until about ten years ago—long enough for me to remember him. Of course, I never really saw him, but then again, I was also only an apprentice. After he handed over control of the company to Helene and Christian, he became a little reclusive and it's said a little crazy too. Ms. Ternheim drove out to the country at least once a week to check on him."

"Do you know more about her father?"

"Not much. When my mother was dying, she sometimes spoke about him. He paints pictures and is mute. I know Ms. Ternheim was very worried about him. But she didn't talk about him often, and when she did, it was more in a general way. Where he lives now must be very idyllic."

"What was Ms. Ternheim's relationship with her brother like?"

"Well . . . basically, they stood eye to eye when it came to the company. Of course, they sometimes had their disagreements. But they always worked closely together. Although . . ."

"What?"

Anna's hands tensed. "No, nothing. They had a good relationship."

Hannes knew there was more to this, but it was clear he would be unable to get it out of her now. "What do you know about the CEO's private life?"

"She didn't have much time for a private life. She loved her sports car, so sometimes she went on road trips. She was always talking about cars with the men in our company. Oh, and she loved the outdoors, especially the shore. She once told me that's where she could best unwind."

"Do you know if Ms. Ternheim rented or purchased a place recently?" asked Hannes.

"I don't think so."

"Did you ever hear anything about her friends?"

"No. She never mentioned any friends or acquaintances. I think she was somewhat of a loner."

"Did Ms. Ternheim have a partner?"

Anna squirmed in her seat and rubbed her nose. "Well . . . no . . . I don't think so. I never heard that there was a man in her life. As I said, she had no time for friends or a relationship. She was always here or on business trips."

Again Hannes felt she was not telling him everything. She spoke in a very low voice and repeatedly glanced at the center of the room.

Fritz and Ms. Wagner were standing there while Irene was typing on the computer.

"Did Ms. Ternheim have any enemies?"

"Was the newspaper right? Was she murdered?"

"That's a fairly routine question," he said after a pause. "I have to ask it."

"Well, I can't imagine someone was so at odds with her that he'd kill her. Although . . ."

"What?"

"Oh, nothing. Lately, she seemed a little absent. Left the office early, which wasn't typical. Sometimes I'd come into her office while she was on the phone, and she'd seem upset. It was unusual because she only made business calls and was always extremely professional."

Hannes rubbed the bump on his forehead. "Ms. Stahl, thank you for this information and taking the time to answer my questions. Still . . . I have the feeling you're not telling me everything. From what you've told me, I can see you liked Ms. Ternheim very much and that she treated you very well. Anything you can tell us is important. By helping us, you're also helping her."

Anna took another quick look around. Hannes noticed Ms. Wagner looking suspiciously in their direction.

"What would you say if we were to meet at a neutral location? Somewhere you can talk freely?"

"You're right." Her voice was a whisper. "How about tonight?"

Hannes was ecstatic, although he had hoped to start training again after getting cleared by his doctor. But he was convinced Anna was keeping secrets. "All right. Do you have a place in mind?"

"Do you know the Chameleon on the south part of town?"

"I do. How about six?"

Anna nodded, and they shook hands.

***

Back at the station, Fritz and Hannes sat in silence in the cafeteria. On their way out of Lagussa's headquarters, the people in the hall had shot them several furtive looks. The whole building had seemed to be whispering.

"It wasn't easy to calm down Mr. Ternheim," Fritz said after he had emptied half his coffee and Hannes had devoured a sandwich. "He's convinced we leaked the story to the press. He's really keeping his head as far as the death's concerned. I haven't noticed any signs of grief, or maybe he just has a lot of self-control. If Ms. Ternheim was wired the same way, then the atmosphere must have been pretty chilly there."

"I'm not so sure," Hannes said and briefed Fritz on the different perceptions of the two assistants.

Fritz nodded. "Ms. Maler's opinion doesn't surprise me. As I was chatting with the head secretary in Ms. Ternheim's office, she told me Ms. Maler would not stay following her probation period. Ms. Ternheim argued in favor of waiting out her six-month contract so she could look for a new job without any stress. It's obvious Ms. Maler hasn't met any of the expectations set forth in her job interview."

"Ms. Stahl seemed a little scared to speak candidly. She kept looking over at her colleagues and spoke very softly. I'm meeting with her alone tonight. I'm convinced she has more to say. Is that okay, or should we do it as a team?"

"Go ahead. She'll probably be more willing to talk if there isn't an old bag sitting next to her. Do you have any idea what she might be keeping secret?"

"No, all I found out was that the relationship between the Ternheim siblings had cooled a little lately. Were you able to coax anything from Mr. Ternheim?"

Fritz shook his head. "The guy clams up the moment he's asked a personal question. According to him, his sister was totally focused on the company, just like him. Neither of them had much of a private life. In fact, both are unmarried and single."

"That's crazy! What kind of a life is that? I don't think I could ever be so consumed by a job that it becomes my whole life. That doesn't mean I don't want to achieve something professionally or be invested in my job. Don't get me wrong . . ."

"You don't need to justify yourself," Fritz said and laughed. "And you don't have to explain the value of free time to me. The sooner I'm done with this crap, the better off I'll be. I get what you mean about work-life balance. But the Ternheim family doesn't seem to know how to strike that balance. If Old Ternheim was anything like them, that might explain his somewhat antisocial behavior."

"Speaking of which, why did the old man not tell his son immediately after finding his daughter dead on the beach? Or did he not recognize her?"

"Good question. Apparently, the father and son don't have a very cordial relationship and haven't been in contact lately."

"That's unusual. You'd think after something like this, it'd bring the family closer together."

Fritz shrugged. "Interpersonal relationships don't seem to matter too much in this family. Let's hope you can get the assistant to chat this evening. For what it's worth, she didn't seem entirely uninterested in you."

Hannes quickly changed the topic. "What did Mr. Ternheim say about the body's anomalies?"

Fritz took a long sip from his coffee cup. "He can't explain them. His sister had always had an aversion to tattoos, and it seems unlikely she'd have become fond of them now. I showed him a reasonably tame photo of the tattoo, but he couldn't make anything of it either. He's already told us that she never dyed her hair and at least until last week still had her natural color. The traces of the sedative surprised him too. She was grounded and always had her life under control."

"Other than murder, what other explanation could there be for the condition of the body?"

Fritz shrugged again. "I still wouldn't rule out a suicide or accident. But of course you're right, there's already a lot of evidence that points to foul play. And it's extremely unfortunate that the few people associated with Ms. Ternheim don't know anything or don't want to talk. I couldn't get anything useful out of Ms. Wagner, and there was nothing interesting in Ms. Ternheim's office either—not a single personal item. Mr. Ternheim denied the possibility that his sister's death could have anything to do with the company. One of us has to pay old Ternheim another visit. If he didn't recognize his daughter, which I think in spite of the dyed hair is extremely unlikely, he must be officially informed of her death. And in any case, we've got to get him to talk, because he ought to have a lot to say about this, especially if she regularly visited him and took care of him."

"So who's going to visit the old man?"

Fritz leaned back in his chair. "I delivered the bad news to the brother, now it's your turn. It's part of our job, and you better get used to it! Also, I think you have a better shot of forging a rapport with him. Just consider our last visit."

"What are you going to do in the meantime?" Hannes asked.

"I've been following the only other lead we have so far. Mr. Ternheim did share one interesting fact with me, which may give our case some momentum: Guess who Ms. Ternheim bought her chic penthouse from three years ago?"

"You mean . . . It can't be!"

"Oh, it can. The transaction was conducted by the same agent who was also spotted at the crime scene and who disappeared once we started poking around. Also interesting is the fact that the transaction didn't go too smoothly."

"Why, what happened?"

"Schneider had apparently pocketed the commission without paying taxes on it. He was caught because Ms. Ternheim had included these costs in her tax returns and the revenue service conducted a routine audit. They then took a closer look at Schneider. It turns out that he was regularly evading taxes."

Hannes shook his head. "How stupid is this man? He ought to have expected that his clients would deduct his commission from their taxes. Eventually, someone would have caught on!"

"Well, usually when this happens, there's an agreement between the real estate agent and the buyer. The agent reduces the fee, doesn't issue an invoice, and doesn't have to pay the taxes."

"That may be, but Ms. Ternheim was obviously not interested in such a condition."

"Schneider claimed the opposite, which Ms. Ternheim denied. Fortunately, she actually had an invoice; but unfortunately, that invoice was surprisingly low. In any case, Schneider was found guilty of tax evasion. He luckily escaped a prison sentence, but the fine was probably pretty hefty and put him into some serious financial trouble."

"In other words, he rues the day he sold Ms. Ternheim her penthouse!"

"Not just that, he probably regrets meeting her at all. And that's why I'm going to find him."

THURSDAY AT NOON

Hannes felt uneasy as he left the city. He had little desire to see the crazy old painter or his paintings again, especially on his own. Since no unmarked vehicle was available, he was stuck with a patrol car. At least it meant old Ternheim would immediately recognize him as a police officer and refrain from attacking.

Even if he didn't really suspect Ben of having something to do with the leak, Hannes had called him a few minutes ago, anyway, only to get his voice mail.

It was ninety-one degrees outside, and the air-conditioning was on full blast. After speeding past the Olsen farm, Hannes abruptly slammed on his brakes and did a one-eighty. He thought it might be a good idea to pay the farm another visit. Since the press had already divulged the victim's identity, he no longer had to withhold that piece of information.

Hohenberg Farm seemed deserted as he pulled up in front of the big barn. The sun beat down from its perch, and Hannes left the air-conditioned vehicle. He smelled manure and heard the animals in the barn. The front door opened just before he reached it, and Mrs. Olsen came out to meet him, wiping her calloused hands on her apron.

"I heard it this morning on the radio," she said. She blushed and looked at him with big eyes. "When they mentioned the business-woman had been found on a secluded beach, I immediately said to my husband: that must be the dead woman from our beach! Poor old painter. That means he found his own daughter dead. My God, how awful! I immediately sent my husband over in case he might need something. His daughter was the only one who took care of him."

"Did your husband see Merlin? Because I'm on my way there."

"Oh, that's nice of you to look after him. No, he didn't see him, but he visited about two hours ago. He put a basket with food by the door. Now he's out on his combine harvester."

"Mrs. Olsen, did you or your husband remember anything else? Ms. Ternheim unfortunately had very few acquaintances, so we don't know much about the deceased yet."

She wrinkled her forehead. "I'm afraid I can't help you there. In all these years, she only once bought eggs from us, and she was very curt when she did. Apparently, she was in a hurry."

"When was that?"

"Oh, it must have been two or three months ago. Otherwise I just saw her pass by in her car."

"How long would she normally stay with her father?"

"Usually not very long, maybe an hour. She mostly came on week-ends. Not that I'm a busybody, but it's very rare that someone comes out here. Not to mention that she also drove a flashy car. Lately, though, she was coming here more often and staying longer."

"When did you last see her driving here?"

Mrs. Olsen thought hard. "It must have been last Wednesday morning, because the farm machinery salesman visited us shortly there-after. We're thinking of buying a new tractor. Yes, I'm sure of it. She was heading back just as he drove away."

"So that means she didn't drive by on Friday, Saturday, or Sunday?"

"I don't think so. I was at the farm the entire time and would have noticed when she came or went. But of course I don't sit by the window all day."

If Ms. Ternheim had committed suicide—and with each passing hour, he was even less inclined to believe this—how would she have gotten to the beach? She definitely didn't walk. There was no way she could have made it from the nearest town to the beach in a business suit and high heels. And where was her sports car?

"I just thought of something else," Mrs. Olsen said. "I've told you before that it's rare for people who don't live in the area to come here. But I've repeatedly seen a young woman. Sometimes walking with a backpack, other times on a bike."

"Hmm." That didn't strike him as too out of the ordinary. But in the absence of any other useful leads, he asked, "Does the woman behave strangely? When was the last time you saw her?"

"I've always wondered what she does out here. I saw her last Saturday. She was walking along the road with her backpack, heading toward the lighthouse."

According to Maria's calculations, Ms. Ternheim was presumably dispensed with on Saturday.

"Around what time?"

"Oh, sometime late in the morning. I'm not sure of the time, and I didn't see her come back."

"Did you ever speak to her? Do you remember what she looks like?"

"No, I've never spoken to her. She looks young and walks at a very lively pace. She's slim, with long brown hair—I can't remember much more about her."

Hannes thanked Mrs. Olsen. He got back behind the wheel and dialed the number for directory assistance. Within a few seconds, he was connected to Lagussa's main switchboard and then put through to Mr. Ternheim. The head secretary answered.

"Hello, Ms. Wagner, this is Officer Johannes Niehaus, Mr. Janssen's colleague. This question might strike you as a little strange, but could you tell me if Ms. Ternheim's car is parked in the company lot or anywhere nearby?"

"I don't know. If the car's here, then it would be in her reserved parking spot."

"Could you please check to see if Ms. Ternheim's car is parked in the lot?"

For a moment, there was silence. "I'll send Irene down to the parking garage. What's the best number to reach you?"

While Hannes waited for her call, he contacted Fritz. From the corner of his eye, he could see Mrs. Olsen looking through the window at him.

"Hello, Fritz, it's Hannes. When you were at Ms. Ternheim's penthouse last night, did anyone see her yellow sports car?"

"No, not that I remember. Why?"

Hannes quickly shared his thoughts and Mrs. Olsen's observations.

"I see," Fritz said. "We should've thought of that sooner. I guess I'm getting ripe for retirement. I'll send a couple of colleagues over to her apartment to look around there again."

"Have you found any trace of Schneider?"

"No, I just went to the doctor. I've been having problems with my back again today. I have to go. I'll be on it shortly."

"Just one more thing, Fritz," Hannes said and informed him about the young woman Mrs. Olsen had told him about.

"Nothing seems to escape her attention. I'm not sure if it's a lead or not. So the woman is often in the area . . . Maybe she just really likes that lonely stretch of beach. But it's conceivable that she could provide us with some clues. Could Mrs. Olsen describe her to our sketch artist?"

"All she can remember is a slender body and long brown hair."

"Then while you're out there, keep an eye out for her. After all, it's your specialty."

Fritz hung up. Hannes had been so busy with the case these last few hours that he had completely forgotten about Fritz's health problems. His condition had been deteriorating over the last few days, even if he did his best to hide the pain. His face had grown more gaunt and ashen with each passing day, and he appeared to be losing weight. Hopefully, he could hold out until the case was solved.

Hannes's cell phone rang. "Johannes Niehaus."

"Hello, Mr. Niehaus. It's Irene Maler from Lagussa. I enjoyed our lovely chat earlier today."

He rolled his eyes. Not only did Ms. Wagner think it beneath her to go check the parking lot, but she had also delegated the return call.

"That's nice of you to call back so quickly. Have you checked on Ms. Ternheim's car?"

"Of course! I'm glad to help the investigation. At least it gives me something to do other than type up letters."

"And? Is the car there?"

"No, of course not," she said.

In the background, he could hear Ms. Wagner scolding her.

"Unfortunately, I have to go now." She sounded annoyed. "There's some extremely important correspondence waiting for me." She lowered her voice. "But maybe I could help more with the investigation this evening . . ."

"That's really nice of you, but right now there's a lot going on. I'll get back to you if I still need you to do something for me. Thanks, and see you soon!"

Hannes hung up. He had always been particularly bad at saying no. He started the engine, waved to Mrs. Olsen—who had still not given up her seat by the window—and turned onto the road leading to the lighthouse. Just as the old structure appeared around the curve, his cell phone rang again.

"Fritz sent us to Ms. Ternheim's place to search for her car. It's a yellow sports car, right?"

"Yes, that's right," Hannes said and pulled to the side of the road. "Did you find it?"

"No. We looked in the garage and surrounding streets. No vehicle fit that description."

Hannes thanked his colleague for the information and shifted into first gear. He wondered why the car had disappeared.

As he pulled up, Hannes noticed that the basket from the Olsens wasn't by the door of Merlin's dilapidated house. Nothing in the clearing had changed since his last visit, though the book was no longer on the porch table.

Hannes wanted to get this visit over with quickly. He knocked on the door. He had deliberately parked in front of the house so the old man would see the police car. He was about to knock a second time when he heard a key turn in the lock. A moment later, the door opened, and Helene Ternheim's father stood before him.

He seemed a little more hunched over than before, but otherwise nothing about his appearance had changed. His woolen cap was still pushed to the side; his threadbare corduroys flapped against his thin legs. He also wore a tattered wool sweater not meant for the summer heat. His clothing and face were dotted by small splashes of color, and the brush in his clawlike hand explained what the old man had been doing.

Merlin stared at Hannes. His gaze wandered between the green eye and the blue eye.

"Forgive me for ambushing you. I'm sure you remember me. I'm a police officer and was here on Tuesday with my colleague. I'd like to discuss something with you—calmly. Shall we sit here in the sun for a minute, Mr. Ternheim?"

Hannes deliberately addressed him by his given name and pointed to the chair on the porch. Merlin shuffled over to it and downed a half glass of vodka. After placing it on the table, he stared ahead at an imaginary point.

Hannes looked at Merlin's large birthmark, and he remembered Fritz telling him that Merlin's son also had a birthmark under his right eye. Did the murdered Ms. Ternheim inherit something similar? Hannes could not remember.

He sat diagonally across from Merlin on the porch and leaned against the rotten railing. "Mr. Ternheim, I'm sure you can guess why I came here. It's about the dead woman you found Sunday on the beach. Do you know who it was?"

The old man only stared into the distance.

"Your son Christian reported his sister, in other words your daughter Helene, missing yesterday. Unfortunately, the dead woman was your daughter. I'm very sorry, Mr. Ternheim."

There was still no reaction.

"There are some things we don't understand. Your daughter had bleached hair, which surprised your son. We also found traces of a sedative in her blood, and her car has disappeared. There was one more anomaly: your daughter had recently gotten a tattoo on her left forearm."

Finally Hannes had his attention! The old man turned his head and looked into his eyes. His facial muscles twitched. But when he remained silent, Hannes gave up all hope of getting him to talk.

"Does this tattoo sound familiar to you? And did your daughter have it for a while? The last time she visited you was on Wednesday of last week, correct?" Hannes realized he was getting nowhere. "We can't make out what the tattoo is supposed to represent, but we believe it's a group of six or seven numbers."

The old man's eyes widened, and his right hand was trembling so much that small drops of paint flew from the brush.

"Mr. Ternheim! We need your help, otherwise this investigation will go nowhere! You know something, I can see it. I'm begging you. This is about your daughter."

Merlin rose from his seat and walked back to the door. He staggered, and Hannes resigned himself to the fact that the old man would slam the door in his face again. But at the door, Merlin turned around. He motioned with his head for Hannes to come inside.

Hannes jumped to his feet and was relieved that his knee wasn't bothered by this sudden movement. He looked forward to training again soon. Then he felt ashamed. He was standing in front of a dead woman's confused father, thinking about sports. He followed Mr. Ternheim inside.

Just like last time, the hallway was very dark because the shutters were closed. Hannes wondered how it was possible to paint in the dim light and reluctantly followed him into the room where the demons and flames had jumped out at him. But the room had changed. White sheets hung over all the frames. Only one image was not covered. Merlin stood in front of it. Without turning around, he waved Hannes over. Hannes looked over his shoulder and caught his breath. It was a black-and-white drawing unlike any of the old man's paintings. A strikingly beautiful woman stared back at Hannes. Despite the lack of color, she almost seemed alive. Her face was drawn with soft, almost loving strokes, and even though she appeared younger in the painting, he immediately realized it was a portrait of Helene Ternheim.

Merlin stepped aside so Hannes could see the whole painting. Hannes gasped. The scene continued below, turning more and more nightmarish the lower he looked. Helene's body was likewise drawn in a realistic fashion, and at her feet blazed images of immense horror that were reminiscent of the ones depicted in Merlin's other paintings. Several hands clutched at her ankles, attempting to drag her into the depths. Farther down were scenes of people being slaughtered and houses burning while figures standing at attention, their right arms outstretched, watched from the sidelines.

Hannes looked over at Merlin. From an artistic point of view, the painting was certainly a masterpiece—even Hannes recognized that. At the same time, it was incredibly disturbing. What did Merlin want to say with the painting? Hannes forced himself to take a closer look and saw women being raped, the faces of children crushed by heavy boots, and kneeling men resigned to their fates, guns pointed at the backs of their heads by Nazis.

"Are . . . are you saying that your daughter was being harassed by Nazis? Has . . . was she threatened?"

Merlin watched him intently.

"You know, this is . . . well, hard to understand. You have to tell me. I know nothing about art and don't know how to interpret this. Who threatened or harassed your daughter?"

Merlin waved him off. Then he walked over to a table and picked up a sketchbook, like the one Hannes had had in school. He drew a face in pencil and held the pad up for Hannes to see. Again Hannes was overwhelmed by the man's skill. In just a minute, he had created an instantly recognizable portrait.

"That's your son! What about him? Talk to me! What are you trying to tell me?"

Merlin shrugged and started drawing again. When he was done, he laid the pad and pencil down on the table and turned to face Hannes. He stood so close that Hannes detected a sour smell in addition to a whiff of vodka. Merlin looked him straight in the eye and nodded without breaking eye contact. Then he turned and left the room. Hannes heard his footsteps in the hall, then the sound of a door, and finally the turning of a key. Apparently, the visit was over.

Hannes looked at the sketchbook and recoiled. Christian Ternheim had been transformed into an angel of death swinging his scythe at him with a diabolical grin.

He was surprised that he had not thought of it sooner. He had already encountered pictures of forearms tattooed with numbers in his history classes. But it was Merlin's portrait of Helene Ternheim surrounded by Nazis that awoke this memory in him.

He was so lost in thought that he nearly collided with an oncoming vehicle just as he was about to turn back onto the main road. After some frantic braking and turning, the car came to a stop only inches from the lighthouse.

After two deep breaths, Hannes glanced at the frightened driver, then got out of his car and walked over to the metallic-green vehicle. He signaled the driver to roll down the window.

"We were lucky," the man said and looked over at the police car.

"May I ask where you're headed?" Hannes said as he leaned on the door frame.

"Certainly," the man said in a falsetto voice. "I'm on my way to my best horse in the stable, so to speak. My cash cow." He chuckled, opened the door, and got out. He was short and only came up to Hannes's chest. He had thinning black hair and a scraggly ponytail. "Louis Laval," he said in a pompous French accent. "I'm an art agent and represent that veritable genius who's retreated into this desert."

"If by 'genius,' you mean the old man who manages to make hell look like paradise compared to his paintings, then you're right," said Hannes.

Laval laughed. "Yes, his pictures are certainly one of a kind, no? But I'll tell you what: Merlin's hugely sought after by collectors. He has a real fan base that eagerly awaits his new work. I just came back from the US and the Americans are crazy about him. Unfortunately, he's so shy I can't take him to exhibitions. That's too bad! It would double the price of admission."

"So there are actually people who hang his pictures in their homes?" Hannes asked.

"You better believe it! Let me tell you, there's never been anything like his style of painting. Try to describe it. Expressionist? Maybe in part! But you can also find features of naturalism and realism—that is to say, the total opposite of expressionism. You will also find sporadic elements of impressionism and other styles. He cannot be lumped into any one category and has his own inimitable style."

"I see. Do you have a few of his masterpieces?"

"That would be a tremendous waste. All of his paintings have gone for tons of money!"

"You wouldn't know it by the way he lives," Hannes said.

"Don't be fooled. His eremitic lifestyle is self-imposed. Money's not important to him, especially since he was financially secure before his time as an artist. He used to lead a pharmaceutical company and—"

"So a little money comes your way since it isn't important to him?"

"I'm not driven by the money! I discovered Merlin years ago by accident. And it wasn't easy to get him to share his paintings with the world. It would have been a crime against art to keep these masterpieces hidden. I saw his first paintings in a newspaper column entitled 'What's So-and-So Up to These Days.' There were only two fuzzy black-and-white images, but I knew right away I had a mission to fulfill. And it was not easy. Since he doesn't talk, I had to negotiate with his two children. They wanted to keep his paintings from going public. But I prevailed! His son was furious. Since then, Merlin has been a fixture in the art world."

"Why does he call himself Merlin?"

"That was my idea!" said the little man, who was becoming more and more unlikable. "Great, no? I thought the artist who painted these extraordinary pictures needed a mystical name. His son didn't like that, but our contract expressly acknowledged my right to choose an artist's name for his father. Ultimately, his son was probably glad the images were not sold under his real name."

"So what do you want from your cash cow today?" Hannes asked. He could not share the man's enthusiasm; Merlin was hardly a fitting name for the old artist. Sure, his paintings were special and mysterious, but Hannes had always associated the real Merlin with a bright, cheerful figure and not a creator of hellish agony. Whatever the outcome of the investigation, one thing was already clear: the positive image of the magician Merlin had lost its innocence for him, and this strange excuse for an agent was the one to blame.

"What do I want with him? Well, to pick up the goods! I've already sold six paintings, and the buyer hasn't even seen them."

Hannes shook his head in disbelief. The world was certainly a colorful place. "You should be careful. He's a little upset."

Laval chuckled. "Don't worry, I can handle him. I've been dealing with him for years."

"Well, that may be so. But now the circumstances are a little different."

"How so? Did something happen to him? Tell me!"

"Haven't you checked the paper today or listened to the radio?"

"No! I came straight from the airport. What's wrong?"

"Mr. Ternheim, or Merlin, found his daughter dead on the beach last Sunday."

Laval froze. He stared at Hannes, his mouth open. "That . . . that can't be!" He shook his head.

"When did you last see his daughter?"

"Nine years ago on the day the contract was signed. That was also the last time I met her brother. I have regularly heard from him in the meantime, only because he has done everything possible to void the contract. But our exclusive deal is valid for another six months. After that I'll probably have to deal with his son somehow. My God, his daughter, how awful! I hope it has not upset Merlin so much that he can no longer paint?"

"Don't worry, I have a feeling his talent hasn't suffered. I've got to go now. Do you have a business card in the event that I need to contact you?"

Laval took a gold-colored card from his shirt pocket and handed it to Hannes. It had an ornate "L" to the left of his first name that extended downward to incorporate his last name. His address and phone number were diagonally opposite his name.

"Tell me something, is that your real name or have you also adopted an artist's name?"

"In the art world, you need a name that has a ring to it, even better if it has a French touch. My actual name is Ludwig Lachmann. I kept my initials."

Hannes smiled. "Do you know why Mr. Ternheim doesn't speak?"

Laval shrugged. "No idea. Ever since I've known him, he hasn't said a word. But every artist has some kind of quirk. Whenever I come here, he leaves me the finished paintings and disappears into the forest. I once asked his children about his silence, but they wouldn't tell me anything."

"How long were you in the US?"

"Two weeks. I organized an exhibition tour in ten cities. It was hard work!"

Hannes quickly said good-bye and waited until Laval had turned off the main road. He glanced at his cell phone and discovered that he'd missed five calls from Fritz in the past few minutes.

THURSDAY
AFTERNOON

Fritz was back on the case. He limped to his car after leaving the doctor's office with painkillers. He took a water bottle from his glove compartment and washed down two small pills. While waiting for the pain in his back to die down, he drummed his fingers on the steering wheel to a melody from the radio, lost in thought.

So there actually was a connection between Schneider and Ms. Ternheim. It was his only viable lead, but how was he supposed to track Schneider down in this sprawling city if he hadn't already taken off? When Fritz's back pain had finally grown tolerable, he decided to head to the outskirts of town. He had to pick up Schneider's trail somewhere, maybe starting with his home.

Just as he was about to squeeze his Jeep into a parking space along the wall surrounding the mansion, the driveway gate slid open. A red Mini waited to pull out. Fritz shifted forward. The driver waved for him to move over as he stationed his Jeep in front of the driveway. Fritz shut off the engine and awkwardly got out of the car. As he approached the Mini, a window came down and a perfumed cloud of smoke blew in his direction.

"Can't you see that I'm trying to leave?" an outraged Mrs. Schneider screamed. "Who do you think you . . . Oh."

"Hello, Mrs. Schneider. Sorry to keep you. May I have a word with you?"

Mrs. Schneider glanced at her gold watch. "Is this going to take long? I have a tennis lesson in twenty minutes."

"We're still looking for your husband. Has he been home since we last met? Why hasn't he contacted us?"

"No, he hasn't been home," she said and took a nervous puff of her cigarette.

"Oh? He was away last night? Where is he now?"

"I have no idea."

"So he wasn't at your party last night?"

"No, and I haven't heard from him either. Why don't you call him if you want to speak to him so badly?"

"I'd love to, but unfortunately his office is still closed, and I forgot to ask you for his cell phone number yesterday."

"Let me give it to you. Hold on."

She wrote the number down, and Fritz cleared his throat. "You know, I'm a little surprised. Your husband hasn't been home for more than a day, his business is closed, and you haven't heard from him, yet you're headed to your tennis lesson rather than reporting him missing?"

Mrs. Schneider held out the piece of paper; her hand trembled a little. "My husband and I have a modern relationship. It's not unusual for him to have some important business matter he has to attend to and be unreachable for a while. The police would have their work cut out for them if I got worried every time this happened."

Fritz recognized the nervousness in her eyes, a look that did not match the sharp tone of her voice. A clear sign of a lie. He had seen this look hundreds of times.

"Well, that's the downside to modern relationships," he said, pretending to be sympathetic. He stuffed the paper with the phone number in his pocket. "Should you see your husband again soon, please remember to tell him he should contact us. But I don't want to keep you any longer from your tennis lesson. Have fun and enjoy the rest of your day!"

With that, he went back to his car and reversed a few feet into a parking spot. The red Mini turned onto the empty street and disappeared behind a curve. Fritz pulled out the piece of paper with Schneider's number and typed it into his phone. Moments later, Schneider answered.

"Thanks for calling Schneider Real Estate. Unfortunately I can't take your call at the moment, but please leave me a message after the tone . . ."

Fritz considered leaving a message but hung up and called an old colleague at the station instead.

"Marko, it's Fritz. I just got the cell phone number for the only suspect we have in the Helene Ternheim case. Could you get a court order to tap his line? It's very urgent."

After providing the details, Fritz pushed his seat back as far as it would go. With a sigh of relief, he reclined and waited for his colleague to get back to him. He couldn't do much more at the moment. He tried to reach Mr. Schneider every few minutes, but all he got was his voice mail.

Fritz was startled by the sound of Beethoven's Ninth Symphony. His phone was ringing. He slapped his cheek and looked at the dashboard clock. Almost an hour had passed! Although he had not seen his colleagues responsible for monitoring the house, he doubted they had missed his nap. There was a good chance there would be a new story about Old Fritz making the rounds at the station.

"Fritz Janssen," he said into the phone.

"It's Marko. We got the judge's permission. But between you and me, since we knew the judge would grant us permission anyway, we got started a little early."

Fritz hummed in satisfaction. He could always rely on Marko.

"Unfortunately, the phone's turned off, so we couldn't listen in or locate its position."

"Okay. Just keep at it and let me know as soon as you have something."

Fritz sank back into the seat and wondered if there was anything useful he could be doing. But his doctor had failed to inform him of the painkiller's drowsy effect. Half an hour later, another phone call woke him.

"Marko again. Mr. Schneider's phone has just been switched on. He called a landline belonging to a Leonie Kustermann."

"That's his assistant! What did he say?"

"That he's leaving in twenty minutes and they'll meet at three o'clock as they'd agreed. He reminded her to bring the documents and to be sure no one followed her. She answered 'Got it' and then the call ended. After that, he immediately turned off the phone again."

"Did he indicate where he was or where they were supposed to meet?"

"No. They probably discussed that before. But I can tell you his approximate location. Each cell phone tower represents a defined cell or area of coverage, and we determined the position of the tower he used to connect to the network. Using the signal's strength and reception angle, we were able to limit the area even further. He's currently in the southern outskirts of town, somewhere near the former container terminal where the new residential development is being built. Unfortunately, only a few towers have been installed there, so we're unable to isolate his whereabouts any further."

Fritz started the engine. "I'm headed there now. He's leaving in twenty minutes, you said?"

"Exactly, only now he's leaving in fifteen minutes. Should we send backup? There may be some officers already in the area who can get there quicker."

Fritz bolted from the parking spot. "Just let me know if Schneider switches his phone back on!"

He placed his flashing police light on the roof and raced along the quiet residential street. He called Hannes and cursed when he only got his voice mail. He drove through the city at breakneck speed, trying every minute to get ahold of Hannes until he finally reached him.

"Man, Hannes!" Fritz yelled. "What are you doing?"

"I was just—"

"You can tell me later! Where are you right now?"

"At the old lighthouse near old Ternh—"

"Get back to the city as soon as possible! Drive to the home of Schneider's assistant, Leonie Kustermann! Twenty Post Street! Understand?"

"Yes, but what—"

"Don't ask, just drive! And hurry, damn it! She's supposed to meet Mr. Schneider at three o'clock."

"How do you know?"

"Quit asking questions and get moving! I'll explain later. I have an idea where he's been hiding, but he's leaving in a few minutes to meet his assistant, and I have no idea if I'll be able to catch him in time. So follow his assistant, but be careful she doesn't notice you! Schneider warned her she might be followed. Got that?"

"Sure thing, I—"

Fritz hung up.

Hannes realized Fritz had already hung up and quickly started the patrol car. Fingers trembling, he tapped the destination address into his GPS and raced toward the city.

Since Hannes had no idea what kind of car Ms. Kustermann drove or if she would need it to get to the meeting place, he realized he would have to catch her as she left her home. He also had no idea what she looked like and hoped she would walk, because he didn't see how he could tail her in his blue-and-white police car without being noticed. Unsure what to do, he pulled into an open parking spot, which was fortunately obscured by a van but still allowed a reasonably clear view of the front door of her building.

Hannes turned down the radio. He couldn't just follow the first woman who left the apartment building. Since Fritz wasn't picking up his phone anymore, he couldn't ask him for advice either. Hannes hoped the unknown meeting place was closer to Ms. Kustermann's apartment than Schneider's whereabouts. Otherwise, he had already missed her.

At that moment, a large garage door creaked open to the right of the building, and a silver Peugeot slowly pulled out. He leaned forward in excitement, but just as quickly relaxed when he realized the driver had gray hair. Nevertheless, seeing the car gave him an idea. His colleague Sven, who was also a competitive boxer, worked in the traffic division. Hopefully he was on duty today!

The switchboard put through his call, and Hannes's hope waned after the eighth ring. Just as he was about to end the call, Sven picked up.

"Sven! I'm glad I caught you! It's Hannes. Can you do me a big favor?"

"What kind of favor?"

"I'm supposed to shadow a suspect, but I have no idea what she looks like. I was hoping she'd use her car and that I could recognize her that way. Can you give me the license plate for a Leonie Kustermann who lives at 20 Post Street?"

"Um, yeah. Hold on."

Hannes heard Sven put the phone down and did his best to stay patient.

After several minutes Sven said, "What's the woman's name again?" "First name: Leonie. Last name: Kustermann. Her address is 20 Post Street."

In the background, he heard the faint clicks of a keyboard. As Hannes looked at his watch, he groaned to himself. The real estate agent and his assistant were due to meet each other in less than ten minutes!

"Find anything? Man, I'm running out of time here," he prodded Sven and prayed that Ms. Kustermann actually owned a car.

"Okay, here we go. Leonie Kustermann, 20 Post Street. It's a blue 2006 Golf." He gave him the license plate number. "Looks like she has quite the lead foot and has received several speeding tickets. She was also recently caught running a red light."

"Yeah, and?"

"Not only was she caught, but she was photographed. It happened just a month ago."

"Seriously? That's awesome! What does she look like? Young? Old? Hair color?"

"It's only a grainy black and white. She looks somewhat young, mid- to late twenties. She has long, light-colored hair. She also wears glasses and is smoking a cigarette in the photo."

"Sven, you're the greatest! I owe you a beer sometime, or a protein shake, if you'd prefer."

"Beer's fine with me," said Sven with a laugh. "Good luck tracking her down!"

Hannes exhaled and took another look at his watch. Seven minutes left!

Then the garage door started up again. Maybe this was it.

Fritz had managed to track down Schneider. In addition to Marko's help, fate had also smiled on him: Schneider's black BMW 3 Series, which Fritz had recognized from the incident at the fishing harbor, had passed him in the opposite direction. Fritz had clearly spotted it on the bridge that led to the new housing development where the former container terminal once stood. But when he used the access road to a construction site to make a U-turn after the bridge, a truck rumbled up behind him and blocked the way back to the main road.

Fritz jumped out of his car, waving. He stormed over to the truck and yanked the driver's door open.

"Move! I have to get back on the road," he said.

Two bearded faces turned to him. "You want to see house? House not finished yet."

"No!" shouted Fritz. "Road! I want to get onto the road!" He shoved his badge in the two construction workers' faces, and their eyes widened.

"We done nothing! Have papers! Everything okay!"

Fritz stamped his feet. Luckily for him, another worker from the construction site wandered over.

"What's going on?"

Fritz held out his badge. "These two idiots are blocking me! I'm chasing a suspect!"

The man quickly addressed the two men in Czech. With a deafening roar, the truck shifted into reverse and the driver backed it out into the street. A thankful Fritz patted the man on the shoulder and ran back to the Jeep. Gravel flew everywhere as he made a quick U-turn and sped off in the right direction.

Fortunately, this stretch of road wound its way through a desolate former port area. Fritz ignored the 35 mph speed limit as the quivering needle in the speedometer approached eighty-five. He couldn't get much more out of his old car. A light flashed, and Fritz pulled his hair. A speed trap. Damn it.

A few minutes later, he entered an industrial zone, but Fritz reduced his speed only slightly. A truck exiting a refinery was just barely able to stop in time and slammed on its horn. Fritz dropped back down to

55 mph. At the first intersection, he made the spontaneous decision to continue following the main road because the other roads dead-ended at industrial facilities. Two minutes later, his suspicions were confirmed. Directly in front of him was a moss-green Toyota, but about two hundred yards ahead, he saw the black BMW convertible.

Hannes paid close attention to the garage door as it came up. He eagerly reached for the ignition in anticipation of a blue Golf. But instead of a car, a bicycle appeared. Discouraged, he pulled his hand away from the key. But the person pushing the bicycle caught his attention.

Female, since he could easily see her large breasts, probably in her late twenties, long light-blonde hair, a cigarette in her hand, and a bag slung over her shoulder. Yet she wasn't wearing glasses. Hannes's doubts vanished as the woman cautiously looked around. Maybe Ms. Kustermann only wore her glasses when driving. With only two minutes left, he had very little choice. Either he had missed Ms. Kustermann or she was leaving late. He preferred risking a mistake rather than sitting around doing nothing.

He quietly opened the door. Of all the possibilities, a bike was the worst! It was impossible to follow her in the police car without being noticed, and if he walked, she would easily lose him.

As the young woman got on her Dutch city bike and slowly rode away, Hannes began trotting after her along the sidewalk. The cyclist repeatedly turned and looked around, forcing Hannes to pay attention to the distance between them and use the parked cars as a screen. Given her odd behavior, he was absolutely certain he was following the right person.

Hannes was relieved that his knee was not causing him any problems. At the end of the street, Leonie turned down a narrow path that ran along a small creek and flicked the cigarette away. After looking at her watch, she began pedaling harder. Hannes picked up his pace.

The straight, narrow path didn't offer him any camouflage, but she apparently felt safe now and only looked ahead. At the end of the path, the stream disappeared under a small bridge, and she swerved the bike to the left back onto the road. Hannes also turned left but jogged down the sidewalk on the other side of the road. Sweat was pouring down his face, leaving a taste of salt on his lips. Pedestrians turned around to look in surprise at the young man running in the summer heat in jeans.

Hannes glanced down a side street and spotted Leonie dismounting in front of a row of shops. He turned and smacked right into a jogger, causing them both to fall. He tried to get his bearings and found himself half lying on top of a young woman. She moaned and pushed Hannes away. She had a bloody knee.

"Are you blind or what?" she snapped.

Hannes turned to look at her and froze.

"It's you!" cried a familiar voice, and Hannes's ears turned red.

"Maria! I'm so sorry. What are you doing here?"

Maria looked at her elbow, which had also been grazed, and then at Hannes. "I'm off this afternoon and was on my way to see a friend. What are you doing jogging around here? Don't you have a murder to investigate?"

Hannes had momentarily forgotten the reason for his jog, and now he peered cautiously around a parked car. The bike was still standing in front of the shops, but Leonie was nowhere to be found. He carefully got up and explained the reason for his bizarre appearance.

"And now I've probably lost track of Ms. Kustermann," he said in frustration.

"Well, I'm sorry I got in your way," Maria said sarcastically and gently picked a small stone from the wound in her knee.

"I'm sorry, I didn't mean it that way. I was just so focused on chasing the suspect. I'm probably just a bad cop," he said.

"I'd say so," teased Maria as she pushed a strand of hair from her face. "Because if you're trailing that green bike, you just missed the owner coming out of the pharmacy."

Hannes looked just in time to catch the bike turning down a side street. "Sorry, but I have to follow her. Let me make it up to you! How about dinner?"

"I'll think about it," Maria said.

Hannes sprinted toward the side street. He sensed Maria watching him from behind and hoped she appreciated her view of him as much as he had of her.

Fritz was careful to track Schneider's BMW without being noticed and initially stayed behind the green Toyota, which seemed to be following Schneider's same path.

A few moments later, the black convertible suddenly accelerated and made a series of quick turns onto several side streets only to end up back on the main road. Fritz was surprised to note that the green Toyota was still following Schneider's car and had also picked up the pace. Apparently, someone else was interested in following him, but who and why?

Schneider accelerated and blew through the intersection by the old water tower before disappearing behind a bend in the road. A moment later, the light turned yellow and Fritz accelerated and swerved into the opposite lane. Fortunately, the driver coming from the opposite direction had stopped at the traffic light, so the road was clear. Fritz easily passed the Toyota, glancing at the driver—a man with his eyes fixed on the road ahead.

Fritz zoomed by and was relieved when he saw Schneider's car in the distance. Schneider made a sharp left onto a street of row houses on one side and a public park on the other. Fritz cautiously turned down the street and stopped behind a parked Jeep. He watched as the black

BMW slowed and eventually pulled into a parking space. Schneider got out, glanced around, and trotted across the street to the park.

Fritz opened his door and followed, staying behind the parked cars in case he needed to take cover. He was so focused that he didn't notice the green Toyota turn down the same road and pull into the last free parking space.

Hannes was running out of breath and wondered whether his break from training had taken its toll. It was already well past three o'clock, and the cyclist struggled to pick up her pace. She turned down a dirt path in the public park. The path wound through a small forested area, and Hannes was glad to escape the sun. His jeans clung to his legs, and his shirt was drenched in sweat. Birds chirped all around, and he could hear the laughter of children in the distance.

Suddenly, the bike turned onto a small path that led down to a hollow. From previous jogs, Hannes knew the path snaked around a shady pond before heading uphill again on the other side. Up ahead, on the shore of the small lake, stood a man in white linen pants and a red polo shirt. He was looking at the water, so Hannes could only see his profile. When the woman stopped and got off her bike, the man turned to her, and Hannes was now absolutely certain it was Florian Schneider. The past two days had clearly taken their toll on him. His once-straight posture and arrogance had given way to sagging shoulders and an exhausted face.

Hannes was surprised to see Leonie Kustermann wrap her arms around him. Schneider tried to push her away in embarrassment. She pulled a manila envelope out of her bag and handed it to him. He took out a small stack of papers and leafed through it while Ms. Kustermann watched.

Hannes took advantage of this opportunity to sneak closer, using the bushes as cover whenever possible. He forced himself to breathe quietly so as not to betray his position. His pulse gradually returned to normal, but after the long run he felt hotter and sweatier.

He gently pushed a branch aside to get a clearer view. They talked in hushed voices. Schneider stuffed the papers back into the envelope and affectionately stroked Ms. Kustermann's arm to calm her. Unfortunately, Hannes was too far away to overhear them.

He noticed a small movement near a thick oak tree, which stood directly opposite him on a slope behind the couple. He pulled his cell phone out of his pocket, chose the camera function, and zoomed in on the tree. A grin crept over his face as an owl-like head appeared on the screen, peering from behind the mighty tree trunk. Old Fritz had managed to track down Schneider. He was certainly one tough cop!

The conversation between Schneider and Ms. Kustermann became more heated; Hannes directed his attention back to the pond. She was furiously waving her arms and violently pushed him. And then it happened: there was a loud crack opposite Hannes, and Schneider and Ms. Kustermann turned around. A man, who had apparently lost his footing, skidded down the slope and landed only a few feet from the water.

"I knew it!" shouted Schneider. "I told you I was being followed, but you wouldn't believe me!"

Enraged, he dropped the envelope and stomped over to the fallen man. He leaned down and angrily grabbed him by the shirt collar, then shook him so forcefully that Hannes became seriously worried and wondered who the man was.

"How long have you been spying on me?" Schneider yelled, his fist raised.

Then there was another loud crack followed by the sound of rustling leaves. "Police! Let go of him immediately!" Fritz made his way down the slope, aiming his gun at Schneider. Ms. Kustermann let out a scream and clapped her hands over her mouth.

Schneider stood up and glared at the detective. "You again! At least you came at the right time. Arrest this guy immediately!"

"Why?" Fritz asked as he slowly approached.

"Because he's probably the one who's been following me for days! Here!" Schneider kicked at a digital camera that the small pudgy man was holding. "He's been taking photos!"

Hannes left his hiding place and walked up. Fritz looked at his sweat-soaked clothes. "Glad you could make it," he joked but could not hide his approval.

"It just keeps getting better and better," Schneider said. "So three people have been following me this whole time!"

"Apparently," Fritz said. "And I bet you know why."

"No, I have no idea why!"

Hannes picked up the discarded envelope and pulled the papers out. "Property Description" was written at the top of every one. He realized the documents were for a simple real estate deal.

Fritz took a closer look at the stranger for the first time. His wire-rimmed glasses were slightly crooked as a result of Schneider's attack, and grass and mud were stuck to his sweaty bald head.

"Who are you and what are you doing here?" Fritz asked him.

The man timidly fixed his glasses. "I'm a private detective," he said, and an angry Schneider immediately started punching him.

"Enough!" shouted Fritz. "Stop or I'll shoot!"

Blinded by rage, Schneider continued to pummel the man. Hannes rushed forward and pulled Schneider off. He dragged him away and tossed him into the small pond. After a few seconds, a sputtering Schneider emerged from the water.

"You have my respect," Fritz said behind him. "That side job of yours certainly doesn't hurt your athletic prowess. But handcuffs probably would have sufficed."

"Would you really have fired on him?" Hannes asked.

"At my age, I'm not going to throw myself in front of some deranged man. See to the private detective. He needs medical attention."

Hannes determined that the whimpering detective hadn't suffered any major injuries.

"What do you want from me?" Schneider asked Fritz in an exhausted voice.

"The same as yesterday. I want to talk to you about the dead woman we found on the beach. We had planned to visit you yesterday, but you vanished."

"Listen, I already told you the other day that I didn't—"

"Well, since then, there have been some crucial developments. A witness has come forward and identified you and your boat. He claims he saw you at the aforementioned stretch of beach. You dropped anchor and argued with a blonde woman on board. A few hours later, a blonde woman was found dead on that very beach. The victim was Helene Ternheim, and you've done business with her before."

"That's quite the story you got there. I don't even know a Helene Ternheim."

"No? Then how is it that you sold this supposedly unfamiliar Ms. Ternheim a penthouse on Sun Street down by the harbor three years ago?"

"Ah, I remember that penthouse, what a unique place! But I don't remember the name of the buyer. All I heard was that she worked for a large corporation."

"Don't lie to me," Fritz said. "You're claiming it was purely by chance that you were at the same spot where Ms. Ternheim was later found dead?"

"Why would I have killed her? The sale went smoothly. And since then, I've had nothing to do with this woman. So what reason would there have been?"

"That's what I'd like to know. Maybe it was about money? Evidently, you can't get enough of it."

"So now envy's a reason to arrest an innocent man?"

"I'm not envious, and certainly not of you. Who do you think we are? The Keystone Cops? I hate to disappoint you. I've made inquiries about you, and we discovered something very interesting. Because of the agreement of sale with Ms. Ternheim, or rather because of unpaid taxes on the commission, you got into quite a lot of trouble. Suddenly the sale doesn't seem to have gone too smoothly."

Schneider's face turned white. "That . . . that was years ago. I was convicted and paid my fine—not without any difficulty, I might add. Besides, I had a deal with her. Unfortunately, she wanted to double dip and save money on my commission and on her taxes."

"Ms. Ternheim told a different story. Why did you issue an invoice if there was a deal?"

"I was naive. She told me she needed the invoice to keep her finances in order."

"Weren't you pretty mad at her? Maybe even to this day?" Fritz said.

"Of course I was mad at her, but not enough to wait three years to kill her."

"There are one too many coincidences, don't you think? So who was this blonde on your boat?"

Schneider stared at Fritz.

"Well? You don't want to tell me?"

"It was me" came the answer from behind him.

Fritz turned and looked at Ms. Kustermann. "You don't need to lie for your boss and get yourself in trouble."

"I'm not . . . I was the one on board." Hannes noticed that Leonie, in spite of her impressive bust size, had a very girlish demeanor.

"Why?"

"What kind of a question is that?" the private detective asked. "They're clearly having an affair!"

Suddenly, the young woman burst into tears. "We're . . . we're not having an affair . . . We love each other. We're a couple."

"Leonie, please," Schneider said, but she slapped his hand away.

"And we were fighting because I'm pregnant, and he wants me to have an abortion!" She crouched into a ball and cried uncontrollably.

Fritz remembered Tom's description of the fight on the boat and cleared his throat.

"Is that true?" he asked Schneider.

"Yes, it's true."

Fritz rolled his eyes. "Why have you been hiding from us?"

"It wasn't from you! I got the feeling I was being watched. I was afraid Leonie and I hadn't been careful enough and my wife had become suspicious."

"And as it turns out, she was right about her suspicions," said the private detective.

"So what do you know then?" Schneider said. "My wife's been screwing our gardener for a while now. Do you think I don't know that? But she probably didn't blab about that to you, did she? She started sleeping with the guy long before there was anything between Leonie and me."

"So why are you playing hide-and-seek?" Fritz asked.

Schneider took a deep breath. "My wife and I have a prenuptial agreement. The money I used to start my real estate firm was hers. If we were to divorce, I would have to pay her out; but I don't have the money, because, among other things, I had to pay off a significant fine not too long ago. I need another year or two. But thanks to that guy," he said, pointing to the private detective, "she has me right where she wants me, and I can't prove her affair with our gardener."

Schneider wiped his face, and Fritz took a deep breath. Then Hannes intervened.

"How long have you been following Mr. Schneider?" he asked the private detective.

"Since last Wednesday."

"Did you follow him to his boat on Saturday?"

"Of course! I take my job very seriously."

"I'm sure. Did you follow him on the water?"

"How could I? I didn't know where he was going, and I didn't have a boat."

"Then you must have at least seen who was with him. Was Ms. Kustermann on board?"

"Yes, I saw him get on the boat and leave with Ms. Kustermann."

"Well, there's always a silver lining," Fritz said to Schneider. "This man may have invaded your privacy, but he also saved you from being taken into custody. Take down the private detective's information, Hannes, and have him show you his ID." He turned to Schneider and Ms. Kustermann. "As for you two, I have one last question. When you dropped anchor, did you see anything on the beach or in the water that looked unusual to you? Another boat or people on the beach?"

"Nothing," Schneider said, "absolutely nothing."

Ms. Kustermann shook her head but seemed distant. Her long lashes were wet with tears, and her mascara had run.

Fritz walked over to Hannes, took the private detective's business card from him, and put it in his wallet. "So now we're back to square one."

Hannes was disappointed. "Now what?"

"Now we get the hell out of here. And take a shower. You smell like crap."

As a precaution, Fritz and Hannes accompanied the private detective to his car. Afterward, Fritz spread a towel over the front seat of his Jeep and made a show of rolling down the window.

"At least you're back in shape. Ole, the fisherman, can sleep easy tonight," he teased. "Is your car in front of Ms. Kustermann's place?"

"Yup, it'd be great if you could drop me off there. I was lucky she took her bike. She would've noticed me immediately in a cop car."

"Say, how did you know who to look for? You had no description of her, right?"

Hannes told Fritz how he had found out who she was.

"Excellent work, Hannes! Maybe I'll make a good cop out of you after all."

Hannes beamed, knowing Fritz rarely praised anyone.

"What happened on your field trip?" Fritz asked.

Hannes began to recount his visit to Hohenberg Farm but was quickly interrupted.

"You can skip that; you already told me over the phone. Your question about Ms. Ternheim's car, incidentally, was spot on. I've flagged the sports car as missing, but so far no one's come across it. Tell me how it went with the wizard Merlin. Were you able to get him to talk?"

"No, but I think I've found a way to get to him."

Hannes set the scene of his meeting with the old man.

"Hold on!" Fritz said. "When you told him the tattoo on his daughter's forearm was likely a series of numbers, did he react?"

"Yes, a little oddly."

"How so?"

Hannes told him about the painting of Helene Ternheim and tried to describe Merlin's drawings.

"Interesting. Then what happened?"

Hannes had almost forgotten about his near miss with the art agent at the old lighthouse.

"So there's another player on the field? As a precaution, we should check his flights and hotel stays. It probably won't get us anywhere, but he didn't have anything particularly good to say about the brother even though he depends on him. People have been killed for less."

Fritz stopped in front of Hannes's police car. "Look, just head home and take a shower! You can take the towel and put it on your seat. Just bring it back to me soon—washed! And bring the car back to the station after you meet with Anna."

"I just thought of something," Hannes said and shared his theory about the tattoo on Ms. Ternheim's forearm.

Fritz rubbed his scar. "I understand the connection. But it's probably a bit far-fetched."

His phone rang. He answered and immediately recognized Ms. Wagner's voice.

"Mr. Janssen! I'm glad I could reach you. Please don't think I'm crazy, but I just had to call."

"What's wrong?"

"Mr. Ternheim has disappeared!"

"What?"

"Mr. Ternheim had a one o'clock lunch meeting with our bank consultant. He usually takes these appointments very seriously. But he didn't show up at Fish."

"Where?"

"Fish. The restaurant where they were supposed to meet. Mr. Grundmann, the bank consultant, called and asked if Mr. Ternheim was running late. He had left here at twelve thirty."

"Maybe something's come up?"

"He would never skip a meeting with our bank consultant. I can't reach him on his cell phone, which is extremely unusual. Please don't think I'm being hysterical, but I'd only blame myself if I didn't let you know as soon as possible."

"Ms. Wagner, calm down. You did the right thing contacting me, but I'm sure there's a reasonable explanation. Let me know when you hear from him again."

Fritz hung up. Hannes looked at him quizzically. "What's going on?"

"Ms. Wagner believes Mr. Ternheim has disappeared." Then he explained the circumstances. "He just lost his sister. Even though he seems in control, I'm sure he's not made of stone. Maybe he just needs some time to himself?"

"So why is he not answering his phone?"

"Because he wants to be left alone. Or maybe his battery died."

"I don't know. It doesn't seem like he would just skip an important meeting."

"Okay, I'll look into it. Now go shower. When are you supposed to meet with Ms. Stahl?"

"We said six."

Fritz glanced at his watch. "It's just after four. I'll take care of Mr. Ternheim, and you can do whatever you want until six. Give me a call when you're done. Maybe I'll have some news by then."

Even though he was becoming more and more invested in the case, Hannes was ecstatic. If he hurried, he could still do a quick lap in the canoe before he met with Anna at Chameleon.

Merle had struggled for hours with hunger. She had been able to resist the tray of food that had been shoved into the room after the flashes of light, which, along with the clicking, she was convinced had been produced by some kind of camera. First her clothes had been taken off, then she had been photographed. What would happen next? Whatever it was, Merle wasn't going to let it happen while she slept.

The hatch had been opened again a few minutes ago, and as a tray with the obligatory bottle of water was shoved in, this time a pizza followed. Merle had heard a cough. A male cough? Or was it an illusion? She had also noted in surprise that a gray wool blanket had been set next to her food. A sign of sympathy and human compassion? She had tried again to establish contact with the unknown person, but her questions and pleas went unanswered.

Merle began to worry about her mental state. That afternoon, she had spent an hour banging on the door, screaming, crying, and hitting her head against the wall until blood dripped into her eye. She was suffering from fear, light deprivation, exhaustion, hunger, and lack of human contact.

Another panic attack threatened to overwhelm her. She could not endure the darkness any longer. Her stomach began to cramp and she felt dizzy. She gasped for breath while tears ran down her cheeks. What if this tiny space ran out of oxygen? Logic, however, saved Merle from a hysterical breakdown. If the air couldn't be replaced, she would have already suffocated. There must be a supply of fresh air coming from somewhere. Then she thought she felt a slight breeze coming from the ceiling above her bed.

After several more minutes, her breathing sped up. In order to distract herself from her fears and hunger, she began to recount another episode in her life. She wrapped the blanket around herself and imagined that Björn, her favorite teddy bear, sat beside her on the bed and looked lovingly at her with his black button eyes. He had been a gift from Aunt Amber and had accompanied her throughout her entire childhood. Merle had left Björn behind when she had started out on her new life because she had thought that she could do without his protection. But she needed him now more than ever.

"You know, Björn," she said in a quivering voice, "when Aunt Amber finally called to tell me my father's name, I didn't know if I really wanted to find out. After all, he had abandoned me as a baby and never tried to get to know me. Do you think he ever wondered about me? Still, I'm glad I met him. Now at least I know who I am and where I come from."

In her mind she could see Björn's comforting grin and bundled up part of her blanket to create the illusion of a teddy bear. She stroked the fabric and giggled like a child. The blanket was a little rougher than Björn, but it almost felt like him. She then asked herself if she was finally beginning to lose her mind and if that was the reason why she was conducting a conversation with an imaginary teddy bear. But with the soothing image of her old companion, she immediately dismissed the thought and continued to pet the imaginary fur, while the memory of the first time she met her father flashed before her eyes.

The meeting hadn't gone as Merle had hoped. Under the pretext of writing an article about depression and appropriate treatment options, she had managed to schedule an appointment with him through his assistant. His face had remained utterly devoid of emotion when she confronted him about her true identity. His air of detached coolness was deeply unsettling. Were it not for the birthmark under his right eye, Merle wouldn't have been able to detect any resemblance between them.

Even now the anger grew inside her. "What a jerk! All he said was he and my mother had come to an agreement and that I should not delude myself into thinking I could squeeze any more money out of him. As if that had been my intention! He seemed to feel almost threatened. Fortunately his sister had walked into his office and was flabbergasted when she found me crying. She was so different from him, compassionate and kind."

Her hands tensed and she stroked her imaginary teddy bear even harder. She then relaxed as she recalled the next few memories.

Even though Merle's father had refused to meet with her again, his sister had taken an interest in her and insisted that she call her Aunt Helene: "Because I am, after all, your aunt!" She had even introduced Merle to her father, whom Merle had continued to visit. Initially, she had felt repulsed by her grandfather and his silence, but he quickly broke the ice after he painted a lovely portrait of her. She had also been able to forge a warm relationship with her aunt. At that moment, she longed to be close to her.

"I wonder if she's reported me missing? We were supposed to get together on Sunday. She must be worried sick. What do you mean, Björn? Maybe the police are already looking for me?"

She was distracted by her stomach growling again. She peeled the blanket off her and placed her bare feet on the cold floor. If she ate, she could be drugged again, but if she didn't, she would inevitably starve.

With a heavy heart, Merle took small steps through the darkness. She sat down on the floor and grabbed the pizza. Despite her doubts, she took a bite, followed by many more. As she pictured her aunt and grandfather, she felt overcome with love. But then Christian Ternheim's face appeared in her mind and instantly scared her positive feelings away.

"I know you hate me because I'm your daughter. And I hate you too," she whispered between bites before she crouched into a ball.

Early Thursday Evening

Hannes entered the Chameleon at six on the dot. The lighting in the glass-walled lobby transitioned from yellow to red, then brown to blue, before starting over again. The actual lounge was behind a heavy dark-red curtain and featured small groups of couches and chairs surrounded by walls painted in warm colors. The shelves behind the bar were also lit in alternating colors, which made the numerous bottles seem to constantly change hues.

Despite the large chalkboard advertising happy-hour specials, there was only a moderate number of people at the bar. Hannes headed for a two-top table in the far corner of the room. Soft background music was playing, but he knew from a previous visit that this would change later on.

The bored-looking bartender glanced at him but continued to polish a couple more glasses before he took Hannes's drink order. He shortly brought over a bottle of bitter lemon soda and a glass, and Hannes ordered a plate of nachos. Practice had made him hungry and sleepy; he had pushed himself a little too hard. Fortunately, he had found clean clothes in his locker, so he had been able to head straight to Chameleon without stopping at Ben's place.

He took out a pen and a small notepad and whiled away the minutes sipping his drink. Had they overlooked anything in the case? Why was the body found in such a secluded spot? And why was the victim someone who seemingly had no friends or acquaintances? All they could focus on was the pharmaceutical company, since this seemed to be Ms. Ternheim's only purpose in life other than visiting her father. Hannes's mind kept coming back to the old man's drawing of his son as the Angel of Death. But he was unsure whether it was merely a senile man's fantasy or a valuable clue. He was equally perplexed by the tattoo and could only hope that the bar's cozy atmosphere would keep Anna from stalling and that she would open up and provide him with valuable clues.

It was already six fifteen when the nachos arrived. He was beginning to think the assistant had gotten cold feet. It was a rather unpleasant thought: if she stood him up, then he would leave empty-handed. Hannes dug in to the nachos.

"Anything else?" asked the bartender a few minutes later.

He looked again at his watch: Anna was half an hour late. But what else was there for him to do other than wait? He ordered a nonalcoholic Summer Delight. He hadn't asked for the assistant's address or number, or he would have called or headed to her place.

The curtain by the front door was pushed aside. Anna walked in and looked around the room, and Hannes stood up and waved to her. Clutching her purse, she crossed the room. She was clearly a little upset or nervous.

"Glad you could come," he said. "I was going to get a table outside, but then I thought we'd be less disturbed inside. Besides, they have air-conditioning here. I hope it's all right."

She nodded and sat down, completely tense. Her brown hair was slightly sweaty, and strands of hair stuck to her face. She kept glancing nervously around the room. Her body language exuded apprehension. But this was not normal apprehension: Anna was clearly terrified.

The bartender placed Hannes's cocktail on the table. "Do you know what you'd like?" he asked her.

"Something with alcohol. I could use it right now."

"Of course, no problem," the bartender said. "I recommend the Caribbean Dream. It's so good."

"Sounds good, I'll take it," Anna said.

"A Caribbean Dream goes well with today's heat," Hannes said. To lighten the mood, he opened with some small talk about the weather. Her Caribbean Dream soon arrived.

"Well, does it taste like a party?" he joked and raised his glass.

Anna sucked so hard on the straw that nearly a third of the orange liquid was gone. She exhaled in satisfaction and relaxed a bit. "That feels good. Today was really crazy!"

"I can imagine. The news must have come as quite a shock."

"That's true. It's still all so surreal. I've never experienced anything like it."

"Neither have I."

Anna stared at him, puzzled.

"Yes, that's right," he said and laughed. "My boss could tell you one crime story after another, but this is actually my first case."

He briefly explained his background and soon realized it did more to make her feel at ease than any small talk about the weather.

"Did you have a lot to do at the office today?" he asked.

"No, not really. The whole company's kind of shocked by what happened. Hardly anyone could work today. Or do you mean why was I late getting here? It had nothing to do with work. I . . . The tires of my bicycle were flat, so I had to lug it here."

"I always have my pump with me except when I need it," he lied.

"Actually, I have a small pump in my bag, but . . . Oh, never mind."

She retreated back into her shell and looked even more unapproachable than she did that morning. As he looked at her, he felt as though he were sitting opposite a frightened squirrel. He wondered if he had made another mistake. "Why, what was the problem?" he asked.

Anna leaned forward. "The tires had been slashed; no bicycle pump would have helped."

"Oh . . . There are some really nasty people out there!"

"This is the first time something like this has happened to me. Lagussa's surrounded by other office buildings, so there are never any shady characters around. And besides . . . Never mind. To be honest, I've been wondering why you asked me here. I don't know anything that could be of help. I'm sorry, this was such a stupid idea! I'm just wasting your time. You have better things to do."

She reached for her purse.

"Wait, Ms. Stahl!" he said. "You made several allusions this morning, and then you show up half an hour late this evening with a frightened look on your face. Now you're suddenly trying to back out and are telling me you have nothing to say. I'm sorry, but I don't buy it! We're grasping at straws right now and know almost nothing about Ms. Ternheim's private or professional life. We're trying to find out as much as we can, and I just want to hear what you wouldn't say in front of your colleagues this morning. And besides, I'd like to know why you're so afraid."

She burst into tears, and the bartender shot Hannes a dirty look.

"I'm sorry," Anna said, wiping her eyes with a handkerchief. "It's all just happening at once. Yesterday everything was fine, and today I'm caught up in this strange story."

"But you're not really caught up in it. You just have to tell me about your boss, and you'll probably never see me again."

Anna blew her nose. Then she rummaged in her bag and pulled out a folded piece of paper which she pushed across the table.

"This note was stuck to my bicycle seat," she said.

He unfolded the paper: *Silence is golden, talking can be deadly.*

"Did you tell anyone about our meeting tonight?" Hannes asked.

"I only told my best friend, who also works at Lagussa. We went through training together. I told her at lunch in the cafeteria. But she is absolutely trustworthy. It's possible someone overheard our conversation—the cafeteria was pretty packed. I'm so stupid."

"Well, you didn't know. Why did you tell your friend about our meeting?"

Anna blushed and looked at the ground. "Oh . . . just . . . We just talked and somehow, I don't know. I wasn't thinking and didn't pay attention if anyone else was listening."

Hannes sensed another reason. He glanced at her knotted hands. She wasn't wearing a ring.

"Whoever placed the note and slashed the tires had to know which bike was yours. How many people at Lagussa would recognize your bike?"

"In the summer, I ride it almost every day and lock it at one of the stands by the main entrance. Most of my coworkers have probably seen me with my bike."

"Well, I'm glad you still came," he said. "Did you notice if someone followed you?"

"No, I kept looking around, but I didn't see anyone."

"Hmm. Usually things like this don't amount to much," he said. "Would it be possible for you to stay with your friend tonight?"

"Yes, sure! She doesn't even know what happened. I came here as soon as possible, but I didn't know if I should tell you. But now I realize the scope of all this . . ."

"Don't worry, we'll take care of you," he said, even though he felt the note wouldn't be enough to justify police protection. "Do you trust your friend completely?"

"Of course, otherwise she wouldn't be my best friend! She's completely innocent, and if you met Tina, you'd know what I mean."

"Does she have any connection to the Ternheims?"

"No, definitely not! Tina works in logistics, there's no overlap with management."

Hannes decided not to press her any further but still wanted to draw his own conclusions. "Be careful! I came here by car. After our conversation, I'll take you to your apartment, so you can pick up a few things, and then I'll drop you at your friend's place. And don't worry, I know how to shake off pursuers," he said with a grin.

She looked at him skeptically. "But you just said that this was your first case . . ."

"Policing 101," he said. "We covered numerous practical exercises! Besides, I already demonstrated once today that I haven't forgotten what I learned."

He persuaded her to order another cocktail and a sandwich. He had apparently managed to make her feel safe again and hoped that he actually had the situation under control. As a precaution, he decided against any alcohol and ordered another Summer Delight, while Anna opted for a Caribbean Lover. Was she trying to tell him something?

He engaged her in harmless small talk and felt this helped further reassure her. After the bartender placed the second round of cocktails in front of them, he steered the conversation back to business.

"Ms. Stahl, this morning I got the feeling you're very happy working at Lagussa."

"Oh, please call me Anna. Otherwise you make me feel like an old woman. We're about the same age, anyway."

"Sure," he said. Anna wasn't really his type, so why did he become more nervous the more she felt relaxed? "However, you're a little generous in saying that we're about the same age: I'm pushing thirty-three."

She cocked her head and looked at him. "Huh? How old do you think I am?"

"That of course is the most dangerous of all questions," he said and laughed. He made a point of sizing her up and realized she came off pretty well. She had slightly tanned, flawless skin and wore only a subtle amount of makeup. A few small freckles dotted her straight nose, and her smooth brown hair was casually tucked behind her ears. Earlier that morning, he had noticed her athletic figure.

"Well? Finished looking?" she asked, and he realized he had been eyeing her in silence.

"You, uh . . . Since you've already been working at Lagussa for almost ten years and started right after graduation, I'd guess twenty-seven."

"Ugh, such a cop," she said and laughed. "I gave you too much information before. Still, you're a little off: I'm twenty-nine. But that's not because I was held back in school. After training, I traveled the world for a year. You could still pass for someone in his twenties . . ."

Now she was clearly flirting: there was no mistaking the look on her face. He had hoped the alcohol would loosen her up, but he had not expected this.

"I've had this question on my mind the entire day," he said, trying to collect his thoughts. He could see the expectation in her eyes as she leaned toward him. "You said Ms. Ternheim had seemed a bit absent lately. When did you first notice the change?"

"Well, she was never really an extroverted person; she only occasionally came out of her shell. But she was always friendly, focused, and extremely present. I first noticed something had changed about two months ago. She started leaving the office earlier and earlier, at least by her standards. In the mornings, she would seem somewhat bleary-eyed and would barricade herself in her office for hours at a time. Normally, she would have meetings or would come out to ask us to do something for her. Then I started noticing how she would stare off into space whenever I spoke to her. She would ask me afterward to repeat myself."

"Was it just a phase or was she like that for the whole two months?"

"Last week, she had almost returned to her former self, and I hoped she had finally recovered from whatever it was. She was looking forward to tomorrow's charity gala for children suffering from leukemia. The cause was very close to her heart."

Hannes remembered Ben telling him he would be staging a protest at the gala, and winced.

"What is it?" asked Anna.

"Oh, nothing." He struggled with his bad conscience. "Are you involved in this event?"

"Our event coordinator takes care of it primarily, but I make sure management's ideas are adhered to. Basically, I supervise it all and make sure everything goes to plan." She sighed. "It's been a real tough job lately. I've had to hit the brakes a couple of times, so it doesn't devolve into some kind of party and we don't lose track of the reason behind the gala."

He felt even guiltier and wondered if he could talk Ben out of his protest. "Do you have any idea what could have triggered the change in Ms. Ternheim?"

Anna squirmed and stared at the table.

"Anna, please! You have to tell me what you know."

"Will it stay just between us?"

"I can't promise that. If it's crucial to the investigation, then I at least have to talk to my superior about it. But I promise you that we will treat your information as sensitively as possible."

"No one at Lagussa can find out. Think of the note on my bike, and Mr. Ternheim could even fire me!"

He thought for a moment and then nodded. "Okay."

"Promise?"

"I promise," he said and hoped he would be able to keep it.

"I have two theories. One private and the other professional."

"Tell me the private one first."

"Well . . . there were rumors going around the company for some time. As you know, Ms. Ternheim was not married and never had been. Even at public and official events, there was never a man by her side. The staff started talking, and I would hear bits and pieces until I was promoted to executive assistant. After that, the gossip stopped the moment I was near." She smiled. "But my friend Tina naturally kept me in the loop. There was a rumor going around that Ms. Ternheim was a lesbian. I couldn't picture it at all because she . . . Well, let's just say she didn't fit your stereotypical idea of one."

He thought of Elke, who also wouldn't be pegged as a "stereotypical lesbian."

"But once I started working closely with her, my opinion began to change." When she saw the look on his face, she laughed. "No, no, she never made any advances. But I did notice how she was quite familiar with a certain colleague, and then there was this one time that I came back to the office after going to the movies because I had forgotten my house keys. It was late at night and I saw her intimately embracing this colleague on the sofa in her office. The door to the office was open, so I saw everything. Fortunately, they didn't notice me and I immediately left."

"Which colleague was it?"

Anna looked around. It was clear she was struggling. "You can't tell anyone I told you!"

She had him sitting on the edge of his seat, and all he could do was nod. But he would have never guessed her answer.

"It was Ruth Wagner."

"What? The head secretary?"

Anna smiled, and to his surprise, he also noted how her smile made him soar. "I had caught them touching each other affectionately at a meeting before and thought I had been mistaken."

"Well, Ms. Wagner has certainly gotten herself under control pretty fast. I would have expected a more emotional reaction."

"Don't fool yourself! Ms. Wagner and Ms. Ternheim were very similar. Ms. Wagner is always under control. When her twin brother died, she was back in the office the day after the funeral and you wouldn't have known at all. However, I did see her in the ladies' room this morning looking like she had been crying."

Hannes looked at Anna and took a moment to think. "How long had this been going on?"

"No idea. The first time I noticed was about six months after I became an executive assistant."

"How did they interact when other people were around?"

"They were very proper and always polite. You couldn't tell if you didn't suspect anything. For me, it was obviously different. Since I had caught them together, I noticed little things. Ms. Ternheim, for example, always gave her assistants a glass of champagne on her birthday, and we got her a small gift. Ms. Wagner always organized this gift. Last year it was a brooch. Ms. Ternheim wore it every day since. Sure, everyone sensed a certain familiarity between the two, but that's not unusual after working together for so many years. I'm pretty sure no one else at Lagussa thinks there was something going on between them. And it has to stay that way."

"I understand. But what does Ms. Ternheim's change in behavior have to do with her relationship with Ms. Wagner? It didn't cause any problems in the past."

"I don't know if one thing has to do with the other," said Anna. "But their relationship began to cool off significantly around the same time Ms. Ternheim's general behavior changed. There were several times when she pointed out mistakes Ms. Wagner made very explicitly in front of other colleagues. They grew more and more distant."

"Couldn't that have to do with the changes in Ms. Ternheim's attitude?"

"She wasn't like that with the other employees. Although she seemed absent and not fully engaged, she was still very professional with us. No, I think the crisis in her relationship had other reasons. I know Ms. Ternheim met a man at some point in the last few months."

Surprised, Hannes leaned forward, hitting his cocktail glass and spilling it across the table. Anna jumped back, but a few drops splattered on her blouse.

"I'm sorry. Man, I'm clumsy!"

The bartender appeared with a rag and wiped up the mess.

"Ugh, I'm sorry. Could I have another cocktail? Anna, how about you?"

She nodded, laughing.

"So you're saying that Ms. Ternheim has never been married, had a secret lesbian relationship with her assistant for years, and most recently was with a man?"

"I didn't say they were together, but she repeatedly called him and probably also met with him."

"How do you know this?"

"He kept calling. Since external calls are diverted to me, I was the one who answered every time. When I asked Ms. Ternheim who the caller was, she avoided the question and said something along the lines of an acquaintance. After that, he didn't call her office anymore, but I'm sure he called her on her cell phone. Sometimes Ms. Ternheim's phone would ring, and I could see his name on the display. I was always asked to leave the room."

"But maybe he was just a platonic friend. Maybe she did have some kind of social circle."

"Well then, why hadn't he contacted her before? Sure, maybe he was a regular friend, but not a longtime one. In any case, Ms. Wagner heard me ask Ms. Ternheim about the man, and their relationship cooled off after that. That's why I felt guilty. I suppose she was jealous and yelled at Ms. Ternheim."

"Anna, this is really important information! We finally have a lead on someone who played a role in Ms. Ternheim's life. Do you still remember his name?"

"He called so often that I noted the name. He introduced himself as Mark von Wittenberg, and whenever I put him through, Ms. Ternheim would immediately shut her door."

Hannes quickly jotted the name down in his notepad. "How do you know they met?"

"'Know' is too strong of a word. But sometimes she rushed out of the office after he called. I once randomly saw her meet a man by the Charles Memorial. I wasn't spying on her, if that's what you think. I had the day off because my brother came to visit. I wanted to pick him up at the train station and you have to pass the monument on the way."

"Could you see what he looked like?"

"No, at least I can't remember. I only glanced briefly because I didn't want her to see me. That definitely would have been awkward."

"Did they hug or kiss?"

"No, they stood opposite each other, and he showed her something in a folder. That's all."

"Was he her age?"

Anna shrugged. "Like I said, I can't tell you anything about his appearance."

"Would you recognize his voice?"

"No idea! I remember only that it sounded a little hoarse, as if he had a slight cold. And there always seemed to be static on the line whenever he called, which made it hard to hear him. I never spoke to him for long because he always immediately asked for Ms. Ternheim."

"Good." Hannes took in what he had just heard. "What did you—"

"Wait, one more thing: these calls began around the time Ms. Ternheim started to change. As I said before, she was a little rattled after that. But lately she sometimes seemed even . . . Maybe I'm interpreting this all wrong. But she seemed downright scared. She sometimes had this look of terror in her eyes. Especially after she had spoken to this man. But maybe I'm imagining it."

Hannes took her observations seriously. "You mentioned something professional as well. What might have upset her at work?"

"Well, it's only indirectly professional. But it has something to do with Lagussa."

"Were there any issues with customers or business partners?"

"No, not at all. I mean, there are always issues, but nothing out of the ordinary. On the contrary, it was pretty calm. It's not about the company today, but about its past."

"I don't understand," he said, but he already had an inkling.

"Lagussa is a very old company. However, it's been incorporated under several names. There was a drug scandal sometime in the mid-nineties, long before I joined the company. It was around that time the company changed its name to Lagussa. That's not unusual after a scandal."

"What kind of scandal?"

"I don't know the details. Apparently there was a drug which had serious and unexpected side effects. There were even some deaths. Ultimately, it was settled out of court and the victims were compensated. The story still remains taboo at the company. Back then, it probably made the headlines, so it should be easy to find out more."

It was clear Anna did not want to go into further detail about this. "And you think this story might have something to do with Ms. Ternheim's behavior?"

"No, that was all settled. There was no trial, because everyone involved had to waive the right to sue in order to accept payment. Since the compensation turned out to be very generous, everyone accepted. What I'm talking about is even further in the past."

"And what's that?"

"I don't know exactly. I've never heard anyone talk about it. It must be a well-kept secret. Some sort of shocking story from the time of the Third Reich."

Hannes remembered his conversation with Ben. "What makes you say that?"

"As Ms. Ternheim's assistant, I've always had to go into her office, sometimes even when she wasn't there. For example, when she called from a meeting and demanded some numbers or other information, I would have to search her desk."

"Aha! And that's when you saw something that wasn't meant for your eyes?"

Anna nodded. "I knocked over a bag under her desk a few weeks ago. I was going to put everything back until I noticed the contents."

She took a break from telling her story when the bartender came over with more cocktails. Her cheeks were slightly flushed, and she kept folding and unfolding a napkin. After the bartender left, Anna took a deep breath and continued. She lowered her voice so Hannes could barely hear her and had to lean in, which didn't bother him.

"There were two books that dealt with the role of industry in the Nazi era, one of them explicitly on pharmaceutical companies. There were also a lot of photocopies, mostly of old documents. A few bore the letterhead 'North German Chemical and Pharmaceutical Works,' which at some point or another I had heard was Lagussa's initial name when it was founded. Afterward, I looked it up in the company history. The information on the early period is pretty brief and monosyllabic, but the company name is there."

"What kind of documents were they?"

"I didn't look too closely. I was sweating bullets under that desk. If Ms. Wagner had walked in on me . . . What I saw was handwritten correspondence with official authorities and the Nazi Party, and then lists of employees and purchase orders. And some black-and-white photos." Anna gulped, and goose bumps ran down her arms. "Some photos seemed harmless. They showed men shaking hands with other men in Nazi uniforms. But there . . . there were also really horrifying photos. Of people who were totally disfigured being presented by doctors. Or emaciated people on an assembly line with the company logo emblazoned on the wall in the background." She put her head in her hands. "I will never forget those images. And you know what I noticed over and over again? Many of these people had tattoos on their forearms."

For a while there was silence. Hannes also had to collect himself. His theory seemed to be confirmed. So was that the reason for the tattoo on Ms. Ternheim's arm? Did the numbers on her forearm represent a connection to a dark chapter in Lagussa's past? Anna couldn't have known anything about the tattoo—it hadn't been mentioned in the press.

"What makes you think it has to do—"

"Well, because she probably didn't know about these things and only found out by accident. After all, it was members of her family who must have somehow been connected to the Nazis. Lagussa constantly presents itself as a responsible and clean company. Its employees, patients, and business partners don't know anything about this. I searched the Internet and found nothing."

"You mean, the shock of this discovery could have unsettled her?"

"Not just the discovery! I had already said that she and her brother saw eye to eye when it came to the company, and that is no exaggeration, even if they were never warm with each other. But their relationship got even frostier toward the end. There were several times when I overheard them fighting."

"And do you think these fights were about the company's history?"

"I'm certain of it! Only last week, they shouted so loudly that they could be heard with the door closed. Fortunately, my coworker, Ms. Maler, was away from her desk. She would have immediately started gossiping about that."

"What could you hear?"

"I can't repeat it to you verbatim, but she accused him of shutting his eyes to the truth, and that it was their duty to deal with this Nazi shit. He replied with something along the lines of 'And even if it is true, no one cares about that today! Why do you want to ruin our reputation?' She replied that he was a self-righteous asshole and that she'd deal with it on her own if he continued to refuse. And . . ."

"And?"

"And then he threatened her. He said, 'If you feel that's really what you have to do, I can't be held responsible for the consequences of your actions. Our family built this company into an empire, and I will not let your bad conscience destroy it!'"

LATE THURSDAY EVENING

For once, Hannes was very pleased with himself. His suspicion that Anna Stahl had important information had been confirmed, and then he had actually managed to extract the information from her. Since he didn't want to unsettle her or interrupt her train of thought, he had barely written anything on his notepad. But the conversation was burned in his memory.

He now had three new leads. The first was Ms. Wagner, the jealous or at least jilted lover. Although Hannes could not imagine that the older woman was capable of murder, let alone physically able, it was still possible she had hired someone. At the very least, she knew more about Ms. Ternheim's life than she had initially let on and could further contribute important information—if she was willing.

The second lead was more nebulous, but at least he had a name. First thing tomorrow morning, Hannes would look for Mark von Wittenberg, who had recently met with Ms. Ternheim and had frequently called her.

The third lead clearly pointed to Ms. Ternheim's brother. As managing director of Lagussa, he felt enormously pressured by his sister and had threatened her. Could her death be one of the consequences of her actions? Was Mr. Ternheim trying to shield his company from potentially irreparable damage, even if it meant sacrificing his own sister?

Hannes would have preferred to drive back to the station to look at the photos of the tattoo on Ms. Ternheim's arm in greater detail. He felt the numbers had to be an important clue to solving the case. Instead, he looked over at Anna in the passenger seat.

"I'm sure no one's following us," he said.

Anna turned toward him, exhausted. "That's good," she said, yawning. "Tomorrow will be extremely busy; I can't wait to get to bed."

Back at the bar, she had called her friend Tina, who had immediately offered her pull-out couch. All the parking spots were taken on Anna's street. Hannes decided to double-park the police car, which he still needed to return to the station, and turned on his hazard lights.

"Take your time packing," he said, "I'll wait here."

"You can come up if you want," she said. "I need some spare clothes for tomorrow because I won't be able to make it home before the gala. You can help me carry my things."

Hannes was a bit uneasy about this, but he also didn't want to come across as ungentlemanly. He followed her into the three-story building. The hallway was well maintained but dimly lit.

"The light's broken down here," said Anna. "The super was supposed to call someone a long time ago. Normally it looks much more civilized."

"I was recently made homeless," he said and told her about the snake and how he had sought asylum in Ben's garden cottage.

"And you want to protect me?" Anna said, then giggled, sounding slightly drunk.

"Hopefully it wasn't a python that stuck the note on your bike," Hannes joked.

She opened the middle door on the second floor and flipped the light switch. Hannes entered behind her and stood in an open hallway which led to a living room.

"Wait here on the sofa, you can leave your shoes on." Anna disappeared into the bedroom.

"It's best if you take enough clothes for two nights," Hannes called out to her from the other side of her bedroom door. "You shouldn't come back here alone after the gala. To be on the safe side, you should spend another night at Tina's. Oh, and please remember not to tell anyone you're staying there. Don't even talk about it in the cafeteria." He was unable to keep his eyes from wandering to the gap in the doorway.

"Sure, of course," she said from her room.

She stood behind the open closet door, so Hannes couldn't see her. However, he could not overlook the fact that she had just put on fresh clothes. Her skirt, blouse, socks, and underwear flew onto the bed. Hannes escaped with his tomato-red ears into the living room. He sat down on the white couch and looked around the tastefully decorated room. No signs of a boyfriend.

"What is it?" asked Anna. Hannes looked toward the door. She was now wearing dark-blue jeans and a white top. Her outfit emphasized her slender figure. He realized he was looking at her for too long without saying anything.

"Oh, it's nothing! I was just thinking about last night and how pathetic I must have seemed."

"Well, if someone lost his tarantula here, I'd be the first one to leave. It's more eight-legged creatures that I'm afraid of. Let me quickly pack my bag and then we can go."

A few minutes later, she entered the living room with a sports bag and a garment bag. Hannes took them from her and threw them over his shoulder.

"Hey, be careful! My dress for tomorrow night's in there. It can't get wrinkled."

Hannes held the garment bag in his outstretched arm. Anna snorted.

"What?" he said. "This way your dress won't get wrinkled!"

"That's true, but you look silly." She grabbed the garment bag from him and pushed him out the front door into the hall.

"You probably don't iron clothes that often, do you? Otherwise you would have been more careful," she said.

"I rarely iron my workout clothes. There are no points for presentation in canoeing, fortunately."

"But if there were, you'd shoot for the stars. Damn it! I forgot my shoes for tomorrow night." She quickly turned around and hurried back to her apartment.

Hannes stood in the stairwell and listened as she rummaged through her shoe rack.

"Here they are!" she shouted and presented him with black high-heeled shoes.

"But they're a little scuffed at the toe," said Hannes. "Do you want to get some polish?"

"No need. I'm done."

She pulled the door shut and hurried down the stairs, with Hannes chasing her. Suddenly, she stopped and he almost ran into her. He instinctively dropped the bag and grabbed hold of Anna before she fell down the stairs. For a moment, her eyes locked on his muscles.

"That was close," she said, and Hannes could feel her warm breath on his face. It still smelled faintly of the fruity cocktail.

"Why did you stop so suddenly?" he asked.

"I left the garment bag lying in front of the shoe rack." She bounded up the stairs again. "Go on down, I'll be right there!"

Hannes picked up her bag and placed the black shoes on top. When he got to the police car, he opened the trunk and threw the bag and shoes in. When he turned around, a green tricycle was parked behind him and a wide-eyed little boy stared at him.

"Are you a policeman?" he asked with excitement.

"Well, what are you doing out here so late? Yes, I'm a policeman."

"How come you don't have a uniform?"

"I only need my uniform when I'm chasing bad guys."

"Have you caught a lot?"

Hannes laughed and knelt down. "Not yet. You know, there aren't too many bad guys. Most times people do silly things, but really bad things don't happen too often."

"I've done silly things before," the boy said. "Mommy was making pancakes, and I wanted to taste the bowl. Then it fell on my head, and we had to eat sandwiches."

A loud laugh came from beside Hannes. "Finn, what are you doing outside? It's getting dark."

"Nah, it's not dark yet at all," said the boy.

"Right," Hannes said and grinned. "You've still got five minutes. Besides, you're a big boy!"

"Exactly!" Finn said. "And you know what? When I get bigger, I want to be a policeman too! But I'm always going to wear a uniform, because I'm going to catch a lot of bad guys."

Anna ruffled his light-blond hair. "I think so too. You'll definitely catch a lot of bad guys."

"How come you have one blue eye and one green eye?" Finn asked Hannes.

"You know, my mother has really great green eyes and my father really nice blue ones. I couldn't decide which color, so I have a green right eye and a blue left eye."

"Makes sense," Finn said. "Then no one has to be sad, because Daddy always says that I have his eyes, and then Mommy looks sad."

"Finn! Finn, where are you?" came a voice from across the street.

"He's here, Sandra!" Anna shouted. "I'll bring him over!" She handed Hannes the garment bag. "I won't take long. Is that okay?"

"Sure," Hannes said and made a show of carefully laying the garment bag on top of the sports bag. "I wouldn't want him to run into some bad guy on his way home." He leaned forward and whirled an excited Finn into the air.

"Finn?" came the voice from across the street, this time clearly worried.

"Don't worry," Anna said, laughing. "Finn's having a blast!"

Hannes put the little guy back on his tricycle. "Okay, safe journey home. And remember, always pay attention to the traffic rules! Otherwise, I'll have to write you a speeding ticket."

Finn giggled and rode off. "I always—I mean, almost always—drive very carefully. Bye-bye!" He turned his tricycle around and waved with both hands while pedaling. He almost crashed head-on into the police car, but Anna stopped him at the last second.

Anna returned a few minutes later. "So, is that true?" she asked.

"What do you mean?"

"Your eyes. Can you actually inherit one color from each parent?"

Hannes laughed. "No, I just made that up for him. It's a pigment disorder called heterochromia iridis. There's only pigment in one eye. It's rarer in people than dogs, for example. As you can imagine, it wasn't always easy going to school with different-colored eyes. My nickname was 'Alien.' I hated my eyes back then."

"I hope you don't hate them now," Anna said. "After all, they suit you. They give you an air of mystery."

Hannes searched for a more innocuous topic. "I hope your neighbor didn't want to know why a police car was waiting for you?" he asked.

"Of course she wanted to know! But don't worry, I didn't tell her the truth."

"So what did you tell her?"

"That you're my new boyfriend! I had to tell her something. And that's the most harmless explanation. Now she's even more curious. And as for Finn, I'm his favorite neighbor." She climbed into the passenger seat. "Once you catch this bad guy who stuck the note on my bike, I'll tell her we broke up because I can't cope with your dangerous lifestyle."

On the way to Tina's, Anna talked about her yearlong trip backpacking around the world. Hannes was fascinated, because he had always dreamed of doing the same. He had always put it off, however, for the sake of canoeing, which probably also served as a convenient excuse for him to avoid traveling by himself through foreign countries.

"I don't mean to pry, but how did you afford it? You don't make a ton of money when you're a trainee, right?" he asked, amazed at the variety of countries and attractions she had visited.

"My parents didn't give me a single cent. I'd work, and as soon as I made enough money, I'd travel somewhere else. There are various agencies that specialize in work and travel. Of course, not all the jobs were great. Once, I worked on a garlic farm in Australia. I reeked of garlic for days, even long after I'd quit. I then flew to Vietnam and was afraid I'd be kicked off the plane because of the smell."

Hannes enjoyed listening to her travel stories. His own life suddenly seemed small and unexciting. Obviously he had underestimated Anna when they'd first met at the office. *And she probably overestimated me*, he thought.

"Turn left up there," said Anna. "Then take the first right, and we'll be there."

Hannes turned and stopped in front of Tina's redbrick building. "I'll carry your things in," he said and reached for the garment bag.

"That one," Anna said with a grin, "I'd prefer to carry myself. But it would be nice if you could carry the other bag."

The door buzzed open immediately after Anna rang Tina's doorbell, and then half a flight up, the door on the terrace floor opened.

"Anna, what in the world!" shouted a girlish voice. A woman about Anna's age with very short black hair appeared at the top step. She looked at Hannes. "So you're Anna's guardian?" she joked and warmly shook his hand. "I'm Tina, pleased to meet you. Why don't you come in?" She immediately struck Hannes as very kind, and he was convinced his initial distrust had been completely misplaced.

"There hasn't been much to protect so far," he said, "but I think it's still better if Anna stays with you. Unfortunately, I have to get going, my boss is waiting for me."

"Sure, Anna can stay with me. I love it when she stays over. Nonstop girls' night!"

"Not tonight." Anna shook her head. "Big gala tomorrow. I just hope I can sleep with all this excitement."

"You will," Tina said and patted her arm, then took the bag from Hannes and walked into her apartment. "And if you can't fall asleep, I'm sure I have something to help calm your nerves. There must be a bottle around here somewhere."

Anna looked at Hannes. "That reminds me. I forgot to tell you that Ms. Ternheim was so nervous lately she started keeping a bottle of sedatives around."

Thursday Night

Hannes trudged through the garden to Ben's cottage, which was shrouded in complete darkness. A crunching underfoot told him that little Nicolas's sand shovel had bit the dust. He would have to replace it another day.

He opened the door and turned on the light. He looked in every room to make sure he was actually alone and Ben wasn't passed out somewhere. He took his shoes off and was about to take a shower when his cell phone rang.

"Hey, Fritz, what's up? Just got home."

"You haven't returned the patrol car yet, have you?"

"Nope, didn't get a chance. I'm exhausted, sorry."

"No problem," Fritz said and chuckled. "The station just called, and I told them that you'd be bringing the car back tomorrow. Now Torsten and his partner have to cram themselves into the oldest car we have in the lot. I love the thought of that!" He was downright cheerful.

"Did you track down Ternheim?" Hannes asked as he wrestled out of his clothes.

"Yup! You'll be surprised to hear where. How's it going with you?"

As usual, Fritz knew how to make Hannes curious by withholding actual information; and Hannes knew that asking Fritz questions only made him withhold longer.

"Good," Hannes said. He reluctantly postponed his shower and sat down naked on the cool floor. "Anna Stahl really gave us something to work with. She had more to offer than I expected. Did you know, for example, that Ms. Ternheim had a relationship with Ms. Wagner? Or that in the last few weeks she was contacted by a Mark von Wittenberg? Or that she had been digging into Lagussa's past and found something her brother didn't particularly like. And—"

"Wait, wait. You seem to have hit the mother lode. Where are you?"

"I'm still at Ben's."

"Okay, I'll be right over. Can we talk somewhere private?"

Hannes wanted a quick shower first. "No problem. Ben's not home yet, but even if he does show up, we can go in the guest room. When will you be here?"

"Ten minutes," Fritz said and hung up.

Hannes quickly jumped into the shower. The day's colorful images flashed through his mind, making him lose track of time. He turned off the water and wrapped a towel around his waist. Still dripping, he stepped out into the hallway only to run into Fritz.

"Ah, so that's what a model athlete looks like," Fritz teased. "Well, take your time getting dressed. I'll wait for you on the patio."

Hannes went into the guest room and rummaged through what Ben had packed for him yesterday. Earlier that afternoon, he had quickly pulled out his gym clothes and didn't stop to take a look at the remaining contents of the bag.

He pulled out his oldest pair of jeans and a black T-shirt but could find no underwear. "You've got to be kidding me," he said and opened the outer side pocket. He found two pairs of long underwear and opened the other side pocket. All he found was a baseball cap he hadn't worn in years. "That's great, Ben," he said. "Should I use my hat as a loincloth?"

Without thinking twice, he walked into Ben's bedroom. Ben did say Hannes could use whatever he needed, which hopefully included a fresh pair of underwear.

He began to open Ben's drawers at random, even though it seemed a little wrong to him. There was no underwear, although he did find some dog food. Then Hannes opened the last drawer. Maybe Ben didn't use underwear? That would explain why he hadn't packed any in Hannes's bag.

Hannes noticed Ben's nightstand had a drawer. He pulled it open and was amazed! Peeking out of a plastic bag at the rear of the drawer were two large stacks of twenty-euro notes. He shook his head in wonder. There had to be several thousand euros here. He knew Ben didn't have any financial worries, but why was he hoarding so much money?

Hannes left Ben's bedroom with a doubly guilty conscience. Not only had he rummaged through his personal belongings, but he had also discovered the cash. However, he had other problems at the moment, and his lack of underwear proved secondary. He hastily slipped on his T-shirt and stepped into his jeans, trying to ignore the unusual feeling. He opened the front door.

"Did you go clothes shopping?" Fritz joked.

"No, no," Hannes said. "Ben packed my bag a bit haphazardly, and I had to sort everything out."

"When does he get back?"

"No idea, he could be here any minute."

Fritz stood up. "Then let's do this as quickly as possible. Shall we go into the living room?"

Hannes shook his head. "We can sit out here. The owners of the big house are on vacation, so there's no one around." He slumped into a chair and stretched his legs out.

"What a long day, huh?" Fritz said and fell back into his seat too. "Tell me how your meeting with the executive assistant went."

Hannes recounted his evening at the Chameleon and Anna's temporary move. He left out the flirting and personal interactions between them.

When Hannes finished, Fritz was silent. "You definitely did the right thing," he finally said. "Maybe the threat was just a stupid prank that has nothing to do with the case, but you never know. Anyway, she should be careful over the next few days, and we should keep an eye on her. You're the best man for the job." He winked at Hannes. "Do you think Ms. Stahl told you everything or does she know more?"

"I'm pretty sure she told me everything."

"Well, this is very interesting information. The fog surrounding Helene Ternheim is slowly beginning to clear. Her relationship with Ms. Wagner and its subsequent cooling off is certainly news to me. At least now I understand why the head secretary is so tight-lipped. If this story got out, it would be the scandal of the year among the staff! Does Ms. Ternheim's brother know about their special relationship?"

"I have no idea." Hannes was angry that he had left some questions unanswered. "I'll ask Ms. Stahl tomorrow."

"Do that. Christian Ternheim seems very suspicious to me. His reaction to his sister's death seems strange. He also didn't report her disappearance until much later. Now we know he threatened her before her death. That brings me to something else I'd like to share with you. As you know, Ms. Wagner contacted me this afternoon to report the head of the company missing. So I went directly to the company's headquarters, because the missing-person report was a good excuse to talk with Ms. Wagner in private. Unfortunately, I went about it the wrong way, thinking I could charm her. She's definitely outstanding in her role as the discreet, loyal secretary and left me banging my head against the wall. Her concern for Christian Ternheim seems to be genuine. She practically pleaded with me to launch an immediate search."

"And? Where did you start?"

"Where was I supposed to start? It was clearly too early for an official missing-person report, and I assumed he was having a tough time coping with his sister's death, even if he didn't show it. So I chose to do something else first. Since I still have the spare key to Helene Ternheim's penthouse, I stopped by again to take one more look around. I hoped I'd get a better idea of who this woman was and could focus on things I had previously overlooked. It's often worked for me before. As I entered the living room, I made an interesting discovery: a picture had been removed from the wall and was lying on the table, and in front of the open safe was Christian Ternheim!"

Fritz took pleasure in seeing Hannes's curious fidgeting. He closed his eyes before continuing.

"May I ask what you're doing?" Fritz had said.

Christian Ternheim had turned around, startled. "What are you doing here?" he said and smoothed his suit. "You can't just waltz in here."

Fritz strolled into the room, casually swinging the key to the apartment. He peered over Ternheim's shoulder into the vault and noticed jewelry boxes and several sheets of paper before Ternheim slammed the door.

"Well, you were the one who had a copy made for me. As you can see, we take the investigation of this case very seriously. Have you found what you were looking for?" Fritz asked.

"What makes you think that I've been looking for something?" Ternheim said.

"Ah." Fritz shrugged. "It just seemed like you were. You were so engrossed in your search that you failed to hear the front door open. Now tell me about this safe in your sister's apartment."

"Helene only kept personal items in it."

"Exactly. And maybe some of these items could shed light on the events of last weekend."

Ternheim shot the detective a dirty look. "Please, take a look and see if her jewelry or birth certificate might help you in your investigation. I have to leave now, anyway." He grabbed a laptop bag from the table before heading into the hallway.

Fritz looked with interest at the bulky bag and then said, "By the way, Ms. Wagner is very worried about you because she hasn't been able to reach you. You should have left her a message!"

Mr. Ternheim muttered and slammed the front door.

"And? What was in the safe?" Hannes asked.

"Exactly what Mr. Ternheim said. Jewelry and various documents, but nothing of much use to us. The question is: What was in the safe before Christian Ternheim showed up?"

"Maybe it was the contents of the bag that Anna . . . um, Ms. Stahl accidentally knocked over in Helene Ternheim's office a couple of weeks ago?"

"I don't think that's too far-fetched. After being threatened by her brother, Ms. Ternheim certainly wouldn't have left these things out in the open. Too bad he knew about the safe."

"Do you really think her own brother—"

"Mr. Ternheim lives only for his company. And he thought the company was in danger. So it wouldn't hurt to devote a little more attention to him. So here's what we'll do tomorrow: check out this art agent and speak to Ms. Stahl again. Then, do some digging into Lagussa's past. There are certainly lots of documents and publications on the Nazi era which deal with the company's role back then. I'll have another conversation with Christian Ternheim and Ms. Wagner, and I'll handle Ms. Stahl's statements with the necessary care. I don't want to have to see another woman's body on the medical examiner's table."

"What about the man Ms. Ternheim frequently interacted with?"

"That's right, Mark von Wittenberg! It's unclear what kind of role he plays. I'll do a background check on him tomorrow and try to track him down."

"If Christian Ternheim's behind his sister's death, then the tattoo on her arm makes sense," Hannes said. "Ultimately, the rift between them was caused by Ms. Ternheim's research into the company's Nazi past. Mr. Ternheim wanted to keep all this covered up, and maybe he tattooed his sister as a kind of punishment. The numbers remind me of what was done to the prisoners of the concentration camps."

"Yeah, but you said he wants to bury the past. Why would he call attention to the company's dark history?"

All of a sudden Socks came out of nowhere and jumped onto Hannes's lap, licking his face. He then did the same to Fritz, enthusiastically wagging his tail.

"Hello! Do we have guests?" Ben appeared on the patio.

"Hi, Ben, this is Fritz Janssen, my boss," Hannes said.

"Just Fritz," he said and shook Ben's hand. He carefully studied him, eyeing his dreadlocks, eyebrow piercing, and slight beard.

"What a night," said Ben. "Two police officers on my patio. It's not every day this happens."

"No need to worry," said Fritz. "I was about to leave, anyway, then there'll only be one officer keeping an eye on this beautiful property."

"Oh, stay as long as you like, it's no bother," Ben said. "There's some beer in the fridge. The perfect thing for such a beautiful summer evening."

"No, thanks, I have to drive," Fritz said.

"One beer? Even a detective could still drive after one beer . . ."

Hannes was surprised at how quickly Fritz accepted and leaned back in his chair.

"Great," Ben said. "Be right back!"

Hannes followed him inside and caught up with him in the kitchen.

"Say, Ben," he whispered. "You kept what I told you last night about the dead woman to yourself, right?"

Ben turned around in astonishment. "Sure, man! You told me not to tell. I didn't even mention it to the people in my group. Why?"

"Well . . . There was an article in the paper this morning and—"

"You can't be serious! I'd never tell the press or anyone else."

"Of course you wouldn't," Hannes said in embarrassment. "I just wanted to make sure."

"You should chill out," Ben said, shaking his head. "Police work's probably made you paranoid. Friends stick together. Even though I might be a little unconventional and some might think I'm crazy, you can always count on me. Okay, why don't you take a couple of beers outside. Your detective looks a little thirsty; one bottle won't do the trick."

How right Ben was. Half an hour later, Fritz put his empty bottle on the ground and cracked open another.

Ben grinned at Hannes. "Tough day, Detective?" he teased Fritz.

"When isn't a day tough?" Fritz said, scratching Socks behind the ears.

"At least you've got a fan," Hannes said, pointing to Socks.

"I've always gotten along with dogs. Except once when I wasn't too careful approaching a Rottweiler." He pointed to the scar on his face. "I still carry around a memento from the encounter. But my love of dogs wasn't affected."

"How come you don't have your own?" Ben asked.

"I'd love to, but with my strange work hours, I'd never be able to keep up." Fritz looked at Socks's black collar, which read "I bite Nazi asses." He grinned at Ben. "So you already trained your dog in your holy war?"

"Unfortunately, Socks's bite reflex doesn't even work on cats. If he came across a group of skinheads, he'd probably run away or lick their hands."

The conversation turned to the neo-Nazi scene. Fritz and Ben agreed that simply monitoring it would be totally irresponsible, though their means of dealing with it varied.

"You can't stand up for freedom, tolerance, and justice and break the law yourself," Fritz said.

"Unfortunately our laws sometimes protect the wrong side. Besides, no one pays attention to candlelight vigils," Ben said.

"But isn't it ultimately just a handful of idiots?" Hannes said. "Maybe it's even more effective to ignore them than to give them attention and media coverage? Isn't that what they want?"

"But you can't forget how easy it is to seduce people," Ben said. "You see that everywhere, be it politics or religion. Even here in Europe, populists have been wildly successful despite the fact that this continent has a lot of experience with fanatical right- and left-wing ideology."

"Most people yearn for guidance," Fritz said. "They want others to determine their lives for them, at least when all is said and done. In politics, the only people who are respected are so-called 'strong' leaders or politicians who show the way. It's hardly surprising these people don't have a basic understanding of democracy."

"That's the problem," said Ben. "People love to be told what they should do. And the worse they have it, the more grateful they are for a strong hand to push them."

"That said, we don't exactly have it that bad here in Europe," Hannes added. "Sure, there's always some economic crisis and unemployment is rising, but still most people have it good enough that they can't be enthralled by some dictator."

"Economic crises aren't the only reason people turn to extremism," Fritz said. "It's also about personal crises. Look at the faces on the bus. How many people look happy?"

"They're probably just tired," Ben joked. "But it's true. There are plenty of studies which suggest that people in poorer countries are happier than we are. But when did you last hear politicians discuss the question of how we actually want to live? Emotional needs are basically irrelevant. It's all about growth, recovery, optimization, and efficiency. If you work day after day in some office like a robot, there's an inner emptiness that reality shows and dramas on television can no longer fill. Take a look at the nonsense the masses tune into night after night. You can't consume real feelings, you have to live them."

"But that's exactly what our society has forgotten how to do," Fritz said. "You need someone to advise you on how to be 'happy.' At some schools, students can now choose Happiness as an elective. How sad is that? Have we become so far removed from real life that we have to introduce happiness as a school subject? How can society not understand something so fundamental?"

"Now some charismatic, eloquent politician appears who knows exactly how to appeal to people," Ben said. "Do you really think we would be completely immune to a politician's temptations and promises today?"

"Okay, okay!" Hannes laughed and raised his hands. "I give up. At the next neo-Nazi march, I'll be standing in the front line of the counterdemonstration, I promise. But speaking of robots—I spent way too long spinning on the hamster wheel today. And Fritz has already given me a list of things to do tomorrow. It's been lovely chatting, but I have to hit the hay."

"Man! But we've only just started planning the revolution," Ben joked.

"No, my young colleague's right." Fritz rose from his chair. "I just have to use the bathroom and then I'll be on my way."

"It's straight ahead." Ben showed him the way and handed Hannes another beer. "Come on, you Goody Two-Shoes. Let's have a nightcap!"

Hannes hesitantly accepted.

"You're not going to party all night again, are you?" Fritz asked when he came back out.

"I talked him into one last round. Let me get you one from the kitchen."

"Thanks, but I have to go."

"How far is it to your house?" asked Hannes.

"I'm usually only there on weekends. I still rent a room on the west side of the city. It'll take me fifteen minutes to get there," Fritz said, then hobbled across the lawn.

Ben watched in disbelief. "Cool guy! He has a funny way of walking."

"Back pain," Hannes said. "It seems to trouble him a lot."

"Anyway, your boss isn't half bad."

"Yeah, I lucked out. Although we had a rough start, I've grown fond of the old guy. I'd run through fire for him."

"Which brings us back to the subject of leaders," joked Ben.

"Don't start! I don't think I can handle another ideological debate right now. On a completely different topic: I met an executive assistant today at Lagussa. She's responsible for the charity gala tomorrow. What are you guys planning? She's been a tremendous help to us and is really sweet too. You're not going to give her any trouble tomorrow, are you?"

"Don't worry!" Ben winked. "Only one person will be in trouble tomorrow, and it won't be her."

Thursday Night into Friday Morning

A mother loves her child unconditionally. But what if that child is not the result of love but of violence and hatred? Does the innocent child also bear the burden of guilt?

At least, that is how it feels. Painful looks. Withheld caresses. Nonexistent affection.

Contempt, disgust, insults.

"You're the product of Satan! The devil is in you too!" screams the trembling mother. She looks with hatred at the terrified child standing in front of the broken plate he had dropped. He had only wanted to help clean the dishes from his meager supper while standing on his tiptoes in front of the tall sink.

Her fist raised, the mother comes closer; the fearful child flees.

"You good-for-nothing!" she shouts and slaps the little head so hard that it hits the edge of the sink.

Red veils the child's vision as it mixes with his hot tears.

FRIDAY MORNING

Fritz had a leisurely start to his Friday. Since his now daily medical checkup had been scheduled for nine, he didn't get out of bed until eight, which was late by his standards. Although he had been an early riser all his life, he needed a few minutes to find his way around the small room of his city apartment.

Even though he often denied it, he had enjoyed his job most of his life. Only right now, he wished he was on the other side of the world. *I can do it*, he said to himself as he stared in the mirror at his bloodshot eyes and stooped posture. *Pull yourself together and just see it through.*

He turned on the cold water in the shower and got in. Afterward, he sat down and had breakfast. The morning paper was still wildly speculating about Ms. Ternheim's death. He was glad the press didn't know that the notorious Old Fritz was leading the investigation, otherwise his phone would be ringing nonstop. He could never get used to the public side of his job. And he despised tabloid journalists.

It was nearly eight thirty. Lauer should be at the office. Fritz gave him a call on his cell phone to avoid speaking with Mrs. Meier.

"Yes, Fritz, what's up?" Lauer asked.

"Morning, Steffen. I want to give you an update on the Ternheim case." He gave him a quick rundown of the facts.

"You're assuming it's a murder?"

"I never rule anything out until the case is solved."

"Oh come on, Fritz. You wouldn't be spending all this time on it if you thought she died of natural causes. And I already have an idea who you've set your sights on now."

"Oh really? Who's that?"

"Let me guess: you strongly suspect the brother. Am I right?"

"Maybe. But you have to admit he comes across as a very strange character."

"After what you've told me, I agree. All right, pay a little closer attention to him, but be considerate and sensitive. After all, he's an influential figure and could get us in a lot of trouble."

Fritz didn't give a damn whether a suspect was an influential person or not.

Lauer asked, "How's your new partner?"

"Excellent, I have to say. He's a quick learner and goes the extra mile."

"You see! And you wanted to get rid of him. Can you two manage by yourselves?"

Fritz knew it was a rhetorical question, so he called Lauer's bluff. "How much backup can you give me?"

"Let's see: Werner's on sick leave; Willi's working with Johanna and Robert on the two construction murders; I had to assign Laura to Bastian and Frank, who are both up to their necks in shit with this hanged junkie case; Manfred's on vacation starting today; Birte is—"

"All right, I get it! Just wanted to tease the offer."

"If you need support, you'll get it. You know that," Lauer said.

"Good to hear. There's one thing I could actually use some help on."

"What's that?"

"Can you have someone do a background check for me? It's a man Ms. Ternheim was recently in touch with, a Mark von Wittenberg. I'd like to know more about him and his contact info. I have to go to the doctor right now and then do a little more investigating."

"All right, I'll put one of the new guys on it. Oh, and Fritz?"

"Yes?"

"I've been watching you lately and I'd have to be blind not to realize something's not right. If you need a break . . ."

"I'm fine! At least, fine enough to solve this case. Then we can talk."

"Okay." Lauer sounded relieved. "Keep me posted!"

"Only if you keep the press off my back."

Fritz left the doctor's office around ten, convinced the doctor couldn't really help him. He had faithfully gone to him for decades, but that was mainly due to laziness and familiarity.

Fritz had lain awake the night before, his thoughts consumed by Christian Ternheim. Now he decided to pay the managing director of Lagussa another visit, this time unannounced. And this time he also wanted to take Ms. Wagner to task. He was annoyed that these two were hiding behind a wall of silence. He would find a way to make them cooperate.

As he entered Lagussa's lobby, he paused at the reception desk, which was manned by the same young woman as before. She had just received a call. She apparently recognized the detective because she nodded and gestured for him to wait.

"I know the way," Fritz said and walked to the elevator.

As the doors opened, the young woman came rushing up to him. "Excuse me, but you can't just go up like that. I have to sign you in and—"

The doors closed, cutting her off. As the elevator started to move, he looked through the glass walls as the woman rushed back to the reception desk and frantically picked up the phone. Fritz was greeted on the twentieth floor by Ms. Wagner, who was already expecting him. She stood with her arms crossed in front of the elevator.

"Mr. Ternheim can't speak at the moment! Why didn't you schedule a meeting?"

Fritz had had enough. He pushed past Ms. Wagner and looked around the room. Ms. Maler's and Ms. Stahl's desks were empty. Alarmed, he turned around.

"Where are your two colleagues?"

"Ms. Maler called in sick again today, and Ms. Stahl's discussing the final details for this evening with Mr. Ternheim. I'm afraid you came here for nothing."

"I wouldn't say that," Fritz said and grinned. "You're one of the reasons I'm here."

Ms. Wagner nervously played with her fingers. She then retreated behind her desk and sat upright in her chair. "I have other things to do. Besides, I don't know what else to tell you." She made a point of turning to her computer screen and typing at random.

"If you don't want to talk to me, I'll just have to start with Mr. Ternheim. I'd be more considerate given that he's in a meeting, but unfortunately my time's running out, and you leave me no choice!" Fritz marched to the managing director's door.

Just as he was about to turn the knob, he heard Ms. Wagner clear her throat behind him. "Wait! What is it you wish to ask me?"

Fritz grinned. He had outwitted her. He grabbed an office chair from Ms. Maler's desk and rolled it in front of Ms. Wagner's desk. He looked at her in silence and considered what was going on inside her head. She kept glancing between his pale eyes and her chair.

"Ms. Wagner, I understand that you wish to protect the Ternheim family and business. However, you mustn't forget one thing: the CEO of this company is dead, and I'm only trying to figure out why she's no longer here and who may have played a role in her death. Your understandable loyalty to Ms. Ternheim should not be a reason to run me around. You'd be a greater help to her if you cooperated."

Ms. Wagner had turned pale. "So it's true?" she said. "You think she was murdered?"

"There's some evidence suggesting murder. However, I can't evaluate the evidence properly unless I learn more about her. You have worked closely with her for years and should therefore know more about her than what you've shared so far."

"I told you everything I know! Ms. Ternheim wasn't someone who involved her employees in her private life. She was careful to keep her work and private lives separate."

"I don't believe that," said Fritz.

"And what makes you say that?"

Fritz decided to attack head-on. "Ms. Wagner, as you can imagine, we've been questioning people in several departments. There are always lots of rumors going around. Often, people love to gossip about what goes on at the management level, and it's no different at Lagussa. We learned something very interesting, and that's why I don't believe you."

Ms. Wagner was visibly nervous and avoided his gaze. "You shouldn't put much faith in rumors," she said and fumbled with her gray bun.

"Don't you want to know what the rumor is?"

Ms. Wagner pursed her lips.

"There is, for example, a very credible rumor that you and Ms. Ternheim had a relationship for years," Fritz said.

Ms. Wagner's facade immediately collapsed. All color drained from her face.

"But . . . how . . . how can . . . but we were so careful," she whispered.

"Apparently not careful enough," said Fritz. "A colleague saw you outside the office and shared his observation with us."

He deliberately sought to point to a male figure so Ms. Stahl would not get in trouble. It was then that Ms. Wagner finally lost her composure. She hid her face in her hands and began to sob. Embarrassed and slightly guilty, Fritz looked at the wall.

He handed her a handkerchief and changed tactics. "Ms. Wagner, I'm very sorry. I lost my wife many years ago. I know how you feel. And I promise to keep your relationship confidential."

"Relationship? It was love, not just a 'relationship.'" Her voice was filled with contempt. "Over the years, something grew between us until it finally became more than just friendship. You can't imagine how much I've suffered because Helene didn't want to be open about our love. She was so afraid of the public reaction and what her brother might do. He's so conservative that he probably would have never spoken to her again. He completely controlled her."

"Does that mean he still knows nothing?"

"Unless the rumor got all the way to him, then no, he knows nothing," she said. "But I suppose he'll hear about it from you. And in that case, I can clear my desk."

"This matter will remain confidential, even with Mr. Ternheim," Fritz said. "Provided, of course, you finally give me some insight into Ms. Ternheim's life."

He could feel the relief that now radiated from Ms. Wagner. "Agreed," she said. "But let's go into the next room, I don't want Mr. Ternheim to see me like this."

Fritz followed her into a small meeting room. "Would you like something to drink?" she asked. Fritz requested a glass of water and a cup of coffee before he settled into a comfortable swivel chair. Ms. Wagner handed him the water. Her hands shook so much that some of it dripped onto the mahogany conference table. She sat down beside him. The coffee machine gurgled in the corner of the room. After placing a filled coffee cup in front of him, Ms. Wagner explained how the two women grew closer on a business trip and what pain it caused them to live their love in secret.

"What was Ms. Ternheim's private life like?" he asked. "So far, we have no names of friends or acquaintances. You surely must know something about her social life?"

"You'll find it hard to imagine," said Ms. Wagner, "but Helene was a very, very lonely person. She had no friends or other people close to her. Just like her brother. Helene was only close with him and her father—and that was precisely her undoing."

"What do you mean?"

"The two of them completely monopolized her! Her father was very strict and overbearing. Their mother died of a disease at a young age. Violence was a constant presence during their childhood. It must have been a joyless existence. They attended a Catholic boarding school, which is still known for its discipline. Immediately after graduating high school, their father sent them to a private university in England where they completed their degrees in record time. Even at school, Helene and her brother were outsiders because they'd been conditioned to be that way since early childhood and never learned how to have a casual social interaction. Christian is two years younger than Helene, so when they were in school, she always took care of him. All they had was each other. That probably explains why they had such a close relationship.

"After college, their father put them to work here at the company. Their whole lives were geared toward their taking over the family business. But no matter how hard they tried, they could never make their father happy. Heinrich Ternheim was so distrustful of his children that he didn't retire until he was eighty-three. But he continued to exert his influence on them and kept coming by to check on things. How frustrating and humiliating this must have been! It was only when their father devoted himself to his painting that they finally got some breathing room. Despite this, Christian tried to prevent the public from seeing his father's pictures. I've seen a few in the paper; they're sickening—a reflection of his soul, in my opinion."

"And yet Ms. Ternheim regularly looked after her father," Fritz said.

"That's true. She always defended him, although she never experienced any love or affection from him. Once she told me her father didn't choose to be that way because he had grown up in a heartless family. For the Ternheims, it was always about the business and money. Helene was the exception. For example, the company's commitment to the fight against childhood leukemia was her initiative. She had to force her brother into it. I think he now sees this activity as a clever PR stunt, but for Helene, it was a cause close to her heart."

"But then isn't it surprising she got along so well with her brother?"

"That depends on what you mean by 'got along.' She had no one else! Family was it for her. And in a family you have to stick together. That was her motto and how she had been brought up. It took me a long time before I could teach her about life's joys. In recent years, she began to blossom, and we were happy together until . . . until that man entered her life."

"What man?" Fritz asked, thinking of Mark von Wittenberg.

"She only spoke of him once. But she repeatedly called a man and arranged to meet with him. She became more standoffish and shunned my presence, and our dates became less frequent. When I asked her what was going on between her and this man . . ." She started to cry. "Excuse me," she whispered. "She told me it was nothing, and that I shouldn't get involved. I was furious because I realized she wasn't being open, and she reacted harshly. She screamed at me, saying it was a private matter and I shouldn't stick my nose in it. And just like that, she changed. As if the years we'd spent together never existed."

"Have you seen the man? Or do you know his name?"

"No. But take a look at her cell phone. You should be able to find his number."

"Unfortunately, Ms. Ternheim didn't have her phone on her when we found her. Does her brother know about this man?"

"I couldn't tell you. Their relationship changed in recent months. They argued frequently. Helene went totally nuts. She even started taking a sedative, which she'd never done before. This man must have done something to her. She sometimes seemed outright terrified. But I could no longer get to her."

Again, she burst into tears, and Fritz waited until she calmed down. "I have one last question. We heard another rumor that Ms. Ternheim had been digging into Lagussa's past and had come across something."

"You mean the scandal in the nineties? That's not new. At least Helene wasn't solely to blame for that. She and her brother were responsible for the drug, but the ultimate blame lay with her father. Enough people had warned him not to release the drug. In the test phase, there had been isolated abnormalities and signs of long-term side effects. He swept all that aside. He always pointed to the drug's potential and insisted on a quick launch. After all, he had invested heavily into the research. Initially, it actually helped a number of people, but then came the first side effects, and eventually there were rumors in the press. And then it all went downhill. But I don't think Helene had found anything else about that."

"Actually, I don't mean the drug scandal. It was a story further back in the past."

Ms. Wagner looked clueless. "I know nothing about it."

"Unfortunately, I don't either," Fritz said. "I'll leave you alone now. You've really helped me better understand some connections. Can you think of anyone else she might have met who could provide us with more information?"

"As I said, Helene was probably one of the loneliest people in the city."

"Acquaintances from the past? Maybe from college or school? A boyfriend or . . ."

"No. I mean . . ." Ms. Wagner looked at her hands in discomfort. "I'm just doing this for Helene. I had to swear to her that I'd never tell anyone."

"I'm sure Ms. Ternheim would have understood," Fritz said.

"I can think of only one name. In college, she had met a young student from Denmark. His name was Lennart. I don't remember his last name. He was a year ahead of her, and they got to know each other while working on a group project. Gradually a romance developed between them. Then one evening, they, um . . . well, you know." Ms. Wagner smoothed her skirt in embarrassment. "Anyway, Helene felt safe because her brother had class all day. She knew he was jealous of her and had always met with Lennart in secret. But the professor was ill, so class was canceled and . . . suddenly her brother was standing in the doorway while Helene and Lennart were having sex! Her brother was completely beside himself. He grabbed Lennart and threw him out. Then he took care of his sister. He called her a bitch and threatened to tell her father she was sleeping around. Then he threw himself on top of her and brutalized her. Do you understand? Christian Ternheim raped his own sister that evening. Several times!"

Fritz headed for Christian Ternheim's office door, his head spinning. Ms. Wagner had been able to provide him with a theory that explained the scars on the forearm: "After Helene was raped, there was always a little piece of her that was broken. She stopped doing well in school and spiraled into a severe depression. As you can imagine, in a family in which power was all that mattered, this was met with little understanding. Although the Ternheims had made a fortune selling psychotropic drugs, it was unthinkable that someone in their family would have psychological problems. During her worst stage, Helene cut herself, finally forcing her father to take notice. She was placed in a psychiatric ward. These past few weeks I was afraid that she had fallen into her old patterns. Despite the summery temperatures, she wore long-sleeved clothes and made sure her sleeves were rolled down. A few weeks ago she was reaching up to straighten a picture on the wall, and I noticed that her left wrist was bandaged. I immediately asked her if she had hurt herself, but she quickly pulled her sleeve down and muttered something about an accident."

Fritz tried to hide his disgust when he sat opposite Christian Ternheim. Was he upset by the loss of his sister? Was he secretly relieved that Lagussa's dark past was safe?

Ternheim drummed his fingers on the table, waiting for the conversation to start. As always, he was clean shaven and dressed in an expensive suit. His gray hair was combed into a tidy part.

"Did you find any leads on my sister's murderer?"

"Why are you so sure your sister was murdered?"

"Isn't that obvious? She disappeared without a trace before turning up dead with dyed hair and a tattoo. Her car's gone, and she had no personal belongings on her."

"Oh, well, I prefer to reach my own conclusions," said Fritz. "By the way, you forgot some things, like the sedative and the scars on the forearm."

"See! All these anomalies should be enough to believe it was murder," Ternheim said. "Instead of wasting your time here with me, you should be searching for the culprit."

"You know, a few things struck me as odd."

"What isn't odd about Helene's death?"

"I find it odd, for example," Fritz calmly continued, "that you failed to inform me that your sister had recently begun taking a sedative. Didn't you say she seemed in control lately?"

"Have you spoken with her doctor? Ever heard of doctor-patient confidentiality?"

"The fact is we now have a harmless explanation for the trace of sedative in her blood. Harmless at least to the extent that it was probably not administered by a third party. Less harmless, however, in the sense that she was obviously under tremendous personal stress. Can you tell me anything about that?"

"Stress? We're always stressed, or do you think it's a breeze running a global pharmaceutical company? Maybe it was a bit too much for her lately. After all, we are planning a product launch, plus there were the preparations for today's gala—not to mention the never-ending regular work."

Fritz shook his head. "I wonder if you aren't making it a little too easy for yourself. We've looked at the scars on her wrist more closely. They clearly predate the time of death, so she must have gotten them before she disappeared."

"Yeah, and? Who knows, maybe she got caught on something?"

"I don't think so. This scarring is characteristic of small self-inflicted cuts."

"How dare you! Just because my sister was taking a harmless sedative from time to time, you try to push her into the psycho corner. It's ridiculous to think that my sister would have cut herself like . . . like a teenage girl!"

"So, is that it? Wasn't your sister already hospitalized for depression because of prior cutting?"

The color in Ternheim's face went pale. "Who told you that? Where the hell did you hear that?"

"You said it yourself," Fritz said, smiling. "We're supposed to step up our investigation, and that's exactly what we're doing. I'm a cop; I know how to dig up information."

Ternheim swiveled around and looked out over the city, struggling to keep his composure. "All right then." He turned his chair around. "In recent months, my sister was in contact with a man. She changed over that time, became irritated, distant, pensive. I was the one who finally suggested she try a sedative. But I highly doubt she sliced her arm on purpose. Something must have happened with this guy. She was afraid of him. I think he threatened her."

"Do you think that or do you know it?"

"I'm only speculating because my sister didn't talk about it."

"Do you know what the man's name was?"

"She mentioned a von Wittenberg."

"Ah. So she did speak to you about him?"

"No . . . yes . . . I mean, she told me she was in contact with him, but nothing more."

"And do you have any guess as to what he wanted from your sister?"

"Like I said, she said nothing about it."

"But there was another issue your sister wasn't quiet about, right?"

"What are you talking about?"

"As I already said, as a cop, I have amazing sources. Is it true that your relationship with your sister was a little tense the past few weeks?"

"I just explained why!"

"But isn't it also true that your sister had recently been revisiting Lagussa's past? And I don't mean the drug scandal in the nineties. I mean the thirties and forties. You surely must have known your sister was gathering information on this . . . dark chapter in your company's history."

Ternheim glared at Fritz.

"Mr. Ternheim, isn't it true your sister uncovered evidence of collusion between your ancestors and the Nazis and wanted to come clean? But you didn't want to jeopardize the company. Wasn't this the real reason for your estrangement?"

"I don't know where you got this story from," Ternheim said. "That is utter nonsense. People would have found out a long time ago if there had been any unseemly practices! Lagussa was and is an exemplary company known for its community involvement. Ms. Stahl will give you a ticket to our charity gala this evening; you can see for yourself."

"Maybe it was clean back then, but not by today's standards."

"Even if it were true, which it's not, what does that have to do with your investigation?"

"Insofar as the relationship between you and your sister deteriorated due to her research. Perhaps you even threatened her? You told me yourself she was afraid. Maybe of you?"

"So this is what it comes down to! You don't have the slightest idea who's behind Helene's death and are now trying to pin the murder on me? How obvious!" He laughed.

"I'm not pinning anything on anyone. You took your time before reporting your sister's disappearance and were extremely reluctant to publish information about it. Of course, I wonder why that is. So far we haven't gotten much help from you."

"So, you're treading water, and I'm the scapegoat? Of course, then you can close the file, and Detective Janssen has solved another case. But fine, if you want clues, I'll give you clues! Of all the people Helene knew, you should only be looking into one man, because—"

"Oh no," said Fritz. "Please not again with this Mr. von Wittenberg! I can assure you we're already looking into him."

"I'm not talking about him. However, another thought did pop into my head because of him."

"So, why don't you share your thought process?"

Ternheim sighed. "At first I thought Mr. von Wittenberg was someone we knew. I noticed she had been talking on the phone with a man and was becoming more and more troubled. It was only after I learned his name and knew that she had met him that I cast this suspicion aside."

"What was your suspicion?"

Ternheim hesitated, then pulled himself together. "As you know, our father paints some . . . well, let's just say special images. An art dealer named Laval became aware of him by accident and did everything he could to get my father as a client. My father was flattered because the dealer praised his paintings and called him an undiscovered genius. Helene and I were strongly opposed to the idea that these images be made public. What kind of picture would they paint of our family and company? People would think he's nuts. Eventually this guy managed to persuade my father to sign. His contract runs out in six months, and now the situation has radically changed. There were a couple of incidents that led to our father being declared legally incompetent and Helene and myself his guardians. That means the contract cannot be renewed or extended without our consent. Mr. Laval, whose real name is Lachmann, contacted us three months ago to discuss an extension. But I told him he could shove it and that he was to leave us alone. He then called my sister a few times—he probably thought she was weaker. I know Laval threatened my sister at least once, stating he could make life very difficult for her if she continued to hinder our father's success."

LATE FRIDAY MORNING

The alarm woke Hannes. He had lain awake the night before, thinking of the events of the day.

Socks was barking, and Hannes sat up. A pounding headache brought tears to his eyes. He gathered his clothes, remembering he needed to ask Ben for some fresh underwear.

Socks came darting out of the living room when Hannes walked into the hall. Ben's bedroom door was open, offering a view of his rumpled, empty bed. He went into the bathroom and discovered a note on the mirror: *Had to leave early today, but will be back around noon. Can you take care of Socks? Thanks and see you later! P.S. There are some rolls in the kitchen.*

Hannes sighed. Ben had a lot of nerve! He had a ton of work to do, still no clean underpants, and now a dog. He looked down at Socks, who wagged his tail.

"Well, Socks, wanna go do some policing?"

A tired face stared back at him in the mirror. His hair was disheveled. Fortunately for him, there was a bottle of aspirin sitting on the shelf. He took two and hopped in the shower.

Upon exiting the bathroom, he called his landlord to inquire about the status of the snake situation. As expected, the landlord had no update. Hannes decided to spend one more night at Ben's.

He ate breakfast and wondered what he should do first. He needed to return the police car. Then he would do a background check on the art dealer before investigating the pharmaceutical company's past. He had to catch up with Anna and bring Socks back at some point, and he needed some underwear.

Hannes drove to the station. Socks sniffed around the room as Hannes returned the keys to the patrol car to Mrs. Meier.

"I'm really sorry I didn't return the car until now, but I had to take care of this dog yesterday. He's a stray, and I didn't have much luck finding his owner."

Fortunately, Mrs. Meier had a soft spot for dogs.

In the corridor Hannes ran into Marcel, who had asked Fritz on Wednesday for advice on a missing-person case.

"Did that young woman turn up?" Hannes asked.

"You mean Merle von Hohenstein? No, still no trace."

"Good luck," Hannes said and opened the door to his office. Socks was easy: after quickly exploring the office, he curled up under the desk and dozed off.

Hannes spent the next hour doing a background check on Lachmann. He found no record of his real name or his pseudonym. So he continued searching the Internet, but the only hit on Ludwig Lachmann was an already deceased economist of the same name. The search for Louis Laval, meanwhile, yielded some information.

An article in an art magazine celebrated him as the discoverer of the genius Merlin, and in an interview he spoke about the success of a recent art opening in Amsterdam. However, most results were related only indirectly to Laval and primarily focused on Merlin. He had a veritable fan base around the world with lots of international bloggers touting his work.

On one fan page, a few buyers had uploaded pictures of them posing in front of their purchases. One group photo made Hannes think he was looking at members of a sadomasochism club, and in another photo, a bald, bare-chested man covered in tattoos stood in front of a painting with his right arm raised. Curiously, he came across very little criticism of Merlin's painting style, even if one Swedish art historian stated his work was "truly eccentric but also an intolerable perversion of the soul."

As for Laval, he found nothing revealing about his origin or his career. One interview indicated his age. Since that article was already several years old, Hannes estimated Laval was about forty-eight.

Hannes was about to give up when he stumbled across a post in an art forum entitled "Art or Junk?" Someone with the username "ashiro" had written:

```
Of  course  Merlin's  images  are  art.
He  works  the  canvas  with  an  extreme,
if  not  diabolical,  intensity  that  is
unparalleled. Unfortunately, it's damn
hard to get ahold of an original image,
and I was once even shortchanged by Mr.
Laval, his ridiculous agent. He promised
me a masterpiece and went on and on about
a one-off opportunity to buy one of the
artist's coveted originals. He claimed
to have several interested parties, so
I had to decide on the spot and pay a
5,000 euro deposit. Since I had often
tried unsuccessfully to acquire one
```

```
of Merlin's images, I agreed. What I
received was a 4" x 6" sketch, not the
painting I had expected. Has anyone had
a similar experience?
```

Several people confirmed that they had also fallen victim to the same trick and strongly advised against purchasing from Laval without having previously seen the real painting. One user, however, did not seem to have fallen prey to Laval's scheme:

```
Ha-ha, how stupid can you be? Laval's
known for controlling the market by
selling sketches and thumbnails, sight
unseen, at inflated prices. Pretty stupid
if you fall for it . . .
```

Hannes considered this new information. So Laval conducted business in a way that could possibly be described as shrewd. But it seemed more likely he was just scamming people.

He called the airline Laval had flown and asked for some information about flight times. Since the employee refused to comment, citing official procedures, he asked a colleague from the federal police for assistance, who promised to look into the matter as soon as possible.

Hannes needed some coffee. He stood and Socks jumped up to follow him. "If only I could wake up that fast," Hannes said and patted his head. He stepped into the hallway and almost collided with Maria.

"Do you have it out for me or something?" she joked. "This is the second time this week you've run me down. I have a nice memento from yesterday's incident, by the way." She showed him her scratched elbow and then lifted her white skirt to let him see her bruised knee.

"I'm really sorry. What are you doing up here? Bored with the autopsy table?"

"Not at all. I just got a very interesting case. An extremely over-weight young man was mauled by his two attack dogs. Let me tell you . . . Wait, and who are you?"

Socks had attracted her attention, and Maria knelt down to pet him. "Last weekend, there was a knife fight at a soccer match. Unfortunately, a sixteen-year-old, the son of a prominent politician, got caught up in the fight. Now the chief of police wants to hear my test results in person."

"I see. A case of a politically explosive nature . . ."

"That's the way it is." Maria got up and smoothed her skirt. "Was your chase yesterday successful, or did I get all scraped up for nothing?"

He told her what had played out by the pond.

She laughed. "That's a good story! Didn't go so well for the lovers, though. I have to get going now, your chief is waiting for my report in a couple of minutes. Nice running into you! And I haven't forgotten that you still owe me dinner." She winked and hurried down the hall.

Back at his office, Hannes entered the words "Lagussa," "history," and "Nazi era" into the search engine. He changed the search words several times, but even the most diverse combinations did not turn up any information pointing to a connection between Lagussa and the Nazi regime. Then he remembered that the drug company had changed its name several times and was previously known as North-South Pharmaceuticals. His new search resulted in a flood of additional links, and after scanning through several articles, he got an overview of the drug scandal.

In 1992, North-South Pharmaceuticals released the drug Xonux, a prescription psychotropic drug meant to treat anxiety disorders. Unexpected side effects were first reported in 1995, but the company attributed them to prescription errors made by doctors. Supposedly other drugs had been prescribed at the same time even though the combination resulted in harmful interactions. The first deaths associated with Xonux occurred a year later, and a media storm broke loose. Several scientists suspected that North-South Pharmaceuticals had doctored market-entry studies and had not taken early signs of dangerous side effects seriously.

A few months later, the company voluntarily removed the drug from the market and got away with just an official warning. Xonux was linked to several heart attacks and strokes throughout the world, some of which were fatal. According to information from the media, it was never quite proven that Xonux had actually been responsible for these side effects. Nevertheless, a health minister stepped in, and North-South Pharmaceuticals agreed out of court to pay compensation totaling in the millions.

A thought popped into Hannes's head, but before he could make sense of it, it slipped away. He was about to search for background information on the company's first name, North German Chemical and Pharmaceutical Works, when Fritz called.

"I have a funny feeling that Mr. Ternheim's hiding something and wants to shift my attention to this art dealer," he said. "Have you checked Laval out?"

"Yes, but I found very little information about him." Hannes briefly described the meager results. "I'm still waiting to hear back about the flights, but I can't imagine he's involved in Ms. Ternheim's death. He's definitely a crook, but he seems too clueless for murder."

"Fine. Take a look into Christian Ternheim's background. I'd like to get a clearer picture of him. By the way, I got two tickets to this charity gala for tonight. We should definitely show up and take a look around."

"Um, yeah, well, actually . . . I thought I could go out on the water today. My knee seems to be better. And besides, I have nothing to wear."

"True, you can't show up in a tracksuit," Fritz joked. "How about this: get there one hour before the official start, so at six. The venue's at the old casino. Try to talk to the young assistant again. Ask her if Mr.

Ternheim knew about the relationship between Ms. Wagner and his sister and if she remembered anything else. Then we briefly catch up, and I give you my blessing to go practice. I can handle a cold buffet on my own."

Hannes was relieved when he hung up. Socks nudged his hand. He remembered he hadn't packed any dog food. He let Socks slurp from his water glass so his stomach was at least filled with something. "Ten minutes, Socks, then I'll drive you home."

Hannes devoted himself once again to the Internet, though he failed to find anything on the North German Chemical and Pharmaceutical Works despite several attempts. He shut down the computer and headed for Mrs. Meier's office with Socks on his heels.

"Mrs. Meier, I need a car again. Do you have something nice for me in the park—"

"Right now, all vehicles are on the road," she said.

"I've found the owner of this poor dog and want to return him as soon as possible."

"Dogs can walk. You kept him penned up all morning in your office. His bladder's probably ready to burst."

Hannes glanced down at Socks. Maybe she was onto something.

"Well, you're probably right, we'll walk. One more thing, is there a clothing store around here?"

She frowned. "You want to go shopping while on duty? Has the CEO's killer been found?"

"Uh, no, but . . ." He was becoming more and more convinced that Mrs. Meier was a witch, and quickly turned around before she could read his thoughts. He walked down the stairs with Socks, and as soon as they had exited the station, Socks sprinted to the first hedge and lifted his leg for a full minute.

***

"Well, how's my four-legged friend?" Ben asked. He was sitting on a chaise longue in front of his cottage and laughed as Socks nuzzled him. "Sorry for leaving Socks with you without asking, I couldn't take him with me this morning."

"Don't mention it!" Hannes said. "Socks was well behaved and even conquered the heart of the greatest secretary-cum-witch of all time. Hey, um . . . can I borrow a pair of your underwear?"

Ben burst out laughing. "Well, no one's asked me that one before."

"Hero that you are, you forgot to pack any underwear in my bag," Hannes said.

"Oh, okay, now I understand. Does that mean that you've been going commando all this time? Man! How does it feel?"

"Fine," Hannes said. "But before I chafe any more, I'd love to have a pair . . ."

Ben disappeared into the house and waved to Hannes to follow him. He pulled out a pair of black boxer shorts from a drawer in the living room and threw them to him.

"If you need a new pair, help yourself. But put them back washed, please!" His laughter followed Hannes to the bathroom, where he quickly slipped on the garment before stepping back out.

"How's the case going?"

"The Internet has turned up almost nothing."

"What, you have no other means of getting information?"

"Of course, but it depends on what you're looking for. If a person or company has always been clean, then they won't be in our system. Police state, my ass! Right now, I wish it were one."

Ben shrugged. "Maybe you should ask the Federal Intelligence Service or the credit card companies. I'm sure they have a ton of information."

Hannes had an idea. "You told me about Lagussa's Nazi past. How did you find that out?"

"So, your boss left you to do the hard work?"

"You guessed it," Hannes said. "Please, share a few of your sources with me!"

"I'm afraid they're not official sources, but I have some time this afternoon. If you want, I can help you with the research. And, no, I wouldn't blab about it to your boss. You'll probably get somewhere with my help."

"All right," Hannes said. "But what I need are facts."

"I'll give you facts," Ben said. "I can assure you that we conduct a thorough investigation before staging any protest. We won't be picketing an innocent business tonight."

Hannes felt guilty the moment Ben mentioned his protest against Lagussa. "By the way, I'll be at this gala for a little while this evening. Don't you think it would be a good idea to hold off until we've solved Ms. Ternheim's murder?"

"The two have nothing to do with each other. This is a unique opportunity, and we don't want to miss it. If I showed you everything we know, you'd probably agree."

Hannes doubted it but did not press the issue. He played fetch with Socks while Ben made some lunch. Half an hour later, he placed two steaming plates of spaghetti in front of them, filled Socks's bowl, and turned on his laptop.

"You're not going to find what you're looking for using a regular search engine. I told you already that everything was covered up. But maybe Lagussa's just been lucky until now and no one has ever thought to take a closer look at the company. We only stumbled on it by accident when an informant leaked to us a list of companies that supposedly had special status under Hitler. The validity of this list was pretty questionable because much of our research led nowhere. That doesn't necessarily mean that the list was wrong, just that we were unable to find anything out about most companies on it. Lagussa, however, was a different story."

He pushed a forkful of spaghetti into his mouth and continued while chewing. "We're part of a network of various groups, such as victims' organizations, social institutions, and other private initiatives. That way, we all have access to a larger amount of data, documents, and eyewitness accounts. We've also created an Internet forum where we can exchange what we know, and this is where we began our search."

Ben opened a website. After he logged in, a new window opened with several forums. "Here." He pointed to a link called "Lagussa—Active Player during the Nazi Regime?" "We started this thread and asked if anyone knew anything about Lagussa. Several people quickly responded, saying they could help, including someone whose father had been a forced laborer at Lagussa, or North German Chemical and Pharmaceutical Works as the company was then known. He described in detail the torment his father suffered. There was little concern for the health and safety of the workers. The smallest alleged transgressions were punished with abuse, arrest, or deprivation of ration stamps."

"Why were the Nazis even interested in the company?"

"Chemical knowledge was a prerequisite for the production of war materials. Plus, the Nazis were interested in vaccines against poisonous gases and diseases like typhus. They were looking to increase the strength of their troops during the war."

"But Lagussa manufactures psychotropic drugs. Were they trying to protect the soldiers from depression? Given the nightmares they witnessed, that would make sense. But I don't see the Nazis being too concerned with philanthropy."

"No, you can safely say they didn't know what philanthropy was. The Nazis had ulterior motives for everything they did. For example, they were very interested in stimulants, because they hoped to shorten the amount of time soldiers needed to sleep and increase the amount of time they spent on the battlefield. You also have to realize that Lagussa only focused on producing psychotropic drugs in the early seventies. NGCP made a lot more than just drugs at the time, and even if the company wasn't one of the big players, they certainly weren't going to say no to the Nazi's contributions."

"How many forced laborers worked for the company?"

"It's impossible to give a realistic estimate. As you can imagine, many records and documents disappeared after the war. According to most estimates, eleven million people were abused as forced laborers in the German Reich and the occupied territories. Look here! We've created an archive where we store documents related to NGCP so anyone who has access to the site can add and view documents. Here we have two documents from 1941 in which NGCP requested a total of 150 laborers, most of them from Poland."

Ben also showed him correspondence between Nazi authorities and NGCP. In most cases, it was about the allocation of raw materials. There were also several photos of an assembly line. Even if the photos were grainy, "North German Chemical and Pharmaceutical Works" could clearly be made out on a wall in the background.

"Of particular interest is this letter here," Ben said and opened a short document dated January 23, 1940. "The addressee was a bank which handled the accounts for the Nazi Party. It acknowledged a transfer of more than 100,000 Reichsmarks. That was a princely sum, especially since, as I said, NGCP was only a medium-sized company."

"Who ran NGCP then?"

"The company was run by its founder, Heinrich Ternheim. He was the grandfather of the current managing director. But the father of Helene and Christian Ternheim also had an important role in the company at that time. Heinrich Ternheim, today better known as Merlin, was born in 1919 and was only fourteen when the Nazis came to power, so he grew up with the National Socialist ideology. It comes as no surprise that he joined the Hitler Youth at fifteen. At eighteen, he became a member of the Nazi Party and manager at the company. His managerial responsibilities later saved him from being drafted during the war, even though he would have been a prime candidate given that he was twenty-one."

"Clever," Hannes said.

"Right. The Ternheims may have supported the Nazis for years, but they let others take the fall. And in more ways than one. In addition to the use of forced labor, there is still another deep, dark chapter in their past: testing on humans!"

Hannes's pulse quickened. His compassion for the old painter waned. "So not only did they use forced labor, but they also experimented on people?"

"Not on the forced laborers. Cheap labor was far too valuable. No, there was another group of helpless people with an almost inexhaustible supply: concentration camp prisoners!"

Hannes began to feel sick.

"The first concentration camps were established as early as 1933. At first, only political opponents were imprisoned, but that changed. Anyone who didn't meet the sick image the Nazis had of people could now expect to be interned. Anyone sent to the camps also ran the danger of being used for medical experiments. Vaccines were tested, chemotherapy drugs injected, and wounds like ones caused by incendiary bombs inflicted—often without anesthesia. Even children were tortured in the most bestial of ways. Most victims died an agonizing death; others were eliminated in the gas chambers. Few survived, and most remained physically and psychologically destroyed for the rest of their lives."

"And NGCP was involved?"

"They didn't conduct the experiments themselves; the camp doctors were responsible for that. But here's a delivery receipt that was leaked to us. It shows that NGCP sent some sort of drug to the medical officer of a concentration camp." Ben opened another file. "Unfortunately, we don't know what kind of drug. It's only referred to as Compound 3282. This is also the only delivery receipt we've seen so far."

"And what are these?" asked Hannes, pointing to some image files.

"Those are images of test subjects." Ben opened one. "This man here actually survived the ordeal. He was one of the unfortunate ones they experimented on with the incendiary bomb wounds. The picture was taken five years after his release. As you can see, he's disfigured."

Even Ben's voice had faltered; Hannes gulped.

"Since we do not know what NGCP delivered to the concentration camp, we can only guess what suffering the drug inflicted. NGCP definitely had nothing to do with incendiary bombs. I bet it was a tuberculosis vaccine: researchers have proven that the company was working on one then."

"Why wasn't NGCP held accountable during the trials?"

"At first, the focus was on the major war criminals, and NGCP was a small fish. Plus, this delivery receipt only recently surfaced."

"Maybe it's a forgery?"

"I don't think so. Why would it be? Who would have an interest in pinning something like that on Lagussa? Once this document was uploaded, another witness came forward. His mother was a victim of concentration camp experiments. She'd told her son when he was growing up that she had been injected with something that had four letters printed on the packaging. He couldn't remember these letters for a long time—after all, he was just a child. But he told us he heard her voice in his head as he read our documents. He's certain those four letters were NGCP."

"So the woman survived?"

"Yes, but with serious side effects. According to her son, she suffered from so-called concentration camp syndrome, a type of post-traumatic stress disorder. In addition to physical ailments, she suffered from anxiety, depression, and nightmares. She took her own life."

They sat in silence. Only Socks's panting could be heard. The sun shone on Hannes, and it was inconceivable to him how completely different this country must have looked seventy years ago.

"Do you understand now why I'm committed to fighting neo-Nazis? It's bad enough to hear about these events and to know that they actually occurred. It's even harder to bear the thought that my own grandfather was murdered by these criminals."

Hannes nodded. He understood Ben only too well.

"So you see, Luther's famous words also apply to me." Ben found his irresistible grin again. "'Here I stand; I cannot do otherwise.' That's why I can't take your new friendship with the young executive assistant at Lagussa into consideration. I have to go through with it tonight. We've created a website containing all the documents that show the company's connection to the Nazi Party. It will go live tonight. I have to go again, but you can browse through the archive on your own. Maybe you'll find something. I'll write down my username and password. Without the password, you can't log back in to the forum. Can I leave Socks with you again?"

"Sure. When will you be back?"

Ben pushed himself up from his chair and went outside to grab his bike. "I don't know yet. Just lock Socks inside if you have to go somewhere. But make sure he goes beforehand!"

Ben whistled softly as he pushed the bike across the lawn and disappeared around the corner. Hannes watched him go, lost in thought, then grabbed the laptop.

FRIDAY EVENING

How she loathed this darkness! When Merle had painted her room black as a teenager and blocked out all the light, the darkness had protected and comforted her. Now it posed a constant threat.

After eating the pizza, she had walked around the room for hours and anxiously waited for the onset of fatigue. Her watch battery had died, and Merle had lost all sense of time.

Now she was sitting back in front of the steel door, trying to force the edge of the wooden food tray into the door's narrow gap to use as a lever. She kept failing until finally the tray became slightly wedged. She pushed with all her might against the other end, but the wood broke and drove a splinter deep into her right hand. In pain, she grabbed hold of the big splinter and pulled it out.

"At least now I can end this all myself," she said and laughed. And to prove it, she placed the pointed end of the splinter against the veins in her wrist and pushed. That would do.

But then rage boiled over. Before she hurt herself, she wanted to attack the man who had put her in this hole. She would wait by the door and jump him the next time he opened it.

She sat feverishly on the floor and concentrated on the world outside the door. She constantly struggled to regain control of her thoughts, which drifted in the most absurd directions. After she had been sitting there for about an hour, her ears pricked: she could hear the familiar footsteps. They seemed a bit slower than usual, but she could also be mistaken.

Merle knelt by the small hatch.

She heard someone kneel outside. Merle held her breath. She was quite sure her kidnapper was a man. Her assumption proved right when the hatch was lifted and a hairy man's arm was visible. As the accompanying hand shoved in a new tray, Merle lunged forward. The man shouted as she clutched the hand and tried to pull it forward. She could feel her nails digging into the strange flesh. Shortly thereafter she could hear violent swearing. The man tried to release himself with his other hand. She desperately defended herself and shouted as loud as she could through the opening. The man let go of her wrist and poked her in the eye. She screamed and covered her face with her hands.

A moment later, the flap came crashing down, and the bolt was pushed forward. There would be no food this evening.

At five forty-five, Hannes parked in a garage near the old casino. He had put his gym bag in the trunk because the boathouse was on the other side of town. Even though he wanted to get out of there before the official start of the event, he had stopped to buy a white button-down shirt so he would look somewhat presentable. He had also purchased a pack of much-needed underwear.

As he walked toward the old casino, he saw no signs of suspicious activity. In front of the stone staircase that led up to the columned entrance, a long red carpet had been laid out and was flanked on both sides by bushes in white planters. Two young men were demarcating the entrance with elegant white wooden fences, while the last Styrofoam boxes were being unloaded from a catering van. Bright flags with Lagussa's blue logo fluttered in the wind.

Nobody took notice of Hannes as he ran up the steps and entered the imposing building. He scanned the area and noticed a brutish security guard in a black suit, who politely stepped in Hannes's way.

"Excuse me, but the doors don't open until seven. I unfortunately cannot let you in. Do you have a ticket?" He scrutinized Hannes, whose tattered jeans didn't exactly go with the clean white shirt.

"Uh, yeah, I do, but my colleague has it," Hannes said.

"Then you have to wait. As I said, the doors don't open for another hour."

"I'm not here for the gala. I would just like to have a word with Ms. Stahl."

"Who?"

"Well, she organized the event. Ms. Stahl from Lagussa."

"I apologize," said the security guard. "I have strict instructions not to let anyone in before the event without a security pass."

Hannes was about to pull out his police badge when Anna came around the corner. "Hannes, I had no idea you were coming. What are you doing here? The event doesn't start until seven."

"I wanted to talk to you briefly. I unfortunately cannot attend, but my boss has already promised to guard the buffet."

Anna showed the guard her security pass. "It's fine, I'll take responsibility for him."

The man stepped aside, and Hannes followed Anna down the hallway. She seemed frazzled and kept looking at her watch.

"Tonight we have a lot of prominent guests, politicians and people from show business, so we have strict security measures."

"Do you have some time right now?" Hannes asked.

"Not really. I have to speak with the sound engineer. The sound check was awful. But that won't take long. If you walk through the ballroom, you'll see a large glass door on your right. It leads to the terrace and a small garden. We set up a bar there. Get yourself a drink. I'll be with you in a few minutes, okay?"

"Of course! I won't keep you for long, promise."

"Cool, I have to run!"

Anna hurried away, and Hannes smiled as he gazed at her figure-hugging black cocktail dress.

Hannes entered the main hall where the waitstaff was busy making last-minute preparations. Several long rows of tables were covered in dazzling white linens, while the crystal glasses and silver cutlery produced a glittering sea of stars in the light of the chandeliers. The chairs were also covered in white cloth, and there were probably enough for several hundred people.

At the end of the hall was a large stage for the band. Several technicians were busy setting up two cameras and discussing the correct angles and settings. Hannes almost regretted not attending the event. He strolled through the rows of tables and stepped through a wide glass door onto the terrace, which was festively decorated with several high tops and a lavish bar.

Since the servers were still busy stocking the bar, Hannes decided against a drink and leaned against a table. The sun was low in the sky, plunging the little garden into soft light. He could hear gently rippling water. Hannes closed his eyes and enjoyed the warm sunshine. When he opened them again, Anna was in front of him.

"Quick nap?"

"It's all so dreamlike. Everything looks great!"

"Thank you," she said and smiled. "I'm quite happy. Mr. Ternheim has the highest standards, and I don't think he'll be disappointed."

"Does the sound equipment work now?"

"I hope so. The engineer swore everything is under control. If not, I'll strangle him."

Hannes chuckled.

"How come you're not staying for the gala? I'm sure you'd like it. We hired a great band. Once the speeches are over, it should be fun. The food is supposed to be excellent."

"I'd really like to stay." Hannes told her about practice for his upcoming race.

"Oh, well, that's understandable," she said but looked a little disappointed.

"I'll watch it later on TV," joked Hannes. "I saw some cameras being set up."

"That's right," she said. "Since it's a charity gala and celebrities are making donations, the media wants to cover it. A lot of reporters are coming too."

"A successful PR stunt, then. Do some good and talk about it . . ."

Anna frowned. "Sure, you can see it that way. But it's for a good cause, and there's no reason why it shouldn't be publicized. Anyway, what did you actually want to talk about?"

"I've been thinking about our conversation. In particular, I was wondering if Mr. Ternheim knew anything about the relationship between his sister and Ms. Wagner?"

"Shh, not so loud!" Frightened, she looked around and lowered her voice. "I don't know. But if he did, he wouldn't have been thrilled. Sometimes he makes crude homophobic remarks."

"If he did know, could that have been a reason for their estrangement?"

"For sure! But she wouldn't have told him about her relationship."

"Does anything else stick out to you? Anything about the relationship between the siblings?"

"Why? You don't suspect . . . ?" She was aghast.

"No, no, it's just routine."

Anna was now on guard. "I in no way wanted to cast suspicion on Mr. Ternheim. I think the rift between them was about her research into Lagussa's past. He probably overreacted. You should know that Mr.

Ternheim is somewhat paranoid. He's always smelling a conspiracy and doesn't trust anyone. I can give you an example, but it has to remain just between us. Mr. Ternheim received an anonymous tip that someone wants to crash this event tonight. And by 'crash,' I don't mean show up uninvited. I mean there's going to be an incident. Mr. Ternheim didn't tell me anything specific. But he insisted that security be tightened and has been tremendously nervous all day. I mean, let's be honest, who would use a charity gala to provoke a scandal? Sure, there are always wackos, but it's very unlikely."

Hannes had to grab the table to steady himself and struggled to keep a straight face. "Where did he get this information?"

"An anonymous call. The person warned of a scandal. The caller wouldn't . . . Oh, here he comes."

Mr. Ternheim walked over to the table, his back stiff, and looked sternly at Anna. "I've been looking for you all over! There's some confusion with the guest list. Could you take care of it?"

"Of course, right away," she said and shot Hannes an apologetic look. "Please, excuse me."

"Uh . . . yes, of course, no problem. Thank you for . . . for the talk," Hannes said.

After Anna hurried away, Mr. Ternheim said, "Are you looking to rub elbows with the rich and famous?"

"Not at all, my boss will be taking over for me. I'm just waiting here and then I'll be on my way."

"Maybe it's good we have the police here tonight." The director stared into the distance.

"Why's that?"

"Sorry?" Ternheim said. "Oh, it's never bad to have law enforcement around, right? After all, there'll be an illustrious group here. What were you discussing with Ms. Stahl?"

"Nothing. As I said, I agreed to meet with my boss here and randomly bumped into her. We've been investigating various aspects of your sister's case separately and have to exchange information."

"Yes, my sister . . . Actually, it's her event tonight. Maybe I should have canceled everything. It's strange we're *celebrating* without her."

"Mr. Ternheim, your sister was pretty tense lately. So much so that it struck many of your employees as unusual. Was she threatened or did anything seem strange to you?"

Mr. Ternheim gazed over the little garden. "I have to put this show on first and then sleep on it. Even though it's the weekend, I'll be in my office tomorrow. Come in the morning with Mr. Janssen, and maybe I can tell you more. Oh, speak of the devil. I'll leave you two alone so you can brief each other. The first guests will be arriving soon."

He gave Hannes a limp handshake. Hannes would have expected a viselike grip, but maybe the past few days had left their mark on him.

Fritz quickly said hello to Ternheim, then walked over to Hannes. He was wearing a long-sleeved light-blue shirt and a black pinstripe suit that looked a bit dated. He had casually thrown the jacket over his shoulder.

"Well? Have a nice chat?" he asked.

"There are certainly more pleasant conversation partners, but he did say he'd maybe have new information for us tomorrow."

"Well, well! Look at you!" Fritz eyed Hannes with interest. "You really seem to have a knack for difficult characters. With me, he's as tight-lipped as they come."

"I guess. He said he needs a night to think it over."

"Then let's hope his thoughts lead somewhere, and it's not just a diversionary tactic. Did Ms. Stahl have anything more to add?"

"No. However, she did hint that Mr. Ternheim is not particularly tolerant of homosexuals and doesn't believe he knew of his sister's lesbian relationship. And he's apparently afraid something will happen this evening. Someone gave him an anonymous tip. Security has been tightened."

"You can say that again. And I had completely forgotten about your buddy's protest. Did he tell you what he and his group are up to?"

"No, he wouldn't divulge anything."

"I hope you remember who's buttering your bread."

"He honestly didn't tell me anything!"

"All right, all right! I believe you. So, what have you found out about Lagussa today?"

Lounge music began playing in the ballroom, and a few guests walked out onto the terrace. Hannes thought he recognized a famous fashion model, but he wasn't sure.

"It seems they're letting people in now. Maybe we should stand off to the side?"

"I don't care," Fritz said. "Let's head into the garden, the guests will hit up the bar first, anyway. Besides, I can hardly be seen with you!" He glanced at Hannes's outfit.

"Don't worry, I'll be leaving shortly. Why would I buy a suit for an hour?"

"A man should always have a suit in his closet," said Fritz.

"All right, boss."

Fritz groaned and sat down on a garden bench.

"How's your back?" Hannes asked as he sat down beside him.

"The usual, not worth mentioning. So, what's up with Lagussa?"

"Lagussa's definitely really good at business. Last year, the company generated a profit of 324 million euros. It's active worldwide, but its core market is Europe, which isn't surprising. According to the OECD, about 20 percent of workers in industrialized countries suffer from mental illness, a majority of them from depression. Worldwide, over 120 million people are affected. So Lagussa is in a very lucrative market. And that's just the total sales for psychotropic drugs. I found an old figure from 2008—back then, consumers spent a shocking 100 billion US dollars on such drugs."

"Brave new world, huh? We shape the world according to our expectations only to realize at the end of the day that it's not quite what we wanted. Then we down these pills in order to put up with all this shit, but keep doing the same thing. In the past decade, the number of prescribed antidepressants has doubled, and mental disorders are the most common reason for hospitalization and people going on disability."

Hannes stared at him in amazement.

"What? You think I don't read the paper?" said Fritz, somewhat miffed. "I may be out for the count, but I still pay attention to what's happening around me. Anyway, continue!"

"Well, most of what's out there on the Internet is about the drug scandal in the nineties. The most interesting thing, however, is that both Ternheims were responsible for the drug's release. It was called Xonux and was supposed to be some miracle drug for anxiety disorders. However, it was quickly suspected to be responsible for heart attacks and strokes, some of which were fatal."

"I know plenty about the scandal. It was in the papers for weeks. I still remember it. More interesting is what you possibly found out about the company's involvement in the Nazi era."

"Back then it was the North German Chemical and Pharmaceutical Works, or NGCP. What was on the Internet was circumstantial, and there was no evidence of cooperation with the Nazis."

"So you're saying you didn't find anything?"

"No, I actually did because I then found a very competent source."

Fritz was unimpressed when he learned who that source was. "Did you talk to Ben again about our investigation? I thought I made myself clear!"

"No, I didn't tell him anything about our work. He already knows we're dealing with Lagussa. All I said was that I was having trouble finding anything out about their history."

Fritz grumbled but became more attentive the more Hannes told him about the contents of the forum and archive.

"The photos were really the most difficult. It's unbelievable that Heinrich Ternheim and his father collaborated with the Nazis when you see that old man today."

"Just look at all the guys brought to trial for war crimes," said Fritz. "Most of them are pretty feeble, yet they committed crimes against humanity. You can't just look at people—you have to imagine them at the time they carried out their deeds. That's the only way you can remain objective."

"Could it be that Anna found the same documents in Ms. Ternheim's bag?"

"You mean that someone leaked these documents to Ms. Ternheim? It's possible. But I don't see her being particularly active on this forum."

"The only way to find out would be if we had Anna take a look at the content of the website."

"Ah," said Fritz with a smile. "So you're on a first-name basis with Ms. Executive Assistant . . . I must say, you seem to have great people skills. Or is there more to it?"

"It's possible that this Mark von Wittenberg, the man who was recently in contact with Ms. Ternheim, is also a member of this forum," Hannes said, ignoring the banter. "Maybe he forwarded the documents to her or tried to blackmail her with them? And maybe it was he who warned Mr. Ternheim about the protest tonight."

"Why would he do that? If he'd wanted to blackmail Ms. Ternheim, why would he warn her brother about a demonstration?"

"Maybe he didn't blackmail her. Maybe he tipped her off in order to get Lagussa to do something."

"Maybe, maybe, maybe," said Fritz. "That's a little too many maybes for me. Christian Ternheim is probably the only one who can shed light on this, but he's bought himself another night to think. Look and see if von Wittenberg was active on the forum, then we'll know if we can change these maybes into certainties."

"You may read the paper, but you don't know your way around the modern world. You usually use a screen name on a forum. Anonymity on the net—heard of it before?"

"You see? That's why I have you. We complement each other," Fritz joked.

"Have you found anything out yet about Mr. von Wittenberg?" asked Hannes.

"Not yet. Our boss put a rookie on it, but so far, he hasn't found a lead."

The terrace had now filled. Fritz looked at his watch. "This shindig gets underway in fifteen minutes. It's best you make yourself scarce, otherwise you'll have to walk through the packed hall during the ceremony. You should spare yourself the looks you'll get . . ."

Hannes nodded. Together they went up the stairs, and Fritz put his hand on Hannes's shoulder.

"I'm going to treat myself to a beer at the bar, otherwise I won't be able to take the speeches. Have fun out on the water! Incidentally, don't think you're off tomorrow just because it's Saturday. Let's meet at nine"—Fritz glanced at the bar—"say ten at the office. Steffen's already threatening to assign us backup. We desperately need a break in the case!" He gave Hannes a gentle nudge in the direction of the glass door and snaked his way to the bar.

As Hannes walked through the ballroom to the exit, he saw many famous faces. In one corner he saw the governor, who was excitedly chatting with Christian Ternheim. He wondered if Ben was there mingling and grinned at the thought.

***

"We've come together here tonight because we're united in the same goal: the fight against childhood leukemia!"

Christian Ternheim walked away from the podium. A short film played on the screen behind him, showing the emergence, spread, and symptoms of the disease. When the film was through, there was a collective stunned silence in the hall. Some guests wiped their eyes. Mr. Ternheim stepped back up to the podium.

"As you know, Lagussa specializes in psychiatric drugs, so we're unable to contribute actively to the fight against this terrible disease. But as a modern company with deep roots in the community, we believe it's our duty to get involved."

Applause broke out, while a camera moved closer to Mr. Ternheim.

"Many of you have supported us in this commitment for years. I therefore wish to extend a special thanks to you. Without you, none of our successes would have been possible!"

There was more applause.

"Thank you . . . I would also like to thank another person who is sadly not with us tonight. A woman whose commitment to the fight against childhood leukemia was the impetus for this evening's event. My sister unfortunately passed away a few days ago in a tragic accident. She would have been proud of this evening and seen it as encouragement for her tireless efforts. Now it's up to us to continue her legacy. I . . ." He paused for a moment. "I ask that you rise from your seats and quietly commemorate my sister for a moment."

Chairs were noisily pushed back and flashing cameras recorded the silent crowd.

"Thank you," Ternheim said into the microphone. "But we should also not forget the heroes who are the stars of this evening: the countless children suffering from leukemia all over the world. We have already achieved a great deal! Last year, for example, we opened a treatment center in South Africa and . . ."

Fritz's thoughts began to wander, and he glanced around the room. While the majority of the audience listened attentively, a famous actress whispered with a soccer player, a television presenter yawned, two business leaders were quietly chatting, and the hottest C-list celebrity couple was staring googly-eyed at each other. The cameras were trained on every person of note in the room, all of whom tried to appear both dignified and concerned as the shot was taken. Fritz shivered and hoped the evening would end soon.

At that moment there was a loud bang. Some guests shouted.

Fritz carefully scanned the room. The blast had sounded like a cannon, and it was now followed by the rhythmic sounds of an army marching with heavy boots on asphalt. This was clearly not part of the presentation. A sharp whistling gave the impression that bombs were being dropped. Fritz knew these sounds from wartime documentaries. A loud explosion was followed by the rhythmic steps growing closer and closer.

On stage, the screen lit up, and white text moved slowly across a black background.

Lagussa

Multinational
Long-Standing Tradition
Supports Mental Health
Committed to the Fight Against Leukemia
Several-Time Winner of Employer of the Year *Award*

But do you have all the facts about Lagussa?

The whole truth requires a look back to the Nazi era.

Financially Supported the Nazi Party

Used Forced Labor
Conducted Medical Experiments on Concentration
    Camp Prisoners
War Profiteer
Never Brought to Justice

The cover-up is over!

For evidence of Lagussa's dark past go to:

www.truth-about-lagussa.de

The room filled with rumblings and whispers. The photographers jostled at the edge of the stage and photographed like crazy. People took out their smartphones and typed in the web address. Fritz noticed frantic activity behind the tinted windows of the control room. He commended the protest and could not explain how Ben's group had managed to do this without being noticed.

Suddenly everything fell silent, and the screen went black.

A moment later, a visibly shaken Ternheim reappeared on stage and grabbed the microphone. He cleared his throat several times and waited for silence.

"Distinguished guests, we ask your pardon for this incident, which was apparently engineered by a group of troublemakers. It's shameful that a charity event would be disrupted in this manner! Our security team has everything under control. We ask that you continue to enjoy the evening. We will take a short break. Please, take this opportunity to find refreshments at the bar. We will continue with the program in a half hour. I thank you for your understanding."

"What about the allegations surrounding Lagussa's past?" shouted a journalist. "Is it true that Lagussa was in cahoots with the Nazis?"

Ternheim visibly wrestled with the question. "Tomorrow we'll hold a press conference to discuss the incident. This evening honors our fight against childhood leukemia. Let's not provide a forum for the actions of a few rebels."

Murmurs of both approval and disapproval could be heard. Fritz got up and left the room. The stairs to the control room were blocked by two security guards, prompting Fritz to pull out his badge. The two men moved aside. He seemed to arrive at the control room at just the right time. A young man with horn-rimmed glasses was being held in a headlock. Mr. Ternheim was also in the small room, heatedly talking to an employee who was apparently in charge of the audiovisuals, while Ms. Stahl stood next to him, her face pale. The man in the headlock was gasping for air.

"Are you trying to squeeze him to death?" Fritz said to the muscular security guard.

"You stay out of this. He's the one responsible for this mess!" He grabbed the young man by the hair and yanked his head back and forth.

"That's enough," Fritz said and pulled out his badge. "Let go of him now! Mr. Ternheim, call your rabid dogs off!"

Finally, they let the man go. He rubbed his neck and breathed deeply.

"Damn, it wouldn't have taken much more! What are you? Vigilantes?" said Fritz as he knelt down next to the young man. "Everything okay?"

The young man gave a strained nod.

"Get him a glass of water," Fritz said to one of the security guards, then turned to Ternheim. "I have to say, you should be glad I barged in here. That could have been bad! How did the boy gain access to the control room?"

"He tricked us," said the AV guy. "Somehow he got a fake ID. He lied to me and said I was wanted downstairs to be informed about a change of program. He claimed it was just a small detail, so I quickly ran downstairs. There was, of course, no one, and when I tried to get back into the room again, the door was locked and the guy launched his thing!"

Fritz nodded and glanced over at Ternheim, who looked completely distraught, his face wet with sweat. "Mr. Ternheim? How would you like to proceed? If you'd like to press charges, I'll call a couple of colleagues."

"Yeah . . . no . . . I don't know!" He shrugged in despair. "That would probably be best, I suppose. What do you think?"

"Well, it depends. Maybe you should talk to your PR department. If the allegations are true, then it might not be worth it. But you also don't need to decide now. We should take down the man's details as a precaution."

"Then let's do that. But could you maybe take care of it? There's already been enough turmoil. I don't want our guests to be upset by the presence of uniformed police officers."

Fritz shrugged. "That's not really my job, but okay." He turned back to the young man, who had been given a glass of water, and pulled up a chair. "I suppose you don't deny being responsible for this incident?"

"Responsible? Responsibility is a good word. Lagussa must finally take responsibility for the crimes committed during the Nazi era. Do you know that this company and the Nazi Party—"

"I didn't ask you about the history of Lagussa. What's your name?"

"Frank Richter."

"Do you have an ID on you?"

Frank pulled a wallet out of his pocket and fumbled for his ID card.

"Can I have a pen and paper?" Fritz asked the AV guy and took down Frank's information. "Did you pull this thing off by yourself? Are any of your fellow activists still in the building?"

"I know my rights and refuse to answer any questions."

Fritz sighed. Apparently, he was dealing with a battle-hardened activist. "You're hereby banned from the premises and will leave the building immediately! The two gentlemen you've just met will escort you out. No more violence."

"Mr. Ternheim, we should talk in private," Fritz said as the control room emptied. "It's quite possible there may be more people here involved in this, and they might have even more surprises in store for you. Maybe you should consider canceling the event."

Ternheim shook his head. "This evening needs to end on a high note, and there are a number of prominent guests who have come especially for this gala."

"Whatever you say. It's your decision. Nevertheless, we should talk briefly about the incident. Obviously Lagussa's high on the list of an anti-Nazi group. Perhaps the death of your sister has something to do with it."

"All right. Do you have your phone on you? I can contact you later. Let me discuss what to do next with Ms. Stahl and then calm a couple of guests down. Later, we can talk in private."

Two hours later, Fritz strolled between the high tops on the terrace. The official program was over and the band was playing light dance music. Guests had already begun leaving, and the incident was still the main topic of conversation.

Fritz saw Anna scanning the outdoor area in search of something. He waved to attract her attention and then made his way over.

"Oh, hello, Mr. Janssen! Have you enjoyed the evening?"

"Certainly. I hope you won't get in trouble because the event didn't go as smoothly as planned?"

"At the moment, Mr. Ternheim is taking out all his anger on the poor guy in charge of the audiovisuals, even though he didn't really make a mistake. But I'm no fool. Tomorrow, it'll probably be my turn."

"It's good that I ran into you. Mr. Ternheim and I wanted to talk in private this evening. He hasn't called. Do you know where I can find him?"

"Strange, I haven't seen him since our conversation in the control room."

"He was going to call me, but so far . . ."

Anna looked worried. "I've tried several times to reach him, but he isn't picking up. Maybe he's stuck in a conversation with an important guest."

"He must be around here somewhere. I'll see if I can find him. But I don't want to stick around much longer. Tomorrow's looking to be another long day."

"If I see him, I'll remind him he was supposed to get back to you," she promised and headed toward the stage.

Fritz decided to take a stroll around the grounds. He felt weary to his bones. He nibbled from the buffet and popped a strawberry in his mouth. He saw Anna again, and she looked tense.

"Did you find Mr. Ternheim?" she asked.

"No, and he hasn't contacted me either."

"I'm really worried now! None of my colleagues has seen him, and some guests have asked about him. And he can't be reached by phone. It just goes straight to voice mail."

"Maybe he left?"

"He wouldn't do that, not with this guest list! Besides, his car's still in the parking lot. You know, this may sound a little paranoid, but what if more of these activists infiltrated the event and—"

"You mean he might have been kidnapped?" Fritz asked. "Honestly, Ms. Stahl, I can't imagine that. This group wants to draw attention to Lagussa's past, and tonight, they succeeded. But I don't think they're the type of people who would kidnap someone. But I can talk to my colleague who has . . . well, certain contacts in this group."

"I'm probably just imagining things," she said. "But his disappearance is strange. He knows how important the host is on nights like these."

FRIDAY NIGHT

After a grueling session out on the water, Hannes peeled off his soaking clothes, hopped into the shower, and put on a tracksuit. Even if he overdid it, he still wanted to visit the gym for an hour in order to catch up on his routine. He was just about to push his gym bag back into the locker when his phone rang.

"Hi, Fritz, what's up?"

"Listen, what did Ben and his colleagues actually have planned? They caused a scandal at the beginning of the gala, but I'm afraid they might have had something else up their sleeves too."

"Why, what happened?"

Hannes grinned as Fritz gave his version of the events. Ben wasn't lying when he said the newspapers would report in detail on the story.

"What makes you think something else is going to happen?"

"Because the activist in the control room was not alone, and Mr. Ternheim has disappeared."

Hannes laughed. "Are you suggesting Ben kidnapped him?"

"What do I know? It's just . . . Wait a minute, hold on . . . Yes, what is it?" Fritz seemed to have put down his cell phone; Hannes could hear muffled voices. Then he heard Fritz say, "Damn it, what are you saying?"

Hannes sat down on a bench and waited.

"Hannes? Get here now! Mr. Ternheim was just found. He's dead!"

"You're kidding me! What . . . Where . . . ?"

"Get here as fast as you can. I'll call for backup."

"All right, I'll change and—"

"No, get here now!"

When Hannes arrived at the old casino, there were already several emergency vehicles parked in the circular driveway in front of the building. A worried Hannes wrinkled his forehead. Things could get quite unpleasant for Ben. Apparently, it had been a bad idea after all to stage his protest against Lagussa. He quickly headed for the building. A senior colleague who had also been on the beach on Sunday recognized him and raised the police tape. "I'm warning you, he doesn't look any better than his sister did on that damn beach."

Hannes nodded and gulped. Two deaths in one week. Was he really cut out for this?

When he got to the scene, he saw Anna, who was leaning against a column, her face pale. She stood up and walked over. He felt uncomfortable wearing such inappropriate clothing while she was standing across from him in her elegant dress.

"What's going on?" she whispered. "I . . ." Her voice cracked and she began to sob. He stood in front of her with his arms hanging by his side.

"She discovered the body," a colleague whispered to him in a sympathetic voice.

Hannes continued to stand there like a statue before finally taking Anna into his arms and leading her to a small bench. She hid her face in her hands and could not hold back the tears. He decided against comforting her with words and stroked her back instead. Slowly, her body relaxed, and she leaned against him.

"Feeling better?" he asked.

She nodded, and he rested his hand on her shoulder.

She raised her head and looked at him with moist eyes. "We hadn't seen him for hours. So I thought I'd look up here. I remembered that Mr. Ternheim had insisted on a room where he could talk in private with key guests. That's why we rented the conference room as well."

Anna seemed to stare past Hannes and fell silent. He moved a little to get her attention. She blinked and turned toward him, and her eyes filled with tears again.

"The door was closed . . . I knocked. When no response came, I opened it . . . and saw him lying right there," she said, her voice choked.

"Hannes!"

When he looked up, Old Fritz was standing in front of him.

"Please come with me. I want to show you something."

"I'll be back soon," Hannes said to Anna, squeezing her arm. He got up and followed Fritz across the hall. Anna remained on the bench, staring at the floor.

"Will she be all right?" Fritz asked.

"I think so. The sight was too much for her. She's devastated."

"Not surprised. Take a look for yourself."

Maria came to meet them at the doorway, wearing white latex gloves. With a languid flick of the hand, she brushed a strand of hair behind her ears. "Be careful, Hannes, it's not a pretty sight."

He wondered if he had a reputation for being queasy after the incident on the beach. As a precaution, he kept some distance from the center of the room, where a figure lay surrounded by several colleagues from forensics. When one of the colleagues stood, Hannes flinched.

Ternheim's face had gone blue; the fixed eyes stared at the ceiling. The body was twisted slightly, and the sleeves of his suit and shirt were pushed up on his left arm. Even from a distance, it was possible to see that the skin was branded on the forearm with black numbers. Hannes immediately thought of Helene Ternheim's forearm.

He cautiously stepped closer and kept his eyes fixed on the dead man's arm. This time, the tattoo wasn't so clumsy: there were no red marks. Six numbers stood out on the pale skin. Four of the numbers were clearly recognizable, while the other two were slightly blurred. Again, it didn't appear to be the work of a professional. Slowly his gaze traveled up the body, and his breath faltered. What he couldn't see from the doorway leaped at him from up close. The mouth was wide open and seemed to be stuffed with something.

"Heavy stuff, right?" said Fritz, rubbing his scar.

"What's he got in his mouth?"

"Not only his mouth. Bank notes were stuffed all the way down his throat. He suffocated to death. Slowly."

Goose bumps ran down Hannes's arms, and he turned away from the gruesome sight. "But . . . why didn't he resist? His hands aren't tied. Was he knocked out?"

Fritz shook his head. He had a sallow complexion but otherwise appeared in control. "The medical examiner guesses a strong sedative was used. He must have been given a high dosage so he was unable to defend himself."

Hannes glanced at the body again. "The tattoo. Are they the same numbers that were on his sister's arm?"

"We don't know yet. We haven't compared them, especially since it was so hard to make out what was on her arm. But we found something else over in the corner."

They rounded a large conference table, and Fritz pointed to a small object on the floor. It reminded Hannes of a small hairdryer but was significantly narrower and had a metal tip.

"What is that?" Hannes asked.

"A tattoo machine, and according to our medical examiner, a fairly new one."

"How could anyone be so stupid to leave this here?" Hannes asked.

"Maybe he—or she—was in a hurry and was afraid of getting caught? But you're definitely right: that was a major mistake. Our forensics team found fingerprints on it."

"And?"

"And what?"

"Did we find a match?"

"We don't work that fast!" Fritz stepped aside as a colleague from forensics came by and carefully placed the tattoo machine in a plastic bag.

"We'll be done shortly, Fritz," he said. "The body will be brought to the medical examiner's. Maria's already on the way there and will conduct an autopsy. We couldn't find his cell phone."

"Thanks! Hannes, please see to it that Ms. Stahl gets home safely. But under no circumstances should she stay in her own apartment. If she received that death threat from the same person responsible for this, then we have to keep a careful eye on her."

"Sure," Hannes said. "What should I do after that?"

"Get some sleep! Tomorrow some clues will hopefully turn up. Try not to sleep in this time. Meet me in my office at nine."

Hannes left without protest. Anna was still as he had left her and looked at him with big eyes. His stomach was in knots, and when he saw the distraught look on her face, he was overcome with sympathy.

"I'll take you home, okay?"

She nodded. He helped her to her feet; she seemed completely numb. "I just want to go to bed."

They walked out to his car. When Hannes got in and started the engine, she leaned back in her seat and closed her eyes.

"It's good you're staying with your friend," he said. "You shouldn't go back to your place."

Anna opened her eyes. "Tina's at a wedding and won't be back until tomorrow."

He shifted in his seat. He didn't want Anna staying alone in her friend's apartment. He weighed the options until he had worked up enough courage to propose an alternative.

"If you want, you can sleep where I'm staying tonight. I'm sure Ben won't mind another guest. I can sleep on the couch in the living room and you can have the guest room."

Anna looked relieved. "That would be really nice," she said. "Tina's apartment is quite large and I don't want to be there alone."

"I can understand that. Let's pick up some of your stuff and head to Ben's."

As Hannes opened the door to Ben's cottage, Socks ran toward them and jumped around. The house was completely dark; evidently, Ben wasn't back yet.

"Do you have any alcohol?" Anna asked. "I could use something before bed."

"There should be beer here," he said and went to rifle through the fridge. When he returned to the front door with two beer bottles, he found Anna snuggling with Socks on the patio.

They sat in silence for a while, lost in thought. The garden radiated a peaceful serenity and seemed to have a calming effect on Anna.

"I've never seen a dead person before," she said. "It's a strange feeling when you've just seen these people alive, and then suddenly they're lying there lifeless and . . . there's nothing left in them."

Hannes nodded. "I just don't understand why . . . Now Mr. Ternheim too," he said. "I was almost certain he had something to do with his sister's death."

"Well, that's definitely been sorted out," Anna said. "Don't you have any other suspects?"

"Not really. But maybe we overlooked something. What do you think?"

She shrugged and held Socks tighter. "I have absolutely no idea. I especially don't get the tattoos. What are they supposed to mean?"

Hannes almost told her that Ms. Ternheim's forearm also bore the black numbers, but he didn't.

"Do the tattooed numbers mean anything to you?" he asked.

"No, why?"

He explained his suspicions.

"You're right! The photos I saw in Ms. Ternheim's office had concentration camp prisoners with numbers tattooed on them. And that was the reason for tonight's protest! Maybe they didn't stop with their little film screening."

Once again, Hannes's thoughts returned to Ben. He seemed to lack any sense of respect and had staged his protest as planned. He would have to ask Ben some extremely uncomfortable questions in the next few days.

"I don't think so," he said and was surprised at his certainty. "But you're right about one thing. Someone's definitely targeting Lagussa. Would any competitors resort to this?"

"You seem to have a pretty poor opinion of the pharmaceutical industry. We're not the mafia!"

Anna insisted, despite his protests, on sleeping on the couch in the living room and let him have the guest room. As she closed the door behind her, it was already well past midnight and Ben was nowhere to be found. As a precaution, Hannes wrote a note explaining Anna's presence and hung it on the door. He left the patio lights on so Ben would see the warning. Then he quietly closed the door to the guest room and undressed down to his new underwear.

Exhausted, he turned on his side and shut his eyes. He heard footsteps on the patio. Then the door opened and someone quietly entered the hall. A little later, water running in the bathroom and the sound of a closing door confirmed that Ben had made it home.

He couldn't even think of sleep. For a long time, Hannes tossed and turned. Then he heard a noise at the door. The knob turned, and a faint light streamed into the room.

"Hannes? Are you awake?" Anna whispered.

He sat up in bed. "I'm awake. Having trouble sleeping too?"

He could hear the sound of bare feet getting closer, and then Anna sat down on the bed. "No, I fell asleep immediately, but then I had a bad dream."

"I'm not surprised. Anything I can do?"

"No. Well. It's just . . . I don't want to be alone. I have this constant fear that someone will come and . . . and do something to me. Can I sleep with you? Don't take this the wrong way. And if you'd prefer not to, that's perfectly fine. Then I'll get Socks to join me on the sofa."

"Uh, sure. No, that's fine, no problem!" He found it difficult to keep his voice under control. "Socks is probably in Ben's room, anyway."

He slid to the side and lifted the blanket. Anna quickly slipped into bed.

"Thanks, you really did save me today," she said.

Despite the long day, her hair smelled fresh. Hannes struggled to control his breathing. What was she expecting? Was this an invitation? Then he noticed Anna had fallen asleep. This new sleeping arrangement was not very conducive to his efforts to get some rest. Anna muttered something in her sleep and shifted. Her breath hit his cheek, and her hand rested on his bare chest. She winced and moaned softly without changing position. Obviously she was still plagued by bad dreams. He put his arm around her. Anna instantly calmed down and began to breathe deeply again. Hannes slowly began to relax and enjoy the situation. It had been a long time since a woman had curled up next to him.

FRIDAY NIGHT INTO SATURDAY MORNING

Finally awake! From a dream that could not be shaken off for years. However, relief is short-lived. The sadistic director of these dreams has just devised a new variant: a nightmare embedded in another nightmare.

The eyes peer from a face dripping with sweat at the beloved body lying peacefully sleeping under a blanket only a few inches away. The face is relaxed, the hands folded.

Suddenly this body struggles to breathe, hands clutch at the chest, and then—cruel immobility. The ever-familiar chest rises and falls no more.

Fear, chaos, panic, screams. Someone shakes the motionless body. Strange men in orange jackets, electrodes of a defibrillator placed on the bare chest, the lifeless body jolts. Again and again.

Then, silence and emptiness. Forever.

SATURDAY MORNING

A loud knock roused Hannes from sleep. Anna was still asleep, but the pounding at the door finally woke her. She pushed the blanket aside. Hannes watched the rise and fall of her chest, veiled only by her shirt. He carefully climbed over her and walked to the front door. He was surprised when he opened it and found Fritz flanked by two colleagues in uniform.

"Did I oversleep again?" asked Hannes.

"No, I'm not here because of you. I'm here because of him!" Fritz pointed at Ben, who was just coming out of his bedroom.

"What's going on?" Ben asked and rubbed his eyes.

"Yeah, Fritz, what is going on? What do you want from him?"

"Mr. Sattler, you're under arrest," Fritz said. "Please put some clothes on."

"What?" Hannes gasped. "Why do you want to arrest Ben? Because of the protest yesterday?"

"If you consider the murder of Mr. Ternheim a form of protest, then you're absolutely right."

"I have nothing to do with a murder," Ben said, outraged.

"See to it that he puts on clothes and doesn't escape through the bathroom window!" Fritz said.

"Fritz," whispered Hannes, "what makes you think Ben has something to do with Ternheim's murder? Just because his group briefly hijacked the event doesn't mean they killed the managing director."

"You may be right, but the fact that your friend's fingerprints were found on the tattoo machine is pretty damning."

Hannes froze.

"You heard right. Forensics examined the fingerprints last night. They were a little smudged, but could still be used against our database. Ben's prints are a 95 percent match with those found on the machine. The remaining 5 percent you can attribute to the smudge. He probably tried to wipe it clean but missed a spot."

"But, I . . . I can't believe it! Ben wouldn't—"

"How long have you known him? A week? And that's enough for you to judge whether he's capable of murder?" He forced a laugh. "I've arrested murderers who spent years leading normal family lives, and no one, not even their wives, had the slightest suspicion. Besides, I didn't say he had to be the killer. But he at least held the tattoo machine in his hands, maybe while someone else stuffed Mr. Ternheim like a Christmas goose. Thirty banknotes were removed from his mouth and trachea."

The idea that Hannes had been fooled by Ben was unfathomable for him.

"We were able to find out more about this group too," Fritz said. "The boys managed to fake ID cards. It's unclear how they came across an original to use as a template. They set everything up in the afternoon so all they had to do in the evening was plug in the cable and play their message in the hall. They probably hid somewhere in the building until the start of the event. Your friend is pretty recognizable, and an employee was able to recall a young man with blond dreadlocks."

Hannes leaned against the door frame.

"You all right over there?" Fritz yelled to his colleagues in the hall-way, who were waiting outside Ben's bedroom door. "What's taking so long?"

The police officers shrugged. "Hurry up!" one of them yelled and pushed the door open. "Holy shit!" He ran into the room.

Fritz rushed to the end of the corridor, followed by Hannes.

Except for the officers, the bedroom was empty, and the window was wide open.

"Watching the bathroom window doesn't mean you can leave him alone in here! Damn it!" Fritz ran to the window and scanned the area behind the house. "He's gone."

He led Hannes into the hall, while the other officers spoke franti-cally into their radios and gave a physical description. "It is unbeliev-able," he said. "The guy was sitting in front of us the whole time, and when we finally realized who he was, those two idiots let him escape. Ben probably let you stay because he knew you were working on the case. He even helped with the investigation by giving you background information on Lagussa. He just wanted to find out what leads we were foll—"

He paused as the door to the guest room opened and Anna came out in her underwear and a T-shirt. Fritz looked back and forth between her and Hannes.

"That's . . . I should . . ." Hannes said. "It's not how it looks."

"It's true," Anna said. "I was afraid to be alone last night, and that's all there is to it."

"Uh, sure," Fritz said, scratching his head. "Anyway, Hannes, put something on, I'll be out here."

"What's going on?" Anna whispered as Hannes ushered her back into the room and closed the door.

He tried to explain the new twist in a whisper.

"You mean I spent the night in the murderer's house? That he was the one who stuck that note on my bike?" She collapsed on the bed and stared at Hannes in disbelief.

"I'm sorry," he said. "Evidently, I'm not so good at reading people. I've only known Ben a few days. I probably should've wondered more why he was so quick to offer me the room. Now I'm going to look like a complete moron to everyone at the station."

He put on some clothes. Anna watched him in silence.

"Where should I go now?" she asked. "Certainly not home. But I can't stay here either."

"Can you stay with another friend for the day?"

"Probably. I'm beginning to feel like a criminal myself, running from one hiding spot to the next. Can't I get some personal protection—from you?" She gave a mischievous grin.

"In extreme cases, yes. I don't think you're at risk. Ben knows we're on his heels, and you've already told us everything you know. Spend the day with friends, I'll contact you later, and then we can decide what to do."

"All right. Let me put some clothes on first."

Hannes left the room and walked over to Fritz in the living room. Suddenly, the young police officer ran in.

"Fritz, you have to look at what we found in the bedside table." He waved a plastic bag, which Hannes immediately recognized.

Fritz picked up the bag and looked inside. He showed the contents to Hannes. "Those are twenties. The notes removed from Mr. Ternheim were all twenties."

Colleagues from forensics had arrived and began to comb the house. "Is there a café near here?" Fritz asked. "I skipped breakfast today."

"There's a bakery down the street. Should I go get us something?"

Fritz looked at Hannes in irritation. "What do you mean 'get'? Do you think we're just going to sit out on our main suspect's patio and have a leisurely breakfast? I hope you realize you'll have to move back into your apartment today."

"There's a small café on the way to my apartment. They do a good breakfast," Hannes said. "Let me get my stuff out of the guest room."

"Do that," said Fritz. "And bring Ben's laptop, which we're seizing as evidence."

"Aren't you supposed to be catching this Ben guy instead of sitting here having breakfast?" Anna teased as she sat down opposite Hannes and Fritz at the small café.

"Can't catch criminals on an empty stomach," Fritz said as he sliced a croissant down the middle. "Besides, we have guys on it. Everyone's keeping an eye out for him, and if that doesn't work, we'll put his picture in the paper and on television. Hannes, do you know anyone from Ben's activist group? He could be holing up with one of them."

"Nope. They're kind of just a random group."

Socks looked at Hannes with sad eyes and whined.

"There, there, it's all right." Hannes patted Socks. "I don't know where Ben is either, but we'll find him soon."

"I think the poor guy's hungry," Anna said, and Socks licked his lips and barked twice.

"You're right! He wasn't given anything to eat."

Hannes quickly ran to a small supermarket and returned with a pack of dry dog food. Anna had asked the waiter for a bowl of water, and Socks scarfed down his breakfast.

Hannes suddenly had an idea. He grabbed Ben's laptop and started it up.

"What are you doing?" asked Fritz.

"There's Wi-Fi here. I want to show Anna the documents about Lagussa's Nazi past collected by Ben's network."

"And what good will that do?" she asked.

"If they're the same images and documents that were also in Ms. Ternheim's bag, then we can assume the material came from Ben's circle."

"Or from Ben," said Fritz. "Maybe he even passed himself off as Mark von Wittenberg."

"You once accidentally saw Ms. Ternheim meeting with this mysterious von Wittenberg guy, right?" Hannes said. Anna nodded. "I know you only looked briefly, but was he a tall young guy with blond dreadlocks?"

"Definitely not. He stood with his back to me, so I couldn't see his face, but he definitely didn't have blond dreadlocks. He also didn't look too young."

"How can you be so sure if you didn't see his face?" asked Fritz.

"No idea. It's just a gut feeling, probably because of his posture. Anyway, it couldn't have been Ben."

"That means it was someone else from the group, if they're the same documents," Fritz said.

"It doesn't necessarily mean it was someone from Ben's group," Hannes said. "Several groups have access to the forum and archive. Damn it! I of course forgot the piece of paper with the log-in information. Without the password, I can't get on."

"Try www.truth-about-lagussa.de," said Fritz. "According to the video from last night, all the information is supposed to be posted on the site."

"Oh, that's right." Hannes typed in the address and the page loaded. "That actually all looks very familiar to me. Anna, take a look, please."

She held the laptop in her lap and concentrated on the screen, opening file after file.

"Well," she finally said. "I recognize some of this—photos, for example, and then this document here and the delivery receipt." She turned the computer so the detectives could see the screen. "But I didn't look too closely at the papers in the office, and it's been a while."

"Hmm, so maybe, maybe not," Fritz said.

"I don't think so," said Hannes. "There was nothing about this elsewhere on the Internet, and the documents on the site come from a variety of sources and whistle-blowers. No one person could have had all of them without first downloading them from the site."

"But why would someone from this network give Ms. Ternheim the documents if there was already a plan to expose these things?" asked Anna.

"That's exactly it," said Hannes. "I don't think it was someone from Ben's group! Mr. Ternheim received an anonymous warning last night. Maybe the same person provided Ms. Ternheim with the information— either because the person read in the forum that a protest was in the works and he just wanted to warn Ms. Ternheim, or because he wanted to take action against Lagussa, just not publicly."

"Maybe blackmail?" Anna said.

"This is all wild speculation," Fritz said. "Of course we should consider all angles, but we have a prime suspect we need to focus on now. Whatever role von Wittenberg played is beside the point."

"Who's going to take care of Socks?" asked Anna.

Hannes sighed and looked at Fritz. "I'll have to take him . . ."

"Absolutely not," Fritz said. "We can't take care of a dog now too. Ms. Stahl?"

"I guess," she said. "I can watch him today, but you'll have to take over tonight, Hannes."

"Agreed," he said. Then his phone began vibrating on the table, and he picked it up. He listened to the caller for a minute without speaking. "Are you absolutely certain?" he asked and then thanked the caller. "I don't think we should focus just on Ben. That was a colleague from the federal police. I asked her to look into the flight info for Merlin's dealer."

"I completely forgot about that guy," Fritz said.

"There's no doubt about it. Laval lied to me. He returned from the US last week on Friday and not, as he claimed, the day before yesterday."

"Here!" Fritz slammed two photos down on Hannes's desk back at the station. The two of them sat side by side and leaned over the close-ups. "The left image shows Helene Ternheim's arm, the right photo was taken last night of Christian Ternheim's arm."

"What happened to your arm?" asked Hannes, pointing to a giant bandage.

"Oh, nothing. My neighbor has a small cat. I can't stand those things. But the neighbor accepted a package for me, and when I picked it up, that fur ball sunk its claws into my arm. Now you know why I prefer dogs . . . But back to the Ternheims, Hannes."

Hannes grinned, then grabbed the two pictures to take a closer look. "We can only decipher three numbers off Ms. Ternheim's. The first is a four, the next two are illegible. Then come an eight and a two. And the last we're not sure about."

"That's right," said Fritz. "The first four numbers are clearly visible on Mr. Ternheim, a four, a one, a three, and an eight. The other two aren't very clear."

"So the four and the eight are in the same position on both arms," Hannes said. "And here: the second number on Ms. Ternheim could be a one or maybe a seven."

"And the fifth number on Mr. Ternheim resembles a two," said Fritz. "It appears it's the same sequence. The question is, what's the last number, and why do both victims have it?"

"And the next question is why Mr. Ternheim had money crammed down his throat. Maybe Anna was right, and it's the result of blackmail?"

"Possible," Fritz said.

"At least it's now definitely clear that Ms. Ternheim was the victim of a violent crime," said Hannes. "What does the senior medical examiner have to say about Maria's assumption that Mr. Ternheim was also drugged with a sedative?"

Fritz moved with a groan. "Still nothing. You're visiting Maria at noon. The results should be available then."

"And what do I do until then?"

"Grab a car and drive out to see old Ternheim. Someone has to inform him of his son's death."

"Why me?"

"Because I have a doctor's appointment. After that, I'd like to keep an eye on our colleagues to make sure the search for Ben is done properly. I don't want him to get away again. We should get a move on. The boss called me last night. He wanted to give us backup when he learned of the second death. It took me a while, but I convinced him to hold off. I explained that having to bring additional colleagues up to speed would be more of a hindrance. Steffen gives us until Monday. If we haven't solved the case by then, Isabelle and Per will be joining us."

"Fine, I'll head out to the country," Hannes said.

"Here!" Fritz pushed the photographs over to him. "Show old Ternheim these photos, perhaps he can make sense of them. And tell him how his son died. Perhaps it'll mean something to him."

Hannes felt an inner restlessness as he drove along the winding roads. He scanned the scenery as if Ben might emerge at any moment. He was still shaken by the morning's events and racked his brain for a plausible explanation of why Ben's fingerprints were on the tattoo machine.

At the old lighthouse, he stopped and got out of the car. The idyllic hilly landscape stretched as far as the eye could see, and the morning sun warmed his face. He walked around the old walls and sat down with his back against the warmed stones. Waves gently lapped the shore below, and a large ferry cruised along the horizon.

Hannes closed his eyes and concentrated on the sounds around him. No voices, no cars. He was surrounded by the faint roar of the ocean, the melodious chirping of small songbirds, the screech of the seagulls, and the slight rustle of the wind in the branches of a birch tree. The air tasted salty and sweet, and Hannes wished he could sit there forever. The chaos of the day gradually faded, and when he opened his eyes twenty minutes later, he felt refreshed and clearheaded.

He walked back to his vehicle with renewed energy—because Mrs. Meier was off on weekends, he'd managed to score a brand-new Audi—and headed down the narrow path that led to the old man's cottage. Just before the road entered the small forest, there was another brief view of the beach below. Hannes slammed on the brakes.

In the distance, a solitary figure sat perched on a small boulder looking out over the sea. Hannes got out of the car and stood at the edge of the cliff. He instantly recognized the hunched back, staff, and woolen cap.

Hannes locked the car door and looked for a safe way to descend to the beach. He couldn't see a path and wondered how the old man had gotten down there. He decided to walk a little farther until he came to the edge of the forest, which stretched to the cliff. Various storms had broken the branches of the crooked pines, and Hannes had to climb over torn-up roots and felled trunks. He stumbled upon a narrow path with logs serving as steps which led down to the beach.

Hannes strolled across the sand to the small rocks and stopped beside the old man staring at the water. Lying in the sand beside him were wax pastels and a sketchbook, the paper untouched, and a silver flask.

"Hello, Mr. Ternheim," Hannes said.

Ternheim looked him in the eye, nodded, and turned back to the water. Was this really the same man who used forced labor at his company and had supported the rise of the Nazi Party? Who had tested his drugs on prisoners?

Hannes sat down beside Ternheim, crossed his legs, and looked at the water. "A beautiful place."

The old man nodded.

Hannes looked at his cane and ran his fingers over the carved figures. "Do they mean anything?"

Old Ternheim carefully laid the cane across his knees. His wrinkled, clawlike fingers ran almost lovingly along the notches. "Life," he whispered. Hannes had to lean in to hear him. "My life . . ."

He spoke! Hannes was shocked. The old man continued to caress the carvings, as if doing so brought forth memories. A stunned Hannes stared at him. He had done it! The old guy had finally spoken.

"Your life?" Hannes asked. "These figures represent your life?"

Old Ternheim looked him in the eye. Hannes shuddered. His eyes didn't seem to correspond with the rest of his body: they seemed simultaneously young and old. The intense blue of the iris merged with the deep-black pupils, which flashed with small golden flecks of light.

The old man grabbed Hannes's hand and pulled it toward the bottom of the cane. His touch was unpleasant and reminded him of dried fruit. He placed Hannes's index finger on the lowest notch, then led him slowly and gently to the other end of the cane.

"From then till now," he said. His vocal cords appeared to be completely out of practice, and he had great difficulty producing the sounds.

Hannes nodded. "So you carved different episodes of your life into the wood?"

For a moment there was silence. Ternheim looked out over the vast sea. "What was. And what is."

Hannes looked at the upper end of the cane, which the carved figures had already almost reached. Not too much space was left for more moments. He leaned forward and inspected one of the symbols more closely. Even if it was an older and already somewhat faded carving, Hannes could clearly make out a swastika.

"Mr. Ternheim, I bring you more sad news. Last night your son was found dead during a charity gala. He was murdered, and we're sure the death of your daughter was not an accident."

He let Old Ternheim absorb this. He sat completely still for a while and then sighed. His head fell forward; his eyes closed. He raised his head and looked over at Hannes. The golden flecks of light in his pupils had disappeared.

"How?" he asked.

"Both were slipped a sedative. Helene was drowned, and Christian choked to death on a bunch of twenty-euro notes which were crammed down his throat." Hannes felt it best to speak bluntly now. "Their left forearms were tattooed," he said, unfolding the printouts of the photographs. "Please take a look at these photos. The left image is of Helene's arm, the right is Christian's. It's a six-digit number, and we assume the first five digits are: four, one, three, eight, and two. The last number is indecipherable. Do these numbers mean anything to you?"

Ternheim stared at the photos in silence. A tear fell onto the paper. "Crime and punishment," he whispered. "Crime and punishment."

"What do you mean?"

The old man did not answer.

"Mr. Ternheim, your children have been murdered, and I want to find out who did this. You have to explain what you mean. Are you talking about what your company did in the Nazi era? If so, what do Helene and Christian have to do with it? They weren't even born then."

"The past . . . casts shadows." After looking a second time at the two photographs, Heinrich Ternheim folded them and handed them back to Hannes. "Maria and Josef," he whispered.

"What do they have to do with it?"

"Maria and Josef. Look for them!"

Hannes scratched his head. What did Jesus's parents have to do with this case?

Suddenly the old man grabbed the sketchbook and a black pastel. With quick strokes, the image of a barn appeared before Hannes's eyes. He watched as the crippled but astonishingly nimble fingers sketched a car half hidden inside the barn. Hannes shook his head. Ternheim then grabbed a yellow pastel and colored in the car. Hannes looked at the drawing. The vehicle was low to the ground, and he immediately remembered the sports car.

"Is this your daughter's car? Do you know where it is?"

"Crime and punishment," he said again and pulled a knife out of his pocket. He tucked his cane between his legs and began carving another figure at the top. Hannes watched him carefully sculpt the wood.

Hannes got to his feet. At that moment, the old man's hands hesitated, and he turned to him. He fumbled around in his pocket and pulled out a photo. The terror-stricken eyes of an emaciated and pale young woman in gray-and-blue striped pajamas peered at Hannes. He instantly recognized her. He had seen a photo of her three days before and had found her extremely attractive but couldn't remember her name now.

"That's the woman who's been missing for a week! Where did you get this photo? Who is she?"

"Merle . . ." he said. "Young and innocent. In great danger . . ." He gathered his art materials and walked away.

Hannes quickly called Fritz and informed him of the latest development.

"That's very interesting," said Fritz. "I'll let Marcel know immediately. He should find out if there's any connection between Merle von Hohenstein and the Ternheims. And you said she looks like a prisoner in the photo?"

"I'm not sure, but she seems terrified and is in a room with no windows. Apart from a bed, I couldn't see any other furnishings. Something's definitely not right! We need to find her!"

"At least she's probably still alive. I'll tell Marcel that this missing-person report needs to be given immediate priority. Did you keep the photo?"

"Of course!"

"Then come back to the station and give it to Marcel. Why didn't you grill the old guy to find out where he got the photo and what he has to do with this woman?"

"You know he's not one to talk. Besides, I tried, but he—"

"Okay, okay. Just come back to the station."

As Hannes walked back to the car, he wondered what crime and punishment, Maria and Josef, and Merle in danger had to do with the case and how it all fit together. He tossed the small drawing of the yellow sports car onto the passenger seat and started the engine. The car bounced along the dirt road, and Hannes accelerated after turning at the lighthouse. *The murders have something to do with Lagussa's past,* Hannes thought. But what role did the old man's children play in all of this? Maybe it wasn't about Helene and Christian. Maybe they were just pawns meant to get at the old man. But that also didn't make sense. Why wouldn't the killer just target the actual criminal? Merlin lived such an isolated existence that it would be easy to surprise him. Maybe the murders were meant to be an attack on the company. Maybe the two Ternheims knew too much. But how did Merle von Hohenstein fit into this story?

A slow-moving tractor appeared on the road and Hannes was forced to slow down. The stretch of road was too narrow and winding for him to pass. Mr. Olsen turned around and waved, then stopped the tractor and got out. Hannes did the same.

"Hello, Mr. Olsen! No rest for the weary, huh?"

The farmer laughed and wiped his hands on his pants before he shook hands with him. "It's been a long time since I've had a true weekend. The days of the week don't matter to us. It's the weather that counts."

"Well, you've been pretty lucky with the weather."

"I wouldn't say that! The heat isn't good for the plants, and the bad weather last weekend destroyed part of our crop. They're predicting another thunderstorm for tomorrow, so we still have a lot to get done today. Hey, I was listening to the radio this morning. Is it true that the hermit's son was killed too?"

"That's correct. The company's now left without a CEO, unless the old man sees fit to take the helm again."

Olsen shook his head. "What drama! Within days, an entire family is destroyed. I can't even begin to imagine what it must be like to learn that your own kids have been murdered." His eyes fell on the small drawing in the seat. "Did Merlin draw a picture of our beautiful countryside?"

"No, no, that's just . . . Hold on, do you recognize the building?"

"Of course! There aren't very many barns around here, and the drawing's very detailed. That's Mats Petersen's barn. When he died, we bought the fields from his heirs. The buildings, however, have been abandoned for years."

Hannes remembered his first visit to the Olsens' farm. "You said on Tuesday that this road leads behind the lighthouse to an old farm. Is that the farm in this painting?"

"Yes, I'm absolutely cert—"

Hannes jumped in the car. "Thank you, you've been a huge help!" he said, shifted into gear, and took off. The lighthouse whizzed past him on the left, and a few yards later the asphalt was so torn up that Hannes was forced to a crawl. Fields extended into the distance on either side of him, separated by short hedgerows. After cresting a small hill, he saw three buildings standing close to one another. The road ended at the entrance to the old farm. A rusty gate blocked the drive-way. Hannes got out and opened the gate. He stepped into the yard and looked around. The farm was the complete opposite of the Olsens' tidy place. Nature was already reclaiming the area. Sprawling plants covered the ground and climbed up the walls of the buildings. The roof of the smallest building had already collapsed. Bits of brick were scattered everywhere. The main building still seemed reasonably intact, but Hannes was convinced that even when it was inhabited, this farm was no jewel. The windows were covered in dirt, and everything seemed gray and unwelcoming.

Hannes turned to the third building, which was apparently once used as a barn. It was clearly the barn captured on the paper. He walked toward it. The sloping corrugated tin roof was riddled with large holes, and stones had fallen out of the walls. The barn door had been secured with a new chain and a modern padlock, which made Hannes suspicious.

He slowly circled the building and tried peering through a window, but he could only see outlines through the dirty panes. He ran back to the car and grabbed a blanket from the trunk, which he used to rub the window clean. Since the pane was caked with dirt on the inside, he still couldn't see into the room, but the outlines were at least a little clearer. In addition to some agricultural equipment, he could make out the outline of a car hidden under a tarp.

Hannes grabbed a rock and chucked it as hard as he could at the window. The glass shattered and flew everywhere. Hannes wrapped his hand in the blanket and pushed the few remaining sharp pieces of glass out of the frame. He pulled the window up and crawled through the small opening. He slid down to the ground and waited for his eyes to adjust to the dim light.

The interior of the barn was filled with random boxes and old farming equipment. And his eyes hadn't been playing tricks on him: a gray tarp blanketed a low car. Hannes lifted the tarp and felt a tire. He quickly unhooked a few more hooks, which had been used to attach the tarp to the body, and threw the cloth halfway across the car roof to uncover a yellow Corvette from the seventies. A look at the license plate confirmed that it was Helene Ternheim's missing sports car.

The chain and padlock fell to the ground with a loud clatter. Fritz then carelessly tossed the bolt aside. Hannes had told him over the phone what he had found, and the old detective had immediately swung into action.

"Forensics will be here any minute, but we should take a closer look around this barn as quickly as possible. We've already lost enough time," he said. "Hopefully you haven't touched anything?"

Hannes shook his head. "I only pulled back the tarp, otherwise everything's as it was."

"Incredible," Fritz said as he pushed open the barn door to reveal the half-covered sports car. "We could have been looking for ages! How did the old guy know the car was hidden here?"

Hannes shrugged. "Mr. Ternheim doesn't just toss around information, you know." He told Fritz about the brief conversation on the beach and then showed him the drawing.

"Crime and punishment and Maria and Josef?" said Fritz. "The crime I get, after what you've told me about the company's past. But what's with the Bible reference?"

Hannes shrugged again. "At least he got his voice back. Maybe next time he'll be a little clearer."

Fritz rubbed his chin. "We can only hope! Especially with regard to this missing Ms. von Hohenstein. If she really is in danger, then we have to get the old man to talk. Well, we'll definitely search the entire farm. Maybe she's being held in one of the buildings."

"It's still a mystery to me how Merlin came across this photo," Hannes said while Fritz circled the Corvette and scrutinized it. "Pretty dented for an expensive car, huh?" he added and pointed to the front of the vehicle. He followed Fritz, then knelt down in front of the fender and pointed to some dents and scratches. "Ms. Ternheim seems to have been quite the driver. There are scratches all over the place, and here you can see some green paint left over from a collision."

"Forensics will take a closer look," Fritz said as he pulled a handkerchief from his pocket. He walked to the driver's side door and gripped the handle of the yellow sports car with the cloth.

"I'm sure it's locked," said Hannes.

Fritz carefully pulled the door open and looked inside. "Not much to look at," he said. He turned halfway around, and just as he was pulling his head out of the car, he bumped it against the roof, lost his balance, and fell into the car seat. "Damn it! Now I've contaminated the evidence. This damn car roof!" A red mark now graced his forehead, and Fritz stuck his arms out toward Hannes. "Pull me out; I don't want to touch anything else."

Hannes grabbed his hands and pulled Fritz out of the car.

Fritz stood stooped over in front of him and placed both hands on his lower back. "I really can't keep doing this," he said.

The sound of an engine could be heard outside. Fritz forced himself to stand up straight. "And just as our colleagues get here! I hope they can still do something with this."

Half an hour later, the barn was a completely different picture. Forensics carefully combed the entire building, and as a precaution, a few of his colleagues searched the two other houses, but they found nothing. A tow truck arrived and hauled the Corvette back to the city for inspection.

"Here's something," came a voice from the farthest corner of the barn.

Hannes followed Fritz, who hurried to the woman in the white overalls. She had just pulled an object from a wooden box.

"A purse!" shouted Hannes. "And it looks pretty new. Maybe it's Ms. Ternheim's?"

"We'll see," said Fritz. "Can you spread out the contents somewhere?"

"Let's go outside. We put down a plastic sheet out there," said the red-haired woman as she carried the purse outside. Her face betrayed her irritation after she unclasped it.

"What's wrong?" asked Fritz.

"That's what's wrong," she said, turning it so the men were able to look inside. "An acid, I suspect. It means we can't do much with the contents." She gently fumbled around the purse and pulled out a slurry of what was once paper, some cosmetics, and a cell phone.

"Shit!" said Fritz. "Can you get any data out of it?"

"Maybe we can save the SIM card and at least access some of the backed-up data. It depends how much acid seeped through the casing. But you can forget about everything else!"

"There's always a problem," Hannes said.

"I don't get why you're complaining," Fritz said. "You just solved one part of the puzzle! This new problem makes the investigation more exciting. After all, you got a confused, mute old man to talk and thus found the car. And you managed to stumble upon a connection with a missing-person case. Good job!"

Hannes's face brightened upon hearing the rare praise. "You're right," he said. "I'll give the photo of Merle von Hohenstein to Marcel before I see Maria. I'm supposed to meet with her at noon. I want to decipher those tattoos."

"Oh, speaking of tattoos, that reminds me. Our colleagues have taken a closer look at the tattoo machine and compared it with the color and the engraving technique used on Ms. Ternheim's arm. It was either the same instrument or an identical model. So Ben's our prime suspect in two murder cases. Unfortunately, there's still no trace of him. But I think I just got an idea of where I can find him."

***

At the same time, a dramatic scene was unfolding just a mile away. Ludwig Lachmann, aka Louis Laval, was exasperated with his most important and—truth be told—only artist.

Although the genius Merlin was again true to himself and didn't exchange a single word with the dealer, his body language was clear when Laval handed him a new contract. A determined Old Ternheim shook his head and pushed the paper aside.

"But what do you want?" Laval said. He found it more and more difficult to control himself. "We've worked well together in recent years. Our contract runs out soon, and if you want your images to sell in the future, we need a new agreement. You do want to sell your pictures, right?"

The old man again shook his head. Then Laval heard for the very first time the voice of the man who had been the source of his now squandered fortune.

"Just one more picture," said the old man. "The last picture." And that was all that he would say. He nodded toward the door.

"You're throwing me out? After all I've done for you?" said Laval. "Without me, you'd be nothing—nothing! Is your son behind this change of mind? He's dead, in case you forgot, just like your daughter. And . . . and . . ." The little man was at a loss for words. Then his eyes narrowed. "Is there someone else? Are you going to work with another agent? You'll regret this!"

He stormed toward the door and then turned around once more. His hand trembled as he pointed it at Old Ternheim. "I'll see to it that not a single picture of yours is ever sold again! Mark my words."

The door slammed behind him with a bang. Merlin turned back to the large easel in order to finish his last work of art.

***

If Hannes and Fritz had left the abandoned farm just a few minutes earlier, they probably would have seen Ludwig Lachmann's green sedan turn onto the road at the lighthouse and speed away.

Fritz gazed at the lighthouse: he had always had a soft spot for light-houses. Then his eyes returned to Hannes's car in front of him, which coasted along the winding route. *It's time this guy buys himself a new car. Then he won't get carried away whenever he uses someone else's,* he thought.

As he passed by Hohenberg Farm, Fritz thought he felt the gaze of the old farmer's wife on him. There was little in this desolate area that escaped the woman.

At a small intersection a little farther on, Hannes took advantage of the straightaway and accelerated, while Fritz slowed down and despite the complete isolation put on his turn signal. Let the speed demon race back to the city! Whenever he was in the area, Fritz liked to stop by his boat and take a fifteen-minute breather.

After parking his Jeep, he wandered over to the dock and could already feel the stress melt away and his mind clear. He looked lovingly on the old cutter. He had invested so much work and material into the boat and was proud of it. His handiwork had paid off.

"A real beaut," came a voice from beside him.

Startled, Fritz took his eyes off his *Lena*. "Oh, Ole. I didn't hear you sneak up. True, *Lena* is one hell of a girl. How's your old *Seagull*?"

"Back on the water. Thankfully, the damage looked worse than it really was. But still, you should have let me teach that pompous fool a lesson or two."

"Be glad I held you back. The guy probably would have sued you. He badly needs the dough."

"Well, in any case, he won't be showing up around here anytime soon. What really annoys me is that I had helped him out with a rope the day before. I even gave it to him!"

"Oh? On Saturday? When he was here with his blonde?"

"Blonde? I didn't see any lady."

"Eh, someone else saw her," Fritz said and then told his old school friend how the private detective had been shadowing the real estate agent.

"Oh, now I understand," said Ole as laugh lines fanned out around his eyes. "I had been wondering about this dark-green car, an Asian make. It was over there in the parking lot. It got here shortly after the boat did. I was a little suspicious and took a look inside. There was a little guy sitting in there." Ole roared in laughter. "But he didn't see anything—he was sound asleep!"

"When was that? Had Mr. Schneider, I mean the boat owner, already cast off?"

"He had just left. I helped him untie the boat before I peeked at the car. Like I said, I'm angry as hell that I help—"

"Forget about that! Did you see a woman on board? Or at least, a woman go on board?"

"What's it matter to you? No, I didn't see a woman, but of course—"

"That little bastard of a private eye! He told us he had observed everything, but he was sleeping on the job and actually didn't see anything! Are you absolutely certain he was asleep?"

"Yes, of course! His mouth was wide open and he was drooling."

Fritz frantically rummaged through his wallet. "I have that guy's business card here somewhere! Damn mess. If I only . . . Oh, wait, here it is!" He quickly dialed the number on the card. "Yes, Detective Janssen! Remember me?" he said into the phone. Then he let out a fierce torrent of accusations and threats of criminal consequences.

As soon as he hung up, Fritz called Hannes to brief him on the latest development.

"The guy admitted he was snoozing?"

"First he waffled, but then he conceded. He said the only woman who could have been with him was the assistant, Kustermann, because the two were constantly by each other's side. He was afraid his client would hear about his blunder and that's why he lied to us. But now he's afraid of the consequences this might have for him. So start looking into Schneider again. His work, cell phone, home, wife, neighbors—whatever. Track him down!"

"Sure," Hannes said. "I'll call you later."

Ten minutes later, Hannes called back. "Schneider's disappeared again! His cell phone was turned off, and his wife picked up at home. Or rather his soon-to-be ex-wife, if I'm correctly interpreting her outrage. She didn't mince words. She's already put the private detective's work to good use. She kicked her husband out, and as far as she knows, he's headed for the mountains with Ms. Kustermann. But she has no idea where or for how long. Mr. Schneider better hope we get to him before she does because—"

"Okay, so put out an APB. Monitor his cell, contact the various units, get the federal police involved, and so on. Ask Lauer. He'll tell you how you need to proceed. And check if there's any connection between Ben and this real estate agent."

"All right, boss," Hannes said. He was beginning to feel overwhelmed, especially since he could no longer get that photo of a terrified Merle out of his head.

The flap had been open for a few minutes. Merle's eyes had grown accustomed to the light. She was mesmerized by the sneakers she could see outside the door. She had given up hope. Her desperate yet unsuccessful attack the previous day had dashed her dreams of escaping.

She didn't care anymore what the guy on the other side of the door wanted from her. All she wanted was for it to be over. This way or that way. Let him stick her in ridiculous clothes, photograph her, and lace her food with sleeping pills. As far as she was concerned, he could stand in front of that door for hours. She had lost all will to resist.

The feet moved a little closer. Merle heard a soft metallic noise, but she couldn't pinpoint its source. Her gaze traveled up from the door, and she thought she saw a small spot of light at eye level. Suddenly it was gone. Shortly after, the sneakers moved to the left out of Merle's field of vision, and the small dot was back.

A peephole, thought Merle. *So what? Go ahead and watch me, I don't care. I don't care about anything anymore!* Her fingers stroked the splinters of wood chips she had saved from the broken tray. *The next time you look in here, you'll be surprised at what you'll see . . .*

The sneakers reappeared and a hand pushed two items into her room. Merle's face was devoid of emotion. She simply stared straight ahead. *What is that?* She already recognized the tray of food and the bottle of water. It seemed to be fries. But what was the elongated object next to the food? She looked closer. A flashlight! She would finally have light! Merle felt life course through her once more.

She looked back toward the door and saw a brief movement behind the little peephole. If he would at least talk to her! She could barely remember how another human voice sounded. Her pleading eyes stared at the door as if she were trying to hypnotize the man on the other side. And when a voice finally spoke to her, Merle wasn't sure if she had only heard the softly spoken words in her head or if they had been said aloud.

"It'll be over soon, Merle. You don't have to wait much longer for the end."

SATURDAY AT NOON

"This doesn't count as the dinner you still owe me, right?" asked Maria as she stirred her latte in a small café near the medical examiner's office.

"No, of course I didn't forget, but right now there's just too much going on. Maybe next week?"

"So you want to solve the case by next week? I've heard a buddy of yours is the prime suspect and managed to evade arrest."

Maria's question hit a sore spot. Hannes could imagine what kind of impression his colleagues had of him now. The rookie who puked when he saw his first body and then lived for a week with the Ternheims' murderer.

"It seems all they do down at the station is gossip," he said. "Unfortunately, it looks as if Ben is at least in some way involved."

"That doesn't sound very convincing . . ."

"Imagine that there's sufficient evidence to suspect that a friend of yours is guilty of killing someone. Wouldn't you search for explanations as to why she couldn't have done it?"

"And do you have any explanations?"

"No. But I also don't have any explanations as to why he would do it. Of course, there's no disputing the fingerprints on the tattoo machine, but why everything else?"

"These are things I don't have to think about, fortunately."

"Well, what did Mr. Ternheim's corpse tell you?"

Maria put her glass down and leaned back in her chair. "First, I can tell you the death occurred at about nine last night. The sedative is the same one we found in his sister's blood, but at a much higher dose. It's Letharmol, which is used to treat anxiety as well as relieve pain."

"How easy is it to get this stuff?"

"You need a prescription."

"How's it taken?"

"Either in tablet form or as drops. It's extremely fast and in higher concentrations can cause serious side effects like muscle failure and cardiac arrest."

"So what was the cause of death?"

"Asphyxiation. He likely suffered a lot. And he was pumped so full of Letharmol that he was completely helpless, his muscles paralyzed."

"And how long would it take to tattoo his arm like that?"

Maria shrugged. "I don't think whoever did the tattoo knew what he or she was doing. So it's hard to say. As a beginner, it'd probably take at least half an hour."

"Damn, that's long! Whoever did this must have nerves of steel. Someone could have walked into the room at any time."

"That's true. But maybe it was done by a professional who wants to throw us off by screwing up the tattoo."

"How do you know so much about tattoos?"

"I have three. Here, for example." She pulled her shirt up a bit so he could see her tanned, flat stomach. Curled around her belly button was a little dragon with two small flames shooting out of its mouth. "Don't you want to know where the other two are?" she asked. "One on the shoulder and another on the ankle. What do you think?"

He didn't know how to respond and laughed.

**

Hannes found some time for practice and headed to the boathouse after his meeting with Maria. This time he properly returned the patrol car and walked to his apartment. He didn't know if it was snake-free, but he had no choice. Anna had said she would bring Socks by at seven, so he only had an hour to sort out his thoughts.

He kept thinking of the young woman who was being held captive in a room somewhere. How did Ternheim get her photo, and what did Merle von Hohenstein have to do with him? Hannes had given the photo to Marcel after returning to the city, but his reaction had been lukewarm: "I can't see anything that would be of much help. The room's empty. It could be anywhere." Hannes had remembered Mrs. Olsen's statement about often seeing a young woman in the area. Marcel had promised to show her Merle's photos to see if there was a possible match.

Hannes walked into his apartment and was greeted by that slightly musty smell that comes when a place has gone without fresh air for days. He opened all the windows. Fruit flies swarmed around a rotten apple on the kitchen table.

He sat down with his laptop and a pitcher of ice-cold mineral water on the tiny balcony. He trusted that Ben was no murderer, and he couldn't for the life of him see a motive for killing the Ternheims. Although Ben fought neo-Nazis, the siblings showed no such leanings. Their father and grandfather were to blame for the company's link to the Nazi regime, so why would Ben wipe out the next generation? Was there a connection he didn't know about?

He decided to search the forum that Ben had showed him. He had retrieved the paper with the log-in information, so he had no problems opening the page. He immediately clicked on the link to the archives and scanned the contents, file by file.

He stopped when he came across the photos of concentration camp prisoners. One of the prisoners was holding out his skinny arm, and Hannes could see a series of numbers tattooed on his forearm. As he was well aware, prisoners at Auschwitz had their respective numbers tattooed on their forearms. He quickly counted six digits. If the two murders were actually related to Lagussa's Nazi past, then the tattooed numbers were definitely a message. Only what was the message?

He went back to the forum's home page and scrolled through the various topics. Lagussa was just one of many headings. One entry interested him in particular: Where is a list of concentration camp prisoners and their numbers?, a user called "tapeworm" had asked.

Several people had replied to this question, and a member named "Ralfa64" recommended a website where you could search for concentration camp prisoners according to various criteria, including names or numbers. Hannes clicked on the link, which opened a search page. He quickly entered the five numbers they could decipher on the Ternheim siblings into a field marked "Prisoner number." He was unsure what to choose as the sixth number, so he entered zero. No matches. He got the same result when he tried a one and then a two. After typing three and clicking search, a name appeared. Stunned, he fell back in his chair.

"What do you mean you found a Maria?" said Fritz over the phone.

"Old Ternheim had muttered something about a Maria and a Josef. But he wasn't talking about the Bible! I found some website where you can search for former concentration camp prisoners. I entered the numbers tattooed on the Ternheims' forearms and added a three for the sixth number. And I got a hit! Now hold tight: the number belonged to a Maria Löwenstein."

Hannes heard only breathing on the other end.

"Did you hear me? The painter recognized the numbers. He must have known it had something to do with Maria Löwenstein. We've solved the mystery of the tattoos! The murders are actually connected somehow to Lagussa's Nazi past. Maybe the murderer tried to extort the two Ternheims, but they refused."

"A stroke of genius," Fritz said. "Did you find out anything about Maria Löwenstein or a connection between her and the Ternheims?"

"No, I haven't started researching."

"The question now, of course, is who is this Josef? Maybe her husband?"

"Hold on, I can search for that right now." He tucked the phone between his ear and shoulder and entered Josef Löwenstein into the search.

"Nope, nothing. If he was her husband, then he wasn't in the concentration camp."

"Or he was at another concentration camp. Or he isn't in the database. Try to find out what you can about the prisoner. Maybe you'll stumble across a Josef Löwenstein."

"Okay, will do. Gotten anywhere searching for Ben?"

"No, we visited the home of Frank Richter, who was caught in the control room. We wanted to question him since he might have been involved with the murders. But we didn't find him or Ben. Maybe Richter has gone underground now too. We will definitely keep an eye on the apartment and expand the manhunt to include Richter. We've just checked the addresses of two other activists who've been arrested with Ben at demonstrations. The two allegedly claim they haven't seen him for weeks, and there was no evidence of him in their apartments."

"What about Ms. Ternheim's car?"

"Nothing yet. The guys from forensics are trying to save her phone's SIM card, but they probably won't get anywhere. The acid really penetrated the device."

"All right, I'll get back to you when and if I find out anything else about Maria Löwenstein or Josef."

"Do that. And if you run into Jesus while you're at it, say hi for me." Fritz hung up.

Hannes's theory initially seemed to lead nowhere. Although he was able to find information on a total of six different Josef Löwensteins, all of them deported to concentration camps, he was unable to connect a single one of them to Maria Löwenstein.

His phone rang.

"Hannes, it's Marcel. Isabelle and I were just at the farm. Mrs. Olsen is certain that the woman she saw walking along the road was Merle von Hohenstein. But that was all she could tell us."

"Then maybe she's still in the area. What are you going to do now?"

"We'll ask around and distribute pictures of her. We'll also visit the old painter again. We have to get him to talk!"

"Good luck," Hannes said. "I suspect questioning the other residents will get us nowhere. But keep us up to date if you find anything else out!"

Hannes heard excited barking on the street, then the buzzer rang. Hannes opened his door. Socks came running up the stairs and jumped in his arms, almost knocking him over, and tried to lick his face. Anna reached the landing.

"Hey, I saw a small Italian restaurant around the corner. What do you say about getting some pizza? We'll need to stop by Ben's place first, though. I think I left my purse there."

"Sure, no problem."

Socks sniffed around the apartment, and Hannes brought the laptop inside. Anna peered over his shoulder. "What are you up to?"

"Digging into the past. But I wasn't getting very far. Let's go."

On their way to the pizzeria, he told Anna about his day, even though he felt guilty sharing the details of their investigation. But the pressing need to speak to someone not involved in the case was overpowering, and it felt good.

"I'm glad to have police protection, and Socks took care of me too. He's a happy guy."

"I'm just glad he's not lying depressed in the corner because Ben's gone."

"Yeah, but after what you told me, he's probably used to Ben being away."

As they approached Ben's place to retrieve Anna's purse before heading to the restaurant, they saw a small group of people standing in front of the gate. They were talking with the two policemen assigned to guard the residence.

"Hi, Hannes!" Kalle shouted. "Did you bring any food with you?"

Hannes was confused and then noticed Ines and Elke. "What are you doing here?"

"What do you mean?" said Elke with a laugh. "You weren't the only one invited!"

He slapped his forehead. "I had totally forgotten!" He turned to Anna to explain. "Ben wanted to host a small party at his place tonight."

"So why are you here if you forgot about the party?" Ines asked.

"I, uh, stayed with Ben a few nights and left some stuff here," said Hannes. "Oh, Anna, this is Ines, Elke, and Kalle. I met them all on Monday night, including Ben."

"Found yourself another girlfriend, eh?" Kalle whispered loud enough that Anna could hear.

"We got to know each other over the course of the investigation," Anna said. "No girlfriend."

"That's not what you told your neighbor the other night," Hannes joked.

"See what can go wrong in just two days?" she said and winked.

"And does this friendly guy belong to you?" asked Kalle, pointing to Socks.

"No, Socks is Ben's dog, we were just watching him."

"Where's Ben hiding?" Ines asked. "We're curious about his little house, but your cop buddies won't let us in."

"Oh, that's right, you don't know . . ."

"Huh?" asked Elke. "Did Ben get into a fight with neo-Nazis?"

All eyes were on Hannes, who was already sweating. He took a deep breath and said, "Ben's on the run." He then gave a quick rundown of the situation. Everyone was shocked.

"And there's no possibility of a mistake?" Ines asked.

"The fingerprints matched."

"What if someone framed him?" asked Elke. "Ben isn't the type to commit murder!"

"So what do we do now? We brought wine and champagne, but something to eat would be nice," said Ines.

"There's a small park around the corner," said Kalle. "This is no time for a party, but we can at least have a small picnic."

"Uh, I think I should head home now," Anna said.

"Nonsense, you have to eat something! The park's a perfect place to enjoy the evening. Where are you heading, anyway?" Hannes asked.

"Tina's back from the wedding, so I'll have a safe roof over my head," she teased.

"Still, you should join us," he said.

"All right. We were going to get some pizza, anyway. We can have it in the park. But I still have to look for my purse."

After finding Anna's purse, Hannes and Anna went to buy the pizza, then the whole group met up at the park and sat down together in a circle. Ben was the topic of conversation for a long time. Elke was unable to come to terms with what appeared to be an open-and-shut case. Hannes sat in silence for most of the time as the topic made him feel uncomfortable. Elke seemed to notice he was taking this all to heart and made a point of paying attention to him that evening. Anna got along well with Ines, especially once they both realized Anna had spent several weeks traveling through Africa as part of her trip around the world.

"I'm sorry tonight didn't go as planned," Hannes said when they were all ready to leave.

"It's not your fault," said Elke as she wrapped her arms around him. "We'll try again soon. I'll give you a call! You're welcome to join too," she said to Anna.

Hannes and Anna stayed behind as the others made their way through the dark park.

"There's still a bottle of champagne left," she said. "Should we try to enjoy the rest of the evening?"

Hannes agreed, and they sat and sipped the champagne.

"It's strange," Anna said. Hannes could see her green eyes glowing in the dark. "The two murders got me thinking. I spent the entire day lost in thought." She rubbed a blade of grass between her fingers. "You know, I thought about what I really want to do with the rest of my life. Before, I always had one goal: go to school, get a degree, find a job, and so on. There was always something, and there was always change because, well, that's normal. But now? I've been doing the same thing for so many years. I have a secure job, but I still don't know what's coming next. So is that it? Have I already achieved my goal in life? Somehow that sounds wrong to me. Funnily enough, I only realized this when I was standing in front of my dead boss. You never know when life ends; it's out of our hands. So the question is, what's left?"

"Or what's to come," Hannes said.

"Precisely! We don't know. Either there's something or there isn't. But in both cases, we should take advantage of our lives as much as possible. When I think about the last few years, there are very few moments that stand out to me. All those years passed without anything special."

"Now you sound like my grandmother. She always said, 'Hannes, when you get older, the years just slip through your fingers.'"

Anna smiled. "Bad, right? I sound like an old woman already! But it's true. I tell myself that the biggest challenge of my life can't be how to spend my best years living so safe."

"But that's what our society's built on. Most people strive for this kind of life."

"Safety is very nice, but isn't it also incredibly boring? How much do you miss out on because you're following a known path? Shouldn't life be a challenge? Shouldn't we try to discover, to experiment as much as possible? Instead, we spend our days doing monotonous work and then at the end ask where all the time went. Sure, you have weekends and holidays to recover from work, but you're often so exhausted you don't have the energy to go explore."

"But there are also people who feel comfortable in their job."

"You mean the lucky few who were able to turn their passion into a profession? I don't hate my job. And I know I should be grateful to even have a job, especially in these difficult economic times, and so on, and so on. But ultimately we just spend way too much time at work. And when you think about it, most of it's just repetition and serves only to profit the company. You can slave away for years working for a company, and if you're lucky, you'll get recognized for it. But once you can no longer do what they ask, they get rid of you! It happened to my aunt. She was at the same company for forty years, was committed to the company, and never complained when she put in overtime. Then came new management, and she was laid off. Since then, she's been taking pills made by Lagussa . . ."

"But I think many people want security and structure in their lives. Look around: we all work, day after day. That's how our system functions. If people were so unhappy with this situation, our free society would have undergone radical change a long time ago."

"Free society? You're free only if you obey the rules—that's not true freedom. The minute you want to follow a different path, you're faced with limitations. A lot of people are afraid of that. We're also distracted enough to never even consider if we're happy or not. I only recently read that last year Germans watched an average of almost four hours of TV a day. On average! That doesn't leave much time for reflection. Most go to work, where they have used their mind or body for the benefit of a company, and then they come home. Before they go to bed, they veg on the couch and watch lame TV shows that promise glamour and adventure—which very few people will ever experience. The shows are sold as reality. Then there are religions and substitute religions, and every now and then publicly organized mass drunkenness like Oktoberfest, all of which makes people lazy and content."

"So if it's a big conspiracy, then who's behind it? I don't think business leaders meet regularly in Frankenstein's castle to discuss how to keep people subdued."

"I don't think so either. A conspiracy has nothing to do with it. We have ourselves to blame. I think we believe too many things are unchangeable, and we tell ourselves, 'We have this system, so we must deal with it.' They forget that it isn't God given, that we were the ones who created it. Who says it always has to be a question of growth, profit, efficiency, money, and more growth? These ideas are almost considered natural laws. It sucks! We see what's wrong, we see that this system doesn't lead to a happy, contented life. I see that every day at the company. Sales figures reach new record highs year after year because many people can no longer cope without our drugs. People must now adapt to the system, otherwise it makes them go crazy."

Hannes realized once again that there was a lot more to this woman than he had realized. He remembered that he'd recently had a very similar conversation with Ben and Fritz. One of Ben's arguments sprung to mind.

"I agree with you on many points. But the real problem is that no one speaks about these things. Look in the papers, watch the talk shows—these fundamental questions are never discussed."

"Of course not, because we've weaned ourselves or have been weaned. The profiteers of the system cleverly realize that anyone who formulates such thoughts could easily be branded as a crazy fool, a communist, or an enemy of progress. But there's no progress without critical thinking! And yet you're ridiculed whenever you express such thoughts.

Isn't it ridiculous that anyone thinking beyond the norm is criticized? Shouldn't everyone be doing this?"

"What questions have you asked to get yourself labeled this way?"

"Well, the fundamental question: What does a system that's geared to the needs of people and nature look like? So far there hasn't been one. Communism worked just as poorly as capitalism does. Capitalism didn't win, it was just left over. I think that says it all."

"And what should this new system look like?" he asked.

"I don't know, but the starting point should be a discussion about how we want to live. What's important is that we all have a good life that we can happily look back on. We just waste it as foolishly as we do any other commodity or resource." Anna looked at her watch. "I have to get going now," she said. They'd nearly emptied the bottle of champagne. "If I don't show up, Tina's going to be worried."

"You should take a taxi. Let's walk to the street."

"All right, Mr. Policeman," she teased with a smile. "What do you have planned for tomorrow? I promised Tina I'd have a girls' day out with her. Sleep in, leisurely breakfast, go to the beach."

"Sounds good," said Hannes. "I'll probably still be hunting for a murderer with my boss, and if I'm lucky, I might be able to get in an hour on the water."

They had reached the street, and Anna hailed a taxi.

"I hope you solve the case soon," she said. "I can't imagine how it will be on Monday at the office with all the management gone! It's almost as if someone wanted to exterminate the Ternheims. Like a personal vendetta."

Hannes nodded, reflecting on what she said. "Get home safely," he said.

Anna opened the door to the cab and turned to look at him. Her expression was serious but caring. "Get a good night's sleep. Try not to dwell too much on the case or Ben. You can't see into people." Suddenly

Anna stood on her tiptoes and gave him a gentle kiss on the cheek. "Thanks for everything," she whispered and got into the cab.

He stared down the empty street long after the taxi had disappeared and felt incredibly alone.

Saturday Night into Sunday Morning

Memories are the photographs of our lives.

Whenever we remember, images appear in our minds. We can perceive bygone smells, tastes, and sounds or feel a gentle caress with a shudder.

If one of our senses is awakened with the proper key, it can spark an instant flashback and project the corresponding image onto our internal screen. But only during special moments does memory think it appropriate to press the shutter button. They can be happy and joyful moments, or painful and agonizing ones.

My personal photo album almost exclusively contains dreary black-and-white photos. I have to flip through it at length before I stumble upon a friendly snapshot.

I know whom to thank for this circumstance—and have decided to rip out page after page from my dark book of memories. Revenge is my tool.

But revenge is not sweet; it has a bitter aftertaste. Although it can provide a fleeting moment of relief, it passes quickly. Guilt and shame enter the battlefield. And above all, fear.

Fear that it can no longer be achieved. Fear that all will be foiled before the grand finale. I must finish. I must tear the last page out of the Book of Books. Only then can there be peace and quiet.

There is only this one way, even if it proves painful to heal the wounds. Yet there is no other possibility. I have learned that time alone does not heal wounds.

Soon it is finished.

EARLY SUNDAY MORNING

Hannes spent most of the night thinking about the murders and a lot about Anna. Just as he had finally fallen asleep, Socks jumped into the bed and began to whine. Hannes stroked his soft fur, and Socks snuggled next to him. He listened for a while to his quiet breathing and finally drifted to sleep.

Hannes was awakened by a loud knock on the front door. Socks jumped out of bed barking and ran into the hall. It was ten o'clock. Hannes put on a T-shirt and shorts and went to the door.

Fritz seemed happy and bent over to greet Socks. He had a pained expression on his face as he stood back up.

"How's your back?" Hannes asked.

"It's fine. I brought some breakfast; if we're working on a Sunday, we deserve a nice start." He waved a paper bag in the air. "What, did you work a night shift? Any new insights?"

"No. I'd completely forgotten that Ben had planned a small party for our fairground friends last night. We gathered for a picnic in the park instead. So I still have more research to do." Hannes hid the fact that Anna had been there. "Did you get anywhere yesterday?"

Fritz shook his head. "The search for Ben and Frank Richter has intensified. If he isn't found today, we'll have to contact the media for help. And Lauer said he'd double the number of officers working on the case if we don't find anything soon."

"Maybe that's not so bad, we're not getting anywhere."

"Twice the number of officers means twice the number of mistakes. Besides, the need for coordination increases. Not to mention, we would have to bring everyone up to speed. But we still have a few hours. So, breakfast?"

"Yeah, come on in. You can you sit on the balcony while I get some plates," Hannes said. He was still half asleep.

"Coffee wouldn't be half bad either!" Fritz called to him.

Hannes scooped ground coffee into a filter. He switched on the coffee machine and gathered some plates. Then he carried the tray out and was careful not to trip over Socks, who was running around his legs.

As he stepped onto the balcony, Fritz was shaking two tablets into his hand and tossed them into his mouth. He looked at Hannes and immediately choked. He put the bottle on the table and began to cough violently. Hannes put the tray down and pounded Fritz on the back.

"All right, all right! You don't need to hit so hard," Fritz said when he caught his breath. With tears in his eyes, he stared at Hannes. "And you volunteered at a nursing home? Are you sure it wasn't a slaughterhouse?"

"Better a broken rib than suffocating, right? What are you taking?" Hannes looked at the prescription bottle; the name seemed to ring a bell. Still, he was unable to identify the drug.

Fritz grabbed the bottle and shoved it into his pocket. "Painkillers," he said. "Yeah, I admit it. Right now the back pain is so severe that I need drugs. But don't say a word to Steffen, otherwise he'll take me off the case and send me to rehab."

"That might be for the best."

"Says Mr. 'I get back into my boat with a broken knee as quickly as possible!' When I'm on a case, I can't let go until it's solved. My health can wait. And with this magic pill here"—he patted his pocket—"I'll be able to handle the pain for however long we still need."

"So you think we're close to solving the case?"

"Of course! We have a prime suspect in Ben, and this Laval character seems to play a strange role. We've got to track down Ben and find out what's going on. Now I understand why you didn't want to move out of Ben's place," Fritz said with a wink. "The view really doesn't compare." He nodded toward the shabby gray apartment building across the way where a scruffy man in sweatpants had just lit a cigarette on the balcony.

"As soon as we close the case, I'll be on the market for a new apartment. By the way, I'm sorry I don't have much to add to breakfast. My fridge is almost empty. I haven't had a chance to go shopping."

"Not even coffee?" Fritz said with a grin.

"Of course! At once, my lord, and please excuse the poor service!"

A few minutes later, they were sipping coffee.

"You're taking it too much to heart," said Fritz as he smeared jam on a slice of bread.

"What do I take too much to heart?"

"Ben. He weighs on you—and don't think I don't understand."

"Yeah?" Hannes said as he reached for some bread.

"Early in my career, my best friend's girlfriend was found murdered in the park. Her name was Monika, and she was always the life of the party. We had wild parties back then, even if that's hard for you to imagine. She was brutally raped before she died. I was working with three others on the case, and in addition to the investigation, I also took care of my buddy every night. He was deeply depressed, and I was afraid he might take his own life, so I moved into his house. My colleagues and I were on that case for weeks."

Fritz took a long sip from his coffee and folded his arms across his chest. "We were about to drop the case when we stumbled on a clue. A homeless man had seen the murder but didn't want any trouble, so he made himself scarce. Fortunately, the man was deeply religious and confessed to a priest who placed solving the murder above the heavenly seal of confession and called the police. The end was ultimately banal. My best friend at the time had brutally raped and murdered his own girlfriend. He felt inferior and thought she didn't pay enough attention to him. He was also insanely jealous. That's when I learned in the most horrible way possible never to trust anyone. The only person you can really trust is yourself."

They both chewed in silence.

"What happened to your friend?" Hannes finally asked.

"He hanged himself in prison. He probably wanted to terrorize Monika in the afterlife, because after the case was solved, his supposed depression went away. He fooled us all."

Again there was silence.

"All right then." Hannes stared into Fritz's eyes. "Then I have lost my innocence and learned my lesson. But I can't say I like the feeling."

"That's the way the world works," Fritz said and ate the last morsel of bread with a sip of coffee. "But I still get the sense you haven't come to terms with Ben's guilt, so let me give you further proof. I did a little more research on Ben last night. Did you know he comes from some small village in Saxony-Anhalt?"

"I thought he was from Berlin."

"Berlin was his last stop. He studied there for a few semesters before transferring here."

Hannes could not figure out what Fritz was getting at. "I didn't know that," he said. "But what's so strange about it?"

"The village where Ben grew up is only a few miles from a small town called Wittenberg. Tell me that's not strange. Who contacted Ms. Ternheim? A Mark von Wittenberg."

Hannes's head swam. There were just too many coincidences. "But the person Anna saw with Ms. Ternheim at the Charles Memorial looked nothing like Ben."

"Ms. Stahl also said she didn't get a good look. Besides, this man didn't necessarily have to be Ben. He could have sent someone else as Mark von Wittenberg, perhaps Frank Richter. After all, it's possible Ben didn't act alone. Maybe there's some connection between him and Laval."

Fritz wiped his mouth and stood up.

"Where are you going?"

"The station. We've got to find Ben. I want to close this case once and for all. I also want to hear the latest about the search for Merle von Hohenstein. But you can stay here and continue your research, even though I think finding Ben will provide us with quicker answers. Call me if you find anything."

"I'd like to work out a little afterward, if that's okay."

"When's this World Cup, anyway?"

"Next weekend, and I really want to use the home advantage to stick it to them."

"Just don't take too long. And keep your phone on you."

Late Sunday Morning

Something was eating away at him, but Hannes couldn't make sense of it. Socks crunched on some cereal as the first few clouds pushed in front of the morning sun, and the wind picked up. A change in weather seemed imminent. Hannes decided to move his research inside and gathered the remains of his breakfast. Socks had inhaled the cereal and now roamed the apartment. Hannes washed the dishes and retired to the couch in the living room.

Hannes opened the forum. He stared at the screen, deep in thought. This time he didn't go into the archives with the stored documents but clicked on the discussion group entitled "Lagussa." It probably wouldn't get him anywhere, but he wanted to know who had already written on the topic.

He jumped when he reached the second page. Ben had told him someone in the forum had a mother who had been a victim of medical experiments carried out by NGCP in a concentration camp. He found the entry under the heading "Medical Experiments by NGCP":

longtime reader, first-time commenter here. when sunflower uploaded ngcp's delivery receipt to the concentration camp, it suddenly occurred to me: my mother was Jewish and imprisoned in a concentration camp. she never spoke much about this time in her life, but when I was older, she told me these sadists tested drugs on her and other prisoners. she was injected daily with something. she didn't know what it was or what it was supposed to do. she had severe side effects, but they still injected her. i remember she told me that on the package of whatever it was there were four letters. for years, i couldn't remember what those four letters were. but after seeing the ngcp delivery receipt, it suddenly clicked. those were definitely the letters my mother mentioned. i can confirm that the ngcp was responsible for medical experiments in at least one concentration camp.

Another comment by "sunflower" appeared the next day:

that's terrible! what happened to your mother after the war? did she get help?

The answer came within an hour:

my mother suffered from post-traumatic

stress disorder. she was ashamed of what
had happened, and barely sought help.
how do you help someone who experienced
something like that? for a while she
belonged to an organization that tried to
help former concentration camp prisoners,
but they were ultimately unable to do
anything for her. my mother took her own
life when i was still a child. we were at
the beach, and she walked deep into the
water and never came back.

The author's screen name was "wittenberge." His first entry was
on May 18, almost exactly three months before the first murder and,
according to Anna, around the same time Ms. Ternheim was first contacted by Mark von Wittenberg. If Mark von Wittenberg and wittenberge were actually the same person, then Fritz's theory was wrong and
he wasn't Ben. After all, wittenberge talked about his mother, and Ben
was too young for his mother to be a concentration camp prisoner.

Hannes searched for other posts by wittenberge and eventually
discovered a thread entitled "Lagussa: Accountable for NGCP's Past?"

of course you can hold lagussa accountable
and should. lagussa is still owned by the
same family that ran ngcp. the senior
head Heinrich Ternheim handed over
control of the company to his children a
few years ago and during the nazi era,
he was already in a position of power at
ngcp. i know this because my mother was
the man's childhood sweetheart. but he
began to adhere more and more to nazi

ideology. he was the one who eventually
denounced my mother to the gestapo, after
which she was deported. he destroyed my
mother's life twice because ngcp did drug
experiments on her and other prisoners.
lagussa and the ternheim clan must pay
for these crimes!

Goose bumps ran down Hannes's arms. It couldn't be a coincidence!
He was certain wittenberge and Mark von Wittenberg were the same
person. But even if he called for revenge, did that make him a murderer?
Was Hannes grasping at straws just to prove Ben's innocence? Ben still
could have been involved. The murderer might not have acted alone.

A small box at the right of the screen began flashing with an IM.

From: emmi

Hi xyz! Online again? Where have you
been lately? Heard about your protest,
that was awesome! Hijack Lagussa's gala,
really top-notch! Lame that the managing
director had to be killed that same
night, meant the act unfortunately fell
into the background. Probably wasn't
worth going...;-)

Clearly Ben's username was xyz.

Hello? Are you asleep? flashed on the screen.

Hannes typed, Nope, sorry, was just in the
bathroom. Thanks for the praise, but you

really don't think we had anything to do with
Ternheim's death?

What? No! It was just a joke! I know you're
die-hard pacifists. Did my information about
the concentration camp prisoners help?

Hannes had no idea what the other user was talking about but still
wrote: Yeah, the research was really useful!

Apparently this emmi had access to information on concentration
camp prisoners. After some hesitation, he typed, I came across
two names that may be directly related to
Lagussa or NGCP. Can you help? I think they're
concentration camp prisoners.

I can try. I have some records up now. What
are the names, and what do you want to know?

He rubbed his forehead. Perhaps this crucial piece of information
would finally get him somewhere.

It's about a Maria Löwenstein. I would
like to know if someone by the name of Josef
Löwenstein was interned in a camp and if he was
in any way connected to her. Perhaps her husband. And what happened to them after the war?

Another IM appeared a few minutes later.

Sorry, the phone rang. I can take a look to
see what I find, but it will take some time.
Will you be online in a while?

About how long do you need? he typed back. He was
ecstatic!

An hour or two. Be glad that the sun's not
out, I had planned to spend my Sunday doing
other things ;-)

Hannes glanced at his watch. It was a little after eleven.

No problem. I have stuff I need to do too,
be back at 1:00. Thanks, you're a tremendous
help!

No problem. I'll log back on then. Out of
curiosity, why the question? Yeah, I know,
curiosity killed the cat ;-)

Of course! This could be a smoking gun! You
give me info, I'll give you info ;-)

Hannes walked away from the computer. Now he could take Socks
for a jog.

After showering, he opened the laptop just before 1:00 p.m. The
wind had picked up speed, whistling past the windows. The thunderstorm had not yet started. The minutes passed without an IM. He
drummed his fingers on the table.

Another call to Marcel delivered the sobering news that the search
for Merle von Hohenstein had hit another dead end. Although a bus
driver had been able to remember her, there was no trace of her along
the lonely coastal roads.

Finally an IM popped up.

Hello, sorry, took a little longer.

No prob, just got back, anyway, he lied. Find
anything?

Yes, I did. Maria Löwenstein arrived at the
concentration camp on November 18, 1942 and
remained there until the camp was liberated in
early 1945. She was probably too weak to be
sent on the notorious death marches during the
evacuation phase. According to the documents
of our victim support association, she was one
of the prisoners they performed medical experiments on. Hence your interest in her?

He was speechless but quickly replied:

Exactly, I came across her name by accident. Do you know if NGCP drugs were tested on her?

The documents are not that detailed. But I did find out some other information. She was born on April 12, 1920, in northern Germany and remained here after the war. Her parents were Jewish and had a small pharmacy. Neither survived the Holocaust. As far as I can tell, not a single one of Maria Löwenstein's close relatives made it out alive. She had no siblings. On May 2, 1949, she gave birth to a son and committed suicide on June 18, 1958.

How did she take her own life?

I dunno, 'suicide' was all that was written, the term fails to take into account her experiences in the concentration camp...By the way, there's an old photo of her in the documents my organization has. I uploaded the picture and put it in the archive.

Curious, he opened the archive in a new window and clicked an image file called loewenstein.jpg. The photo had yellowed a little, but the facial features of the emaciated woman were still visible. She stood at an angle, her eyes lost in the distance. Her age was difficult to estimate: her body looked young, but the sunken eyes and pinched mouth made her seem old. Hannes felt she was somehow familiar.

Thanks for the picture, he wrote back. Did you find any connection to Josef?

After the war, she had a son, and his name was Josef.

It was as if someone had poured a bucket of ice water over Hannes. A shiver ran down his spine.

What else do you know about Josef? What happened to him?
It just says: 'Son was given up for adoption after suicide.'

Could it be that Josef Löwenstein was Mark von Wittenberg alias wittenberge? From the corner of his eye, Hannes noticed additional lines appear on the screen.

I couldn't find anything else, but I hope it helps. By the way, I'd love to be at your next protest against Lagussa...;-) Oh, wait, one more thing: Maria Löwenstein's son had a middle name.

Hannes anxiously awaited the next IM. When the name appeared on the screen, he was stunned. Everything was falling into place, and the answer was right in front of him.

Hello! Are you there?
Yes, and you've been an amazing help! It's all so clear now! After a brief hesitation, he typed, One more thing: Do you have any idea who wittenberge is? He posted info on the medical experiments. Do you know his real name?

Nothing for several minutes. Then suddenly:

Who are you? If you're really xyz, you'd
know it's against the rules to ask about someone's identity. I was wondering what was up
with your odd writing style. You're getting
reported!

Wait! I know the rules, but there's an emergency! I think this wittenberge is dangerous,
that's the only reason I asked!

He hoped emmi would calm down and stared desperately at the
screen. After five minutes, the screen turned dark blue and a window popped up: You have been logged out by the
webmaster.

"That's impossible!" he shouted and typed in Ben's log-in information. A new window popped up: Username and/or password
unknown.

"No!" he screamed. Once again, he carefully typed the username
and password. The result was the same. Ben's account had been blocked.

He fell back into his seat and moaned. Socks jumped up onto the
couch and nudged his hand. The wind continued to pick up, and the
living room was bathed in a diffused light. The storm would not hold
off for much longer. Hannes pushed Socks off his lap and went to
the window. Outside, branches waved violently in the wind. The sun
peeked through the clouds one last time before disappearing behind a
grayish-black wall.

He went over the details again and again. Could it really be true?
The evidence seemed incontrovertible. He went to the kitchen to make
some more coffee and consider his next steps.

He was startled by a loud crash on the balcony. He quickly turned
around, and as he opened the balcony door, a gust of wind almost
ripped it from his hand. A patio chair had been knocked over and was
now leaning against the table. As he picked up an overturned potted

plant, he heard Socks barking. The first flash of lightning streaked above the sea of houses.

Hannes quickly left the balcony and shut the glass door. Socks was still barking, which made him wonder how he had never been so talkative before. He followed the barking into the cramped hallway. Socks was at the front door. When he noticed Hannes, he ran up and wagged his tail.

On the floor lay a white envelope someone must have pushed through the slot. When he opened the front door, nobody was there. He picked up the letter and went into the kitchen, where he took a sharp knife and carefully opened the unmarked envelope. He tore off a paper towel and sat on the sofa. He used the paper towel to pull out the contents of the envelope, certain not to touch anything with his fingers. It was a plain white piece of paper with a few narrow lines of text—a computer printout in a font that imitated handwriting.

> *you've gotten closer than I had expected.*
> *i quickly realized you would figure it all out sooner or later.*
> *i had hoped that wouldn't be the case.*
> *now i must finish this sooner than planned.*
> *don't think it was easy for me to kill someone, it was both*
>   *agony and relief.*
> *and yet i had to do it because guilt must not go unpunished.*
> *i do not believe in divine justice, only earthly retribution.*
> *retribution for murder, for torture, for suffering.*
> *the history of the prestigious ternheim family is one of murder,*
>   *torture, and suffering.*
> *forced laborers, concentration camp prisoners, and patients.*
> *thousands of people have lost their lives or their health for the*
>   *sake of this family's ruthless greed.*
> *my family has suffered from the ternheims' deeds, and many*
>   *times at that.*

and me? i still suffer to this day.
this curse has been with me since early childhood.
i don't believe in happiness because no sooner do i feel it
*   than it is taken away,*
as if the ternheims were my fate,
as if they had been sent into this world to torment me
*   each and every day.*
but i have had enough of letting this clan destroy my life.
that's why i struck before it was too late.
and now i will bring this to an end,
i do it for myself and for all those who have suffered
*   because of this family.*
do not condemn me, just try to understand,
because time heals no wounds.

Hands trembling, Hannes laid the letter on the table. His last remaining doubts had disappeared. Suddenly Anna's words replayed in his head. "It's almost as if someone wanted to exterminate the Ternheims. Like a personal vendetta."

Suddenly everything was clear.

"Damn it! Old Ternheim's next!"

SUNDAY AFTERNOON

"We almost had him!" Henning Federsen banged his fist on the table. They were in a small, shabby room on the fifth floor of the police station.

"We almost had him before," Fritz said. "Say, Henning." He leaned both arms on the desk and looked him in the eyes. "How can a young man who's only been cited for a few run-ins fool the city's entire police force?"

"His cell phone's off, we have little information about his personal life. And he doesn't have a car, doesn't use credit cards, and hasn't been spotted by any surveillance cameras. The city's large enough to hide in. Maybe there's another change in the works," Federsen said. They had known each other since their days at the academy and had experienced profound changes in the police force over the years. "There are plenty of young men today who know how to effectively use their social skills. Our time's coming to an end, and that's probably a good thing. The dinosaurs went extinct, after all."

"The problem is that men like Hannes are far too trusting. They have a hard time imagining that people don't always act the way we expect them to. So, where did you lose Ben Sattler this time?"

"Wait a minute. The last time he escaped, you were there, not me!"

"Okay, okay!" Fritz said. "Where did *we* lose him this time?"

"At a gas station on Fuchsberg Street, on the northeastern outskirts. An officer on patrol had just filled his tank and was about to pay. Inside the store, he noticed a guy with blond dreadlocks duck behind some shelving, then take off."

"Why didn't the officer catch him?"

"The suspect grabbed the officer's motorcycle and took off! Such a rookie mistake leaving the key in the ignition. We'll probably have to expand the search to all of northern Germany."

Fritz took a deep breath. "Did the cop at least notice which direction he went?"

"Away from the city. The coastal road. But he could be anywhere now."

"Maybe you're right. But I'll take a look around just in case. Tell me if you hear anything new."

Federsen got a call, and Fritz left the office. He'd overlooked the fact that he'd left his cell phone on the edge of the desk.

Hannes ran into his bedroom and quickly changed into jeans and a thin wool sweater. He grabbed his tattered jacket and ran out the door, leaving Socks alone. Just as he was turning toward the steps, his neighbor Richard stepped outside.

"Hannes, I haven't seen you in a while. Were you on vacation?"

"No, I've just been really busy," he said and headed for the stairs.

"There's been some excitement in the building after that snake got loose," Richard said as he leaned against the banister, blocking Hannes's path. "Mrs. Kowarz on the first floor drafted a petition demanding that management terminate the snake charmer's lease."

"Did they catch that thing?"

"You didn't hear? The snake was found on Thursday on a nursery school playground."

"Unbelievable. And where is it now?"

"The zoo came and took it."

"That's great to hear. I'm sorry, but I have to go to a meeting and I'm already very late. Say hi to Heike. We'll have to talk more next time."

He pushed Richard aside and raced down the stairs. Richard shouted something down the stairs, but he didn't hear it. He bounded three steps at a time and nearly knocked over old Mrs. Kowarz.

"Sorry, Mrs. Kowarz!" he called to her as he made his way to the basement parking garage. "Your petition's a great idea. I'll sign it tomorrow!"

Hannes barely got his truck to start and took off as he scrolled through the contacts in his phone. He had just found the final puzzle pieces he needed to complete the picture and had to contact Fritz, because Old Ternheim was now in grave danger. He should have been put under police protection a long time ago!

"What?" someone barked at him.

"Uh . . . Fritz?" The voice didn't sound right.

"Fritz isn't here. He left his phone on my desk. This is Federsen. Who's this?"

"Uh . . . Hannes Niehaus. I'm his assistant. So where is he?"

"How should I know?"

Hannes hung up. For several minutes he struggled with whether he should call for backup. But what if he was wrong? Then he would forever be the butt of jokes at the station, and Fritz would no longer take him seriously.

Hannes bolted out of town just as the rain picked up. A few minutes later he turned off the highway onto the sloping coastal road. Low-hanging black clouds cast a pall over the landscape which made it hard to see. Fierce gusts of wind blew branches into the middle of the road, and Hannes had to swerve to avoid them.

Finally, the old lighthouse loomed before him, and he turned down the small dirt road. The old truck skidded across the soggy ground, and in a moment of carelessness, Hannes lost control of the car and slid sideways into a small ditch. He put it into reverse and cautiously pressed the gas, but the wheels were stuck. He hit the gas harder and tried to rock the vehicle but was unsuccessful. He was stuck in the middle of nowhere.

Hannes turned off the engine and listened to the loud patter of rain. He put on his jacket and looked at the cascades of water through the side window before throwing open the door. His shoes landed in a small puddle and were immediately soaked. The truck's wheels had dug deep grooves in the ground and were covered in mud.

Hannes wiped the water from his eyes. Streaks of lightning flashed across the sky, bathing his surroundings in bright light. Then thunder tore through the air. He thought about getting back in the car but decided to throw himself against the storm with all his might and struggled to take small steps forward. When he reached the forest, he was mostly shielded from the wind, and the treetops managed to catch some of the rain. He had to stare at the ground to keep on the barely visible path. Then he started to run, hoping to reach the clearing. A glance at his watch spurred him on. Since he had found the letter, almost an hour had passed, and he had no idea how long the envelope might have been lying by the door.

His wet pants clung to his legs. He continued jogging and was soon out of breath. Just when he was ready to slow down, he saw the small clearing. Then another flash of lightning bolted across the sky. This time, it only took a second for thunder to rattle the earth. Without the protection of the trees, Hannes was defenseless against the downpour. Each step he took caused water to spurt up like a fountain as he hurried toward Old Ternheim's dilapidated house. The shutters were all closed, but the front door was wide open. Not even the crazy old man would be so careless.

Hannes crept up the rotten planks to the small porch, trying to listen for sounds from inside the house. But all he could hear was rain and the howling wind. Then he quietly slipped inside. Water had gotten into the hallway and formed a small puddle by the entrance. The door couldn't have been open for long.

Hannes warily entered the narrow hallway. After the physical exertion, he struggled to calm down. Should he call for Mr. Ternheim? If the old man was alone, Hannes might frighten him to the point of having a heart attack. If he wasn't alone, he would lose his stealthy advantage.

All indecision was cast aside when he heard noises from behind the door on the left. It sounded as though items were being overturned, and an excited voice shouted. Hannes rammed the door so hard he stumbled into the room. The storm let loose a massive roar of thunder. He could only see outlines but almost made out an upright silhouette half hidden by an oversized canvas. The person had his arms raised above his head and held an elongated object. Hannes shouted. But it was too late.

The ax whistled through the air toward Heinrich Ternheim, who was sitting in his chair. Ternheim tried to protect himself by holding up his walking stick. The attempt threw the ax off course, snapping the cane in two. The blade sliced through the tattered upholstery of the chair, while the blunt side hit Ternheim in the temple. He slumped to the side.

The attacker was so consumed by his deadly mission that he took no notice of Hannes. As the flashes of lightning were replaced by a deafening roar, the man pulled the ax from the back of the chair to attempt another blow.

"Stop!" Hannes yelled as he rushed forward.

The man turned, and the ax slipped out of his hands. He ran over to the giant canvas and hurled it at him. Hannes caught it and struggled to regain his footing. The attacker kicked one of his legs out from under him so he fell to the ground, covered by the monstrous image. With great difficulty, he crawled out from under the painting and saw an outstretched arm pointing a gun at Ternheim.

Hannes jumped up and walked into the line of fire. Wild thoughts flashed through his mind as he stared at the gun. What was he thinking? Was he going to lose his life for some ancient criminal? They stood motionless until the man curled his finger around the trigger. The gun trembled. He could not take his eyes off the barrel. Would this be the last thing he ever saw?

Hannes closed his eyes. When he opened them again, he saw a shadow disappear out the door. Ternheim gave a weak moan, and Hannes rushed over to the old painter.

"Are you hurt?" he asked as he felt Ternheim's pulse—a feeble but stable beat. Then he realized his cell phone was in the car.

"The picture . . ." whispered the old man, "the picture shows the truth."

Hannes placed his hand on Old Ternheim's shoulder. "I'll look at the picture later. I have to try to catch up to him. Close the door until I'm back!"

He ran from the room to the porch, where he saw a figure disappear into the woods. The rain had eased, and the thunder sounded distant. The worst seemed to be over.

The man was amazingly agile as he moved through the forest. Branches hit Hannes in the face. Ignoring his injuries, he darted through the woods, gaining ground. The intervals between flashes of lightning continued to grow, and with each illumination of the sky, he seemed to have gained another few feet. He had no idea where they were when the trees suddenly ended, and he recognized his old truck, still halfway in the ditch with its lights on. He had even left the windshield wipers running.

Then he saw the fugitive staggering by the lighthouse. The rain had gotten a little heavier, but in the fields, he could now see the man without much difficulty. The roar of the waves breaking against the cliff drowned out the distant rumbling of thunder. The lightning had moved to the horizon. Hannes shivered in his damp clothes.

He cautiously approached the old walls and circled halfway around the lighthouse. There he stood, at the edge of the cliff, looking out to sea. His back was slightly hunched and his shoulders rose and fell. Hannes also gasped for breath and had to place his hands on his knees to steady himself. Then he raised his head and looked over at the man. About thirty feet lay between them. The wind ruffled his hair.

"Sorry to screw up your grand finale!" Hannes shouted.

The man straightened and slowly turned to face him. Hannes looked into his eyes, which had become so familiar to him in recent days. Eyes that so uniquely reflected the inner life of this man. Eyes that could look amused, angry, thoughtful, compassionate, and melancholy—sometimes everything at once. Eyes which Hannes had looked up to. Now they were empty.

"When did you know it was me?" Fritz asked. His voice sounded tired.

"Really know? Only today. I suspected it yesterday, I just didn't want to admit it! But too many things just fell into place. The brooch in your boat, the yellow paint scratches on your car, the green streaks on Ms. Ternheim's car, and your painkillers, which were used to sedate the two Ternheims. Not to mention your behavior in recent days. Eventually I connected all the dots. After all, you were the one who taught me not to rule out any possibility. At first I laughed at the idea that you could be the murderer, until I found a picture of Maria Löwenstein this afternoon and remembered the photo of your mother in the office. When I learned that Mrs. Löwenstein gave birth to a son named Josef Fritz, all doubt vanished. Why did you do it?"

"Did I not tell you why in the letter? There are some that you can never forgive. What this monster did to my mother cannot be allowed to go unpunished. She was never herself again. Supposedly before her internment, she was a fun-loving and confident young woman. I never knew her like that. Only depressed, absent, angry, sad. She would burst into tears for what seemed like no reason in the middle of the city. Once, when a family friend gave me a pair of pajamas, she got upset because it reminded her of the blue-and-gray stripes on her prison clothes at the concentration camp. That's why I also took photos of Ternheim's beloved granddaughter Merle wearing pajamas like those." Fritz had to take a short breath before continuing. "On one of my birthdays, my mother threw herself to the ground, kicking and screaming. Since that day, I became the leper at school, the kid with the crazy mother. On a summer day when I was nine years old, we went to the same beach where Helene Ternheim was found by her father. My mother couldn't take it anymore. She simply walked into the sea and never came back."

His voice was surprisingly firm. Hannes carefully took a step closer. Fritz raised his hand in warning. "Stay where you are! I have my gun in my jacket."

"Is it true Heinrich Ternheim was your mother's childhood sweetheart?" asked Hannes.

"Ah, so you've figured out who Mark von Wittenberg, or wittenberge, is," Fritz said and nodded. "You know why I fought with Steffen when he assigned you to me? My plan was actually to work the case alone to control everything. Then suddenly you popped up. I knew I had to tighten my schedule because I couldn't distract you forever with false leads."

"You digress, Fritz," said Hannes. "What about your mother and Ternheim?"

"Childhood sweetheart? Sandbox sweetheart is more like it! They were neighbors and practically grew up together. When Ternheim's father became enamored with Nazi ideology, he forbade his son from hanging around 'that Jewish bitch,' as he called her. The two of them continued to meet in secret. There was even talk of running away to get married." Fritz sneered. "But it didn't work out that way."

"Why did he turn his back on her?"

"He was a member of the Hitler Youth. They probably poisoned his thoughts. Then he was promoted to manager at his father's company. The meetings with my mother became less and less frequent and finally stopped altogether. Then one day the Gestapo came to her door and took the whole family. They'd been tipped off in person by a childhood friend. Ternheim probably hoped to curry favor with the regime—and it worked! But that didn't stop his lethal influence on my mother. A few years ago I found out that one of the drugs they tested on her at the camp came from Ternheim's diabolical factory."

"Why did the Ternheims go unpunished after the war? I thought Nazi criminals were brought to justice."

"Justice?" Fritz laughed. "With the number of criminals and collaborators, they would have needed thousands of investigators to bring everyone to justice! They focused on the main perpetrators. Besides, many documents disappeared before the Allies could get ahold of them. Heinrich Ternheim renamed the company and buried the matter. Since his company made huge profits thanks to the Nazis, he could hit the ground running after the war. My mother on the other hand had to make a living as a seamstress and maid."

"Did she tell you all this?"

"Great bedtime stories, huh?" Fritz laughed. "Sometimes she didn't speak for days, other times it would all come gushing out. At least it awoke my sense of justice. That's why I wanted to become a cop—to ensure the justice that my mother did not get. But all too often I've seen prosecutors and judges sacrifice justice in favor of corrupt agreements."

Bit by bit, Hannes inched forward. "How was it for you after your mother died?" He was trying to keep the conversation going and distract Fritz at the same time.

"Oh, the new German government had a simple solution for me. I was hauled off to an orphanage. I was a feeble child, probably a long-term effect of the experiments and other hardships my mother had endured in the concentration camp. I couldn't run as fast as the other boys and wasn't as strong as they were, and my growth was stunted. Of course it was not long until they noticed such shortcomings. Then I became the whipping boy. Even the caretakers at the orphanage couldn't stand this pale, sickly little boy and tormented me as well. I ran away several times, but was always brought back."

"What I don't understand is the history of your name. How did you become Fritz Janssen?"

Fritz smiled. "So that's what held you up? After the war, my mother fell in love with a British soldier who was stationed for several years in Germany. When he was shipped back to England, my mother was already pregnant with me, but she never told him. They wrote each other letters for years afterward, but she never informed him about me. Everyone assumed this British soldier was my father. But there was a reason my mother didn't breathe a word to him about me."

The smile on his face gave way to hatred. "My birth had absolutely nothing to do with the English soldier. Long after my mother died, I found her diary and learned the truth about where I come from. Shortly after the war, Heinrich Ternheim once again entered my mother's life and inquired about her health. She confronted him about his guilt, threatening to go public."

A dark premonition took hold of Hannes, sending shivers down his spine.

"Of course that posed a serious threat to Ternheim's career. He went ballistic, called my mother a Jewish bitch, and threatened her. Realizing she was undeterred, he changed tactics and began to flatter her and offer money for her silence. But my mother was not for sale; she insisted on seeking justice. So . . ."

Fritz's voice cracked, and he shook his head in anger. He cleared his throat several times, and Hannes inched forward again.

"To make a long story short, he began to lash out at my mother. But that's not all. He tore the clothes from her body, threw himself on her, destroyed the last small remnant of life in her. He raped her several times and the result of that . . . that heinous crime stands before you. Heinrich Ternheim . . . Merlin . . . is my father."

Although Hannes had already feared this, it nevertheless pulled the ground out from under him.

"And your mother kept all this to herself? Why? Why didn't she—"

"Why?" screamed Fritz. "My God, Hannes! Some empathetic cop you are! Put yourself in her shoes, and imagine what she'd gone through! After being raped, she was dead inside. With his seed, this devil had smothered the last spark of life in her. It's a miracle she was ever able to write this . . . this . . . experience in her diary. She was troubled by me: every time she looked at me, the memories came flooding back. Once she lost her temper and called me the spawn of Satan. Then she hit me so hard I landed on the edge of the table. That's how I got my scar. The dog bite was a lie. But it's understandable why she couldn't love me, after all that she had been through. Right?"

Fritz fought to control his heavy breathing as he looked almost pleadingly at Hannes, who was unable to say a single word and was ashamed of himself for it.

"Anyway, you asked how I got my name. I was born Josef Fritz Löwenstein and everyone thought I was a German-English bastard. At least that was the expression I heard most often. The first positive experience in my life was a name change: when I was twelve, I was adopted by a couple named Janssen who couldn't have children. For the first time I experienced what love and security were. They had a farm not far from here. I tried to catch up on my childhood there. Since neither had a particularly high opinion of the Church, they always called me by my middle name, not Josef. And it stuck. They were killed in a car accident twenty years ago."

Hannes had dramatically shortened the distance between them. "What I don't understand is: Why didn't you just kill Old Ternheim? What did his children have to do with it?"

"That would have been too easy. I wanted him to suffer as much as I had suffered. He should feel what it's like to lose a family member. And to make sure that he understood, I left several clues. First, Helene died like my mother did: by drowning. I even dyed her hair, because before my mother turned prematurely gray, she had light-blonde hair. I gave Helene a sedative and took her on my boat. Unfortunately, the dose was too low, so I had to tie her hands. I couldn't tattoo her properly because she struggled. Don't you know how easy it is to get a tattoo machine online?"

Hannes shrugged; he lacked the strength to reply.

"Anyway, the tattoo was meant to be another message to Old Ternheim. The numbers, as you discovered, were those tattooed on my mother at the concentration camp. I held Helene's head under water until she stopped struggling. Then I removed the ropes from around her wrists and tossed her overboard where I could be sure she'd be driven by the currents to the beach where Old Ternheim takes his walks. You were already well on my heels when you decided to look at maps of the currents and lists of the ships in the area. One of those unknown blips on the radar was my *Lena*. Luckily I was able to stop you from looking into it further."

"Then why did you also have to kill Christian Ternheim?"

"For the same reason. However, he had been estranged from his father for some time. Did you know he raped his sister? On the day Ms. Wagner called to say her boss was missing, I was alone with her in the office and was able to coax this savory detail from her. He also impregnated a woman he met on vacation and got in real trouble with his father. He once again had to dig deep into his pockets to buy the silence of the poor woman and keep the family name clean. Eventually Christian Ternheim channeled all his ambition into the company. The hasty launch of Xonux was due to his vaulting ambition, even if his father had the final decision-making power. And so Christian Ternheim also had my wife on his conscience."

Hannes gasped in surprise.

"So you didn't find everything out," Fritz said with a hint of satisfaction. "My wife had a miscarriage and afterward suffered from anxiety. Xonux was considered a harmless miracle drug. In the summer of 1996, she suffered a fatal heart attack. I'm convinced this drug was the reason. Despite the warnings, Christian Ternheim had released the drug to satisfy his greed and desire for material success. That's why I let him choke on banknotes. It was purely coincidence that I used twenty-euro notes like the ones we found in Ben's nightstand."

"But why did you try to lay the blame on Ben? What did he ever do to you?"

"Nothing! On the contrary, I really like him, and I find the war he wages against that Nazi shit admirable. But he was also an ideal scapegoat. Don't worry, I wouldn't have let the suspicion rest on him for long. I had to buy time so Heinrich Ternheim could suffer a little longer and I could carry out the last part of my plan in peace."

Hannes stared at Fritz half in fascination and half in disgust. "But Ben's fingerprints on the tattoo machine . . ."

"That was nothing! Do you remember when I excused myself to the bathroom the evening I visited you? I took a bottle from the kitchen covered with Ben's fingerprints. It was easy to transfer prints from it onto the machine. I've been in the business long enough to know how to do a few things."

"The warning sent to Ternheim that something would happen on the night of the gala probably came from you then, right?"

"No, why would you say that? I thought you were behind it because you felt guilty about the assistant. There's no ignoring the sparks between you two. No, it was in my interest for the protest to take place. That way, I could cast suspicion on Ben. The increased security measures didn't make the murder any easier for me. The leak had to come from someone in Ben's circle."

"But why didn't you do more to sabotage the investigation from the start?"

"Then it would have been too obvious! Besides, I slowed the investigation down. I was able, for example, to delay the start by an entire day. Or think of the note stuck to Ms. Stahl's bike, which was meant to silence her because I couldn't be sure how much she knew. Then I tried to stifle your interest in the boat traffic, and this morning, I tried to convince you that Ben and Mark von Wittenberg were the same person. While it's true he grew up in the vicinity of that small town, it was pure coincidence I had chosen the name von Wittenberg or wittenberge. At the time, I didn't even know Ben. But a complete torpedoing of the investigation was also not in my best interest. Certain things about Lagussa and that miserable family had to come to light."

"The leak to the press was your doing too, right? Ben was completely innocent."

"Of course! I wanted to gradually up the ante. Unfortunately, I had to apply more pressure a little more quickly toward the end. Since there would be double the number of detectives working on the case tomorrow, I wanted to bring the matter to a close. I wouldn't last long against three colleagues."

"Why did you hide Ms. Ternheim's car?"

"You know why. Don't you remember the slight yellow scratch on my car? At first, Helene Ternheim trusted me. I got in touch with her and told her I was doing some research into Lagussa's past during the Nazi era. I told her that what I had unearthed would cause a scandal in the wrong hands, that it would be better if Lagussa took proactive measures. She initially doubted the authenticity of the documents, but later she was very interested. But then I noticed she was uneasy in my presence. Perhaps I had pressured her too much. I soon realized I had no other option. So I arranged to meet with her one last time. She was reluctant. So I lied to her, said I had found new documents which were much more damning. In the end, she agreed to meet. When she ran to her car, I managed to block her with my Jeep before she could drive off. Unfortunately, my car was not the only vehicle damaged in the crash. It would be hard to explain the traces of paint from my Jeep on her sports car. So I drove the car on Sunday to that abandoned barn. I of course hadn't considered that Old Ternheim would notice and somehow inform you. Luckily for me, you called. That gave me enough time to trip and fall in the driver's seat before forensics arrived and thereby explain why my fingerprints and DNA were inside the car."

Hannes nodded as he took it all in. "Just tell me one more thing: Why was Heinrich Ternheim so afraid of you, and how did he know your other name?"

"That was a mistake on my part. Ten years ago, I had written him a letter, but I'd limited it only to allusions. This triggered his withdrawal from the company. I couldn't bear the thought that he was living the peaceful, quiet life of a retiree. I confronted him years later, after he gained worldwide fame and admiration for his weird pictures. I knew he had stopped talking and supposedly acted a little confused. I thought he had forgotten my face. At that time, I had no idea that I would—"

"And the sedative found in the Ternheim siblings—I suppose you took them from your own stock?"

"I made another mistake taking those two pills in front of you this morning, but I couldn't deal with the back pain anymore. I immediately feared you would recognize the drug and remember the name Letharmol. That's when I realized I didn't have much time left."

"Why do you take those pills, anyway?" Hannes continued to inch forward. "Suppressing back pain can't be the only course of treatment."

Fritz was silent for a moment. "The back pain isn't the real problem, Hannes. I have prostate cancer—and it has metastasized to the spine. The cancer wasn't diagnosed in time and is incurable. That's why I'm running out of time." He rubbed his eyes before he continued. "Now you know how it all fits together. And you figured out most of it for yourself. Perhaps Mrs. Öztürk from the cafeteria is right. With your different-colored eyes, you can see both past and present. You have shed light on the events of the past and linked them to those of the present. As unlikely as it may sound now, I'm proud of you! You learned quickly and you're not easily outwitted. You've got the instinct, Hannes. You'll be a good cop. I hope in spite of everything that you've learned something from me."

"What about Merle von Hohenstein? You're behind her disappearance, aren't you?"

Fritz gazed past him, lost in thought. "That . . . that was wrong of me. Merle is Heinrich Ternheim's granddaughter. Christian Ternheim slept with her mother; she was the result. Of course, the Ternheims simply bought the mother's silence. Merle only recently found out who her father is."

"Why did you kidnap her? She bears no guilt just because she's Christian's daughter."

"You're right . . ." Fritz's moist eyes were shimmering. "I said I made a big mistake. I was blinded by hatred. It was only in the last few days that I found out her true story. But hindsight is always twenty-twenty. When I kidnapped her, all I knew was that she was that barbarian's granddaughter and probably meant more to him than his own children. She visited him often, and since there are no buses out here, she'd walk from the last stop. I watched her over and over. It was obvious the old man had a soft spot for her." He rubbed his eyes again. "I was sure she was his weak point. I observed Merle for quite some time, waiting for the right opportunity. She always had a water bottle in her backpack. I laced her bottle with sleeping pills when she wasn't looking. Today I realize Merle was just as much a victim of this family as I was."

Hannes was shaken by the scope of his revenge. "I remember you told me at the very beginning that most murders have to do with personal relationships and that it's impossible to see inside another person. You were right. This was a family drama—one that played out over more than these last seven days. But it ends here and now."

"No, Hannes," Fritz said with a smile. "This drama isn't over yet. Something's missing."

With that, he took a giant step back and fell off the cliff. A horrified Hannes cautiously approached the edge and peered over to see the twisted, motionless body lying on the beach fifty feet below.

"But Fritz," he whispered, "where do I find Merle?"

The front door of the ramshackle cottage was still open, and Hannes knocked loudly on the wood to announce his arrival. It was now drizzling, and the wind blew softly.

"Mr. Ternheim, it's Johannes Niehaus from the police!" he called out. "You can rest assured, Josef—Fritz—Janssen is no longer a danger to you!"

Nothing moved. Hannes pushed open the door to the room where Fritz had attacked the old man what felt like an eternity ago. First, he noticed the unusual brightness; the shutters had been opened in his absence, and the giant canvas, which had buried him less than an hour before, stood again in the middle of the room. But something else had changed. The large white sheet that had covered the huge picture lay crumpled in a corner. The canvas was covered in a colorful hodgepodge of shapes and images. The chair in which Heinrich Ternheim had almost been split in two was now placed in front of the painting, and he was sitting in it.

Hannes stood reverently behind him and gazed at the picture. It undoubtedly represented the old man's life. The stages of his multifaceted existence were displayed in realistic detail. What surprised him most wasn't the artistic quality of the painting but its honesty.

The story began on the left side with a young girl and a little boy who ran holding hands over a blooming meadow. Colorful butterflies seemed to flutter from the painting toward the viewer. The scene expressed profound serenity and intimacy. However, it was replaced by the overwhelming imagery of the next scenes. Marching hordes with outstretched right arms made for a nightmarish transition, and in the middle stood a young man whose features were somewhere between those of the boy in the picture and the old man in the chair. Tortured souls in prison uniforms and distraught figures on an assembly line seemed to plead for deliverance. One woman's face was drawn in vivid detail. Her arm was tattooed with a six-digit number and stuck with a syringe bearing the letters NGCP. A whirlwind of paper money directed the viewer's gaze to the right. Two lonely children looked with wide eyes at the viewer while an oversized figure resembling Old Ternheim towered menacingly over them. Tormented people appeared again—the effects of Xonux.

Then a skeleton swinging a scythe separated the heads of Helene and Christian Ternheim from their bodies. And as always, the painter had successfully achieved a realistic effect: there was no denying the vivid likeness of Fritz in that skeleton. The picture ended on the right with an old man standing in front of a canvas on which the painting was faithfully reproduced in miniature. Opposite him was a judge's bench, and behind it was a giant figure in a white robe whose neck was cut off by the edge of the canvas so the head was no longer visible.

"Divine judgment?" Hannes said as his eyes moved to the bottom of the gold frame. In the middle was a brass plaque on which the title of the painting had been engraved: *Crime and Punishment.*

Hannes reluctantly stepped around the chair and looked down at Heinrich Ternheim. He stared past Hannes to the image he must have worked on for months. His face was calm and composed. In his hands, he held the two parts of his broken cane. The top half was now covered in symbols—the timeline had reached its end. Hannes sensed Mr. Ternheim was no longer breathing and carefully closed the old man's eyes.

SUNDAY EVENING

Even Merle had been able to hear the storm. She had overcome her fear of thunderstorms and rejoiced at the sound after days of silence.

She had stopped talking to herself and instead played with the flashlight—so much so that it now only produced a weak glow. She had carefully shone the light over every inch of the space without finding a way to escape. At some point, she had put her fingers in front of the light and cast shadows on the wall, creating short plays with her hands.

Once, there had been a loud blast of classical music, and she had adapted the movements of her hands to the melody. She had been unsure whether this music had played only in her head, just as she had been uncertain whether her captor had really spoken to her the day before or if it was just her intense desire to hear a human voice that had caused that illusion.

It doesn't matter, anyway, she thought and brushed a strand of hair from her face. *But the voice was right. It won't be long, and I'll take the end into my own hands!* She knew she could no longer hesitate. Who knew when her captor would come back and what he might do? She planned to wait for the flashlight battery to die. That would be the sign for her to plunge once and for all into the darkness.

She heard sounds that weren't the thunderstorm. It was a voice and footsteps. She had waited too long! Determined, she grabbed the splinter and held it to her wrist. She hesitated. It was hard to hurt yourself, to take the ultimate plunge. When she heard the noises again, she closed her eyes and thrust. A sharp pain made her gasp and at the same time unlocked her last reserves of strength. She pulled the splinter of wood out of her left forearm and stabbed deeply again and again. Her left hand was numb, and she felt the moisture drip down her legs. Just to be sure, she touched her left wrist with her right index finger, which she then placed in her mouth. The rusty taste produced one last smile. Blood! She had done it just in time!

Exhausted and yet strangely satisfied, she stretched out on the bed. Her arm hung over the edge, and she listened to the steady drip of life flowing from her veins. It was loud, incredibly loud, and the sound completely filled her head. She felt the cold spread through her. Weak and shivering, she pulled the wool blanket over herself. In her daze, she heard excited voices at the door and felt no more fear.

The pounding on the door and the loud shouts barely registered. Suddenly, a light flooded the room, covering her in warmth. *Light!* she thought. *Finally! So it's true we go into the light. It's beautiful . . .*

"My God, here she is! We found her!"

"Look at all the blood."

"She cut her wrist. Where's the damn ambulance?"

"Let me through, quickly!"

A finger was placed on Merle's neck.

"She's still alive!"

ONE WEEK LATER

Summer weather had returned after the storm, and the tinny speakers were blasting the current hits. The flags of the participating nations fluttered in the warm breeze, and a hundred spectators were in the stands. As usual, the crowd was made up almost exclusively of family members of the competing athletes, but in Hannes's case it was different this time.

Anna strolled beside him in the grass. "Why did your boss stick that note on my bike? Would he have really done something to me?"

"No. I can't picture him doing that. He probably just wanted to prevent you from meeting me that evening, because he didn't know how much you knew about Ms. Ternheim's contact with him—as Mark von Wittenberg, that is."

Anna shuddered. "Good thing you were able to connect the dots. It never would have occurred to me to suspect my own boss, especially if he was in charge of the investigation."

"Fritz's biggest mistake was to tattoo his mother's prisoner number on Ms. Ternheim's forearm. He clearly wanted to send Old Ternheim a message, but after researching the number, I figured it out. If I hadn't looked into it, I would have dismissed my theory as too far-fetched."

"I still can't believe that nice man was capable of doing what he did!"

"Me neither. And I think I'm never going to be able to get the images of the bodies—even Merle von Hohenstein—out of my head."

Nor did he think he could forget the tormented look on Fritz's face as the paramedics placed him on a stretcher at the beach. Fritz's plan hadn't worked. Although he was seriously injured in the fall, the cliff had not been high enough for him to evade justice. He was still in the intensive care unit, but would have to move from the hospital to a prison cell after his recovery.

"What about Merle?" asked Anna.

"We found her just in time. She had slit her wrist with a splinter of wood. She must have been so desperate."

"I can imagine," Anna said and shuddered again. "To be locked up for who knows how long in a dark room without knowing why or what's going to happen . . . I don't know what I would have done."

"The irony is, she's now in a psych ward. She hasn't said a single word since we freed her and is completely spaced out. And you know whose drugs they'll be giving her?"

"Lagussa's?"

"That's right! Sometimes I have the surreal feeling that this has all just been a dream and tomorrow I can laugh about it. Fritz was like a mentor to me: he bossed me around, but he also encouraged me. Unfortunately, this is one dream I won't wake up from."

"Well"—Anna shot him a mischievous look—"everything about this dream is hopefully not too bad."

Hannes felt his ears turn red.

"Maybe he wanted to be caught. Maybe he wanted you to be the one who solved the case. Since he had cancer, he probably had no intention of surviving this."

"I could see that."

Fritz had left a detailed written confession on his desk in which he described his crimes as well as Merle's whereabouts, whom he had hidden in an unused room in his basement at his house in the country. He also made no secret of how he had deliberately sought to mislead Hannes or how he'd failed to keep him at a distance.

Hannes had become an overnight hero at the station despite his attempts to stay out of the limelight. The events hit too close to home for him to be happy about his first successful investigation. Steffen Lauer had told him that he had a very promising career ahead of him, but he was unsure if he wanted to go down that path. At the moment, his focus was on an entirely different thing. He still hadn't totally written off the Olympics, and today's World Cup could be the first step. He needed to place in the top three to qualify for the world championships, which took place in a month. If he practiced hard, there would still be enough time for him to qualify.

"What was up with the twenty-euro notes in Ben's nightstand?" Anna asked.

"Oh." Hannes grinned. "There's a simple explanation, but I promised Ben I'd keep my mouth shut." Ben had recently revealed to him that since his pot dealer had once been ripped off with a fake fifty-euro note, he now only accepted twenties.

They arrived at the starting area, where Hannes was greeted by five smiling faces. He did, however, get the sense that Maria's smile was a little forced.

"Here comes our medal contender!" said Ben as he jokingly punched Hannes in the chest. He had read an article about the Ternheim case on Monday and immediately called Hannes. He had cautiously asked if it was safe for him to come out of hiding, and a few hours later moved back into his garden cottage. He'd been holed up with a member of his group who wasn't on the cops' radar. As a thank-you for solving the case and saving him from the line of fire, Ben had given Hannes an oversized hand-rolled joint.

"Not too hard," Elke said in protest to his playful roughhousing, "or Hannes won't make it to the starting line."

"Go get them, tiger," said Kalle, and Ines rolled her eyes.

Maria looked suspiciously at Anna. "Anyway, we'll be the loudest ones cheering you on. Then you can buy me that dinner you still owe me and celebrate your victory." She winked at him. She wore a white miniskirt, which highlighted the full potential of her tanned legs, and a midriff-baring top, which clearly revealed her tattoo. Anna would have looked a little pale and boring next to Maria if not for her mysterious, radiant green eyes and fascinating charm.

"Men's C-1 1000 meter in five minutes," the announcer said.

As his new friends shouted in encouragement, an elated Hannes made his way to his canoe. When the starting pistol fired and the starting blocks holding his boat sank into the water, his arms almost froze. But then instinct kicked in, and his field of vision narrowed. He knew this phenomenon already: at his club, he was known for his tunnel vision. He tuned out all the sights and sounds around him and kept his eyes fixed on a point about fifteen feet ahead. His mind became freer with each new stroke, and he paddled as hard as he could toward the finish line.

ABOUT THE AUTHOR

Photo © 2015 by Ruediger Schapmann

German author Hendrik Falkenberg studied sports management and works in sports broadcasting. The magical allure that the sea holds for him comes alive in his stories, which are set on the north German coast. His book *Die Zeit heilt keine Wunden* (*Time Heals No Wounds*) was a #1 Kindle bestseller in Germany and has been translated for the first time into English.

About the Translator

Patrick F. Brown studied French and German at Georgetown University in Washington, DC. He currently lives in Philadelphia, PA, where he does freelance translation.

6/16